DANCING IN THE PURPLE RAIN

<u>**Other Books by Judy L Mohr**</u>
Hidden Traps of the Internet: Building and Protecting Your
Online Platform

<u>**Judy L Mohr also contributed to:**</u>
Putting the Science in Fiction: Expert Advice for Writing with
Authenticity in Science Fiction, Fantasy, and Other Genres

DANCING IN THE PURPLE RAIN

JUDY L MOHR

Black Wolf
PUBLICATIONS

Black Wolf Publications
PO Box 27008, Shirley
Christchurch 8640
New Zealand

blackwolfpublications.com

Cover Design by E. L. Julian

First Published 2025

ISBN-13: 978-1-7386251-2-3 (paper)
ISBN-13: 978-1-7386251-3-0 (ebook)

A catalog record for this book is available from the National Library of New Zealand.

Turn *can't* into *Watch Me!*
Debbie Mohr (b. 1957, d. 2020)

I miss you, mom.
But I still listen to your important words.

One

I STARED AT THE BROWN package on the table. What form of death would it contain this time? Gun? Bomb? Some biochemical weapon? It really didn't matter. My job was to deliver the package—not question why or how the ensuing chaos would be unleashed on the world.

I sighed as I glanced around the room. Who would be the unlucky recipient of the brown package of death? Would it be the man with the tablet in the corner having a boisterous conversation with someone on video chat? Perhaps it would be the woman who seemed to be at her wit's end as the console at her table refused to take her order—something about exceeding her caffeine allowance for the month. Or maybe it was the young thing who kept getting stopped at the door; the entry scanner flickered between a red X and a green checkmark, then back again.

Those units were always failing in the outer sectors. Twenty years ago, they were outdated technology. Now, they were ancient. Yet, the owner of the joint probably couldn't afford anything else. And if they wanted to stay open for business, they needed something to scan the pharmachips embedded under the skin at the right wrist.

I needed another job. One day, a drop would turn sour and I would be forced to take matters into my own hands. It was bad enough that I was the Pregutor's lackey, delivering packages to people who would die. But I didn't want to be the one who died myself.

I didn't have many options. When applying for a new job, your full medical history had to be supplied with your application. The moment potential employers discovered that I had White Rabbit syndrome, it was all over.

That wasn't its official name, but who would want to hire someone who would frequently get the shakes and lose their grip on reality? So, delivering packages of death for the Pregutor was my lot in life.

Yeah, sucks to be me.

The scanner at the entrance finally stabilized with the green checkmark brightly illuminating at the top of the unit. There was a collective sigh of relief from the patrons lining up to get through the door.

The clock in the corner of my virtual display insisted on counting down to zero. Any minute now, and I would become indirectly responsible for another death.

A soft hiss announced the arrival of my order. It wasn't often that I was in a position to order coffee. Real coffee. Not the brown sludge pretending to be the incredibly rare caffeinated nectar. It was probably why this particular joint was so busy. A line of people snaked around the block, waiting for the clearance to come in.

One thousand credits for this tiny thimble of black fluid—roughly half my food budget for the week. Food wasn't needed to survive, right? All of a century ago, there were some who classified coffee as a basic food group.

The clock in the corner of my vision started to blink. Thirty seconds to the drop. Thirty seconds to attempt to savor the coffee.

A muted ding in my ear announced the arrival of a new message—the one I'd been waiting for. I tapped into the empty space in front of me, a gesture that my glasses recognized as an instruction to open the message. It contained the photo of an unassuming man and the words: ›You know what to do.‹

I scanned the coffee shop for the recipient, running a facial recognition app on each face I looked at, comparing it to the photo from the Pregutor. There was nothing that stood out about the man in the photo. He wasn't the most stunningly gorgeous person on the planet, but he wasn't ugly either. He was clean shaven and possessed hair that was classically styled. Short, well kept. And his eyes . . . As the facial recognition program splashed a green MATCH in the center of my display, I studied the vacant eyes of the man in the photo. There was no brightness to them, like the man had nothing left to live for. Perhaps that was why the Pregutor chose him.

I skulled back the tiny thimble of caffeine, cursing at how I didn't have the time to allow the liquid gold to linger on my tongue. But when there's a drop to be made, time was of the essence.

The clock hit zero, and the scanner unit at the door flashed a red X again. A message on the main scanner panel said that the unit was reinitializing and reconnecting to the Central Health system. No doubt the Pregutor's handiwork. That meant I had roughly fifty seconds to make the drop and disappear before the system rebooted, tracking my movements.

I tapped out a preprogrammed sequence on the edge of my glasses, and my favorite song started playing in my earbuds. *Purple Rain* by Prince and the Revolution. The moment I heard that first strum of the guitar, any emotions or doubts I might have had about the drop melted away, giving way to clear logic.

With a steady breath, and the classic rock ballad muting all sounds from the outside world, I got up from my seat and grabbed the package. I then headed toward the table in the center of the room, weaving around chairs pushed backward in the pathway. I stood before the hollow-eyed man sitting on his own.

The moment he looked up at me, I did my thing. The edges of my vision darkened, and I pushed past whatever questioning thought sat on the surface of his mind. Soon, all that remained in focus were his eyes—those lifeless eyes.

"You better do what the Pregutor wants you to do," I mentally said to him. *"Don't make me come back here and do it for you."*

I dropped the package on the table. Without a word or another thought, I headed for the door. I tapped the edges of my display glasses, and a seal formed to protect my eyes. I pulled up my breather and activated the filters, then pulled up my hood, tucking in the loose strands of purple hair.

The well-known refrain of the chorus played in my ears as I stepped out into the outside world. Walking down the street, I waved my gloved hand in front of me. My virtual display revealed a single icon in the center of my vision. A white rose in full bloom—my employer's logo. I pressed the virtual button, relaying my position back to the Pregutor, along with a timestamp of when the package was delivered.

As I continued down the busy streets, a gunshot echoed behind me, followed by screams.

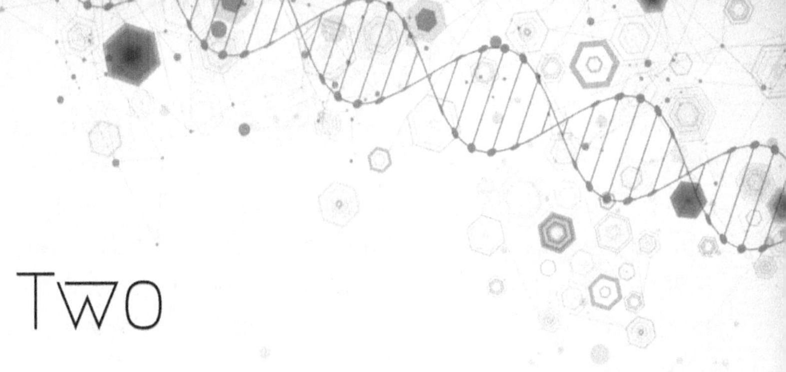

Two

THERE WAS ANOTHER SHOT, AND the gathered crowd outside turned into a mob running away from the chaos. I sped up into a light jog, moving with the crowd farther away from the coffee shop.

A police drone flew down the street, its lights flashing as it hovered over the crowds. I tilted my head down and pulled tight on my right sleeve with my gloved hand, ensuring that the RDF signal blocker was shielding my pharmachip from remote scans. I even altered my gait.

With gunshots fired, there was every probability that the drone would be scanning the crowd, hunting for anomalies. With my chip hidden, I would appear as a dark spot in their scans, something that would be flagged for later review. But as long as any identifiable features were obscured, they wouldn't know exactly who I was. I had to stay hidden . . . at least until I got to the sector checkpoint.

I continued to jog down the street with the rest of the crowd. More drones flew overhead, whizzing toward the source of the chaos. Eventually, the crowd slowed down, many people hunching over, exhausted from the brief brush with mortality. I slowed to a walk, but didn't stop.

Pedestrians coming from the other direction gathered in groups as they all looked to the skies. It never ceased to amaze me how a little chaos would draw out people's curious nature.

A young child kept pushing his mother's hand away as she tried to readjust the child's breather mask. The child pointed to the sky, holding still long enough to give the mother a moment to ensure the child's mask was fitted correctly.

In the plaza just outside the checkpoint, a group of protesters held up signs about all the negative impacts of the pharmachips. How they were controlling people's thoughts. My vid-feed displayed all kinds of assessment threat data, including the elevated body temperatures of the protesters. A red haze surrounded their persons. Xs hung over their heads. The system was unable to identify the exact contagion they carried.

One of the protesters reached out to the crowd with blackened fingers, and the crowd took a wide berth. Guards filed out from the security checkpoint. It would have been nice to believe that the protesters would have been escorted to medical facilities to get treated, but that wouldn't happen. Without the pharmachips that they protested against, proper medical treatment would be denied.

The health centers in Sector 4 could only do so much. Most of the time, medicine in the outer sectors was limited to wild herbs steeped in boiling water. Any medical facility worth a damn was located in Sector 14, and the only way to get into Sector 14 was via a sector pass connected to the pharmachips. No chip, and access through the sector checkpoints was denied. But even with a pharmachip, there was no guarantee that one could get into Sector 14. Entry into the sector was restricted to those with money or sponsorship.

I sighed. As much as I hated being a courier for the Pregutor, without my job, I wouldn't have had money. Without my job, I wouldn't have had sponsorship either. The Rhodon Corporation, with their white rose logo, was my sponsor.

A ding sounded in my ears, alerting me to a new message. I tapped into the empty space in front of me to open it.

>>Fifty thousand credits have been deposited into your account, and a prescription for Miransine has been dispatched. It will be ready for you to pick up from your chosen pharmacy after 4:00 p.m. Payment for the prescription has already been deducted from your account.<<

I did the mental math. Fifty thousand credits minus rent, that thimble of coffee, and my prescription. If I was lucky, I had three hundred credits left to my name. And I had to make that last for two weeks. Definitely no coffee in my foreseeable future. Not the real stuff, anyway.

At least I wouldn't need to worry about the meds that I needed to stave off the symptoms of White Rabbit syndrome.

I glanced at the clock in the corner of my vision and groaned. Eight hours before my script would be ready to pick up, assuming the pharmacy wasn't backlogged, and assuming they had a supply of Miransine and didn't have to order it in. Eight hours. Normally, that wouldn't have been a problem, but it had been near on twenty-four hours since my last dose, and my hands were already starting to shake. In eight hours, the symptoms would be much worse. If I was lucky, the voices would be harmless.

No, I needed to find a source of the active ingredient in Miransine right away. Thankfully, there was a natural source roughly two hours away. It wasn't as concentrated as Miransine was, but it would be enough to tide me over until I could pick up my meds from the pharmacy.

As the crowd moved to the barriers, small pedestals rose out of the ground with scanners. I approached the scanner closest to me and pulled back my right sleeve, holding my wrist to the scanner. A giant green checkmark flashed on the pedestal.

I crossed the threshold into the glass canopy structure that separated Sector 4 from its neighboring sectors. The overhead glass was streaked with dirt and filth. A purplish-brown tinge colored the lines that dribbled down the sides. In places, the purple hue was vibrant. It was further proof that the rain that fell from the sky wasn't just water—like anyone really needed that proof. At certain times of the year, it was only the hoods that people wore that kept their skin from melting off.

Cameras were scattered throughout the facility, taking pictures of those walking through, comparing those pictures to government records. No one went through a secured facility without multiple scans—matching biometrics, measuring the gait of your walk, comparing your photo, and checking many other things too. How it all worked with the goggles and filtered masks in place was a little mystery, but they did it.

A holographic sign blinked into existence before me.

>>You are now entering Sector 4 Inspection Area. Please remove your hood.<<

The last time I tried to proceed through a sector checkpoint with my hood still up, an electric shock went through my system. Just the thought of that pain was enough to send shivers down my spine.

I lowered my hood and glanced at the camera directly above me. If only I could figure out how to pass by those cameras like a ghost. Surely, I would get paid more for my deliveries if I had that knowledge. Then again, the Pregutor might ask me to be the one to pull the trigger, not just deliver the weapons.

A line on the ground sprang into life; a blinking series of arrows on my virtual display told me which security gate to use. Not that I needed the arrows to tell me which way to go. My sector pass granted me the privilege to use exclusive lines dedicated to diplomats and city officials. I never really understood how a courier would be worthy of carrying such an elite pass, but it was convenient. Because of my pass, I didn't have to go through the metal detectors. Good thing too, considering sometimes the packages I carried contained guns—and bombs—and the components to make bombs.

As I bypassed the lines heading to the metal detectors, I could feel the eyes of suspicion on me. Why would a petite woman with purple hair be treated as though she was above the rest of society? Politicians and other city officials didn't have purple hair. And the rich folk never came down to Sector 4.

A security guard came out and stood before me. "I'm sorry, but I will have to ask you to join the lines with the other patrons."

"I have the appropriate pass to be in this line. What's the problem?"

"No problem with your pass. The health scanner is down for maintenance."

"I thought they did maintenance in the evenings, when no one was coming through."

"Unfortunately, the unit dedicated for the express lines is giving everyone the big X, and it has been doing so for the last hour. We can't seem to reconnect to the servers. Until we do, you'll have to use the other scanners. It can't be helped."

I sighed and shook my head. While my sector pass gave me the privilege of bypassing the metal detectors, everyone who went through a sector checkpoint needed to go through one of the health scanners. No exceptions. It was the only way that the city officials could contain disease and stop it from spreading throughout the city.

It wasn't a bad thing. The scanners often picked up things that in the past would have been allowed to fester. The scanner I went through two days ago pointed out a scratch behind my knee that I didn't remember getting—a scratch that was just starting to show signs of infection. A small amount of topical ointment and it was gone. The scanner I went through on the way to Sector 4 pointed out that my audimensase levels were getting high. The system suggested that I take some Miransine to counter the effects. If only I could get to the pharmacy to pick up my prescription.

I looked at the clock display on my glasses again. Gah. Seven hours. And the shaking in my hands was getting steadily worse. And now there was a constant hum inside my head too. The only thing that would make my symptoms go away was mintonal, the active ingredient in Miransine.

I sighed in defeat. "Okay. Thank you." So much for getting out of the sector fast. Instead, I joined the shortest line I could find, standing on the virtual dots spaced two meters apart.

As I waited for my turn in the scanner, I scrolled through the newsfeed, trying to determine if the events at the coffee shop had already been relegated to old news. There were reports about the latest flurona outbreak to ripple through Sector 2—not surprising considering that Sector 2 was the gateway into the city for those looking for a better life. And there were headlines about the latest advances in algae food production and lab-grown protein, but it still wouldn't be enough to feed the entire population of the human race. Many would still die of starvation. But right at the bottom, I found what I was looking for.

>>Two dead at coffee shop in Sector 4. Pharmachip protesters blamed. The identity of the dead still to be confirmed.<<

So that was how the Pregutor was going to play it. It made sense, given everything I had seen. The faulty scanner would have possibly granted entry to the protester. And there were protesters outside the checkpoint saying that the pharmachip was controlling minds. The best way to take down a movement was to fuel hatred and suspicion against that movement. And no one would be looking for a courier in possession of an elite sector pass.

I finally stepped onto the sensor pad of the health scanner and waited. Clear doors closed me into the unit, giving me a false sense of privacy as the unit scanned for any infection and told me the results. Sector border guards would only be informed if I carried some disease that was a danger to others. Thankfully, my audimentia, aka White Rabbit syndrome, was genetic. I could only pass that on to my children, assuming I ever had children.

The soft hum of the machine filled the tiny space.

One, one thousand. Two, one thousand. Three, one thousand.

The scanner took a full body scan, measuring localized body temperature, searching for hot spots and measuring my pulse rate and blood flow. It connected into the tech of my breather, measuring for any ketosis or elevated carbon dioxide respiration. And it connected to my pharmachip, which had an on-board testing system to keep a close monitor of my blood sugars. These scanners were meant to catch anyone who might be presenting symptoms of any number of diseases.

A green checkmark flashed in front of me, and the doors opened, allowing me to proceed to the transport tubes.

Six seconds from the start of the scan cycle to the end. A new record.

THREE

I stood on the platform waiting for the transport tube that would take me toward the city center. Everyone around me had on breather masks and eye seals fitted securely in place. Distinguishing features came down to hair and general physique.

On my left was a man who was twice my size. I only came up to his shoulder. If I stood in the right position, the camera mounted in the ceiling on the other side of him wouldn't see me. The same could not be said about the camera located opposite the platform. The wide-angled lens would easily spot my purple hair. But it would also spot the woman next to me with neon green hair standing next to the man with bright pink hair.

The intercom system crackled into life. "Train traveling to Sector 10 and Sector 11 now arriving. Please stand behind the yellow line."

A single light grew in size in the dark tunnel. As the train pulled up to the platform, there was a soft hiss, the brakes being applied to stop the train.

As the pod doors opened, I stepped into a pod coded for Sector 11. Soon, the door sealed behind me with that telltale hiss as the unit's isolated filtration system kicked in. Yet another means to stop the spread of disease. More importantly, it meant that I could take off my breather and deactivate the seals on my display glasses.

I leaned back in the seat and tried to get comfortable. The train of mini-pods soon exited the dark tunnel and headed to the elevated tracks.

I stared out over the city through the murky haze. The dome covering Sector 14 stood proudly in the center, with smaller domes scattered around it. As the city radiated outward from the Sector 14 dome, the height and extent of shielding from the elements dwindled. The outer most sectors, like the one I had just left, didn't have much protection worth speaking of, other than the buildings that were showing signs of corrosion and disrepair.

We traveled alongside a secondary track carrying a train of mini-pods of its own. As the train hit a junction point, there was a slight shudder as the mini-pod I was in disconnected from the units around it and interwove with the train on the other track. There was another shudder as the mini-pod reconnected.

In the distance, I could just make out the concrete wall surrounding the city, separating Crystal Hills from the rest of the world. Outside those walls would have been gateway facilities, filled with people taking whatever tests the Rhodon Corporation demanded of them. Only the healthiest of specimens would be permitted through the gates into Utopia. Though none of them knew that Rhodon actively took steps to cull the herd of human lab rats to allow another ripe selection in.

It was one of the reasons why my job existed. Population control. Ensuring that Rhodon Corporation could maintain the illusion that they projected to the world—that Crystal Hills was the healthiest place on Earth to live.

A maintenance crew clambered up the outside of the dome for Sector 8, checking it for any damaged spots that might fail in the storms that would arrive in a few months, like clockwork.

The acid rain season—or what I liked to call skin-melting season—would arrive soon enough. If just one section of the dome's exterior failed during the rains, the death toll would be unimaginable, and the reputation of Rhodon would be trashed. And I would likely be sent on multiple courier runs in the cover-up.

I really did need another job.

The train entered the tunnel leading to Sector 11's station platform. According to the screen just above the door, the conditions inside the sector were quite favorable today. The dome's filtration system was working at optimum, with no hint of poison from the outside world found in the sector's air. The environmental controls maintained the constant, even temperature of a moderate spring day. And the humidity factor was just enough to ensure your skin didn't dry out. One could happily walk around the sector without a breather or any protective clothing.

A poor-man's haven. Never mind the rent for the closet I called home was twenty thousand credits a month, but at least I had a place to call home and didn't need to live in the staff barracks underground in Sector 14.

I stepped off the train with my breather hanging around my neck. I still wore my virtual display glasses, but the goggle seals that hindered my peripheral vision were not activated.

I headed to the main plaza area, praying that there were enough credits in my account to get some cressicubes from my favorite vendor. It was the only natural source of mintonal I knew of. It wouldn't be enough to completely stabilize my body, but I had few options left until I could get more Miransine.

I curled my hands into loose fists, hoping to hide the shakes. If others on the streets saw my shaking hands, they would likely assume that I was infectious and call the health police. That was the last thing I needed.

The aroma from Hope Alley called to me. That coffee shop in Sector 4 might have been a busy place, but Sector 11 was a nonstop party. And the food carts in Hope Alley were just the entry.

Steel drums played a historic Caribbean rhythm with an infectious beat that endured to this day. Even the grumpiest moods could be lifted by those rhythms. One just wanted to do a hip sway and some salsa footwork—even when they didn't know what they were doing. With a soft smile on my face, I opened my hands and allowed the rhythm to take me wherever it wanted to. The shimmy of the shoulders would hide the shakes better than anything else I could do.

I followed my nose through the aromas of spicy foods to my favorite cart. The man who ran the food cart was an expert at Japanese–Caribbean fusion. One wouldn't have thought the two would go together, but Hector was a food wizard. "Ah . . . Mike. The usual?"

"Yes, please."

"Coming right up."

I held out my wrist, revealing my pharmachip, so I could authorize payment, but Hector waved my hand away.

"Today, it's on the house."

"Are you sure?"

He smiled and nodded. "It's the least I could do for the one who managed to get my Cecila the medication she needed." He leaned in closer and lowered his voice. "The voices were driving her crazy. Miransine is the only thing that works to stabilize her properly. If you don't mind me asking, how did you get your hands on so much of it?"

I sighed and did my best to maintain my smile. "I guess I have the right contacts." Never mind, I had given Cecila the bulk of my personal supply, but that didn't matter. I knew exactly what voices Hector was talking about. And those voices had been known to lead to suicide. Those voices killed my mother when I was a little girl. I couldn't let that happen to Cecila. As it was, she had already climbed the ledge, threatening to jump, just to silence the voices.

Ten years old, and she was rapidly going insane.

"I'm just glad that she's well again." Though, my own health would go down the toilet if I didn't get my hands on a new supply of Miransine and soon. The constant hum in my head would soon turn into those insanity-driving voices. If I wasn't careful, I would find myself climbing a ledge.

"It won't take long to have your order ready." Hector smiled, then turned to the next person in line to take their order.

I moved to the side, doing what I could to continue to enjoy the Caribbean sounds, but the movements of my dance were forced. My heart was no longer in it.

"That was generous of you."

"Did you say something?" I asked the person closest to me.

They just looked at me with a furrowed brow and shook their head.

"Sorry, my bad." I glanced around to see if it was someone else who had spoken, but the others were either buried in conversations with those around them, or bouncing around in time with the music, completely oblivious to anything I was doing. It had to have been my imagination, though that thought alone put me on edge.

I forced myself to take several deep breaths. I held my hand flat before my belly. Crap. The shaking had gotten worse. A lot worse. I needed mintonal.

One by one, the people waiting to collect their food disappeared, replaced by another who had put in a new order. I only had to wait for five minutes, but five minutes of trying to hide the shaking was more than enough.

I thanked Hector for the food, then made a beeline to a secluded spot. With no fear that anyone might be watching me, I quickly unwrapped the cressicube and took a bite. My hand shook violently. If the food cube had been smaller, I would have shoved the whole thing into my mouth at once. But given the choice between choking and shaking, I preferred the shaking.

From experience, it would take roughly twenty minutes before the effects of the mintonal in the cressicube to kick in. It wouldn't be enough to take away the shakes completely, or the humming in my head, but I only had to get through a few hours until I could pick up my prescription.

I looked at the clock on my virtual display. Five hours to wait, assuming there were no other delays.

"But there are always delays."

I spun around, looking for the one who just spoke to me, but there was no one nearby. "Hello?" I pressed my fingers to the side of my glasses, activating the voice command for my personal AI system. "Alice, run a complete scan of the area. Search for anything that could result in audio disturbances. Radio signals. People nearby that I can't see."

"Scan complete. There are no radio anomalies detected. The closest life force is twenty-five meters away."

"No audio messages that randomly played before?"

"Negative. You have no new messages."

Damn it. It had to have been my imagination. But if that were true . . .

I shoved the last of my cressicube into my mouth, praying that I wasn't finally succumbing to White Rabbit syndrome.

A muted ding sounded in my ears, and the number 1 flashed in the corner of my vision. I really didn't want to know what the message said. No doubt, it was something to do with my climbing audimensase levels.

Another ding, and the blinking light shifted to the number 2. Then another, and another. Number 4.

Damn it. All I wanted to do was to pick up my prescription, then disappear from society long enough to hide my increasing symptoms and to sleep off the *crazy* of the morning. Surely, the fact that I had been on the clock since 10 p.m. the night before would have been enough to say that my working day was done.

"But is a courier's work ever done?"

I spun around again, scanning for the owner of the voice. My heart raced ahead. Three times now, I had heard a voice right there, beside me. And all three times, the owner of the voice was nowhere to be seen.

I was overtired. That had to be it. My audimensase levels were skyrocketing, and I hadn't had much sleep. It had to be just my imagination. Though that thought didn't bring me much solace. The last time I had heard voices like this, I was locked up for psychological evaluation and a full battery of tests were carried out. They upped my Miransine dosage big time after that. Which was why I had so much of it that I could spare some for Cecila. But I miscalculated how much I needed to get by . . . and I ran out.

Another ding and the number of messages now counted in double digits. How many more messages could I ignore before they overrode the call block-out I had put in place? Well, whatever the number was, there was no way I could continue to ignore them for five hours.

Ignoring any concerns about the public seeing my shaking, I darted out of my hiding spot and headed straight for the pharmacy, hoping against all odds that they had already filled my script.

The dings turned into ringing. Damn it! When will I learn to not jinx the good luck?

My shoulders sagged as the caller ID displayed the name Tam Haworth. For the lack of a better term: my boss. Tam not only gave out the delivery assignments, but they also managed the rest of my life. Tam decided when and if I got paid. Tam was the one to oversee my medical treatments. And Tam was the one who ensured that I had the freedom to move from sector to sector in the way I was used to. When Tam said, "Jump," there was only one response. "How high?"

I knew from experience what would happen if I ignored Tam's calls. And it wasn't pretty.

While continuing to walk briskly toward the pharmacy, I reached up to my temple and pressed the answer button on my glasses. "Tam, I'm sorry, but now is not a good time. I'm on my way to the pharmacy to pick up my script. My audimensase levels are climbing—big time."

"I know. Which is in part why I called. You need to report to headquarters immediately. I will have an emergency script filled here waiting for you."

"But Tam, I also need to get some sleep. I've been up—"

"I am sorry, Michaella, but we have a situation that could compromise the security of our entire operation. All members of PentWave are to report immediately. No exceptions. From your present location, it should take you no more than ninety minutes to get through the checkpoints and to report to the team room. If you are not here within two hours, I will send a STAR unit for you."

I closed my eyes and tried really hard to bottle up my frustration. The last thing I needed was a Special Task and Reconnaissance unit rocking up to escort me to who knows where. They would not be gentle. "So, no sleep then?"

"I am sorry, Michaella."

I blew out the breath I had been holding. "On my way." There was no need to say anything else. I just turned around and headed for the transport tubes to Sector 14.

Four

As the doors to the transport tube opened to the underground entrance into Sector 14, I took several deep breaths of the filtered air—the cleanest air in the city controlled by one of the most sophisticated air filtration systems in existence. As much as I hated coming here, or more appropriately hated what coming here meant, it was always a relief for my body to breathe in such freshness.

With the clean air bringing some much-needed energy to my tired muscles, I headed toward the employee tunnels, scanning my pharmachip at one of the five pedestals at the first security checkpoint. Upon stepping into the first of the sanitation bays, I had to splash through three shallow pools of pink sanitation fluid designed to kill any germs tracking in on my boots. Each pool was three and a half meters long, nested in the ground and stretched wall to wall. Even if you took long strides, you were still forced to walk through them, with both feet getting wet at least once—each time. And that pink fluid killed the bugs alright, but it also killed the stitching on your shoes.

How many more passes through those baths could I get away with before I needed to replace my boots? I hung my head in despair, because I didn't have the money to buy new boots. Gah! I didn't want to even contemplate the number of courier drops I would need to make to afford new boots.

I entered the bustling locker room and headed to the far corner where my locker was tucked away. I pressed my wrist to the sensor pad and waited for the telltale click as the locker door released. Dragging out the inevitable, I removed my display glasses, mask, jacket, and gloves, allowing my favorite song to finish playing. It would be several hours before I could listen to it again, so I made the most of it while I could. When the song finished, I placed my earbuds on the shelf next to my display glasses and proceeded to remove my boots and every strip of clothing I wore, including my underwear. I folded each item as I put it in my locker. Nothing from outside Sector 14 could be brought into the sector—not through these entrances, anyway. Food and industrial supplies were brought in through service entrances on the other side of the sector under the watchful eye of trigger-happy grunts.

With all my belongings stowed in my locker, I turned my display glasses to face outwards and enabled the motion-detection recording system. My locker was supposed to be *my* locker, but sector security had the authority to override security protocols to *inspect* any locker they wanted. And a few of those security guys had sticky fingers. Virtual display glasses were encoded with genetic biometrics and were never on the list of things stolen. High-quality boots and RDF signal-blocking jackets, on the other hand . . .

I closed my locker, punching in my personalized lockout code, then headed out into the hall toward the health scanners, naked as the day I was born. It was one thing about working in this place. Any insecurity you might have had about body image vanished as soon as everyone around you was also naked. A little flab here and there was nothing compared to the shriveled-up junk that dangled between some guys' legs. At least my breasts were still *perky*, as I was once told. But as comfortable as I was in my own skin, I still felt exposed and vulnerable—without my jacket to hide the signal from my pharmachip, or a mask to filter the air in the event of an environmental system's failure. Or without my earbuds to play *Purple Rain* to help keep me calm and focused.

I followed the stream of naked sector employees through the sanitation walkways that blasted the body with various rays meant to kill external bugs. All the while, health scanners imaged my insides and compared them to the scans on file, actively on the hunt for internal bugs.

A woman some distance in front of me was pulled out of the line by those wearing yellow hazmat suits with fully sealed face masks. No doubt the scanners detected some infectious bug trying to hitchhike into Sector 14, using her body as the transport.

Everyone around me just kept facing forward, not really paying attention to the pleas from the woman being hauled away. Centuries of pandemic after pandemic had a habit of making people jaded to the desperate souls who carried infectious disease. And an outbreak in Sector 14 would spell disaster for the entire city.

The doctors in the early 2100s were geniuses when they decided to risk aggressive vaccination schemes on pregnant women and their unborn children. Never mind that somewhere along the way, someone stuffed up the cocktail, resulting in audimentia, aka White Rabbit syndrome. But other than the symptoms of audimentia, I've never spent a day sick in my life. Some doctors called me the perfect specimen of health—except for the fact that my brain didn't work quite right.

I stepped into the main health scanner. The last hurdle into Sector 14. The glass door closed behind me and a red X appeared in front of me.

"Please keep your eyes open and look forward," said the technician over the intercom. "The scan will start shortly."

I rolled my shoulders and breathed in slowly, counting to five as I inhaled, then counting to three before I exhaled to another count of five. I kept my eyes forward and my hands by my sides. My fingers lightly tapped on my thighs—an uncontrollable action.

The scan in this machine wasn't like the scans moving between sectors. This one would be a full sequence, taking at least thirty seconds to run. And it would report everything about my physical health to the technicians—including my climbing audimensase levels.

The system hummed and slight vibrations radiated up through my feet as I waited to be released from the cage.

Twenty-nine. Thirty.

The red X still shined brightly, and the doors still hadn't opened.

Fifty-three. Fifty-four.

My heart rate sped up, and my breathing was getting a little shaky. What I wouldn't have done to have my earbuds right then.

Eighty-five. Ninety. One hundred.

"Is there a problem? The scans don't normally take this long."

The hum from the intercom was more like a squeal, and I winced as the technician's voice filled the space around me. "I'm sorry, Agent Davison, we've detected an abnormality in your system. We're just waiting for the all clear from the medical team."

"An abnormality? Like what?"

"Nothing that will compromise the health and safety of others in the sector. But medical want to see you as soon as possible. You're free to enter Sector 14."

The red X was replaced with a green checkmark, and the glass doors in front of me opened.

I exhaled in a rush, then proceeded forward.

That was a record scan length time.

I continued down the hall to the uniform pickup. Each uniform issued was of a different design and color configuration, intended to indicate a person's assigned role within the sector. Some people were issued beige overalls. Others were given white suits or white lab coats. My uniform consisted of a long-sleeved, form-fitted, black tunic and a pair of black tailored pants. On top of the pile rested a pair of thick black socks and a pair of combat boots. While in Sector 14, I was a *protector*, but not just any protector. The deep purple stripes that ran down my sleeves marked me as a member of PentWave, an elite unit that was given the authority to take whatever steps were necessary to ensure the safety of the entire city. I wore those stripes with pride; I worked hard to earn them. I just wished I had known about the terrorist-style tactics that came with those stripes before accepting them.

With my uniform on, I headed to the equipment desk, where I was issued with an earpiece radio and a head unit with a flip-down optical display that rested over my right eye. While in Sector 14, I was part of sector security, but I was only to act on security matters in the case of a significant breach. The entire time I had been part of PentWave, not once had I been called upon to play the role of security guard. Because of it, I always turned down the weapons they wanted to issue me. Besides, in close quarters, a gun was just as much as a danger to me as it was to an assailant.

Fully equipped, I headed down the halls leading to the main entrance into the sector plaza—where all those entering the sector got to see the true splendor that was Sector 14.

Trees dotted around the place surrounded by lush green grass where people could enjoy a picnic lunch. The high-rise buildings were covered in green ivy; manicured garden balconies were scattered up the sides of the buildings. But the most spectacular feature of Sector 14 was the sky—blue with the odd white cloud floating overhead. I closed my eyes and tilted my face upward to enjoy the warmth of the sun.

It was all an illusion, of course. Projector technology interwoven into the dome that sheltered us from the outside world—from the real sky that was dark and dingy, and likely filled with acid rain. Within Sector 14, special environmental controls were used to ensure that all those inside the sector had the luxury to forget about the mess that the generations before them had made of the world outside.

"How many times do I have to tell you that it's not real?" Another soul dressed in a black uniform slid up beside me and nudged me with his shoulder. His bright red hair sparkled in the sunlight.

"Morning, George." For a brief moment, I rested my head on his shoulder.

"Morning, Mike." He laughed as he wrapped his arm around me and pulled me closer, giving me a kiss on the top of my head. "I take it you got called in by the Ham?"

"Yes." I sighed, not surprised by the new nickname for our handler. "Though I would have preferred to have gotten some sleep first."

I pulled away from him and headed across the main plaza toward the tallest building in the sector, where the head offices and research facilities of Rhodon Corporation were housed. I inhaled as deeply as I could, enjoying the smell of white roses lining the walkways.

George walked beside me. "Yeah, well, sleep is for the weak. Hey, did you hear the latest news?"

"What conspiracy theory are they coming up with this time?"

"Not a conspiracy, but rather a story of revenge."

"Oh . . . do tell."

"Well, apparently Dr. Elizabeth Eason is dead."

"Why does that name sound familiar?"

"Dr. Eason was the one we all called the Angel of Death."

"You mean that geneticist who killed audimentia patients, hiding her failed attempts at finding a cure?"

George grinned. "The one and the same."

"But I thought she disappeared a year ago. That she evaded authorities by leaving the city?"

"So did I. But she showed up this morning in a coffee shop in Sector 4."

I about tripped over my own feet. I pulled on George's arm and turned him to face me. "In Sector 4? Are you sure?"

"Positive. According to the news, while in the coffee shop, she was shot dead by the brother of her last victim. After he killed her, he killed himself."

I ran my fingers through my hair and sighed in relief. "I can't believe that someone finally got her."

"Don't you mean that *you* finally got her?"

"What are you getting at?"

"The death of Dr. Elizabeth Eason is not what is making headlines. The news is all worked up about how her killer managed to get a gun into Sector 4 in the first place. An unmarked gun at that. While the news first reported it as the work of pharmachip protesters, they're starting to wonder if those with White Rabbit syndrome are lashing out, turning into a group of organized terrorists." George glanced around, then ushered me into a side alley, away from the crowds moving through the sector plaza. "Mike, while the police are not looking for Dr. Eason's murderer, they're looking for a person with purple hair seen leaving the scene just before the shooting." He reached forward and ran his fingers through my purple hair. "You were there, weren't you?"

When George looked at me with those accusing eyes, it was really hard to stay silent. And I knew he was trying to read my thoughts. But I also knew how to keep him out. Not that it did much good.

He was my best friend. We had been through so much together. And I hated keeping secrets from him. But some secrets—

George sighed. "I thought so." He stepped back, taking several deep breaths, and combed his fingers through his red mane. "Geez, Mike. I thought you said that you weren't going to do anymore drops, that your request to transfer to STAR had been granted. You told me that you were scheduled to get your communications implant any day now. Why would you risk that to do the Pregutor's dirty work?"

"I needed the money. They paid me fifty thousand credits to deliver that package."

He blinked, and his jaw dropped. "Fifty? Shit. It still doesn't explain why you would risk your future."

"What future? We have audimentia, George. It carries with it a death sentence of its own. We're all going to die. Some of us sooner than others." I took a deep breath and held up my left hand. The shaking had amplified since I had come through the staff tunnels. "My audimensase levels have skyrocketed, and I ran out of Miransine." Never mind that I had given the bulk of my supply away to a little girl in greater need. "I took that job so I could pay for my prescription."

"Are you hearing voices?" His voice was just barely above a whisper, like he was not wanting to admit to the worst symptom of audimentia.

I averted my eyes.

"Mike, answer me. And don't you dare try to lie to me. You know I can sense it when you're lying."

My chest grew tight, and my throat felt like it was being constricted. "Yes, but they're not telling me to do things."

"Not yet."

We stood there staring at each other, knowing the truth.

He reached forward and pulled me close to his chest. "We'll figure it out. You don't have to do this alone." He then pushed me back and brushed my hair from my eyes. "I want you to make me a promise. If you are ever presented with the opportunity to get out—to escape this life—take it."

"I promise." But it felt hollow. There was only one way to truly escape my mess of a life. Death.

A buzzing radiated from the earpiece I wore, and a message appeared on my eyepiece display.

>>Do I need to send a STAR unit?<<

There was no sender ID attached to the message, but I knew who it was from.

George sagged and sighed, as he turned and led the way out of the alley, heading toward the Rhodon Corporation buildings.

Five

THE RHODON BUILDING WHERE OUR briefings were held was filled with the boring monochromatic humdrum of a sterile environment. White walls with white ceilings and white floors. There wasn't even the color of photos on the walls, like one saw in those old vid-recordings from before the health reforms of 2096. It was like the mission to eradicate disease raged a war on color—and color lost.

We navigated the monochromatic maze, passing by monochromatic people. White lab coats and black pants, and their black or blond hair. A hint of color leaked into the world through the stripes running down the sleeves of those wearing black uniforms. Blue and yellow. But everyone cleared the path for those wearing the purple stripes with brightly colored hair. We had the elevator to the lower levels to ourselves.

As soon as the elevator doors closed, George groaned. "Have you ever noticed how the only real color in this joint seems to be blue and yellow? It's like no one has heard of the color red." He shook his head, exaggerating his latest dye job. "Only the other day, I caught the gardeners pulling out a red rose bush and destroying it. Like anything but white roses was a crime."

"Painting the roses white?"

"Off with their heads," we said together, then laughed. But he had a point.

There was a soft ding as the elevator doors opened to the main security level. An unusual bustling of activity filled the hall. Those with blue stripes lined the walls in pairs, fully armed, their eyes following those who walked by them. Technicians with their yellow stripes darted past the guards in groups, yammering in their coded language as they tapped into the empty space in front of them and disappeared through holographic walls.

A tactical unit in full gear ran down the hall, forcing George and me, and anyone else who wasn't part of the unit, to press up against the wall in the spaces between the guards.

I reached up to my radio receiver, double checking that I was connected to the main security channel; the channel was filled with the normal chatter. "What's going on?"

George shook his head. "Don't know, but whatever it is, I don't want to know. Let's just get to the briefing."

We resumed our trek through the bustling halls to a small briefing room located at the end of a long corridor. The door was closed and locked, requiring the appropriate security authorization to open the door. This was standard practice for a PentWave briefing. The Pregutor couldn't have just anyone knowing about our terrorist tactics.

I stepped closer to the door and pressed my right hand and wrist to the scanner. A blue light sprang to life to scan my eyes. Why were some security scans happy with just my pharmachip while others required more? It was like the designers wanted to ensure that only those conscious and living were able to open certain doors—a rather important detail for anyone taking part in the activities that occurred on the other side of these doors.

There was a small click, followed by a slight hiss, as a portion of the wall withdrew and slid to the side. With the path now unhindered, George and I stepped inside.

The team room was almost the exact opposite to the hall outside. Its black walls seemed to absorb the ambient light. Those wearing black uniforms melted into the background, even with the purple stripes running down their arms. If someone stood perfectly still, their presence would go unnoticed, until what little light was in the room reflected off their eyes. Digital displays adorned the walls, showing maps of the city, with colored lines of blue and yellow separating the city into fourteen sectors. George nudged my shoulder and pointed to the maps. He wore an expression of "See." Vid-recordings were scattered around the maps, showing security camera feeds from around the city, continuously hunting for threats that needed to be neutralized.

While I could never work out how the Pregutor determined which threats to neutralize (and which to ignore), I knew how the members of PentWave were selected. Every single one of us suffered from White Rabbit syndrome, diagnosed as children and sent to isolation camps, while the geneticists and doctors worked on a cure. Responding well to treatments, each member of PentWave was given special training, so one day we could protect the city as a form of payment for the treatments we had been given. It was our audimentia that united us. And it was the promise of ongoing medical treatment that kept us loyal to the Pregutor, even knowing the nature of the packages we delivered.

I held my hands tightly to my sides, determined to hide the shakes. There was no way I wanted the others to know about my audimensase levels. It was bad enough that George knew about the voices.

There was another hiss of the door as a pure white figure strode in. Tam stood out in their white suit, their pale complexion, and snow-white hair. Even Tam's eyes were white with little black dots for the pupils. An albino, as it was once called, though Tam didn't have any of the other traits that went along with albinism based on what I had read. Tam's vision was as sharp as anyone's. At times, Tam looked more like a ghost. It didn't help that the low light levels created this iridescent glow around their person. The more I interacted with Tam, the more the definition of *human* was stretched.

"Good morning, everyone." Tam passed a data rod to one of the team members. "Please load this for me." They then turned to face George and myself. "George, a quick word."

George followed Tam into the corner of the room. When Tam spoke, they ensured that their back was to the rest of us, and they spoke in whispered tones, quiet enough that none of us could hear what was being said. But whatever it was caused George's shoulders to sag as he hung his head. He then nodded and headed for the door.

Before he left, he placed his hand on my shoulder, encouraging me to look at him. "Remember your promise." There was an intensity in his eyes: determination mixed with fear. I wanted to ask him what was going on, but I didn't dare—not with everyone in the room watching our little exchange.

Aware of the accusing eyes trained on me, I nodded. "I will."

George then tried to smile. As he headed out of the room, he was instantly surrounded by guards. My breath caught in the back of my throat and my heart rate sped up.

Before I could fully process the implication of the guards, Tam sealed the room.

They stood next to the main digital display and pressed their hand and wrist to the wall. They then looked at each of us in turn, daring us to question what we saw, but no one said a word.

It was one of the things I admired about Tam. They exuded a level of command that made it perfectly clear who was in charge. No one spoke unless given permission to speak.

"Michaella, this is for you." Tam held a small medical dispenser spray unit designed to inject a measured dose of medication directly into the bloodstream. "Pull back your hair, please."

I did as I was told, exposing my carotid artery. The cold unit was pressed to my neck, and there was a slight hiss and a pinch. A cooling sensation filled my veins. The sense of relief was almost instantaneous. It would still take a few minutes for the drug to take full effect, but the shakes were gone . . . as was the hum inside my head.

"I expect you to be more diligent in the future." Tam pocketed the dispenser unit.

"Yes, Tam. I'm sorry."

"No need to apologize—not to me, anyway."

The others glared at me, like they were getting ready to lecture me about putting them all in danger.

"Now that you are all here, we have important matters to discuss. In the last week, each of you delivered a package to one of these locations." Tam tapped out a sequence into the empty space before them, and location dots overlaid the city map. Eight dots in total, including one that would have aligned with the coffee shop in Sector 4. "Each of you performed your duty admirably. However, there was one drop that was problematic at best."

Tam tapped out another sequence into the space in front of them. The display zoomed in on Sector 5, one of the outskirt sectors, but one that was well maintained. Sector 5 was where all the city imports and exports happened. It was where the truckers worked, delivering goods to the city from outside manufacturing facilities and transporting any pharmaceuticals manufactured in Crystal Hills to the rest of the world. No one lived in Sector 5; it was too dangerous with all the potential exposure to disease from the outside world. And only those with top-level health records could work there. Like Sector 14, the health scanning of those going in and out of the sector was incredibly strict. And like Sector 14, an outbreak in the sector could spell certain doom for the city.

"The drop was supposed to occur at BioShipping. They are a small exporter, one that specializes in the transportation of hazardous biowaste to the facility at Eudurvinna for safe disposal. It turns out that they were exporting more than just biowaste. The owner of BioShipping has been smuggling out of the city those infected with flurona. We do not know how those with flurona have been able to get into Sector 5, but because these people have been allowed to roam freely, there are now massive outbreaks in Eudurvinna and Lagniappe Fields. The Pregutor sent an undercover operative to learn more about the operations and to ultimately remove BioShipping from the equation. Three days ago, the operative put in a request for the equipment needed to execute the removal. Unfortunately, the drop did not go as planned, and the operative was found dead this morning with a message pinned to his chest."

The image on the screen changed, bringing up the photo of a dead body with a clear view of the operative's face.

The short woman next to me gasped. "That's Lucas."

I glanced at the tiny woman next to me. Jody Kristensen. She was the only other female on our team, but talk about a powerhouse when she wanted to be. It was Jody's motto: the deadliest things known to mankind came in the tiniest of packages. And when it came to Jody, I believed it. She only came up to my shoulder, and she used that size difference to her advantage. But Jody was also a gentle, caring soul, one that was desperate to find love and companionship in this meager life that we led. At one point, Jody found that love in one of our trainers, though it didn't last long.

"Are you sure?" I searched the image of the deceased man for signs of the curly locks and the boyish rough exterior that had once graced the face of one of my trainers.

Jody nodded, keeping her eyes on the display. The little amount of light in the room caught the glistening that hung in the corners of her eyes.

"Jody is right," Tam said. "Lucas Tellis. Former PentWave courier until he was promoted to trainer, then field operative. And according to the medical examiner, his death was not a peaceful one. Whoever killed Lucas injected him with Floxdronolin, a biological weapon designed to thicken the blood to the point where it no longer flows. Once exposed, death is a certainty."

Scuffling feet sounded around the room. If Lucas was unable to save himself from a brutal attack of this nature, what hope did the rest of us have?

"What about the note?" someone asked from the other side of the room. From the sounds of the deep timbres, it was Marcus Gahan, the meanest, badass bully that I had ever met.

He always had to prove that he was the toughest kid on the playground. But for some unknown reason, he stayed clear of me. All I had to do was stare at him, wishing that he would leave me alone . . . and he would.

The image changed on the display to show a closeup of the note found with Lucas's body.

>>Abram Shutton's son lives.<<

"What's that supposed to mean?" Marcus asked. "Dr. Shutton doesn't have a son. Or does he?"

Tam took a deep breath. "The fact that Dr. Shutton may or may not have a son is of little consequence. What is important is the level of doubt and mistrust that this message has managed to sow in such a short period of time."

The video display shifted to the security footage from one of the transport companies inside Sector 5. Trucks were lined up, blocking the roads in and out of the sector. And one by one, the drivers got out of their trucks and disappeared off camera.

"When asked, the drivers all said the same thing. They fear that the one responsible would come after them next. And they all fear that the one responsible is Dr. Abram Shutton's son."

"You said that the courier drop went wrong," I said. "What do we know about the drop itself?"

A vid-recording from a security camera near the entrance for BioShipping came up on the display. The courier came into view and stood at the corner of the building, obscured by the shadows.

Even though there was no uniform as such for couriers outside of Sector 14, there was a commonality to the way we all dressed, namely the colorful oversized, RDF signal-blocking jacket with the hood that hung low over our eyes, the glasses with seals activated that protected the eyes from the elements, and the breather mask. We also wore black leatherette gloves, made from the finest synthetic material that Rhodon Corporation could get their hands on. It wasn't for warmth, but rather to ensure we didn't leave prints on the packages themselves. The gloves added a layer of cover on our pharmachips, too, in case the sleeves of our jackets were lifted and exposed that part of their wrists to the security drones.

Even though we had all been trained in surveillance avoidance tactics, able to hide our identities from standard security, we all knew who it was on the screen.

George.

I closed my eyes and hung my head. I knew the security guards surrounding him couldn't mean anything good.

"Who is that?" Jody asked.

She wasn't referring to George, but rather to the other hooded figure that the courier on the screen was talking to. The courier's movements were jerky, almost like George had been resistant, but eventually George handed over the package, and the second hooded figure disappeared. However, George just stood there, not moving. His actions didn't make any sense. The moment he made the drop, he should have been hightailing it out of there, making a beeline for the sector checkpoint.

Another hooded figure appeared on the screen, coming from the opposite direction that the hooded figure in possession of the package had disappeared. There was a short verbal exchange between George and the new hooded figure—though no sound was recorded—followed by a sense of desperation as George patted down his person.

Marcus whistled. "Holy shit. George delivered the package to the wrong person. How the fuck could he make such a stupid mistake?"

"And who did he actually deliver the package to?" Jody asked.

"Both are good questions," Tam said, "and both of them do not have an answer at this time. We are hoping that George managed to get a good look at the unknown."

Nervous fears threatened to take over my thoughts. "I don't think it really matters who he handed the package over to. I think it's more important that we find out how this unknown made George forget he handed over the package in the first place."

"Why would you think he forgot about the package?" Marcus asked. There was a hint of accusation in his voice, like he was challenging me to reveal something that I shouldn't. Not that I had a clue what he wanted revealed to the world at large.

I pursed my lips and tilted my head to the side. "Tam, could you please rewind and show the drop again?"

Tam pinched their fingers in the air and waved the video back to the start of the sequence, when George stood there waiting.

I inhaled and exhaled in a controlled manner as I moved to the front of the team room and stood next to Tam. "We all know it's George we're looking at. We can't see his face, but we know his mannerisms. The way he stands. The way he bounces and fidgets when he's waiting for something." I waved my hand to fast forward past the exchange with the unknown, then with exaggerated arm motions, the image zoomed in on the courier. "Standard protocol for courier drops is to disappear the moment the drop is made. Don't linger for any reason. Yet George is just standing there—doing nothing. Not even bouncing up and down while he waits. It's like he's catatonic until the real drop arrives." The video footage zoomed back out to the full view, then continued to play. "Watch carefully the way he starts patting down his person. It was a small package he was delivering. We saw the delivery. But a package that size could be stored in any one of five pockets inside our jackets. We all tend to use the same pockets, but how many of you have placed small packages in a different pocket in a hurry?"

"I've done that," Jody said.

"And what did you do when you discovered that the package wasn't where you expected it to be?"

Jody smirked. "I patted myself down, trying to feel for the lump."

Marcus wove around the table to stand next to me. He gestured for the footage of the delivery and the pat-down to replay. After walking it through in slow motion—and in reverse—Marcus scowled. "George might be an idiot, but he's not so incompetent that he would forget about a delivery. Not while on the job, anyway."

An uneasy silence fell over the room. There were times when the treatments for audimentia would result in temporary memory loss. Normally, it was only the short-term memory affected, but Rhodon Corporation had developed treatments and technologies to help restore memory function. That had to be where George was right now: getting treatment for memory loss.

I took a few deep breaths and faced the others. "We need to find this unknown, and we need to find them fast."

The others just stared at me. Some wore furrowed brows that demanded more answers, while others possessed eyes that widened with fear. But Tam's expression was calm, with a slight smile. It was their expression of approval, like I had hit the exact area of concern that threatened us all.

There was someone out there with the ability to make people do things, then forget that they did them.

This unknown was like me.

Six

My eyes were getting blurry as I continued to stare at the virtual displays. The Pregutor had run algorithm after algorithm, checking every system available. Radio signals. Entry logs in and out of Sector 5. The pharmachip records. Video feeds from throughout the sector. Everything on file was pushed through the Pregutor's systems, trying to find a trace of the unknown hooded figure. But there was no sign of them . . . other than the fuzzy zoomed in image from the failed drop footage.

As much as I hated the idea, I had to admire them. I had been trying to figure out how to sneak past sector security undetected for years. And here I was, staring at the proof that some unknown had done it.

I allowed my head to fall forward and rested my forehead on the cool table surface. "It's official. They're a ghost."

"Impossible!" Marcus slammed his fist against the table, causing me to bolt upright again. "There is no way to get past the system undetected. If there was, we would know about it."

"Yet, the proof is right in front of us," I said. "And how much do we really know about the security systems? We're not STAR. They have access to systems we don't."

"Not even the STAR can vanish completely from the Pregutor." Tam waved their hand in front of them, and the displays dissolved into an inert state. "PentWave has been at this for nearly six hours. You all need a break. Get some food and some rest, then report back tomorrow morning."

The door hissed as it slid to the side, and light from the white hallway flooded into the dark room. One by one, the members of PentWave stretched out their arms, loosening their stiff muscles, then headed out the door. But before I could get too far, Tam called me back.

"Michaella, a word."

There was something about Tam's tone that made my heart sink. The reprimand was coming, and the punishment was not going to be pretty. All I wanted was a good night's sleep, but just the look on Tam's face told me that sleep wasn't part of my near future.

I did the best I could to stand tall and not cower. I could easily count on one hand the number of times that Tam glared at me with those accusing eyes. And the fact that Tam's eyes were pure white except for the black pupils only made that accusing stare worse. And every time that I had been on the receiving end of that look, it was because my audimensase levels had skyrocketed—because I hadn't been taking my medication.

Tam pressed their hand to the door sensor and tapped out a code. The door slid shut and a red X appeared over the sensor pad. Priority One Security Lockout. No one was getting in or out of that room until Tam said so.

"Tam, I'm sorry, I—"

Tam's lips pressed into a thin line. "You promised me that you would never go off your medication again. I had a look at the logs, Michaella. Your audimensase levels have been steadily climbing for the past three weeks. That should not have happened if you were taking your proper dosage of Miransine. I want the truth. Why did you stop taking your medication?"

I tried to swallow the lump forming at the back of my throat, but it just wouldn't go away. "I was running low and had to ration what I had left until I could afford a new prescription." I sighed as I hung my head. "But I ran out a few days ago."

"According to the logs, you had more than enough to get you through the next month. How could you possibly have been running low?" The air around Tam wavered. Their white suit seem to glow even whiter. "I want the truth, Michaella, and I want it now."

"Tam, please, I—"

The colored flesh of Tam's lips nearly disappeared as the thin line pressed even straighter. The hard expression in Tam's eyes became cold steel. The air surrounding Tam took on a slight red sheen.

No matter how much I tried to stay strong, I just had to accept whatever punishment Tam saw fit—even if my actions were with good intentions. "I gave some of my last prescription to a little girl who lives in Sector 11."

"And why would you do that?"

"Because the voices in her head were telling her to kill herself, and I couldn't let that happen."

Tam's expression softened, and the white radiance consumed Tam again. A hint of regret wrinkled the corners of their eyes. "Miransine is not for everyone who hears voices, Michaella. Giving this girl some of your prescription was very dangerous—for both the girl *and* for you. We need to bring her in for testing. I need her name."

My heart raced ahead. "Tam, please. She's only ten years old. If she's formally diagnosed with audimentia, her life will be ruined."

"Do you consider your life ruined?"

The silence that hung between us grew thick.

In the end, I sighed and hung my head in shame. "I'm tired of delivering death. It breaks my heart every time. But I don't have another choice. The only other option for me is death, and I can't live with that."

"I am unable to live with that option as well." A hint of a smile broke up the thin line of Tam's lips. "But we still need to test the girl. She may not be suffering from audimentia. There are many conditions that could result in a person hearing voices that are not there, and any one of them could drive a person to take their own life. If you truly care about this girl, you will tell me her name."

I took several deep breaths. "Her name is Cecila. I don't know her last name. But her father's name is Hector. He runs one of the food carts in Sector 11. He makes a mean cressicube."

"The only natural source of mintonal. I take it that the young girl lives on cressicubes."

I nodded.

"That explains why you thought Miransine could help her. Do you know anything about her mother?"

I shook my head. "All I know is that she went missing shortly after Cecila was born. Hector raised her on his own, barely making ends meet. Tam . . ." I took another deep breath. "He can't afford to get medical treatment for Cecila. He can barely afford the housing in Sector 11. I understand what you're saying about Cecila needing testing and needing proper treatment, but . . ."

Tam gave my shoulder a gentle squeeze. "The Rhodon Corporation will pay for the testing and the initial treatments. She is using your prescription, after all, and if you continue to share your prescription with this young girl, *you* could die. As you so eloquently put it, that is not an option that we can live with." Tam took a deep breath and brushed out the creases in their white pant suit. "I need to make a few calls, send someone out to bring the girl and her father here for testing. In the meantime, the Pregutor was pleased with how your mission went this morning."

"About that . . ."

Tam held up their hand. "The police are nothing to worry about. The Pregutor has it in hand. You were the only one who could have done that drop. The Pregutor needed your unique skills." Tam took another deep breath and stood straighter—though I didn't think it was possible for Tam to stand any straighter than they normally did. "And the Pregutor needs your unique skills again. I have another job for you . . . in Sector 2. And you have only four hours to get there."

"What? Sector 2 is in the outer rim. With all the health checkpoints that I'll be required to go through, four hours doesn't leave a lot of time for any transport delays. And that dose of Miransine you gave me before won't last the night. My audimensase levels are still elevated, and they will continue to rise, and—" I stopped myself from telling Tam about the strange voice I kept hearing.

"I am sorry, Michaella, but the Pregutor was very specific. You are the only one who can deliver this package, and it needs to be delivered by the deadline in four hours." Tam sighed. They reached forward and caressed my cheek. It was a gesture that was so uncharacteristic. Normally, Tam was distant—caring, but distant. But the center of Tam's eyes took on a pink hue. A sweet fragrance filled the room. And a feeling of love washed over me, radiating from Tam's touch.

Tam jerked their hand back and brushed down their suit. The fragrance vanished, and their eyes resumed their unnerving pure white state.

"You will need to leave right away, or you will miss the drop. Even if you run, it will take you fifteen minutes to go through the sector-exit health protocols. The package will be waiting for you at the security desk at Gate 4B."

So much for getting sleep. At least the adrenaline had already started coursing through my veins. "Understood."

"And Michaella, report back here after you complete the delivery. The Pregutor will want a full report immediately." Tam released the security lock on the room, and the door slid open. "Please be careful. No mistakes can be allowed to happen during this drop. It is a Level One Drop."

My eyes went wide. Level One Drops were threats of the highest nature. If I failed to convince the recipient of the package to carry out the Pregutor's wishes, I was to carry them out myself—even if it meant my death.

Without another word, I bolted from the room and ran through the halls, heading for the staff tunnels.

Seven

I DARTED ACROSS THE CENTRAL plaza, ignoring disgruntled looks as I pushed past a group of nurses who were in my way. I hopped the last few meters as I removed my standard issue boots. As soon as I entered the employees' tunnels, I stripped down to my naked form. I dumped my gear on the counter for the equipment drop-off, waving my pharmachip over the scanner. And I continued to run through the halls. Thankfully, everyone moved to the side, making a hole for me.

At my locker, I took a quick breather as I waited for the system to recognize my authorization and open my locker. It was then a race to put on my clothing, lace my boots, and grab the rest of my gear. But before I could race to the transport tubes, I still had to go through the health scanners.

I stood in line, waiting for my turn, bouncing on the balls of my feet. No doubt, the people around me thought I was suffering from some condition that made me fidget. Then again, maybe they thought I was doing some kind of toilet dance. But at least, no one would be thinking that I was carrying some contagious disease.

The line got shorter and shorter. It wasn't long before I was at the front and stepping into the main scanner unit. I had to force myself to take a deep breath and calm down. My antsy demeanor would only interfere with the scan.

As soon as the door behind me closed, I started to count. *One . . .*

A green checkmark flashed before me and the doors opened. One second? Finally, something was going right. They were using quick sweeps for a change.

I darted down the hall to the security desk at Gate 4B. "You should have a package for me." I held out my right gloved hand, palm up, and pressed my index and forefinger from my left hand to my pharmachip. A holo-authenticator hovered above my palm. A white rose in full bloom that spun around in slow circles.

The security guard stepped forward with his scanner, then nodded at the beeping noise. He handed over a box that was three inches by twelve inches by seven. This wasn't a box that I could *easily* conceal, but I had ways of keeping the package hidden as I traveled.

I put on my display glasses and activated my special scanner by pressing the button at my left temple. The preloaded software did its job and checked for anything that could cause issues as I moved from sector to sector. The scanner app came back clean, and I tapped at the white rose logo in the center of my vision. As far as the Pregutor was concerned, I was now in possession of the package. I thanked the security guard and headed for the sector transport hub.

I had just over three and a half hours left to get to Sector 2, though I wouldn't know exactly where I was going until I passed the final checkpoint and entered the sector.

"Excuse me!" The security guard chased after me.

Okay, it doesn't matter if I hadn't done anything wrong. Seeing a security guard chase after me was always going to be a little nerve-racking. "Did I forget something?"

"No, I was the one to forget. This was with the package. I was meant to give you this too." The guard held out a small metallic cylindrical tube that easily fit in the palm of my hand. Etched into the side was the white rose logo.

That in itself was confusing, because packages never possessed any markings that could link them back to Rhodon Corporation. If anyone ever found out what the Pregutor was doing, it would lead to massive riots in the streets. No, this package was different.

My brow scrunched up in confusion. Cautiously, I took the metal tube and ran my scanner program again to ensure that the tube was safe to transport between sectors. With the clean light, I accepted the package and was sent an instant message.

>>This one is for you . . . to stabilize your audimensase levels and keep you in full control. Good luck. Tam.<<

I couldn't resist the smile. Tam really did look after those under their care.

I unscrewed the tube and poured two white tablets into my gloved palm. I dry swallowed both tablets, and mentally calculated how long it would take for the pills to kick in. Then I headed toward the transport tubes heading to the outer rim.

EIGHT

I passed through the last checkpoint with the package safely stowed under my oversized jacket. Four tube transfers, all with their own health scanners to go through, and the foot travel through Sector 6, but I made it to Sector 2 with roughly twenty minutes to spare.

Sector 2, one of three border sectors to the outside world. Immigrants entering into Crystal Hills via Sector 2 were subjected to countless medical tests to ensure that they weren't carriers of some disease that could cripple the city. And if they had skills that could be of benefit to Rhodon, they were given sector passes and allowed into the city interior after their quarantine period. Those unable to obtain a sector pass had two choices: leave Crystal Hills immediately and seek sanctuary from the outside world elsewhere; or live in squalor until they gave up and left Crystal Hills, anyway—occasionally leaving in a box destined for the cremation facilities located outside the city walls.

Once upon a time, Sector 2 would have held all the promise of a better life. The archway entrance to the sector checkpoint still possessed the faint outlines of the mural artwork, showing a young family walking into a dome-covered garden. But the child's face had eroded away long ago, covered in streaks of black filth. And the dome depicted in the mural was cracked in places, missing sections—not unlike the real dome structure that was supposed to cover Sector 2.

The support beams for Sector 2's dome jutted out from the checkpoint building, hanging in midair. It was like the city's designers had intended for Sector 2 to be fully enclosed, but they ran out of money to complete the construction. Instead, I had a clear view of the dark purple clouds that hung overhead, a vivid reminder of why so many people sought refuge in Crystal Hills. Without my breather firmly in place, I would struggle to breathe, inhaling traces of corrosive toxins. Without the active seals on my display glasses to protect my eyes, I would go blind at the first sign of rain.

With one last look at the eroding mural, I moved away from the checkpoint terminal and deeper into the sector.

Like clockwork, a ding resonated in my ears and the message indicator flashed in the bottom corner of my peripheral vision. I waved my hand and opened the message. It was a simple graphic with a jagged line surrounding a star.

I pressed my hand to the side of my display glasses. "Alice, are you there?"

"Awaiting orders."

"Bring up the latest street map of Sector 2 and overlay the most recent message received. Then calculate the best path from my present location to the location indicated by the star."

"Processing."

Why Alice insisted on saying things like *processing* when the commands were executed almost immediately was a complete mystery. Within the blink of an eye, there was a tiny map of the sector in the corner of my vision, with blinking arrows telling me which way to go.

"Alice, what is my ETA?"

"Estimated time of arrival: eight minutes."

"Bring up a countdown for the drop."

A countdown timer showed on my display, with nine minutes and twenty seconds remaining.

I blinked. I could have sworn I had twenty minutes left. But time never passed as one expected. Talk about calling it close.

Without further thought, I headed into the depths of Sector 2.

Over the years, the one thing I had learned about drops was to expect the unexpected. And walking around in Sector 2 was no different. I was a courier from the interior sectors, equipped with a filtration breather and high-tech health scanners. I hated to think what the going rate was for my tech on the black market. But my training included advanced self-defense and disarming tactics. Besides, my kit was DNA encoded and equipped with biometric sensors. And if anyone managed to bypass those systems, Alice had a few surprises waiting for them.

My virtual display went into overdrive, washing my field of view with a red haze. An X hovered over the head of every other person I passed on the street, signs of elevated body temperatures and infectious disease. The analysis data indicated that many of them were carriers of flurona.

An old man tripped, and I skated out of the way, doing the best I could to avoid physical contact. Even though my breather and peripheral seals on my glasses protected me from airborne diseases, some diseases were still spread by touch—and I refused to become a permanent resident of Sector 2.

I turned the final corner and stared at the dark entrance to a tiny store. A mortar-and-pestle symbol was painted on the sign out front. Dried sticks and weeds hung in the window.

An apothecary?

It made sense if I thought about it. The Pregutor would take action to shut this place down if it was discovered that they were dishing up whack medicine. There were people who insisted that herbs and dead weeds contained better medicines than could be found in the central districts—a lie concocted by those riddled with disease and no respect for proper hygiene. It was places like this that were partly to blame for the number of pandemics that had spread across the globe over the last two centuries. It was because of places like this that vaccinations were now mandated by the birthing commission. Every child was now administered their first set of vaccinations while still in the womb. Rhodon Corporation even took measures to ensure that there were zero unsanctioned births within the city walls.

One minute and twenty-seven seconds left before the drop.

A tiny bell rang as the door opened and another courier came out. A man with a brown bag in his arms, loaded down with flowers and weeds, stood just outside the door. Even though the man wore a breather and goggles like I did, I would have known his red hair anywhere.

"George?" As far as I knew, he was still in Sector 14, undergoing memory recovery treatment.

"Mike. What a pleasant surprise. What are you doing here?"

"I was about to ask you the same question. How are you feeling?"

He furrowed his brow and shook his head. "I feel fine. Why do you ask?"

"Because . . . you were in the chair."

He shook his head. "No, I wasn't. I haven't been to Sector 14 in over a week."

"That's not true. The entire team was called in this morning . . . for a briefing about your failed delivery in Sector 5."

"My failed . . .?" His joyous nature was replaced by sagging shoulders and a frown. "Oh." He looked up and down the street, then down at the bag in his arms, then at the apothecary behind him. "I guess it was bound to happen eventually."

"George . . ." I bit my bottom lip and shook my head. I scanned the surfaces of the surrounding buildings, searching for the security cameras. The Pregutor would be watching. It was a Level One Drop. If I failed to convince the target to do whatever damage the Pregutor wanted them to do, I was to do it myself—or die in the manhunt that would likely ensue. But seeing George here, I didn't need the final instructions to know exactly who the package was meant for.

I blinked multiple times, fighting back the tears. With the seals on my display glasses firmly in place, I wouldn't have been able to wipe them away. The warmth from my fingers disappeared, and my chest grew tight, making it near impossible to breathe.

George sighed as he put the bag of herbs on the ground at his feet, then he stood tall. He reached up and pulled off his breather and goggles.

"What are you doing?" I tried to stop him, but he grabbed my hands and held them firmly in his own. "George, the toxins—"

"I know." He took a deep breath and coughed, but he smiled the same way he always smiled when he inhaled deeply in Sector 14, like he was breathing in the cleanest air, not the air that would eventually kill him. "With my mask on, I can't do this." He pulled me close to him and pushed back the strands of purple hair on my forehead. The tenderness of his lips made it harder to hold back the tears. "I love you, Mike. I always have. Just remember your promise to me: if the opportunity ever arises to get out, you're to take it."

The clock went to zero, and the message with the final instructions arrived. I didn't want to open it. I didn't need to open it. This was why the Pregutor demanded that *I* be the one to make the drop. It was a test . . . to see where my loyalties lay. And I had to close my eyes for a moment as I tried to deny what was true.

George's fate had been decided the moment he failed to make the drop in Sector 5. But the Pregutor needed to see if I would carry out their orders, even though I was close to the target.

He pulled out of his pocket a thin, stiff card and placed it in my gloved hand. "Do me a favor. Make sure my aunt gets this."

I shook my head as I turned the card over in my hand. "It's just a card."

"It's the Queen of Hearts."

"I don't understand."

George's grin was so wide that it stretched from ear to ear. His teeth gleamed in the light from the overhead streetlamps. "I know." He encouraged me to put the card inside my jacket pocket, then he cupped my cheek as though he wanted to capture one last memory of my face with his touch. "Do it, and never regret it. Do it now."

I shook my head. "I can't do that to you." I frantically looked around the street and the surrounding buildings, hunting for another way out of this. "You need to run. I'll take your place."

He took a deep breath, coughing as he inhaled the toxins. "No matter what you do, they won't let me live. I'm a dead man, anyway. But you . . ." His thumb ran along my chin— the bit not covered by my breather. "Maybe the truth will help. Mike, I chose this. I knew it was a risk, but I did it anyway."

"What are you talking about?"

"I didn't miss the drop in Sector 5. I knew exactly what I was doing when I gave that package to Abram Shutton's son. And regardless of what it might have looked like on the vid-feeds, I wasn't compelled. I was just trying to make it look that way."

I pulled away from him, stepping back. "I don't understand."

He coughed again, but he kept his eyes trained on me. "I'm a member of the resistance, Mike, and I have been for some time."

It was like I had been punched—unable to inhale. "You deliberately took action that resulted in the death of one of our own? Because of that missed drop, Lucas Tellis is dead."

"Not everything is as it seems. We're being lied to. The voices are nothing to be afraid of. We should be embracing them, not taking drugs to suppress them."

"The voices? You're hearing voices? They're making you—"

"They're not making me do anything that I don't choose to do of my own volition. I'm in complete control over my abilities." He stared at me, locking our joint gaze together.

The humming that I had been hearing off and on all day focused into a singular voice. Deep. Soothing. Calm. Unknown. *"You're in danger, Michaella Davison. You have to get out before it's too late. If they ever learn that the drugs are no longer working, that they can no longer control you, they will kill you. You need to remember exactly who you are."*

Blood trickled from his nose, and his body started to tremble.

An alarm started beeping incessantly in my ears as the clock in my vision flashed negative numbers, increasing to a minute and longer.

George tried to take another coughing breath and looked around at the people surrounding us. They glanced in his direction, then scurried away as fast as they could, like they knew what was about to happen.

He then looked to the skies as a police drone came into view. "Your time's up, Mike. Soon, the Pregutor will learn the truth about you, and you'll become a target, just like me. Find Abram Shutton's son. He can help you."

"Abram Shutton doesn't have a son." I glared into his eyes and time seemed to slow down. The edges of my vision went dark.

His lips were moving, but I couldn't hear a single word he had said. Instead, I focused on his eyes, willing him to hear my thoughts—to hear my breaking heart.

George went completely still. His vibrant soul drained away, leaving only an empty shell.

"You betrayed us, George," I said to him mentally. *"Because of you, a good man is dead."* I pulled out the package and passed it to the zombie in front of me. *"You know what to do."*

Without another word, I walked away from him, kicking over the bag of herbs. I waved my hand in front of me and tapped on the virtual white rose icon.

Behind me, there was a ding of the tiny bell hanging over the apothecary door, followed by an explosion and screams.

Nine

I HEADED BACK TOWARD THE sector checkpoint, cut off from my emotions. If it wasn't for my favorite song playing in a repeating loop, I would have been a blubbering mess.

I understood the location, destroying the falsehoods impacting on people's health. And given what I now knew about the drop itself, I understood why it had to be me. But how could George betray the Pregutor like that? How could he pretend to make a false drop and admit that he did it on purpose? How could he kill Lucas?

And who else on the team was a traitor?

I had known the other members of PentWave since we were children. I considered them my family. Even the bully Marcus. But if just one of them could be a traitor, then it was my job—my responsibility—to deal with them, and to remove the threat to the Pregutor and Crystal Hills. No one else could do it.

With determined steps, I charged past the gathered crowd lined up outside the checkpoint entrance.

A large burly man grabbed my arm as I walked past. He snarled, his yellow-stained teeth visible through his cheap breather system. "Where the hell do you think you're going? I've been waiting in this line for three days. No way in hell am I letting you cut in."

I glared at the man. The edges of my vision went dark. "I suggest you let go of me. Now."

His mind was strong. His jaw clinched as he fought against the mental order that I was implanting.

"Don't make me do this the hard way. Trust me. You won't like it. Let go of my arm."

Blood dripped from his nose and his breathing became labored. He coughed repeatedly. It was like his breather unit had failed and he was inhaling the toxins from the atmosphere. He let go of my arm and clasped his chest; his breathing eased. The man looked at me and stepped back into the line.

Whispers echoed up and down the line as the spectators speculated about what I had done to the man. But I wasn't in the mood to explain it to anyone. They would find out soon enough if they got in my way.

"You can be really cold, you know that?"

I halted in my steps and looked back at the crowd, trying to ascertain who would have the audacity to talk to me like that.

"I thought you had a heart, but with the way you just cut off your emotions like that, flaunting your superiority. No wonder they hate us."

I looked at each face lined up in turn. The man who had the gall to grab my arm was still clutching at his chest, trying to hide from my gaze.

I took several deep breaths through my breather. Was it possible that I was hearing voices again? Were my audimensase levels skyrocketing again? I looked down at my hands. Steady. No sign of trembling.

Doing the best I could to ignore the random thoughts, I trekked the rest of the way to the sector checkpoint terminal, heading for one of the guards stationed at the entrance.

As I stood before the guard, I pulled back my right sleeve and exposed my pharmachip. Confused, but not willing to question my actions, the guard held a scanning unit to my right wrist. A few clicks and a beep later, the guard paled and his eyes grew wide.

"Agent Davison. I wasn't aware anyone from Central Health was in the sector."

I shrugged. "Do you honestly believe that we would advertise our presence? Especially in Sector 2?"

"No, I suppose not."

"Just point me to the health scanners so I can get out of this filthy place."

The guard swallowed and averted his eyes.

I sighed. "Let me guess. The health scanners aren't working. Hence, the reason why you've had people waiting outside for days on end."

"Um . . . I am sorry, Agent Davison, but . . ."

"What are your backup protocols?" I asked, hoping against hope that I wouldn't be stuck in Sector 2 because of shitty maintenance practices.

I looked intently at the guard. The edges of my vision went dark again, and the guard's tired eyes took on a vacant quality. "This way."

I followed the guard through the facility and into a secure area. Doors opened in response to the guard's pharmachip. He then led me down a long tunnel, not unlike the staff tunnels found in Sector 14, complete with the foot baths that were known to eat away the threads of my boots. At the end of the hall stood a secure door.

"You might want to activate your goggle's UV filters," the guard said.

I tapped a sequence at my right temple. My display glasses went dark.

The bright light of a UV decon unit flooded the hall. It was designed to kill any bugs that might have been hitching a ride out of the sector on my clothing. With the UV sequence over, the guard opened the door into the neighboring sector.

I stared out into the quiet streets beyond the door, blinking. "Is that it?"

"What else would there be?"

I scoffed and shook my head. With all the precautions taken to keep disease contained to a single sector, the backup protocols for Sector 2 dealt with external bugs only, potentially allowing sick people through the gates. I could have been a carrier of a highly contagious disease for which I was asymptomatic.

"When I get back to the Sector 14, I'll be putting in a report about your poor hygiene practices. No wonder we have a flurona outbreak. When this is over, you'll be lucky if you still have a job."

The guard paled. It was obvious that he had no clue what to say in response.

"I suggest that you pull up your sleeves and fix those health scanners. Now."

"Understood. The scanners will be operational the next time you visit Sector 2." It was an automatic response from the guard to one whom he perceived as a superior. But in truth, I wasn't convinced that he understood at all.

"I doubt I'll ever be visiting again." With a deep breath through my breather, I left the guard and headed into the city streets to make my way to the transport hub—still amazed at how easy it was for me to get out of Sector 2.

That's when it hit. Those with flurona were being smuggled out of the city through Sector 5. No one could figure out how they were being smuggled into the sector. But what if there were piss poor secondary protocols for Sector 5 that the rebels took advantage of?

"So, she's finally figured it out. Now, what are you going to do about it?"

I spun around in circles, searching in every direction for the owner of the voice. "Who's there?"

"No one. Except for the voices in your head."

I looked down at my hands again. No shakes. What the hell was going on?

"I'll tell you exactly what's going on. You killed your best friend, then you used your superiority to con your way out of Sector 2 without going through a full medical screening. Which in some respects is a good thing, because yes, your audimensase levels have gone through the roof. But your mintonal levels are still high. It's why you're not shaking. You've developed an immunity to Miransine, and if the Pregutor finds out, you won't need to worry about what is going on in Sector 5 or in Sector 2, because you'll become a permanent resident of Ward 27. Then you'll wish that Dr. Elizabeth Eason wasn't dead, because she would be your only way out."

I forced myself to take slow, steady breaths, focusing on the chords that played in my ears.

"You have a choice to make, Michaella Davison. You can trust the lies told to you by Rhodon Corporation or you can trust me."

"And who is *me*?"

There was a lingering silence, like the owner of the voice in my head was smirking. *"Abram Shutton's son."*

Ten

I STOOD IN THE STREET, not knowing which way to go. As I saw it, there were two options: that the voice in my head was telling me the truth and I was being lied to about my condition and the medication I had been taking; or I had finally lost grip on reality, and the voices in my head were trying to convince me to harm myself. I did kill my best friend, sending him into that shop with a bomb. But the voices didn't tell me to do that. The Pregutor did.

My optical display flashed, displaying the words: ≫Priority One System Override.≪ Tam's voice replaced the music that had been playing on repeat via my earbuds.

"Agent Davison, report to Sector 14 immediately." The irritation in Tam's voice carried deep, resonating notes. "Your tracker has been remotely activated, and we have eyes on your location." A hover drone dropped from the sky, its camera pointing in my direction. "If you are not here in two hours, I will send a STAR squad to escort you to the facilities at Zatvor. Do I make myself clear?"

My eyes bulged, and I had to force myself to take a calming breath. I looked up at the drone, slightly shaking my head. "Two hours is not enough time to make it to Sector 14 from my present location."

"Then I suggest you run. Your time starts now."

A blue timer appeared on my display, counting down the minutes and seconds to my doom.

Shit. I took off at a sprint. At the best of times, Sector 14 was four hours away. But if I missed this deadline . . . I shook my head, trying to dislodge the thoughts of the horror that awaited me.

There was no time to think. I had to just act, pumping my legs as fast as I could, mentally screaming out to the lines of people at every sector checkpoint to get out of my way. Even if everything worked in my favor, it would take a miracle to make it across the city in time.

"You shouldn't do this," said the voice. *"Michaella, please, we can hide you. You'll be safe with us. Don't do this."*

But I knew the consequences if I didn't report as ordered. So, I kept running as the hover drone trailed after me.

"You need to listen to me. This is a dumb idea."

"I don't care what you think," I answered the voice. *"Just shut up and go away."*

"Michaella—"

"No. Just leave me alone."

But I knew the voice would never go away. Even if the voice was lying to me, trying to convince me to harm myself, it was clear that the drugs were no longer working. Whatever voice was inside my head would haunt me for the rest of my life—however long that was.

Purple Rain continued to play on repeat as I ran. Each bass beat equaled two running steps. The protests from the voice became a hum, drowned out by the choir and the electric guitar. As I rode the last train heading to Sector 14, the voice and the chorus melded into one, making them indistinguishable. And the timer in my vision continued its countdown to the deadline and my final fate.

I exited the transport pod and bolted toward the entrance to the staff tunnels, watching the clock tick down with five seconds left to my deadline. I held out my right wrist over one of the authorization scanners just as the clock hit zero.

A group of armed guards filed out of the entranceway and surrounded me, weapons pointed at me. I had hoped that Tam meant that all I needed to do was scan into Sector 14 by the deadline, but clearly, I was wrong.

I closed my eyes and bowed my head. I reached up to my temple and turned off the music, finally allowing my emotions to run their course. I pulled off my breather mask and my optical glasses, taking a deep breath of the Sector 14 air. I tried to smile, but there was nothing to smile about. Instead, tears escaped from my eyes, but I didn't bother to wipe them away. I fell to my knees.

"I told you this was a dumb idea," said the voice in my head. *"I could have kept you safe."*

A gentle gloved hand rested on my shoulder. "Mike?"

I knew that voice and I knew it well, but I never expected to hear that voice with a caring tone. I looked up at the soldier next to me in full tactical gear. "Marcus."

His eyes were filled with a hint of sorrow. "Are you okay?"

"I don't know. Are you here to escort me to Zatvor?"

He glanced at the others around us, as if he was looking for some help on how to answer the question. "Why would I take you there?"

"Because I was late."

He bent down and encouraged me to stand. "I don't know anything about Zatvor. All I know is that we were told to wait for a courier who was coming in with vital information about the resistance. We were told that as soon as they arrived, we were to escort them directly to the chair room, that they would go through decontamination through the isolation tunnels. Mike, what's going on?"

I looked at the guards around me. Some watched the exchange between Marcus and me, while others encouraged those entering the sector to keep moving.

"You might as well tell him what you did," the voice said. *"Everyone will know the truth as soon as you're in the chair."*

I licked my lips as I tried to regain some sense of composure. "I delivered a package to Sector 2."

Marcus shrugged. It was clear as anything that he didn't understand how any package could warrant the level of security that I was being subjected to.

"George was there."

Any sign of emotion drained from his person. "The failed drop in Sector 5 . . ."

"It wasn't a failed drop. He did it on purpose." My breathing was shaky. My stomach was doing flip-flops. "He was working for the resistance."

Marcus stared at me, like he was struggling to fathom what he was hearing. But there was more to it. I just didn't have the heart to tell him.

"Like how George was hearing voices?" the voice asked. *"Like how you're hearing voices? They'll find out soon enough, you know."* That voice was really getting annoying.

"You were under orders to escort me to the chair room, right?" I asked Marcus, who only nodded in response. "Then let's go."

I pocketed my glasses and breather, then followed the lead guard into the tunnels, through the sanitation bays, and through various decontamination units. Instead of leading me to the staff locker rooms, the guards ushered me down a side hall. I was instructed to remove my clothing and don a plain black uniform. I wanted to cry at the lack of stripes.

Marcus and the team of security guards continued to escort me through the long maze of underground corridors, down passageways that I had never seen before. At times, the walls seemed to waver, briefly revealing a darkened chasm filled with blinking lights.

The whole way, Marcus walked by my side. Not ahead of me, not behind me, but right next to me. Close enough that our elbows could almost touch. At one point, the back of his hand brushed against mine. With each step, my chest grew tight, and a series of questions and doubts flooded into my mind. But these random thoughts were nothing like the voice that wouldn't shut up. Instead, they were centered around doubts of taking one's life—particularly of one viewed as a . . .

A sister?

I looked sideways at Marcus. His lips were pulled tight into a slight grimace, and the wrinkles in his brow deepened. His eyes were filled with something I never expected to see coming from him. Concern.

"What?" Marcus demanded.

"Nothing. I'm just wondering why they sent you and not someone else."

"Because I volunteered."

"Why would you do that?"

He stopped in the middle of the hall, grabbing my arm and pulling me around to face him. The intensity in his eyes grew deeper, like he was trying to draw me in. In all the years that I had known him, he had never once been able to get past my mental defenses—not unless I chose to let him in. So that's what I did.

"I'm scared for you, Mike," he said inside my head. *"They have never insisted on such a show of force after a drop before."*

"We have never had anyone deliberately betray us either," I said mentally in return. *"Lucas is dead because of what George did, but George is no longer a threat. I saw to that."*

"And what about you?"

I took a deep breath and allowed his presence to go deeper into my mind. *"Search my thoughts, Marcus. I'm loyal."*

His gaze intensified, and my vision grew clouded. Marcus suddenly inhaled and let me go, pulling back from my mind. "You might be loyal," he said aloud, "but you think that someone else in PentWave might not be."

"Where there is one . . ." I said.

Marcus nodded. "There's always another."

The guard leading the group turned and stared at Marcus, who only nodded in return. "I know," Marcus said aloud. "I just—" The guard said nothing, but the look on his face grew stern. Marcus nodded again. "Yes, sir, I understand." He then turned to me. "We need to keep moving."

For the first time, I took a closer look at the guards around me. It was hard to see at first, hidden under their tactical gear, but their uniforms bore a thin purple line running down the center of the blue stripes on their sleeves. And none of them wore a radio. Instead, each of them possessed a small scar at the base of their right ears, evidence of a bone radio implant. And they each had a tiny tattoo to cover the scars: a blue rosebud.

Oh, shit. These guards were all just like me. Every single one of them would have once been a courier, diagnosed with White Rabbit syndrome as a child. But these guards would have proven that they could be trusted with state secrets, no longer required to do a pleb's work. These were the guards tasked with the responsibility of terminating couriers who had gone rogue and attempted to run. The fact that I was now surrounded by a STAR unit meant that they expected me to rebel in some way.

I glanced at Marcus and, for the first time, noticed that his uniform bore the same purple thin line down the middle of the blue stripe. He, too, had the scar from the bone radio implant and the blue rosebud tattoo.

When did he join STAR?

I sighed as I tried to focus on the path in front of me. *"Okay, stupid voice, you were right. This was a dumb idea."* But the voice I had been hearing all day chose that moment to remain silent.

At the end of the corridor, Tam waited in their white suit, surrounded by more guards with the blue and purple stripes. The guards in front of me parted, allowing me through.

"Did you know?" There was a slight tremor in my voice.

"Did I know about what?" Tam asked.

"About the nature of the drop?"

"I only had the information the Pregutor allowed me to see."

"But you know everything now, right?"

Tam sighed. "What do you want me to say, Michaella?"

"That you knew it was a test . . . a test of my loyalty to the Pregutor."

Tam stood there, calm, without reaction. "We need to download your latest mission reports into the servers."

"So, that's what we're calling it now: downloading mission reports. Meanwhile, every single time we sit in the chair, we lose a portion of ourselves. Of our memories." I licked my lips as I glanced at the guards surrounding us. Marcus was no longer discernible among them. "But that's the point, isn't it?" I looked intently at Tam, the edges of my vision slightly darkening. "George knew the truth, didn't he? And you're afraid he might have told me something that could result in me questioning my loyalty. That's why I'm here, surrounded by Rhodon's finest. You're afraid that I might follow down the path that George has set before me. That's why the Pregutor wanted him dead, and that's why I was ordered to kill him."

"George killed himself, Michaella."

"But only after I told him to do it." I might have spoken in a soft tone, but I made sure that everyone in that corridor could hear my rising anger. And I should have known that the STAR would raise their weapons aimed at me.

I severed whatever mental connection I might have had with Tam and closed my eyes, allowing my senses to return to normal.

"Put your weapons down," Tam ordered. They then stepped closer to me. "I know you find this hard to believe, but I have always put you and your interests ahead of my own. Please, Michaella, do not resist."

I stared at Tam for what felt like an eternity. The temptation to force my thoughts past their mental barriers was strong. But even if I got the answers I sought, the Pregutor would never allow me to keep the memories.

I drew my shoulders back, though it did nothing to increase my height compared to the guards around me. "You can take my memories, but in my heart, I'll know the truth. There are more dangerous things out there than a plague."

I stepped into the chair room and sat down. The nurses in the room strapped my feet in and applied the restraints to my wrists. I leaned my head back and waited for the strap to go across my forehead.

Tam stepped forward and caressed my cheek. "Like you, I am only following orders." A sweet fragrance filled my nostrils, and a calmness washed over me. I jerked my head away from Tam's touch. The smell vanished instantly, but the calmness remained.

Tam just nodded, then checked the vial that the nurse handed them, and withdrew a measured amount into a syringe. "I am sorry, Michaella. I never wanted this to happen."

The nurse secured the head strap into place, and Tam plunged the needle into my arm. With the cold rush of the fluids, my grip on consciousness was slipping.

Without any further warning, a hum filled the room and an electric jolt shot through my body, thrusting me deeper into the chair.

Eleven

The repeated beeps grew louder.

"Alice, shut up." It was a soft, rough croak, but thankfully, Alice could interpret my incoherent groans and silenced the alarm. Laying on my back, I tested the slits in my eyelids and wiped the crusty sleep from my eyes.

It felt like only seconds had passed, but the alarm started again.

I sighed in defeat. "Coffee. Coffee would be nice right now." I sighed again and continued to stare at the ceiling. The only place in the city where I could possibly afford real coffee was that coffee shop in Sector 4. But because of what I did, because of the package I delivered, that place was likely out of business.

I rolled to my side and tried to focus on the digital numbers that hung in the air.

6 a.m.? Shit! I was supposed to report for work in an hour. It was going to take me at least that amount of time to get to Sector 14 and through the health screening. With adrenaline pumping through my veins, I bolted out of bed and headed to my closet to get my work clothes . . . and tripped over my boots.

I stared at my boots. They took up almost the entire space between the bed and the wall, putting them directly in my path. I never left my boots there for that exact reason. It was too easy to trip over them there. I must have been really tired when I came in.

Without another thought, I grabbed some clean clothes from the closet and rushed to put on my jacket and boots. I went to grab my display glasses and breather off their charging units on my desk . . . only they weren't there.

What the hell? It was possible they had fallen off the shelf, or dropped into the little drawer below the shelf, but my glasses and breather were nowhere to be seen. I even scoured under my bed. Nothing.

I tucked the loose purple strands of my hair behind my ears. "Alice, where the hell are my glasses?"

The soft, muted refrain from *Purple Rain* chimed from my jacket pocket. More specifically, a pocket that I rarely used—an outside pocket that could be easily targeted by thieves.

Confused, I pulled out my glasses from the little used pocket, along with my breather. A thin card came out with them. I picked up the card from the floor and stared at the two-headed Queen of Hearts.

The only person I knew who ever carried cards like this was George. But how the hell did I get it?

Shaking away any doubts, I pocketed the card, then took one last look at the clock. Crap! I had wasted twenty-three minutes looking for my stupid glasses. I put them on and activated Alice's uplink. With my breather in my inside jacket pocket where it belonged, I ran out the door.

I darted through the alleyways and headed toward Hope Alley, determined to get something to eat before heading to the transport tubes. As I entered the food alley, I made a beeline for my favorite vendor . . . but the name on the cart had changed.

Grandma Tilly's Algae?

I spun around, looking in all directions. Had Hector moved his cart to somewhere else?

"What will you have?" An old woman leaned through the serving window.

"Do you know where Hector moved his food cart to?"

"Sorry, deary, but I don't know no Hector. If you're gonna order something, order."

"Do you make cressicubes?"

The old woman narrowed her eyes. "No one makes those. Mintonal is a Class A regulated substance. Are you some undercover cop or something? Is this a setup?"

I shook my head. "No. I . . ." I furrowed my brow and glanced at the people surrounding me. They all stared at me like I had lost my mind. If I was honest with myself, I wasn't entirely sure I hadn't. "Um . . ." I scanned the list of items the old woman had for sale. "I'll take a valkcube." I pulled back my right sleeve to reveal my pharmachip, so the vendor could take the money directly from my account. The old woman gave me the food cube right away—no waiting time. Which had to have been some kind of bonus.

I then darted through the crowds, heading toward the transport tubes. While waiting for my turn, I did the best I could to eat the tasteless, gritty mush that pretended to be food. It didn't contain the mintonal that I knew I needed, but at least it contained all the protein and nutrients my body required to stave off hunger.

When I arrived in Sector 14, I joined the lines to head into the staff tunnels. As I got to my locker, I had another fifteen minutes to get through the health screening and report to the team lounge. It would be close, but I could do it. I had done it before.

"Oh my god, Mike . . . Where have you been?" Jody stood there with her clothes and gear already stowed in her locker. Her hands pressed against her hips. It was a stance that was supposed to make her look like some *badass*, but with her petite stature and standing there naked as the day she was born, *badass* was the last thing that came to mind. "We've been trying to call you for hours."

I tried to ignore the attitude radiating off of Jody, so I could get undressed myself. "I was tucked up in my bed, sound asleep."

"But Trent said he checked your apartment. You weren't there."

I shrugged. "Maybe Trent forgot my address. Because I assure you, I was asleep in bed, trying to sleep off the headache left over from the chair."

Jody blinked. "You were in the chair yesterday?"

I furrowed my brow. "I don't know why I said that. I haven't been in the chair for quite some time."

"Mike, are you okay?"

"Yeah, I'm fine. I'm just . . ." I looked around the room, feeling like someone or something was watching me. But this was Sector 14. The Pregutor had eyes everywhere. "I guess I've been running on empty. Not enough sleep."

Jody narrowed her eyes and glared at me, like she was trying to decide what to do about . . . Well, Jody was always trying to decide what to do about me.

"We better go," she said in the end. "Otherwise, we'll be late. And you know how Tam gets when we're late."

I smiled, and activated the motion-detection recording system on my glasses, closed my locker, then followed Jody out into the hall.

"Hey, have you seen George this morning? There's something I want to ask him."

Jody about tripped over her own feet. The color drained from her face.

"Jody, what's wrong?"

"I thought you knew."

"Knew what?"

"George committed suicide yesterday."

"What?" I pulled her to the side of the passageway, both of us naked and feeling the slight breeze as people glared at us. But I didn't care. Somewhere deep inside, I prayed that Jody was playing a practical joke—her sense of humor was odd and not very funny—but her entire being radiated with concern and fear. "What happened?"

"I don't know all the details, except that George was in Sector 2 and lost the plot. He went homicidal, killing multiple bystanders before killing himself. According to the footage from the drones, he was mumbling something about how the medicine in Sector 2 wasn't good enough. He destroyed one of those herbal dispensaries in the attack. But no one can figure out is what he was doing in Sector 2 in the first place."

I sighed and hung my head as I leaned up against the wall. "He was likely taking medicine to his aunt."

Jody furrowed her brow. "His aunt?"

"From what I understand, his aunt is unable to get a medical pass to enter into the inner sectors. She's really sick. I'm not sure where she lives, but I know George used his status here to bypass some of the red tape to get her the medicine she needs. But with George now gone . . . Does she know?"

"I'm guessing not. I didn't even know he had an aunt."

I bit my bottom lip, trying to control my emotions. "The two of us should go see her this evening—maybe take the others as well. And we should find out what medicines she's on. Source her a decent supply."

"Agreed." Jody took several deep breaths. "I'll coordinate with the others as soon as we're finished here and have our assignments for the day." She moved away from the side wall and rejoined the lines, heading toward the health scanners.

I took a few more deep breaths before doing the same.

The line for the scanners couldn't have moved any slower. But as I moved from dot to dot, I thought of nothing but George. We had known each other since we were kids. Both of us at O'quv Lageri, the training camps for those with White Rabbit syndrome, quickly bonding over the insane idea of dancing in the purple rain. It was George who had introduced me to the classic rock ballad, and it was George who made me want to become something more than just a sufferer of audimentia. He encouraged me to join the couriers for Rhodon Corporation. And he encouraged me to apply to STAR. Without George to kick my ass every time I was down on myself, who would provide my motivational compass?

I stepped into the main scanner and sanitizer unit, the glass upright coffin that it was. Would George be given a coffin for his funeral? Or would they just burn what was left of his body until there was nothing left but dust?

The scanner whirred into life, and I tried to stay focused on the red X in front of me. But my mind drifted to the red hues on the Queen of Hearts card in my jacket pocket, back in my locker.

George had always liked red. It was why he always dyed his hair that color. But he hated how the color was often associated with death. Probably because red was the color of blood.

"Excuse me, Supervisor Blake, I don't understand what this means. The system is saying that her audimensase levels have skyrocketed, and that there isn't enough mintonal in her system to counteract it." It was such an odd comment to get over the intercom, like someone was leaning on the intercom button, but I did the best I could to ignore the technicians.

"It means that she has audimentia," said another.

"You mean she's one of those freaks?"

"Be careful who you say that around. You ever meet one of the STAR?"

"No, but why should that matter?"

"Because every single one of them has audimentia. And if anyone from STAR ever heard you calling them a freak, you wouldn't like the consequences. It's like they can read your mind and make you live your darkest fears."

I furrowed my brow and glanced at the technicians sitting in their comfortable, isolated bubble. The edges of my vision went dark, and their voices seemed to grow in volume.

"Umm . . . Bill, she's looking at us. Do you think she can read our minds?"

"No, you morons," said another technician, entering the room and encouraging one of the other technicians to get out of their seat. *"Those with audimentia can't read your thoughts, but some of them can read lips. Isn't that right?"* The new technician looked directly at me. I just smiled and nodded once.

The other technicians paled as they gawked. The technician with reasoning leaned forward and pressed a button on the panel in front of them, leaning into the microphone.

The hum from the intercom was more like a squeal, and I winced as the technician's voice filled the space around me. The darkness around my vision brightened to a white fill, making me squint.

"You're free to enter Sector 14, Agent Davison. Your scan is clean. And I apologize for my idiot colleagues here. They're still new and haven't really worked with any of the Pregutor's representatives yet."

A green checkmark lit up in front of me, and the glass doors opened.

I took one last look at the technicians, who looked like they were being reprimanded—but I couldn't hear what was being said, and I certainly couldn't read their lips. I tried, but the lip movements didn't make any sense.

No. I had heard them talking, like they had forgotten to turn off the intercom as I stepped into the scanner. But now I had to wonder if something else was going on.

I collected my sector uniform and happily donned the purple stripes. Finding Jody waiting for me, we walked together through the sector plaza toward the Rhodon Corporation buildings.

Bright lights bounced off the white walls and the white floor. The whiteness of the space seemed to be brighter than normal, making me squint continually. I was getting another headache.

As Jody and I entered the team lounge, everyone turned and stared at us. Correction: they stared at me.

"She doesn't know anything." Jody pulled me deeper into the room. "She didn't even know about George's death until a few minutes ago. Just give the woman some space."

"But—"

"Zip it, Trent." Jody held up her hand toward the green-haired beanstalk by the server console. She then waved her wrist over the unit and pushed the number two on the screen. Two cups of black sludge appeared moments later, and she passed one to me. "Drink."

Frowning, I stared at the black fluid masquerading as coffee. Syncoff. I hated the stuff. It had no zing. It might have contained caffeine, but whoever designed the stuff did something to it, creating this hybrid caffeinated/decaffeinated drink that tasted like . . . well . . . flavored mud. I wished I could have gone back to that coffee shop in Sector 4, even if a thimble of the real stuff would clean out my bank account.

"You might as well enjoy that stuff now. If things go the way I suspect they will, it might be a long time before you have anything that resembles coffee—even the synthetic stuff."

"What makes you say that?" I asked.

Jody looked at me with furrowed brows and suspicious eyes. "Are you saying that I shouldn't have told them to give you some space?"

"No. I mean yes. Space is good, but why would you say that it would likely be some time before we would get anything that resembled coffee, even syncoff?"

"I didn't say anything about the syncoff. I know the stuff is shit, but I can't afford anything else."

"Yes, you did. I heard you as clear as—" But Jody's voice possessed a higher pitch than the voice I heard complaining about the syncoff.

"Mike, is everything okay?" She leaned in close. "Please tell me that you're not hearing voices again."

I bit my bottom lip and glanced around the room. Everyone was pacing their own little patch of floor, scowling as they sipped the black swill.

But the voice was so clear.

"So, no one said anything about syncoff?"

"Not that I heard." Jody put her own cup of syncoff down and stood as straight as possible, demanding that I give her my full attention. "Are you sure you're okay?"

"I'm fine." Though I was starting to wonder if I was losing my mind.

In a poor attempt to hide my awkwardness, avoiding the accusing looks from Jody, I scanned the room. "Hey, where's Marcus? The two of you are never far apart."

"He's not here." She casually sipped her syncoff.

"I can see that. Where is he?"

Jody mumbled something that I didn't quite hear properly.

"Jody . . . What are you not telling me?"

"Well . . . Um . . ."

"Out with it. Where's Marcus?"

Jody sighed, then took a deep breath with her shoulders rising to around her ears. She then exhaled in a rush. "I'm sorry, Mike. But after George, I thought you knew. Tam told us that your request for transfer to STAR was delayed, pending investigation—and Marcus was given your place instead."

"Oh." I sighed in defeat. "So, I'm stuck doing the Pregutor's dirty work. For the moment at least."

"I'm so sorry, Mike."

"No need to feel sorry. Being part of STAR was just a pipe dream, anyway."

"There is a bright side, though."

"And what's that?"

Jody grinned. "Only couriers get to dance in the purple rain."

I smirked. It was a common saying among PentWave, because it was only the couriers who were stupid enough to be out and about on the streets in the outer sectors during skin-melting season. Only couriers were given the gear needed to be in the purple rain without developing a nasty rash that would eat away at their skin.

Jody hummed the chorus of the historic song, and I joined her. Slowly, the others around the room joined in too, spreading a joyous, calm nature that helped to ease the tension.

"I am pleased to see that the most recent news has failed to dampen your spirits," said the familiar voice of our handler. Tam stood with their hands resting by their sides. Their white suit and pale complexion almost matched the white doors behind them. "But as much as I enjoy hearing you all sing, I need to disrupt this impromptu party. In light of George's suicide yesterday, each of you will need to undergo a full battery of tests to ensure that you are all stable . . . that the symptoms of your audimentia have not worsened. Jody, if you will please come with me. We will see you first."

Jody nodded and continued to smile, even if it took on a nervous quality. She then followed Tam out the door, still humming the historic song.

The others in the room did their best to continue the joyous mood, knowing that there was no point in worrying about the things that were out of their control. It was only a matter of time before White Rabbit syndrome would take each of us, driving us to the point of insanity.

But not today.

I drank what was left of my syncoff—still wishing that it could have been a thimble of the real stuff.

One by one, the couriers were called out of the room, eventually leaving me to contemplate my lackluster existence alone. It was a long wait in the silence, but I kept singing *Purple Rain* over and over in my head, trying to stay calm.

A technician in a white coat finally came back to collect me and lead me to my ill-fated doom. "Michaella Davison. We're ready for you now."

Twelve

I KNEW I STOOD OUT like a sore thumb against the white walls. Black upon black, with a bit of purple thrown in for good measure, would always stand out in this sterile environment. Normally, I was okay with that, because everything about my appearance was not designed to blend into Sector 14. It was designed to blend in while I was in the outer sectors.

But as I followed the technician, I tried really hard not to laugh. He blended into the background so much that he looked like a bodiless head floating down the hall.

At the end of the hall, the technician waved his wrist over the sensor for the door. The room beyond was like nothing I had ever seen before—not in Sector 14, anyway. It was a sunshine room, filled with brightly colored furniture— oranges, yellows . . . and red. George would have loved this room. And sitting comfortably on the couch in the middle was the whitest of white people I had ever known.

"Good morning, Tam."

"Michaella." Tam gave a slight bow of their head and smiled. "Please take a seat."

Amazed that such a colorful room could exist in Sector 14, I sat on the couch opposite Tam, on the other side of the coffee table. Tam reached forward to a thermal pitcher and poured a cup of deep brown, almost black, liquid, then passed me the small cup.

"Dr. Shutton will likely reprimand me for encouraging you or your fellow workers to consume stimulants like this," Tam said, an unnatural smile spreading from ear to ear, "but that synthetic compound provided in the team lounge . . . You deserve much better than that."

Was it possible that Tam had given me coffee? The real stuff? And not just a thimble? A whole cup?

I tried really hard to contain my excitement as I took the cup and brought it to my nose. The earthy spice energized my senses, and I took a sip. The acidic bitterness lingered on my tongue, cleansing my mind. "Mmm . . . That's good."

Tam continued to smile and slightly bowed their head. "It is my understanding that you were unable to take your time to enjoy the cup you ordered when you were in Sector 4. I wanted to correct that."

"Thank you." I lifted the cup slightly, a toast to my host. I then savored another sip of the black gold. The slight buzz from the caffeine was going to be amazing.

"If you don't mind me asking, why are we in a sunshine room? I mean, I didn't even know that such a colorful room existed."

Tam chuckled, a sound that I thought I would never hear. "Being surrounded by white can sometimes be dreary. I find this room comforting. Calming. It makes me long for the days when one could look up at the sky—the real sky— and take in the sun's warmth. I know that you and your . . . companions . . . joke about dancing in the purple rain, but imagine what it would have been like to be out in the rain without fear of it eating away at your skin." Tam continued to smile as they closed their eyes, like they were imagining another time and place. "Besides, I wanted to have these conversations in a room that was . . . perfectly suited. George would have liked this room."

"I agree." Suddenly, I was no longer interested in drinking the rest of my coffee. My chest grew tight.

Tam took a deep breath. "Shall we begin?"

I nodded, then put my cup down and prepared to stand, but Tam reached forward and encouraged me to stay seated.

"Aren't we going to the chair room?"

"Not today. There are aspects of the chair technology that sometimes misses the important things. The chair is a wonderful tool to help us understand the details of your various missions, but the Pregutor is unable to interpret your emotions . . . your feelings about a given situation. It is your emotions and feelings that help us to understand how we should continue treating your audimentia. So, if it is all right with you, I would like to ask you a few questions about what you remember of your latest missions. How you felt about them."

I sighed and leaned back in the soft cushioned seat, doing the best I could to keep the butterflies at bay. It was times like this when I wished I could have had my tech with me, playing my favorite song to keep me calm. "My missions are all the same. I collect a package from security as I leave Sector 14, and I carry it through the checkpoints to the outer rim. The Pregutor tells me who the recipient is when the timer for the drop runs out . . . then people die . . . because of me. What more is there to know?"

"Do you kill the people yourself?"

"Of course not, but I deliver the weapons."

Tam studied me at length. It was a little unnerving to have those colorless eyes staring at me, as though Tam could see the inner workings of my mind. In the end, Tam leaned forward and pressed their hand to a sensor pad in the middle of the coffee table.

A virtual display sprang to life, revealing images from the news about the incident at the coffee shop in Sector 4. Tam did a series of complicated hand gestures over the coffee table, and the scenes on the display froze and zoomed in on one of the bodies found inside the empty coffee shop. Next to the face of the dead woman, the display showed an employee record for Dr. Elizabeth Eason.

"The Angel of Death."

"That was the nickname she had been given, yes."

"But she's not the person I delivered the package to."

"No. The one you delivered the package to was Jonathan Attewell, an undercover operative of Earth Force." Tam did another complicated series of hand gestures and the hollow-eyed man from the coffee shop came up on the display. "Inspector Attewell had been working undercover for a year, trying to track down a man by the name of Edward Palmer."

"I don't know that name."

Tam waved their hand again, bringing up new records and a photo of another man. "Edward Palmer was a research scientist contracted by the government to develop a device that would target the genes affected by audimentia. His goal was not to reverse the effects of audimentia, halting its progression, but rather to speed it up. If he could control the voices that those with audimentia heard during the final stages of the disease, then he could turn those afflicted into a weapon against the general population. No one knows how far he got with his research, because he disappeared around the time you were born, taking his research with him. Because of the amount of time that had passed, government officials thought he was dead . . . until recently, when he came in contact with Elizabeth Eason."

"So, Inspector Attewell was in that coffee shop to apprehend her."

"Yes, and no. He was tracking Elizabeth Eason, knowing that Edward Palmer was trying to recruit her. Attewell's orders were to take whatever action necessary to ensure that Palmer never forged an alliance with Elizabeth Eason. With her detailed knowledge of the genetics associated with audimentia, Palmer could succeed in turning those with the condition into weapons. But Inspector Attewell had been undercover for so long that he had been cut off from certain resources. We agreed to help."

"Which is where I came in." I leaned in closer to the images dangling in midair in front of me. "Let me guess, things didn't quite go as planned."

"No, they did not, because of this man." Tam waved their hand one last time, bringing up an image of a hooded figure with his face mostly obscured. "The Pregutor is unable to find a match in the system for this man's identity. As such, we have no idea who he is. All we know is that he is able to move throughout the city undetected and without a pharmachip." Tam brought up other images of the hooded figure taken at opposite sides of the city.

"How is that even possible?"

Tam gently shook their head. "We do not know. We had sent George to question the people that this man had been seen talking to . . . Then yesterday . . ." Tam looked at me with that inner-workings gaze again. "Michaella, you were close to George. Is there anything you can think of that would explain why George would act out in such a violent way? Did he say anything to you about meeting this man?"

"No. He . . ." I looked down at my hands. "I haven't seen George in a while."

"When *was* the last time you saw him?"

"When I told him that my application to join STAR had been approved. I guess that was three days ago."

"There has been no communication with him since?"

I shook my head. "I . . . I'm sorry that I can't be of much help."

"No need to apologize. Perhaps George was trying to protect you from the mess that he had found himself in. All I ask is that you do me one favor: if you remember anything, anything at all, come to me."

I nodded.

"Thank you, Michaella. We can complete the remainder of the tests on another day. Right now, you need a chance to grieve. Take the remainder of the day to do whatever you want, see whoever you want to see. Despite everything that has happened, George was still your friend."

Again, I nodded. Then I got to my feet and numbly walked out of the sunshine room and back into the plain white halls. With no assignments or packages to deliver, there was no need for me to stay in Sector 14, so I headed toward the employee tunnels.

In the locker room, I slowly dressed myself in my regular clothing, but before I donned my jacket, I took out the card from my jacket pocket.

The Queen of Hearts.

The longer I looked at the card, the more confident I was that the card had belonged to George. But I couldn't remember when George had given it to me.

"Nice card." Jody slid up next to me, fully dressed in a jacket of her own and her breather dangling around her neck. "Didn't George used to carry cards like that?"

"Yeah, he did."

Jody laughed. "I remember asking him once why he always carried playing cards. I mean, it's not like he was going to play a game with them or anything. He never carried a full deck. He said that they were his protection . . . like playing cards could really protect you from anything."

"But the playing cards were the personal guards of the Queen of Hearts." It was a vague memory of the many conversations I had with George over the years. "The Queen of Hearts," I said again, staring at the card in my hand. He was protecting me. But from what?

"Well, when you're ready to make a move, the others are waiting for us."

I looked at Jody, not quite comprehending.

"George's aunt? We were going to take her some medicine. And tell her about her nephew. Marcus used his new connections with STAR and found her name in the system. He managed to get us everything we needed, including the address where she lives."

"Oh . . . yeah, of course." I stuffed the card back into my jacket pocket and finished donning the rest of my gear, then headed out toward the sector exit with Jody.

Thirteen

I pulled my glove tight and ensured that my breather was firmly in place. I had no desire of ever becoming a permanent resident of Sector 2. There was no shelter from the purple-gray sky and the buildings were rundown with crumbling facades. There was only so much risk to disease that one could live with.

Marcus led the charge through the streets. Other pedestrians scurried out of our way, coughing from the sudden exertion. The health scanners on my vid-display were in overdrive. Bacteria and viruses hovered in the air.

How could anyone live in filth like this?

We stopped outside a dark, concrete apartment building. The years of built-up dirt made the concrete black with purple-gray streaks. The odds were that if anyone ever tried to remove the layers of filth, the place would disintegrate into nothing when the rainy season started.

I glanced at the sky. When would the rainy season start?

Inside, remnants of a bygone era lingered. Vibrations from the passing truck threatened to bring down shards of the overhead crystal chandelier, merely tinkling together once it passed. The light fixtures on the side walls dangled from their wires, the glass panels still whole in places. And dark filth coated the main lobby, with the color of the tiled floor no longer discernible. Many of the tiles were chipped.

Even with breathers and goggles covering our faces, the disgust and disdain radiated through our gestures. The faster we could do what we came here to do, the faster we could get out of here.

"What floor is she on?" someone asked, their voice muffled by the breather.

"Twelfth floor." Marcus stared at the elevator cage in the center of the lobby. "No offense, guys, but I'm not going up in that thing."

"Neither am I." I started climbing the stairs, ensuring that I stuck to the edges, where the safety strips still had some grip. By the time we got to the eighth floor, my thighs were feeling the workout, jumping over the odd missing step. On the tenth floor, I was feeling it in my calves. But the bonus in all this was that the higher we went, the bacterial and viral count in the surrounding environment dropped. In the hallway on the twelfth floor, the bacterial levels were not any greater than what I normally saw when traversing some of the mid-level sectors, though the air was still toxic, blending with the atmosphere from outside.

Outside one apartment, a leafy plant with long spindly green fingers and white centers hung from the ceiling. And it was flourishing. Miniature versions of the main plant dangled on long, arching stems.

Jody stared at the plant with her hand before her, like she was testing to see if it was a hologram. "I don't think I've ever seen a living plant before. Not outside the domed sectors, anyway. How has this thing managed to survive in this environment?"

"Perhaps we can ask George's aunt." Marcus pushed his way to the front of the group and knocked on the door next to the hanging plant. It wasn't long before a washed-out holographic image of an elderly woman appeared in the middle of the door.

"What do you want?"

"Are you Renee Tuthill?"

"Don't know that name. Go away."

"Ma'am, please . . ." I stood close to Marcus, ensuring that whatever surveillance system imaging those in the hallway could see me. "City records show that this is the address for Renee Tuthill. We really need to speak with her. She was the aunt of a dear friend of ours, and we have some news for her that shouldn't be said through a door."

The holographic image disappeared, but nothing else happened.

"Are you sure we have the right place?" Jody said.

Marcus shrugged. "There was only one Renee Tuthill in the sector directory. And according to the pharmachip tracking records, George came to this address often enough. If that woman isn't Renee Tuthill, I wouldn't have a clue where to start."

I sighed and knocked on the door again. "Ma'am, please . . ." But there was no answer.

"We're not getting anywhere. We should just leave. Besides, I really hate being in Sector 2."

"You can leave if you want. I'm staying." I took a focusing breath and stared at the door. Everything in my being was telling me that this was the right place. We just had to convince the woman that we meant her no harm.

I tilted my head to the side, taking in the plant and the dark green door. The tiles at my feet reflected the overhead light, accentuating the checkered pattern of bright white and rich black interlocking squares. At the base of the doorframe were four tiles that stood out among the rest: a tile with a red heart, a red diamond, a black spade, and a black club.

Playing cards.

With a smile, I knocked on the door again. "Excuse me, ma'am, but we've come to speak with the Queen of Hearts."

The hall was filled with silence as the others just stared at me. But before anyone could say anything, there was a soft click, and the door creaked open.

A sliver of a woman's face was revealed through the crack. "What do you want?"

"Are you Renee Tuthill?"

"It depends on who's asking."

It wasn't a yes, but at least it was an answer. "Ma'am, I'm sorry to tell you this, but your nephew, George . . . He's dead."

"I already know that." Disdain laced her voice. "You folk won't leave me alone about it."

"I'm sorry, Ms. Tuthill, but we didn't know if you had been informed of George's death or not. There aren't really any protocols regarding this, because most of us don't have any real family."

"Real family?" The woman grunted. "Who are you? Let me see your face."

I licked my lips, trying to decide what to do. "I'm sorry, Ms. Tuthill, but if I lower my breather, I might not be able to get back through the sector checkpoint." I glanced at the others behind me, fully covered and looking like evil monsters. But I had a vague memory of George wandering around Sector 2 with his breather on, but his hood was lowered, showing off his red hair.

I reached up and lowered my hood, revealing my purple hair. I then deactivated the solid filters on my goggles, so the old woman could see my eyes.

"I know you," the old woman said. "Your name is Michaella."

I smiled—though I was fairly confident that the woman couldn't see my smile. "Yes."

"And you've come to tell me about what happened to my nephew."

"Yes." This time, my answer wasn't so enthusiastic.

"Well, I already know about George's death. I've known since it happened." The old woman looked beyond me to others standing behind me, then turned her attention back to me. "I would invite you in, but you're not staying, not this time. I suggest you lot head back to Sector 14. No doubt, the Pregutor will have some . . . jobs for you. And Michaella . . ."

"Yes, ma'am?"

"The next time you come back, leave the playing cards behind. They would be a total disruption to the tea party."

"Playing cards?" Marcus asked. "What is that supposed to mean?"

"Oh, definitely off with his head." The old woman slammed the door, leaving Marcus, Jody, and the rest of us staring at each other, confused in the silent hallway.

I chuckled. "I like her."

"What the hell was that all about?" Jody asked.

"You don't remember?"

Jody, Marcus, and the others just stared at me, their masked, gawking expressions demanding answers.

"*Alice's Adventures in Wonderland*. The playing cards were the queen's guards."

"Hang on," Jody said. "Wasn't that the archaic children's story that George loved so much?"

"Oh, that thing." Marcus turned his back on the door and headed toward the stairs. "The number of times that idiot quoted that thing . . . He was obsessed with it. Now I know why."

Jody scoffed and pointed to herself and the others. "So, that woman was calling us the idiotic guards of the Queen of Hearts?"

I continued to laugh. "I think so."

"Now I understand why George never told us about her," Marcus said. "She's a grumpy old bat. Let's get out of here. I don't want to stay in Sector 2 any longer than I have to."

One by one, we all turned to follow Marcus out of the building, but before I left, I pulled out the package of medicine we had brought with us and placed it on the floor in front of the door. I put the Queen of Hearts card on top.

Fourteen

I chased after Marcus and the others, doing a funny jogging walk to keep up. Every time I tried to slow down, Marcus would turn around and bark at me for falling behind. But I wasn't the only one struggling to keep up. Jody's legs were like two-thirds the length of mine.

Frustrated with her slow pace, Marcus grabbed her arm and pulled her down the street. "Bloody hell, man," she growled. "What's your problem?"

"I've already told you. I don't like being in Sector 2."

"Neither do I, but you can at least show a little respect. Our friend died yesterday. We should be allowed to grieve at a speed that doesn't require us to run." Jody yanked her arm out of his grasp and glared at him. It was the stare down of the century. And if past experience was anything to go by, Marcus was going to lose.

Thankfully, there was no one around to witness the squabbling duo trying to put on a display of dominance—other than myself and the rest of PentWave, who were all on Jody's side, trying to remind Marcus that we all had a right to grieve in our own way.

I rolled my eyes. When would they learn that Marcus was just being Marcus? Trying to be all macho and never show any sign of weakness? Grief in Marcus's little world would be seen as a weakness.

Ignoring the others, I turned my attention to our surroundings. The brick buildings all possessed the same degree of dark filth that kept the buildings standing. But under the overhangs, just outside the doors of little shops, were small displays that showed what each store offered. Rain gear. Boots for children. Boxes of herbal vitamins and ointments. One store had a display of synthetic hair extensions, promising to turn the wearer into a "new you."

I casually walked down the street, looking at shop after shop, but not bothering to examine their wares; I had no intention of buying anything from Sector 2. But there was something about the street itself that was familiar— something that I couldn't identify.

As I turned the corner, I gawked at a burned-out storefront located at the end of the street. The sign with its mortar-and-pestle symbol dangled from a single eyelet bolt. A bell hung just above the shattered doorframe, waving in the slight breeze with a continual ding. Shards of glass spread across the ground in front of the store. Entangled among the mess were remnants of weeds and dried flowers.

As I continued to stare at what was left of the apothecary, the ghosts of the place insisted on coming to life. I could have sworn I saw George carrying a brown bag in his arms walking out of the store. His ghost stopped in front of me, grinning.

"Mike. What a pleasant surprise. What are you doing here?"

A hand settled on my forearm, and I jumped. I had to force myself to slow my breathing.

"Are you okay?" Jody asked.

I shook my head. "I . . ." A chill washed over me and fought to hold back the tears. It wasn't like I could easily reach up and wipe them away—not without taking off my goggles.

I turned around, only to face the ghost of George again. This time, he had reached up and pulled off his breather and goggles, coughing as he tried to take a deep breath. He pulled me close to him and pushed back my purple hair. Then kissed my forehead.

"I love you, Mike. I always have. Just remember your promise to me: if the opportunity ever arises to get out, you're to take it."

I closed my eyes, begging whatever portion of my mind in charge of these visions to take them away. My chest grew tight; I could barely breathe.

George's ghost stood completely still. Life slowly drained from his eyes, and his vibrant soul morphed into an empty shell.

"You know what to do," I heard myself say as a dream version of myself pulled out a package from inside my jacket and passed it to zombie-George. There was another ding of the tiny bell. I screamed as I curled up and tried to shelter myself from the unknown explosion.

"Mike!" Strong arms grabbed my shoulders, forcing me back to reality.

I inhaled sharply, and my eyes shot open. Marcus stood before me, but he wasn't looking at me. He was looking at the hazy, blue light barrier that cordoned off what remained of the apothecary from the rest of the street. A virtual sign hung in the middle of the field.

››Access restricted. Crime scene. Police line.‹‹

"You're almost out of time, Michaella Davison. You need to remember exactly who you are. Find Abram Shutton's son. He can help you."

Ignoring anything that Marcus, Jody, or the others were doing, I spun around, trying to find the owner of the voice.

"That's it." Marcus wrapped his arm tightly around me. "I'm escorting you back to Sector 14 for a full medical workup."

I pushed him off and pulled away from his uncharacteristic protective embrace. "I'm fine."

"No, you're not. You're hearing voices again, and don't you dare try to pretend otherwise. I know that look. I've seen it before. You're going back to Sector 14. If I have to, I'll pull rank and use my position as a member of STAR."

I glared at him, backing away, then turned to look back at the burned-out building.

"Don't do it," said the voice inside my head. *"If the Pregutor learns the truth about you, there'll be no escape."*

Marcus held his hands out to the side and slowly stepped closer to me. "What's it going to be, Mike? Do I force you back to Sector 14, or will you come willingly?"

"Don't do it," the voice said again.

I took a deep breath and stared at Marcus and the others. "I killed George."

Fifteen

"Don't be ridiculous." Jody wedged herself into the shrinking gap between Marcus and me, putting her hands out to stop Marcus from coming any closer. "You have nothing to feel guilty about. Isn't that right, Marcus?"

The other PentWave members were staggered around the three of us in the middle, their eyes bouncing from person to person, like they were trying to decide which way to look or who to support. Marcus remained silent.

"Marcus? Tell her," Jody said. "Mike had nothing to do with George's death."

Again, he was silent.

I shook my head. "He can't, because he knows the truth." I stared at him, trying to give him every opportunity to answer on his own. The more he remained silent, the more I knew the truth too. The only thing I couldn't figure out was how I could forget something so important, like my role in George's death.

I scoffed. "Of course. The chair room."

"What about the chair room?" Jody looked between Marcus and me. "Oh, shit." She then faced Marcus full on. "You escorted her to the chair room, didn't you?"

For a fleeting moment, Marcus glanced at Jody, then he dropped his gaze. The group around us berated Marcus, insisting that I had nothing to do with George's death, but Marcus continued to say nothing at all.

I smirked, shaking my head in disbelief. Eventually, I headed down the street, away from the burned-out store—and away from the rest of PentWave.

"Where are you going?" Jody ran to catch up with me, dragging Marcus behind her. The rest of the team chased after us.

"To the sector checkpoint. Marcus wants to head back to Sector 14, and he wants me to go with him. So, we might as well get it over and done with."

"Mike, I—" Marcus called out, but I spun around and held up my hands.

"Don't. Just don't." I exhaled in a rush and pressed my hands to my head. A headache was brewing. "Every single one of us has been in the chair at least once, our memories taken as a result. And apparently my last visit to the chair took away my memories of this place. I don't remember being here, yet I can see it so vividly. Only this morning, we were talking about how George lost his mind and destroyed the herbal dispensary. But what if the reason he lost his mind was because I took it from him? What I don't understand is why the Pregutor would choose to take those memories from me. I know in my heart that George is dead because of me . . . and the only one with any real answers is in Sector 14. So, I'm going to Sector 14, but not to be medically assessed. I'm going to find out the truth. Now, are you with me, or are you against me?"

I looked at each member of PentWave in turn, looking them in the eyes. Slowly, they nodded—even Marcus. As a group, we headed toward the sector checkpoint and to the transport tubes that would take us to the city's center.

I shared a mini-pod with Jody and Marcus—riding in silence. Our breathers dangled around our necks. Our display glasses sat in our pockets.

I stared out the windows, not really taking in the city. There was nothing left to take in during my numb state.

"You know that it's highly unlikely that you'll get the answers you seek."

I turned to Jody and Marcus, who also stared out the windows into nothingness.

"You'll likely find yourself in the chair again, whatever fragments of memory you've regained stripped away." It was the voice inside my head. *"The Pregutor doesn't want you to remember, because they can't use you as a weapon if you regain your sense of self."*

But even with the risk of losing my memories again, I had to try.

"Michaella, please. Don't do this. Run while you still can. I can help you hide, but you have to trust me."

I shook my head. *"Trust my imagination?"* I asked the voice. *"I really am losing my mind."*

When we finally arrived at the transport platform in Sector 14, the PentWave team made our way to the employee tunnels. After the first decontamination bay, Marcus peeled off from the group and headed down a different corridor. I was about to ask him where he was going, then I remembered he was now a member of STAR. His personal gear wouldn't be stored in the lockers reserved for couriers.

The wait for the health scanners and the transition into sector uniforms went by in a daze. With each step, my emotions drained into numbness. I didn't even need my favorite song to help me stay calm. I was nothing but an empty shell.

The voice in my head continually begged me to not go through with this, but I couldn't think of anything else to do.

What remained of PentWave stood at the edge of the main plaza together. Marcus was in his new uniform—the blue and purple stripes running down his sleeves—full tactical gear. The rest of us wore our purple stripes and simple security radios. Trent was armed with a pistol and a taser, but the rest of the group was like me—seeing no need for the weapons.

I looked up at the simulated night sky with its blanket of twinkling stars. I had always loved staring at the illusion, but now it carried a reminder of how much had been lost—and the lies we were being told.

All for the sake of maintaining some delusional sense of peace.

"Now where?" Marcus asked.

"We should find Tam," I said. "They've always been honest with us before."

The others agreed, and we headed toward the Rhodon buildings.

The night sky was suddenly replaced with a white ceiling, flooding the plaza with lights. Alarms blared, and lights fitted above the Rhodon building entrances flashed red.

"Atmospheric breach?" Jody asked, but Marcus shook his head.

"It's a Code Black. I've gotta go."

We stared at him with wide eyes. "Infectious disease breach?" Jody said in a squeaky voice.

Those in black uniforms and full tactical gear poured out of the various buildings and bolted across the main plaza. Guards shouted for civilians to dive to the ground and take cover.

Marcus joined the guards lining up in formation in the center of the plaza, rifles aimed toward the public access tunnels. Jody, Trent, and the rest of us in PentWave did what we could to escort civilians to the safety of nearby buildings. I pressed my hand to my radio, concentrating on the distracting chatter coming across the security feeds.

High-pitched whistles echoed from the public tunnels. A naked man ran into the main square. He halted only briefly as he encountered the wall of guards, all with guns pointed at him, but that didn't seem to stop him from darting this way and that, evading shots. It was like watching some animated cartoon, where the bad guys all seemed to have the worst aim ever, and the hero of the story spun through the air untouched. The naked man kicked and punched his way through the lines of guards, fighting like a wild animal, sending the guards to the ground sprawling in pain.

I watched in awe. Here was someone who was clearly unarmed—being naked and all—able to fight off the growing number of guards surrounding him, like they were just rag dolls. I had heard stories of fighters like this, but they were meant to be a source of inspiration for those training to be part of STAR. Yet, running across the plaza was such a warrior.

The man snapped his head in my direction, briefly halting his fight. He was hit by a taser, and his muscles tensed. With a roar, he spun around and kicked the converging guards in the head, then continued his run—heading straight for me.

Desperation radiated off the naked man, like wafts of a salty perfume. As I continued to watch the running man heading toward me, my vision darkened around the edges. His eyes locked onto mine.

"I found you. He said I would, and I didn't believe him. But here you are."

I couldn't explain it. I was hearing the naked man as though he was standing right in front of me—not fighting off the unit of guards still fifty meters away. There was no way that it was possible, especially not with the shouting guards chasing behind him. Yet, I could hear him clearly.

As the naked man continued to evade the guards and continued running toward me, I stepped away from my post against the protests from Jody. I headed into the plaza, heading toward the running man.

My arms hung loosely by my sides. Who was this man? Why was he looking for me?

Soft muted music played around me. It was the classic chords of the electric guitar of my favorite song. My vision continued to grow dark, with only the naked man's eyes clear in my field of view.

Orders came across the radio, but I was unable to process them. Instead, I continued to stare at the man fighting his way toward me, focusing on his eyes.

"You need to stop," I said in my mind, willing the stranger to hear me. *"Stop fighting. Stop running. Stop resisting."*

The naked man came to a complete stop, just standing there, like some switch in his body had been flipped. Time crawled forward, and my vision grew darker.

The man stared at me, locking our joint gaze together. There was something about his eyes, though I couldn't explain it. I just knew those eyes.

The headache that had been brewing since we had left Sector 2 vanished. The voice I had been hearing came through strongly: deep, soothing, and calm. *"You're in danger, Michaella Davison. You can't use your powers like this. Not here. Not now. They don't know what you are fully capable of, but if the Pregutor finds out and if they gain full control over you, there will be no stopping them."*

Blood trickled from the man's nose, and his body trembled. Time rushed forward as the guards tackled the naked man to the ground.

My vision was flooded with light, making me squint, partially blinding me. I pressed my hand to my forehead as the music vanished and the mother of all headaches pulsated behind my eyes. The fingers of my other hand tapped violently against my thighs. When I balled my hand into a fist, my knuckles knocked against my thighs instead.

As the guards pulled the naked man to his feet, he looked directly at me one last time. *"Find Abram Shutton's son. He can help you,"* the man said, though his lips never once moved.

A part of me wanted to chase after the group dragging the naked man away at gunpoint. I needed to know who he was . . . and why he had singled me out. And why he thought I was in danger.

"Because you are," said the voice. *"It's only a matter of time, Michaella, before the Pregutor learns the truth. In this case, the truth won't set you free. The truth will paint a target on your forehead."*

"Have you lost your mind?" Marcus seized my arm and spun me around to face him. "What the hell were you thinking? Did you think you could go all badass and take him on your own . . . unarmed?"

"I'm far from unarmed, Marcus. You know that."

He stared at me with a growing intensity to his gaze.

Slowly, my vision grew clouded—and the headache grew in intensity. I closed my eyes and tilted my head to the side.

"Please, Marcus, stay out of my head." My voice contained a hiss and anger.

There was a growing commotion surrounding me. When I opened my eyes again, Marcus was on the ground staring up at me with wide eyes filled with fear. Other members of STAR surrounded us, all of them with their weapons trained on me.

Jody screamed out from the side, her hands held behind her back, like she was in cuffs. The two guards with her held her upper arms strongly. The other members of PentWave were also being arrested.

"Courier Davison, you are to stand down," said the lead guard.

I shook my head. Strands of my purple hair wafted across my eyes. Uncertain as to what was going on, I raised my hands out to the sides—in surrender.

Sixteen

I sat on the hard metal chair, handcuffed to the table. A gray room with gray furniture. Even if it wasn't white like the rest of Sector 14, it was still colorless and bland. But now, even the guards in their black uniforms stationed at the door seemed to blend into the background. But they didn't disappear. Though I wished they would. The rifles raised and pointed in my direction made it perfectly clear that if they had to, they would make *me* disappear before I could say anything in my defense.

With the cold metal surrounding my wrists, I held no delusions that I was a prisoner.

"Can either of you tell me what's going on?"

The guards were silent.

I snorted. "No, I suppose not. Because in truth, you probably don't know either."

There was a click, and the door slid open. Tam, in their white pant suit, walked in, accompanied by more guards—Marcus among them. His eyes contained fear, but he held his rifle pointed at me, just like the others.

"Tam, please, what's going on? I swear I didn't do anything wrong."

Tam placed a small circular disk in the middle of the table. A virtual display sprang to life, showing the security footage from when the naked man ran through the plaza. The security audio overlaid the video.

The scene was chaotic as security guards chased the naked man around the plaza. On the video, I calmly walked away from my guard post at the entrance to the main Rhodon building and headed toward the main lawn area. There were orders that had come across the radio, but at the time, I couldn't make them out. Now I heard those orders clearly.

"Courier Davison, stand down. Return to your post."

The naked man continued to run toward me on the video, then everyone froze where they were. At first, I thought Tam had halted the playback, but the timestamp in the top corner of the display continued to click over.

"What the hell is going on?" someone said across the radio channels. "Is anyone else seeing this?"

The movement of those on the video lurched forward as the naked man was tackled to the ground.

The screen went black, and Tam stepped into my field of view. "No one knows what or how it happened, but all movement in the plaza froze for over a second. What did you do, Michaella?"

"I don't know." My heart raced ahead.

"Do not lie to me. I need to know what you did."

"I swear, Tam, I don't know."

Tam took a few deep breaths as they rewound the footage back to the moments just before all movement in the plaza stopped. "What were you thinking at this moment? What thoughts were going through your head?"

I licked my lips. My eyes darted around the room. For a moment, I locked eyes on Marcus, pleading for his help, but he responded by readjusting his grip on his rifle.

My fingers tapped uncontrollably against the table, and my head was pounding. "I wanted the man to stop. I wished that he'd stop fighting, that he'd stop running . . . and he did."

"Did he say anything?"

I shook my head. I couldn't be sure. It had to be my imagination. It was the only thing that made sense, because the voices weren't real.

"Michaella, he was less than three meters away from you. Did he say anything?"

"I don't know."

"How could you not know? He was right there, and he was looking directly at you." Tam looked at me with those eyes that demanded answers. "What are you not telling me, Michaella? What happened?"

I sat on the verge of tears. My chest grew tight. I glanced in Marcus's direction, then back at Tam, silently pleading.

"Everyone out," Tam ordered, not once taking their eyes off me. "I know what the protocols are, but they have little merit right now. I want everyone out. Now! That includes you, Marcus."

It seemed to take forever for the room to empty. When the last man left and shut the door, Tam took another device out of their pocket and activated it.

The world around us was suddenly silent, and we were plunged into darkness. A few seconds later, the room was filled with a soft glow emanating from the device in Tam's hand.

"I need you to trust me," Tam said. "I am unable to help you if you refuse to tell me the truth. Please, what happened? What did the man tell you?"

I couldn't stop the tears from falling. "He didn't say anything . . . at least not out loud. I thought I was going crazy. I had been hearing voices in my head all day. And when that man stood before me . . ." I forced myself to take a deep breath and did the best I could to wipe my hair out of my face. "His lips didn't move, but I heard him so clearly. He was staring at me, directly into my eyes, and the edges of my vision went dark like it normally does when I look at someone else like that, trying to get into their head. And that's when I heard the voice."

"What did he say to you?"

I took another deep breath. "'Find Abram Shutton's son. He can help you.' Tam, I thought Abram Shutton didn't have a son."

Tam pursed their lips. "Not anymore."

"I don't understand."

"Abram's son disappeared fifteen years ago. A few days after he went missing, his pharmachip went offline, showing negative life signs. His body was never found."

"So, he could still be alive. Tam, what if that hooded stranger you showed me in the city's surveillance footage, the one that you've been looking for . . . What if that was Dr. Shutton's son? That man from the plaza . . . he knew something. Did security get anything out of him during his interrogation?"

"No."

"Let me talk to him." I held up my hands, bringing attention to the cuffs that held me there. "He might not talk to the guards, but I think he'll talk to me."

"I wish I could, but that is not possible."

"Why not?"

The overhead lights blinked back into life, and the power to the room was restored. Tam pocketed whatever device they had used to take out the power.

"I am sorry, Michaella. The path forward has already been determined."

Before I could ask what that meant, the door burst open and a medical team with a gurney and other supplies came in. Two large orderlies came forward and grabbed my arm, pushing up my sleeve. Tam checked the tablet that the medical team brought with them and signed their signature. The nurse then came forward with a needle and syringe.

I did the best I could to fight against them—to fight against the restraints—but it was no use. Darkness swallowed the waking world.

Seventeen

Small amounts of light leaked into my blurry vision, but the edges were still too dark to make out where I was. And wherever it was, it wasn't my apartment. The shapes and the muted colors were all wrong. There wasn't any color worth speaking about, for starters. It was just white, with the hint of gray that played with the shadows. My apartment was draped with purple.

I blinked a few times, occasionally squinting, trying to regain my focus. I tested the movement in each of my limbs. My muscles were sore, like I had been tensed up in my sleep. When I tried to roll over, a sharp pain radiated down my left forearm. Tubing was coming out of it.

An IV line?

Next to me, there were flashing lights and blurry screens filled with wiggly lines and random numbers. Monitoring equipment.

I was in the hospital. But how the hell did I get here? The last thing I remembered was . . .

My mind was blank. The last thing I remembered was the coffee shop in Sector 4. Oh crap. I must have been exposed to some sort of atmospheric breach while in the outer sectors. That was all I needed.

I continued to blink, letting more light in through thin slits, focusing on the machine with lights next to me. Tubes were cradled in various slots. No doubt, the machine regulated the dosage of whatever drugs they were giving me.

"It's about time."

I about jumped out of my skin and looked around the dimly lit room for the owner of the voice.

"I was wondering how long you were going to be out for."

The room was empty, except for myself and the machines. I had to be hearing imaginary voices again.

"You can stop looking. No, I'm not there, not in person, at least. Yes, you're hearing voices again. And no, you're not going crazy—though you're unlikely to believe me. But you are going to have to trust me. That's assuming that you want to get out of there alive."

I pressed my fingers to my temples. What the fuck was going on?

"I'll tell you exactly what is going on. I keep telling you that you're in danger, and you refuse to listen to me. But this time, if you don't listen and make a move, this could end badly."

"Who are you?" I asked, though I knew damn well that I was talking to my imagination.

"We can worry about the introduction later, after you're out of immediate danger. Right now, you need to get out of that bed and out of that room."

I sat up and brought my hand to my face, trying to wipe away the delirium. My White Rabbit syndrome had clearly progressed to the final stage. It was only a matter of time before the voices tried to convince me to kill myself.

"Seriously? Just get over it and move your ass. As soon as that nurse walks in the door, you'll understand precisely the danger that you're in."

"What nurse?"

The door opened and a large muscular person wearing dark blue scrubs backed into the room.

"That nurse," the voice said. *"Whatever you do, don't let them give you any more drugs. Trust me on that one."*

The nurse turned around, revealing a small tray with multiple tubes on it. "Oh, you're awake." The nurse smiled as he turned on the lights in the room. "I'm Nurse Bennett. I just need to take a few vitals."

I blinked several times as I took in the nurse's features. The well-defined biceps and triceps were not something that was any cause for concern, but the mustache was outside of protocol for any medical professional. It was a requirement that all hospital staff in Sector 14 be clean shaven. It was a matter of perception. Some people believed that facial hair was the sign of a person who didn't care about their personal hygiene. That no-facial-hair rule bled across the lines to other staff employed in Sector 14 too.

Whoever this person was, they weren't a nurse . . . at least, not at this hospital.

The not-a-nurse placed the tray on the rolling table located at the end of the bed. He then pulled a portable scanner from his pocket. "If you wouldn't mind . . ." He gestured to my right hand.

I turned over my wrist to expose my pharmachip, but kept my focus honed in on the not-a-nurse. "So, how long have you been a nurse?"

"Long enough."

"And you've always worked at Rhodon Central?"

"Yeah. It's a great place to work." The nurse tapped on a few buttons on the scanner, then moved to the other side of the bed where the IV monitor machine was mounted. He pulled open one of the dispensary compartments and disconnected the empty cartridge. He then grabbed one of the medicine vials from the tray he brought in with him and connected the tubes in place.

"What is that?"

"Nothing major." The nurse's smile was likely meant to be disarming, but there was something in the eyes that made the hairs at the back of my neck stand on end. "It's just something to help you sleep."

"I just woke up. Why do I need to sleep?"

The nurse gazed at me, like he was trying to stare into my soul. "Because you're tired."

"No, I'm not."

The nurse stood straighter, pulling his shoulders back and holding his head high. His stare intensified. Tentacles of darkness threaded across the edges of my vision. *Fall asleep, you bitch,* the not-a-nurse said, though his lips never moved.

I yanked out the IV line and jumped out of the bed on the opposite side from the nurse. "Who the fuck are you? Because you're clearly not a nurse from this hospital."

He blinked and quickly shook his head. *Why the fuck isn't this bitch going down?* Again, his lips weren't moving, but I could hear him clearly. *How is she able to resist?*

"Resist what?"

His eyes went wide. "Oh fuck," he said aloud. "They didn't tell me that you're a fifth gen."

"What does that mean?"

"Doesn't matter. I'm under orders to get you ready for transport, so that's what I'm going to do." The nurse who wasn't a nurse edged around the bed, blocking any chances I had of bolting for the door.

My options were rapidly diminishing to only two: fight or . . . Well, the alternative wasn't worth thinking about.

The nurse tried to bolt toward me, and I struck out, landing a solid kick to his knee, followed by repetitive strikes to the head. The not-a-nurse blocked my next punch, grabbing my wrist, but I followed through, lifting my arm and ducking in behind him, kicking out his other knee. I then grabbed the tray that not-a-nurse had brought in with him and hit him in the face, and again in the back of the head. He lost his footing and hit his head on the metal framing of the hospital bed as he fell to the floor.

I stood there heaving, with the tray held ready to strike again. I gave the nurse a kick in the side, half expecting him to grab my leg and pull me down, but he didn't move. But that didn't mean that he wouldn't move unexpectedly.

I hit the nurse's head repeatedly with the tray. Blood matted in his hair and mustache.

"Next time you want to pretend to be a nurse, shave the mustache." I staggered back from the body and forced myself to take several deep breaths.

"*Well, that was unexpected,*" said the disembodied voice that had been plaguing me.

"What the fuck is going on?" I hissed.

"*I'll answer all of your questions as soon as we get you to safety. Right now, you're just going to have to trust me. Okay?*"

I nodded. "Okay." Not that I had much choice.

"*Good. First thing I need you to do is to change out of that hospital gown. Take the nurse's clothes.*"

"He wasn't a nurse."

"*Yeah, well, you still need to take his clothes.*"

"Can't I just put back on my own clothes?"

There was a snort. *"Sure, assuming you can find them. Look, you don't have time to argue about this. Just take the nurse's clothes."*

My shoulders sagged as I looked down at the hospital gown I was wearing. I frowned as I took in the size of the not-a-nurse. I was going to swim in that uniform.

"It won't be as bad as you think."

I shook my head. What was it going to take to wake up from this nightmare?

"Oh, get over it. And get moving. Someone will come looking for that brute soon, and you don't want to be there when they do."

I couldn't argue with that. Whether I was going crazy or not, I did bludgeon that nurse—not-a-nurse.

I knelt on the floor and removed the nurse's shoes, then yanked on his uniform to remove it. Floppy limbs and the head swayed in every direction. Quickly stripping off the hospital gown, I pulled the bloodied scrubs over my head. I considered putting on the shoes, but they were way too big and would have been dangerous if I had to make a run for it.

With the not-a-nurse's uniform on, cinched as tight as I could make it, I prepared to walk out of the room and into the main hall of the ward. With my hand on the door handle, I took several deep breaths.

"Michaella, you can do this. Oh, and Michaella . . ."

"Yeah?"

"There's no need to vocalize your thoughts. I'm able to hear you clearly . . . just like you can hear me: inside your mind." There was a hint of amusement in the voice. Of course, my imagination would be amused by the situation. *"I can get you out of there, but you're going to have to trust me, okay?"*

It wasn't like I had much choice. I took one last deep breath, then stepped out into the hall.

EIGHTEEN

"Go LEFT. *Take the second hallway on the right, then the first left. Go quickly. But not too quickly."*

Refusing to question the sanity of following directions coming from a random voice in my head, I headed into the labyrinth of hospital corridors, weaving past open shelves of linen and the odd gurney in the hall. As I moved deeper into the hospital, past patients waiting for rooms of their own, I started to question why no other patients had been in my room. It could have easily accommodated four patients. But now really wasn't the time to question hospital policies.

"How do you know where I should go?" I tried to keep my eyes down as I walked through the corridors past orderlies wheeling patients around.

"We've hacked into the cameras."

I stumbled as my foot stuck to the linoleum. *"You can do that?"*

"Yeah, and be glad we can—because we know that security have been alerted to your disappearance. They're locking all the doors. Pharmachips are required to open them."

"Great." I kept heading down the hall, doing my best to stay calm—though it wasn't easy. *"And how do you suggest I get another pharmachip? It's not like I can cut off someone's arm and carry that around with me."*

There was a snort. *"We're working on it."*

"We? Who's we?"

"Introductions later, remember? Just keep going."

I internally growled. Not only was I barefoot, wearing scrubs that were falling off my small frame, but I was trusting an imaginary voice without explanation. And the voice's attitude was getting on my nerves.

There was a minor hum, like the voice wanted to say something in response to my last thought, but they didn't. *"There's a door to your right. It's a cleaner's closet. Door is unlocked. Go now."*

Without further thought, I darted across the hall to the cleaner's closet and ducked inside. With the door closed behind me, I pressed my ear to the door, trying to hear what was going on outside in the hall. To my surprise, the voices outside were crystal clear, like I was hearing them across a radio.

"The floor is clear," someone said. "No sign of her."

"She has to be here somewhere. We locked down the floor as soon as we lost contact with our operative. Find her."

I took several deep breaths. No matter what happened, crazy or not, there was no doubt in my mind that they were searching for me. And it didn't matter why.

I rested against the door, staring into the darkness of the closet, not daring to turn on the lights. Racks of cleaning supplies and toilet paper lined the walls. I snickered.

With all the technological advancements of society, you would think that they would have come up with something better to use than toilet paper.

"You have no idea what I would do to have a nice roll of toilet paper. I'm stuck using old rags."

"You're still there?"

"Of course. And it's not yet clear for you to leave your hiding spot. See if you can find something you can use as a weapon. You might need it."

"Yeah, fight or die." I sighed in defeat as I grabbed a broom hidden in the back corner. I unscrewed the head from the metal rod handle. *"Who was that nurse, anyway?"*

"Not a nurse." There was a hint of a snort to the voice.

I snorted in return. *"Yeah, I got that."* I tested the weighted balance of my makeshift staff, doing the best I could to give a quick spin in the tiny space. *"The way that guy was talking. It was like he was . . ."* I really didn't want to say it . . . or think it.

"Like he was trying to implant a thought?" the voice asked.

"Yeah. And the way he reacted: it was like he was surprised that it didn't work. He said I was a fifth gen. Do you know what that means?"

"I do, but we don't have time to go into that now. The hall is clear. You need to move. Go right, and head to the fire exit at the end of the hall. But be careful, they have it guarded."

"There isn't another way off the floor?"

"No. All exits are guarded, but the fire exit is guarded by only two guards."

"And what do you expect me to do against two guards?"

"Fight."

I pursed my lips. *"Great."* I held my makeshift staff at the ready, then edged the door open, slowly peeking out into the hall. With no one in sight, I darted into the hall and ran as light-footed as possible, trying to not make a sound as my bare feet padded along the linoleum.

I came to the last corner and pressed up against the wall, then contorted myself to peer around the corner at the two guards guarding the fire exit. They wore standard issue security guard uniforms, with the solid blue stripes going down the black tunic sleeves. They had on tactical gear—helmets, vests, and radios—but they appeared to be lightly armed, with only sidearms and tasers. That didn't mean that they didn't have other hidden goodies.

"Any thoughts?" I asked the voice—not that I was expecting any pearls of wisdom from my imagination.

"Move fast and pray?"

I snorted. Yeah, if there was a god, I hoped he was on my side. I leaned slightly out from my hiding spot and stared down the short hall toward the guards. The edges of my vision darkened, but instead of being afraid of it, I embraced it. I slipped into the hall, holding my weapon at the ready, walking calmly and slowly toward the guards.

"Michaella, what are you doing?" the voice said. *"You should be running."*

But I ignored the voice and continued toward the guards in a calm, slow walk. The guards stared directly into my eyes.

"You don't want to fight me," I said through whatever connection I had with the guards. My vision grew darker along the edges. *"You want to help me."*

One of the guards suddenly drew his pistol and fired. There was clattering and chaos behind me, and the guard continued to fire his weapon at targets behind me. The other guard waved his wrist over the security pad at the door and waved me forward. "Come on! Hurry!"

I sprinted for the open door. Something bit at my upper arm as I squeezed through the opening and it shut behind me. The sounds of gunfire continued on the other side, and I ignored the pain in my upper arm as I wedged the metal rod that had been the broom handle against the door and the floor. I then ran down the stairs.

There was a slight buzz inside my head. It was a sensation that gave off a sense of irritation, but I also got a sense that the voice wasn't irritated with me.

"Now what?"

The door above me burst open. Faces of guards peered down at me. Shit. I bolted down the stairs, determined to not trip over my too-long pants.

The door on the landing directly in front of me burst open, and I pushed it closed with my full body weight as I ran past. But with guards running up from lower levels and guards above me, there was nowhere left to run. Everywhere I looked, guns pointed in my direction.

Fight or die. For whatever it was worth, it became a little mantra.

"Put your hands up," a guard shouted.

I didn't move. Instead, I kept my hands slightly in front of me, guarding my center. I stood with my weight evenly distributed, with my knees slightly bent and ready to spring into action.

Only a handful of the guards around me wore masks. With the filtration system in Sector 14 being the best there was, there really wasn't the need. But I didn't need to see their full faces to see the loathing written across their expressions.

"I said, 'Hands up.'" The guard at the front of the group edged closer to me. He was one of the guards who didn't have a mask on.

"Michaella, we have an idea," said the voice that had been plaguing me since the nightmare began, *"but for it to work, a lot of things need to go right. I hope you can hold your breath."*

Wafts of smoke leaked into the stairwell from the overhead vents. One by one, the maskless guards started to cough. I shook my head and tried to suppress the laughter of insanity. Instead, I inhaled as deeply as I could and held my breath.

The smoke came in more thickly. Alarms blared. The coughing around me grew in intensity, and a guard behind me fell forward, pushing me to the side as he fell. He thrashed on the ground.

"Atmosphere breach!"

"Stand your ground!" shouted another guard through bouts of coughing.

My eyes started to water as I fought against the urge to breathe out.

"Just keep holding your breath," the voice said. *"The recyclers are rebooting now. When you hear them kick in, you need to run back up through the gas."*

"What? Are you crazy?"

"Trust me. Only fifteen more seconds—give or take."

My lungs burned to take another breath, but I didn't dare.

The lights in the stairwell flickered, plunging me into darkness. The only lights left in the concrete environment were the luminescent strips on the edges of the stairs and on the helmets of the guards.

Still holding my breath, I seized a taser from a guard beside me and used it on the first guard who stood in my way. I pushed the twitching guard to the side; he tumbled down the stairs, taking other guards with him. I continued to push my way through the guards, blocking each strike that came at me, slowly climbing the stairs.

There was a clunking sound overhead, and a gush of air pushed in from above. My hair fluttered around, waving in my eyes. The emergency lighting flooded the stairwell, and the doors into the stairwell burst open as hospital staff and patients poured out, trying to escape from the atmosphere leak.

As much as I wanted to believe that I was imagining things, I struggled to fathom how my imagination could conjure up such pandemonium.

With the added people flooding into the stairwell, the guards gave up their pursuit and ran with the hospital staff and patients, heading for the nearest exits, many of them coughing.

I almost fell over a fallen guard as the group kept trying to find their way to fresh air. Avoiding the stampede, I yanked on the collar of the guard's tactical vest and pulled him to the side. I pressed my fingers to his neck. Even though he still had a pulse, there was no hope for him. Foam had formed around the edges of his mouth, and blood was streaming from his nose, ears, and eyes.

I searched through the downed guard's gear. Security units in Sector 14 were trained to be prepared for every scenario, including an atmosphere breach. Even though he wasn't wearing a mask, he would have had a portable filtration unit on his person somewhere . . . if only I could find it. It wouldn't be as effective as a full breather mask, but at least I would be able to take another breath without my lungs being filled with the acidic air.

What I was looking for was in the guard's right top pocket of his tactical vest. With the breather tubes up my nostrils and the portable unit turned on, the hairs inside my nose wavered, forcing me to sneeze, expelling the breath that I had been holding in a rush. I tentatively inhaled, consciously breathing through my nose, but exhaling through my mouth. There was a slight sting on the inhale, but it wasn't anything that I couldn't handle.

"What the hell did you do?" I called out to the voice. I continued to huddle in the corner with the dead guard in my arms, watching everyone run past.

"What needed to be done. I suggest you take advantage of the chaos. But you can't go out the main doors."

"Why not?"

"They're watching the exits. Everyone is being scanned as they exit the building—even the patients."

"Is the atmosphere . . . ?" I couldn't quite bring myself to finish the question.

"The breach is contained to just the hospital. The rest of the sector is fine. Sector 14 has an isolated filtration circuit for each building. We took advantage of that to create a diversion."

"Some diversion."

"Yeah, well, while we might have given you a way out of the hospital, getting out of the sector is going to be a different matter. The sector has gone into full lockdown. No one in or out. And only security pharmachips can open the doors now. We can't get around it."

I looked down at the security guard in my arms. *"There's always a way."*

Without a moment to think, I got to my feet and lifted the guard as high as I could, holding his wrist to the scanner by the door. The door opened onto the main floor. I pulled the guard through with me and into a side room off the main hall. It was an empty hospital room with six beds. It looked as though the patients had recently been in those beds, but they were likely among those who were running down the stairs.

I stripped the dead guard of their uniform, swapping out the oversized nurse's uniform for the black tunic with blue stripes. The uniform was still too big, but not obviously so. I then grabbed the guard's helmet and tucked my purple hair up into it. And I happily grabbed his boots too. They too were a little big for me, but by tying the laces in a certain way, I could make them work.

The security radio channel was filled with chaos, orders flying in every which direction. Guards were ordered to ensure that each floor of the hospital was clear of civilians while they continued the search for me. Knowing they would be searching the building room by room, I dressed the dead guard in the hospital scrubs and labored to lift him to one of the hospital beds, tucking the bed sheets around him—like he was a patient who had fallen prey to the atmosphere breach.

Just as I had finished staging the body, the door flew open and another security guard stood in the doorway. "Find anyone?"

"Just a dead patient." I moved to the side to reveal the staged body.

"Leave them. We're under orders to escort the nurses and doctors with us to the staff tunnels via the service stairwell. I've been told that a STAR unit will be doing a full sweep of the building as we leave. I don't know about you, but I don't want to be around when they show up."

"I couldn't agree with you more." The longer I could avoid STAR, the better.

In the hall, there was a group of nurses and doctors, all in dark blue and black scrubs, all wearing breather tubes like I was. Several of them scratched welts that had appeared on their forearms and face. It would be a trip through the chemical decontamination baths for all of them before their skin would start to heal properly, but that treatment would be given to them in the staff tunnels.

As the group navigated through the maze of corridors to the service stairwell, I walked alongside one of the nurses, who seemed to be struggling the most with the effects that the atmosphere breach had on her skin.

"Will you be okay?" I asked.

The nurse nodded. "Is it true what they're saying? About an escaped prisoner?"

"And what exactly are they saying?"

"Just that they've killed someone. Another nurse. And that it's because of them that we now have this atmospheric breach. Are they really that dangerous?"

I shrugged. "It's not worth taking the chance. Your safety is the most important thing here." I tried to keep my voice calm and filled with authority.

The medical staff smiled. "Well, I, for one, feel safer having you with us."

I feigned a smile, but I continually looked around, while at the same time keeping my face down so the visor from the helmet would keep my face hidden from the cameras mounted on the ceiling.

Nineteen

Blinking arrows ran down the walls as we entered into the staff tunnels, funneling everyone toward the decon units. Guards and technicians lined the halls.

"Strip all clothing and gear and place them in the bins," someone shouted to the newcomers. "This includes your breathers, people. No exception. Security personnel, put your radios and tactical gear on the yellow counter. You'll be issued with new breathers and radios on the other side of decon."

Other than the emergency decontamination protocols, it was like any other day in Sector 14. Coming into the sector, you had to strip. And leaving the sector, you had to strip. It was part of life. So, it was no surprise when the doctors and nurses around me stripped to their naked forms in the middle of the hall, dumping their contaminated clothes into the biohazard bins.

The nurse next to me removed her surgical cap, then brushed her fingers through her purple curly locks. I waited for security to converge on the woman, but they never came. The security guards on the periphery of the room just kept ushering people toward the decon units.

"Nice hair," I said with a smile, removing my helmet and letting my own purple locks fall around my face.

The nurse beamed as she continued to strip.

Without any further thought, I stripped out of the guard's uniform, placing the uniform in the bins and the tactical gear on the yellow counter. I considered grabbing a taser, just in case, but where would I hide the weapon while naked?

We were ushered into the decon units in groups of ten. As the sprays and powders graced our skin, there was a collective sigh of relief. We were then instructed to return to our lockers to don our outer sector clothes, then wait for further instructions.

The nurses and the doctors headed down the corridors on the right. The security guards peeled off to the locker rooms on the left. I followed the security guards, but when no one was looking, I darted into the locker room for the PentWave couriers.

To my relief, my old locker room was empty, but now I was facing a new issue. All the lockers in the room used biometric locks. If they were monitoring the security logs of the staff locker rooms—which I suspected they were—the moment I opened my locker, they would know. So, my own locker wasn't an option, but . . .

"Michaella, this is a dumb idea."

"Shut up. I'm thinking."

There was this buzzing left in the wake of the voice. It was like the voice wanted to protest, but there was nothing the voice could do about what I was planning. Besides, there were some things that I would need if I was going to live a life on the run.

"Like what?" the voice asked. *"What can be so important that you would risk getting caught like this?"*

"For one, I need a jacket."

"A jacket? Michaella, I'll get you a new jacket when you get here. Just find any clothing you can and get out of there."

"I'm not leaving without a jacket."

"Forget what I said earlier. You are going crazy."

The fact I was listening to voices in my head told me I had already lost it. But if I was going to descend into total madness, I might as well go with the gear that would keep me hidden from the trackers.

"Trackers? What trackers?"

So, my imagination didn't know everything. *"A courier's jacket is lined with a special material that masks the signal of my pharmachip and any other tech I might be carrying. All Rhodon Corporation couriers are issued with one. It would do us no good if the packages we deliver are tracked before we deliver them, especially considering the packages often contain death."*

I had expected the voice to respond to that last comment, but instead there was a silence. It was almost too quiet. At least the silence gave me room to think.

I darted across the room to the last row of lockers located at the back. As I stood in front of the locker closest to the wall, I stared at the identification panel and smiled. I brushed my finger along the top. Dust.

"And why is dust a good thing?" the voice asked, finally breaking the silence.

"Because it means this locker hasn't been used in a while. And if I'm right, they won't be monitoring this particular locker."

With a deep breath, I pressed my right hand to the scanner, hoping against hope that my security codes hadn't been locked out. "Security override. Authorization: Davison Kilo-Alpha-Two-Beta. Execute."

There was a soft beep, followed by a click, and the locker door swung open.

I chuckled in relief. "Thank you, Marcus." Reaching into the locker, I grabbed what I could of the outer sector clothing. Marcus's taste was incredibly boring, black skinny pants and a black tunic. But beggars couldn't be choosers. The boots were a bit big, but with the extra pair of socks that Marcus had stashed in the back of the middle shelf, I was able to ensure a snug, comfortable fit. But it was the bulky purple jacket that made me smile the most.

I had always thought that Marcus was a *blue* kind of person, maybe yellow, but that purple . . . I brushed my hands down the sleeves as I put it on. For a moment, it felt like I was coming home. I then grabbed the gloves and the full breather mask that Marcus kept next to his display glasses, but I deliberately left the glasses behind.

Instead, I made an exaggerated show of bowing to the glasses that faced outward. I then gave a funky goodbye wave as I closed the locker and headed out into the halls.

"I don't get it," said the voice. *"You grab the jacket and the breather, but you left the glasses? Why?"*

"They can be tracked. They have a camera recorder in them. And Marcus would have left his display glasses in record mode when he put them facing outward on that shelf."

"Who's Marcus?"

"Another courier, or at least he was. When he transferred to STAR, they would have issued him with a new locker, along with a new jacket—different color, but just as stealthy. I was hoping his locker had been left abandoned. And I was hoping that my security codes hadn't been deleted yet. But Marcus will eventually want to collect his glasses. Then they'll know exactly how I got out of the sector. Part of it, anyway."

I looked down the hall toward the junction where the locker room tunnels converged with the outgoing sector tunnels. *"Do you still have eyes on the security cameras?"*

"We do. It's the only part of the system we still have access to. All other systems have been isolated and locked off."

"Good. Find me a way out of here."

TWENTY

THE CORRIDORS THAT LED FROM the locker rooms converged with the main exit tunnel. A sea of people filled the hall from wall to wall. In all the years I had worked for Rhodon, I had never seen this many people trying to exit Sector 14 at the same time. Then again, there had never been an atmospheric breach either.

While I never really liked being in crowds, the number of people with purple hair brought a little comfort. And the rainbow of jackets moving in the long lines toward the health scanners helped too.

I maneuvered into the middle of the group, slowly moving toward the exit. If I stood in just the right position, the colorful people around me could help me hide from the overhead cameras.

Fully armed guards lined the halls, with their dark blue jackets with thin purple stripes down the sleeves. The STAR. And there, only ten meters ahead of me, was Marcus.

Shit.

"Just pull up your hood," the voice said.

"I can't. Protocol. No hoods are allowed in these tunnels."

I tried to move to the opposite side of the hall, as far away from Marcus as I could get. But as I got closer to him, a high-pitched humming echoed inside my head, and my right eye started to twitch. Instinctively, I pressed my gloved hand to my temple, willing my eye to stop whatever it was doing, but the pain only intensified.

"You!" A STAR guard pointed at me. "Hold it right there!"

"It's her!" Marcus called out.

I had no time to think. I just turned and pushed my way back through the crowd, heading back into the main facility.

"Shit! If you're there and you really have eyes on the cameras, I could use a little help here. Get me out of this maze."

The crowd heading toward the exits seemed to grow, becoming denser. And the STAR were not far behind me. "Just get out of my way," I hissed. Suddenly, the gathered crowd parted, clearing a path. Not questioning my good fortune, I bolted down the hall as the STAR continued to chase me, Marcus with them.

"Take the next corridor on the left," said the voice.

Not questioning it, I skidded around the corner, heading down tunnels that were rarely used.

Shots fired behind me. By some miracle, I wasn't hit. Though I was fairly certain that the jacket I was wearing now had a bullet hole or two in it. Thank goodness Marcus was significantly larger than I was.

I chanced a look over my shoulder as I continued to run. Marcus stood at the end of the corridor with his rifle raised, preparing to fire, but before he could get off a shot, someone pushed his aim upward. The light fixture above me exploded, raining sparks down on my head.

But I kept running. Thundering footsteps echoed behind me.

"Get me out of here, Voice!"

"Next right, then take the left."

I did as I was told and skidded to a halt as soon as I turned the last corner. *"It's a fucking dead end."*

"No, it's not." There was a beep in the distance, followed by a slight hiss, and the wall moved. A thin, dark opening appeared.

I bolted the remainder of the distance and squeezed through the gap that was just barely large enough. On the other side, I pulled hard on the door, and the door sealed with a hiss, followed by a thump. Lights on a control panel next to the door changed from green to red.

I stumbled backward a few steps, staring at the door, waiting for it to open any second.

"The codes have been scrambled," the voice said. *"It'll take a while to decode them. I suggest you make good use of the time that we've given you."*

I nodded, though I wasn't sure *why* I was nodding for this disembodied voice.

"There are no cameras in those tunnels, so you're going to have to describe what you see so we can navigate you through."

Again, I nodded.

"Michaella, I'm serious. You need to talk to me. I can't help you if you don't speak."

"I'm talking to my imagination."

"Do you honestly think those guys on the other side of the door will care if you are talking to your imagination or not?" The banging on the door became rhythmic.

"No." I forced myself to take a slow, deep breath. The air was musty. Stale. *"It's dark down here. It's going to take a while for my vision to adjust."*

"Understood. Just use your sense of touch to start with. If you head down deeper into the tunnel, there should be a junction approximately thirty meters ahead on your right."

"Okay." I turned my back to the door—and the banging—and brushed my fingers along the wall on my right.

After I turned right at the junction, the voice said, *"Take the next left, then another right."*

Without question, I followed the voice's instructions. There was a muffled bang, followed by some shouting.

"Um, I hope you have a way out of these tunnels, because I think they just got in."

"We do. At the end of the passage that you're now in, you'll come to a door. It's old. Very old."

"How old is very old?"

"Let's just say that the door is old enough that it doesn't use an electronic lock."

I knitted my brow together, squinting in the dark. Slowly, the wheel on the back of the door came into view, connected to what looked like locking bolts that went out in two directions horizontal to the ground. I tried to turn the wheel, grunting with the effort.

"I think it's rusted shut."

"You'll have to do your best. That's the only way out . . . unless you want to go back and risk running into those guards chasing you."

"No, thanks." I felt around the ground and wrapped my fingers around a long cylindrical rod. I wove it in between the spokes on the wheel and pulled hard, using my full body weight to help.

The metal groaned, and the locking mechanism gave way. I pushed on the door, wincing every time the metal scraped and screeched. Hot air rushed into the tunnel from the outside, making me cough. I was tempted to pull out the breather that I stole from Marcus's locker, but the neighboring sectors to Sector 14 all had functioning domes and clean air. Instead, I forced myself to take several deep breaths and pushed the door open further.

Dead vines hung over the entrance on the other side. It took a bit of effort to push my way through, but as soon as I could, I closed the door behind me and spun the wheel on the other side, locking the door again. Hopefully, with how dark it was down there, they wouldn't know that I had used that door until I was long gone.

I readjusted the vines, covering up the door again, and headed into the streets with my hood pulled up to hide my hair.

Everyone around me was all focused on their own little worlds. The odd person waved their hands in front of them, commands for their virtual displays. Others held glass tablets, flicking their thumbs upwards. It was older technology, but it still worked well. I just joined the flow, heading farther and farther away from the hidden door.

"Now what?" I asked the voice.

"You need to get to Sector 9."

"Sector 9? But there's nothing in Sector 9."

"I'm in Sector 9. You'll have to traverse the city by foot. If you go anywhere near the transport tubes, they'll find you."

"How do you suggest I get past the sector checkpoints? The moment I step into a health scanner, I'll be caught."

"You won't be using the health scanners. You'll be using the service tunnels."

I stopped walking, and the person behind me bumped into me.

"Watch it!"

"Sorry." I moved out of the way, then continued down the street. *"Are you kidding me? Service tunnels? I could be spreading disease from sector to sector."*

The voice was silent, but there was an irritating hum.

I shook my head. *"Never mind. Service tunnels, it is."* A shiver went down my spine. Was this how I was going to spend the rest of my life? Questioning my own sanity as the voices in my head led me into dark tunnels? I sighed. *"So, I need to get to Sector 9, but where am I now?"*

"Sector 12."

"Okay . . . That's not that too far to go."

"Just don't dilly-dally. It won't take them long to work out how you got out of those tunnels."

TWENTY-ONE

I APPROACHED THE SECTOR GATE on the other side of Sector 12. From where I stood, the guards stood tall, actively searching those passing through the gate. I inhaled as deeply as I could, then blew out a long stream of breath, trying to slow my racing heart.

"*Okay, Voice, you told me that I'll need to use the service tunnels, but how do I gain access to them without drawing attention to myself?*"

"*Do you see the concrete bench in the corner? The one fashioned to look like a tree?*"

I nodded, then remembered that the voice could only hear my thoughts. "*Yes.*"

"*The entrance is just behind that. I'll tell you when it's all clear.*"

I took another slow, deep breath and casually moved closer to the bench. I knelt on the ground just in front of it, pretending to retie my boot laces.

"*Go now.*"

I darted behind the fake tree and stared at a small steel door with a wheel in the center.

"*What are you waiting for? Clock is ticking.*"

As I continued to stare at the door, I remembered my security briefing with Tam about a hooded figure who had vanished without a trace. There was a slight hum to the silence in my head, something that I had come to associate with the voice wanting to say something about my thoughts but choosing to remain silent.

But time was running out, and I could only stay ahead of the STAR for so long.

With all my attention and efforts focused on the wheel, I pulled the door open. With one last look at Sector 12, I slipped inside the maintenance tunnels and pulled the door closed behind me.

I turned to face the darkness, breathing in the musty, damp air. But it was clean, and that's what mattered. I pulled out a light unit I had pocketed from one of the shops on the main street and turned it on to its dimmest setting. Heading deeper into the tunnel, I followed the voice's instructions through the maze to the other side and into the next sector.

Sector after sector, I moved through the city on foot, and I bypassed the sector checkpoints by using hidden passages.

With the final door closed and resealed, and the entrance hidden behind a dumpster, I joined the pedestrian traffic moving away from the sector checkpoint and deeper into Sector 9.

The air in Sector 9 carried an acidic taste that caused an irritation at the back of my throat. I finally pulled out the breather from Marcus's locker and pulled on the straps to ensure a snug fit.

"Now where?"

"Head to the White Rabbit Bar over on Chantal Ave. Ask the bartender for a Shirley Temple."

"I don't know where Chantal Ave is."

"Walk down the main street like you're heading toward the warehouse district, then follow the noise of the party-goers.

That will be Chantal Ave. The White Rabbit is down the end."

"Then what?"

The voice went silent. So too did the buzzing hum. But I had trusted the voice this far. Might as well see how deep this rabbit hole went.

I pulled my hood tight around my face, keeping my head bowed. Hover drones flew overhead, carrying holographic posters of the latest treatments for flurona available from Rhodon Corporation.

»Visit your nearest clinic for more information.«

But what the posters didn't say was that flurona didn't have a cure—or a treatment that managed the symptoms properly. All the clinics were doing was rounding up victims to become human lab rats.

But those with flurona weren't the only human lab rats in the city. I had been a human lab rat all my life, given one experimental treatment after another. I shuddered at the thought.

As the muted daylight gave way to night, music grew in volume in the distance. It wasn't the same Caribbean salsa beats found in Sector 11, but the music possessed a quality that made me long for the sliding electric guitar riffs of *Purple Rain*. As I turned the corner onto Chantal Ave, black ultraviolet light flooded the street. The crowd lining up outside a busy nightclub was draped in a neon glow.

It was a sea of neon yellow, orange, and green, but my own jacket looked black, absorbing the light. I knew that a courier's jacket was designed to blend into the background in the outer sectors, but to disappear into the darkness?

I smiled at this new knowledge.

At the end of the street, a blackened sign swung back and forth over a black door. A rabbit dressed in a vest looking at a pocket watch was barely visible under the filth. The windows were also covered in blackened filth, blocking any view of the interior. But the lights were on, so someone had to be home.

I stood in the doorway of the White Rabbit Bar, staring at the dimly lit serving bar that ran the length of the wall. Tables lined the outer walls, jammed together into little booths. Soft jazz played from crackly speakers in the ceiling, having no issue with being heard over the heavy bass music coming from the neon fest just up the street.

"You don't need the breather in here," the bartender called out. "We have an isolated filtration system."

I nodded, then lowered my hood and took off my breather. I tested the air with a few shallow breaths at first and steadily inhaled more deeply. The air carried a woody scent, laced with something that I couldn't quite place—something sweet. Not too sweet, but inviting.

"That will be the house special you're smelling. Don't even bother trying to figure out what it is. It's a secret . . . and I'm not telling anyone. Not even a pretty young thing like you. So, what can I get you?"

I smiled, a genuine smile—which surprised me, because I didn't have much to smile about these days. "Do you know how to make a Shirley Temple?"

The bartender smirked. "It's been a while since I've been asked for one of those, but sure, I can do that. That will be sixty credits."

I was fairly confident that the color drained from my face as the bartender continued to smirk.

"Put it on my tab." A man sitting at the end of the bar pulled out the stool next to him and invited me to take a seat.

I tried to swallow the lump forming at the back of my throat and edged my way deeper into the bar, but kept my distance from the stranger.

"She looks like the nervous type," the bartender said, as he went about making up the drink.

"With everything she's been through to get here, I'm not surprised. For whatever it's worth, Michaella, welcome to Sector 9."

TWENTY-TWO

"I KNOW YOU, DON'T I? You guided me here, didn't you?"

The man bowed his head and smiled. There were smile lines around his eyes, like he spent so much time laughing and grinning—like he was determined to see the brighter side of life, even though the pocked scars on his hands highlighted how hard his life really was. The dimple in his right cheek only added to a hidden joyful nature. But there was something about the way he held himself that said he was far from innocent—like he had seen with his own eyes the worst humanity had to offer.

Given the things I had done on behalf of the Pregutor, I couldn't call myself innocent either.

"You're real and not just some figment of my imagination." The tension I held in my shoulders drained away. I wanted to collapse in relief. I wasn't crazy. But I had to keep my wits about me. It still could have been a trap.

"I might still be a figment of your imagination. You could be seeing things now—not just hearing them." The edges of his lips twitched as he took a sip of his drink.

I smirked and shook my head. "Yeah, I don't think I would imagine a smart-ass like you."

He grinned, showing off that not-so-innocent dimple. And his smile made his eyes sparkle. Blue diamonds with flecks of purple running through them.

"Here you go." The bartender put the red drink in front of me, complete with a maraschino cherry. I eyed up that cherry with longing. The last time I had one of those was at my welcoming party to PentWave. Tam had wanted to treat the entire team to the candied nature of those pitted fruits.

"Let's go sit in the corner." The unknown stranger didn't wait for me to answer. Instead, he settled himself at a table in the far corner of the bar, his back to the wall and facing the door. He pulled up the sleeves of his well-loved jacket, drawing attention to the blackened creases around the material gathered at his elbows. Purple-brown streaks cascaded around the shoulders—signs that he had been caught in the purple rain a few times over the years. But with his hood down, his black curls flowed around his shoulders.

Could I really trust this man? It wasn't like I had many options. Resigning myself to whatever fate had in store for me, I picked up my drink, then headed to the corner table and slid into the booth opposite the stranger.

"Thank you for the drink."

He smiled, showing off that dimple again. "It's the least I could do. You took a leap of faith in coming here. A bit of hospitality isn't too much to ask for."

Although it was a nice gesture, I really couldn't be bothered with civilities. I was on the run, and who knew what kind of danger this stranger was leading me into? Assuming he was indeed the voice.

"Who are you?"

He snorted and shook his head. "Where are my manners? We've been talking to one another for so long, I sort of forgot that we've never met. The name's Cedrick. And yours is Michaella."

"It's Mike, actually. Only the doctors call me Michaella—and you don't look like a doctor."

"You got that in one. But for whatever it's worth, I'm sorry. I overheard the others calling you Michaella, and I . . ." He took a deep breath as he looked around the bar. "I should know better than to assume anything. Nothing is ever quite what it seems. That especially applies to you."

"How so?"

"Just look at you. You're this skinny, young woman. But even that would be an assumption, because you don't like to think of yourself as a woman, do you?"

"No, I don't. I prefer to think of myself as a human—as much as anyone can be a human these days. But I do think of myself as a she. Nature chose to give me a uterus rather than a dick between my legs."

"Blunt. I like that."

I leaned back and crossed my arms. "So, what other assumptions are you making about me?"

He, too, leaned back, but his posture was open, relaxed. Somewhere in the deep recesses of my mind, something told me that this posture was inviting inquiry. If I wanted answers, all I had to do was ask. And I wasn't going anywhere with this guy until I got some answers.

His lips twitched. "I did promise you answers. So . . ." He looked at the table briefly, like he was trying to gather his thoughts. "I knew they were coming after you, but I thought you were unprepared for what was to come. When I first heard your mind, you seemed so unsure of yourself." He looked up at me, gazing into my eyes, but his gaze was just as relaxed as his posture. "You wanted out, but you didn't know how to get out. I'll admit that I was afraid for you—that you would have had no hope of defending yourself against the Pregutor if they chose to bring their full might down on you. But after seeing what you did to get out of that place . . ." He sat up straight and rested his forearms on the table. It was still an open posture, but no longer one of open defiance. "You've been trained in hand-to-hand combat and surveillance avoidance tactics—and not some basic training either. You're not just a courier, are you? You're an assassin."

I unfolded my arms and averted my eyes. "I have some basic skills, yes."

"How did you get into that guard's head? How did you convince him to help you?"

I pursed my lips as I stared at him, ignoring my drink. "Why don't you tell me? You've been inside my head this entire time."

We stared at one another, and the edges of my vision darkened like they always did. But instead of slipping into this guy's thoughts, the buzzing hum I'd been hearing off and on for the last few days returned and grew in volume. Then it stopped, and the world was plunged into total silence. A sharp prick forced me to blink, flooding the world with a brightness that caused me to repeatedly blink until my eyes readjusted.

Cedrick shook his head. "Now, I understand why they want you so much. You're good . . . but not quite good enough. You can try all you want, but you won't be able to get past my defenses—not without training, anyway. But that's why they want you, because with a little training . . ." He shook his head again, like he was rethinking telling me something. He sighed. "That's why they had you drugged. If you ever learned how to really use your abilities, there would be no stopping you."

"What are you talking about?"

"You're a telepath, Mike, and not just any telepath. You're a fifth gen."

"The nurse called me that. What does it mean?"

"First, he wasn't a nurse."

I snorted. "I kind of got that when he tried to kill me."

"Second, being a fifth gen means that you're the fifth generation of Rhodon's genetic experiments."

I laughed that desperate I-can't-believe-this-shit laugh. "I'm a genetic experiment?"

"Actually, you're a genetic mishap; a mutation they weren't expecting, and one that they have no idea how to control."

"And I suppose you're about to tell me that only I have the power to bring down the bad guy. Without my help, you would always be relegated to operating in the shadows, intruding into people's thoughts."

Cedrick sighed as he leaned back again. "Mike, I know it sounds like fiction, but you have to trust me."

"Why? Give me one reason why I should trust you."

"What would have happened to you if you hadn't escaped from Sector 14?"

I resisted the urge to fidget, feeling a little squirmy in my seat. If I was honest with myself, I didn't know what would have happened. All I knew was that it wouldn't have been good. The way that nurse fought against me . . . The way those guards chased me . . . The way Marcus hunted me . . .

"Look, if you would prefer, you can go back and I'll leave you alone."

"No." It was an instant response. I struggled to believe the bullshit he was telling me, but at least he was willing to tell me something. I turned my attention back to the Shirley Temple and shoved the maraschino cherry into my mouth, savoring the candied taste. "I want to trust you. You did help me get out of that maze. But moving forward, you have to promise me something."

"What's that?"

"That you won't try to talk to me from inside my head without my permission. It's incredibly disorienting."

Cedrick chuckled. "I can do that."

I sipped my drink, letting the bubbles fizz on my tongue before swallowing. "So, you were about to tell me what it means to be a fifth gen."

"Yes, of course. Well, it started two hundred years ago, when they started to use RNA vaccinations to combat rapidly morphing viruses that were wiping out large portions of humanity around the globe."

"You're talking about the Covid vaccines in the 2020s."

He nodded. "The RNA vaccines generated a reverse transcription that modified our genome and started to improve our immunity against other viruses too." He paused briefly. "But they didn't stop there. When the increase in the global temperature caused the icecaps to melt, viruses and bacteria that the human race had never seen before were released. It was pandemic after pandemic."

I sighed and rolled my eyes. "I know all this. Because of the repeated pandemics, the global economy collapsed and governments lost control. War broke out, because there weren't enough resources to go around. And the world was struck down by the worst pandemic yet. It was the pharmaceuticals, like Rhodon Corporation, who saved us, opening their facilities to all those who could help society flourish again. That's what led to the 2096 health reforms."

Again, Cedrick nodded. "And that's what eventually led to the mandated vaccinations of unborn children. To maintain the ongoing health of the population living in the facilities managed by Rhodon Corporation, the medical researchers devised a vaccine cocktail to ensure that the population became dependent on the drugs Rhodon Corporation were developing. With each generation, the resulting mutations got worse."

"So, I'm the fifth generation of this mutation experiment? But there's nothing wrong with me. I'm as healthy as they come."

He shrugged. "Except for the fact that you hear voices." He sighed, then licked his lips as he looked around the empty bar again. The bartender was the only other person present. Cedrick then turned his full attention back to me. "Other than White Rabbit syndrome, you've never been sick a day in your life, have you?"

"No, I haven't."

"That's because they designed you that way. What started as vaccinations became deliberate genetic modifications. The first generation of genetic-enhancing vaccinations held the promise of the healthiest children on the planet. And they were right. The first generation was incredibly healthy, just like they promised. And they were smart, too—very smart. Many of them became scientists for Rhodon, further developing their medical miracle treatments. But every time you make a change to one gene sequence, you have no idea what the ripple effect will be. They made changes to the cocktail given to the general population. And whatever was given to that original generation reacted to the standard vaccination sequence, mutating it and making additional changes to the human genome—changes they weren't expecting."

He licked his lips again, leaning forward on his arms again, this time inviting me to lean in too. "The second generation was born with an enhanced level of empathy. The third generation had the ability to affect the emotional states of those around them. The fourth generation could hear the thoughts of others—and in some cases, implant thoughts. But the fifth generation . . . Let's just say that they have no idea what a fifth gen is fully capable of. But Rhodon has found a drug to suppress a fifth gen's abilities, even if it is only for a limited period. It's not much, but it gives them some level of assurance as they try to work out what it is we can do and how best to use us to their advantage."

"Us? You talk like you're part of these so-call genetic experiments too."

"That's because I am. Or at least, I was. I'm a fifth gen, Mike, just like you. The oldest fifth gen alive."

I looked at Cedrick with caution. There was every possibility that he was playing mind tricks on me, conjuring up some vivid story to explain what was complete madness.

"For the moment, let's say I believe you—that you and I are some sort of genetic experiment. And let's say that Miransine is really a suppressant, targeting telepathic abilities specifically. Why now? Why would you try to reach me now? What's changed?"

"Why don't you tell me? What do you remember about your last mission?" He reached into his pocket and slid a card across the table.

I stared at the two-headed Queen of Hearts, its red hues dominating the image. I continually swallowed back the lump that threatened to close off my breathing. Cautiously, I reached forward and touched the card. "Where did you get this?"

"From a friend to the cause. She said it would help you remember what you know to be true."

I looked at him, uncertain what to say and fighting to hold back the tears. But as I stared at the card, I kept seeing George in my mind, blowing himself up. And I knew I was somehow involved, but I couldn't remember the details. My memories sat on the surface, but no matter how hard I tried, I couldn't quite access them. I pulled my hand back and pulled my sleeves down tighter over my hands, ensuring that my pharmachip was covered.

"I'm sorry," Cedrick said. "I don't mean to make you feel uncomfortable." He reached forward and pushed the card toward me. "But it was important to her that you get this."

I forced myself to take several deep breaths before reaching forward to take the card—fingering it—staring at it. "You were right, by the way. I have been trained in hand-to-hand combat and surveillance avoidance tactics. It's a requirement of *all* couriers for the Pregutor—especially those of us who are part of PentWave. We're an anti-terrorist group, tasked with taking out terrorist threats before they cause a problem. And the way in which we take out the threats . . ." I stared directly at him, demanding his full attention. "Yeah, I, like the rest of my team, have the ability to implant thoughts into people's minds, so they become suicide bombers, mass shooters . . . killers. The people selected to become the weapons have limited connection to their targets, but they are those who the Pregutor has determined can be easily manipulated. We work covertly. We slip in and out before anyone notices us. And the ones tasked with the investigation of the bombings . . . How can you track someone who has the ability to manipulate thought?"

Cedrick blinked several times. "You know. You've always known."

"About the genetic experiments, no. But now that I think about it, it makes sense. And being fifth gen . . ." I snorted. "It's probably how my team got its name." I shook my head and chuckled. "Not very imaginative. But if you were asking about my knowledge of my abilities? Yeah, I knew. I don't know how it works, just that it does. And when I really set my mind to it, no one is able to stop me from slipping into their thoughts. Not even the other members of my team. That's why the Pregutor chose me." I fingered the glass of my drink, wiping off the condensation from the outside. "I think you're wrong about what Miransine does. I don't think it was designed to suppress the ability to implant thought. I think it was designed to suppress the ability to *hear* thought."

Cedrick looked off into the corner. "That makes sense. You wouldn't want your soldiers to be hearing what lies you were weaving."

"It's more than that." I shook my head slightly and rolled my shoulders as I inhaled deeply. "I've been taking various drugs since I was a child, only five years old. But as I got older and started to use my abilities, my body burned through the mintonal faster than they could keep up. I have been on one experimental treatment or another for years, and each one lasting a shorter time than the previous one. My powers are getting stronger, and I think they know it. They were just hoping that by the time I fully understood what I could do, that I was fully indoctrinated into whatever they had planned for me." It wasn't a question, but a realization.

There was a silence that hung between us. I got the sense that he wanted to be my *knight in shining armor*, rescuing the *damsel in distress*. But this damsel was more than capable of rescuing herself.

"Now what?"

"You'll need training. And I can help you with that." He smiled, with that twinkling hope shining through his eyes.

I tried to suppress the grin threatening to spring forth. "You're not going to ask me to try to bring down some bad guy, are you?"

Cedrick smirked. "On that front, I can't make any promises. Once you know the truth—the full truth—you might decide to go running off to play vigilante on your own. But for now, my primary objective is to make sure that you stay alive."

"So, there's more *truth* than these genetic experiments that you thought I knew nothing about? What more is there?"

Cedrick shook his head. "Not yet. Not only is it not safe, but you're not ready."

I looked around the empty bar, and I noticed the darkness. At first, I thought it was a sign of the sector, rundown and downtrodden. As I looked closer, I saw the signs of fortification and deliberate dinginess on the windows placed to hide what was going on inside from those who were outside. This wasn't a randomly selected location for this meeting. This place was chosen because Cedrick felt safe here. But safe from what?

"Cedrick." The bartender pointed out the dirty window to the military vehicles driving down the street.

"Time to go." Cedrick pulled up the hood of his cloak. "Don't forget the card."

TWENTY-THREE

I DIDN'T BOTHER FINISHING MY Shirley Temple, as tasty as it was. I just pocketed the Queen of Hearts, then pulled up my hood and followed Cedrick out into the city streets. I went to put on my breather, but Cedrick told me not to.

"The air in Sector 9 is not too bad, which is one of the reasons why I told you to meet me here."

If his idea of *not too bad* was having an acidic taste to the air that irritated the back of my throat, I didn't want to know what he thought of the air in Sector 2. But I had other reasons for wanting to put on the mask.

"Without the mask, I'll easily be recognized." I pointed to the 10-foot holographic image of myself hanging over the street, projected by a hover drone. The image told the world that I was a wanted person, armed and dangerous. The award for any information that could lead to my capture was five hundred thousand credits.

Cedrick whistled. "If I didn't know it was a complete lie, I would turn you in myself. Regardless, you put that mask on, you'll give yourself away. Residents of Sector 9 don't own that sort of tech." He reached up to my hood and pulled it tighter around my face. "I really wish this jacket wasn't purple, but at least you're not the only one wearing the color." He looked out over his shoulder to the party-goers headed toward the neon club, all wearing purple jackets. "Let's go." He grabbed my hand and pulled me out into the streets. "Stay close, and whatever you do, don't let go."

"Why?"

He shook his head. "Trust me."

"Not like I have much choice."

He rolled his eyes, but he gave my hand a squeeze as he continued to pull me down the street—to where exactly, was still a mystery.

The giant image of myself stared down at me, like it was daring me to keep defying the powers that be. Every blank space of wall bore smaller images, rotating to give full side and frontal views. My purple hair seemed more purple in the holographic images than it was in real life.

Police drones stalked overhead, lights flashing, recording anything and everything that moved. Soldiers with scanners walked down the streets, stopping pedestrians at random, scanning their pharmachips. My heart raced ahead. My jacket might have shielded my pharmachip from the overhead scans, but if any of those soldiers stopped us and insisted that they scan my pharmachip . . .

Cedrick pulled me into an alleyway and pushed me up against the wall. "Do you trust me?"

He stood before me, staring at me with an intensity in his eyes that I had never seen from anyone before. There was a desperation in them. And he was so close that his cologne nearly overpowered my sense of self-control. The woody notes made me long for the forest cavern that my mother had taken me to when I was a little girl, before I started having the blackouts at summer camp.

I blinked, wondering where the memory came from. But before I had a chance to process it, Cedrick leaned into me and kissed me full on the mouth.

My head spun, unable to think. I had never kissed anyone before, and certainly not like this. It was filled with such passion. I should have been resisting—I didn't know this man—but instead, I melted into the moment, placing my hands on his waist, pulling him closer, curling my arms around his back. My body was following its own instincts and my brain had no say. As the kiss grew in intensity, I never wanted it to end.

Then it did.

Cedrick pressed his forehead to mine. "It's safe now. The soldiers are gone." He took a long, steady breath, then backed away from me, grabbed my hand, and pulled me back into the streets. While the images of me still graced every blank wall space, the giant image overhead had disappeared. So, too, had the police drones and the soldiers.

Still in a slight daze, I glared at the back of Cedrick's head. "What did you do that for?"

"Your mind was too chaotic for me to mask it properly. I had to distract you."

"By kissing me?"

Cedrick winced. "Sorry. I couldn't think of anything else to do—not anything that would be as effective that quickly."

"What if I had hit you?"

"Still would have worked. Distraction is still distraction."

"And I could have given you a black eye."

"But you didn't." He looked back over his shoulder with a mischievous grin that grew from ear to ear, accompanied by a suggestive wiggle of his eyebrows.

I pursed my lips, then pulled him to a stop, forcing him to turn and face me. "Why did you need to distract me? I was well aware of the danger."

Cedrick took a deep breath. "Can I enter your mind?"

I didn't know how to respond to such an odd question.

"You made me promise that I would never try to talk to you from inside your head without permission. What I have to say, no one else can hear."

I glanced at those around us. It wasn't a lot of people darting down the streets, but it was enough. I nodded.

"One way to hide from others is to implant the idea that they don't see you. But your mind was screaming to be heard. A part of you wanted to be seen. I had to distract you from your thoughts long enough so the soldiers would listen to my suggestions and not yours."

"So much of what we do is instinct," he continued aloud, "which is why you need training."

He just looked at me while I took the time to process what he was saying.

"We good?" he asked, breaking the silence.

I nodded, looking everywhere else but at the man in front of me. The heat in my cheeks rose, and I pulled my hood tighter around my face, hoping to hide any blushing features.

Cedrick smiled and grabbed my hand. "Good. Now, we need to get off these streets before the soldiers come back."

Cedrick led the way through a maze of streets and dark alleys, then out through courtyards filled with vendors. Then back into the dark alleys. With each turn that we took, I got more turned around. And I could have sworn that we were going around in circles. So many corners all looked the same.

I gripped his hand tighter, fearful that if we became separated, I would have no idea of how to get back to civilization. Following a complete stranger down dark alleyways wasn't the smartest thing I could have done, but what other option did I have? I could have gone back to where the soldiers were searching for me and turned myself in, but I really didn't want to know where that would have led. Besides, I wanted answers, and Cedrick appeared to be willing to provide them.

We turned another corner and passed yet another dark, familiar doorway. "Have we passed this corner already?"

Cedrick just looked over his shoulder with a beaming smile but kept moving.

"Where are you taking me?" I pulled him to a stop, insisting that he turn to face me.

"To somewhere safe."

I examined every detail of his body language. His eyes were fixed on me, but they possessed a slight dilation of the pupils. His breathing was calm and even, but his hand was clammy. And his other hand twitched in a rhythmic pattern against his thigh.

Morse code.

"Son of a bitch." I stepped back from him, not sure where to run. "Who the hell are you? Who are you really?"

He held out his hands before him in surrender. "Mike, I'm trying to help. Honest."

"By leading me around in circles? Sector 9 isn't that big, and the soldiers are crawling around searching for me. Yet, somehow we've managed to evade every group of soldiers, except for that first lot just as we came out of the bar. If you are leading me to somewhere *safe*, as you call it, then running around in circles in this maze is not going to do it. Who are you?"

Cedrick dropped his hands and sighed. "Everything I've told you is true. I'm with the resistance and I really do want to bring you somewhere safe. But there's a minor problem."

"And what might that be?"

"You can't know how to get there."

"Excuse me?"

Footsteps echoed around us. Those dressed in dark clothing revealed themselves, closing in on me, but staying just out of reach.

I allowed my hood to drop, giving me the ability to use my peripheral vision. It was fight or die all over again.

Cedrick sighed. "I know what this looks like, but you have to trust me, Mike. They're tracking you. That jacket of yours is doing a fantastic job of keeping your precise location hidden, but how do you think they knew to look for you in Sector 9? We're fighting a war here. It would be suicide for us to show you exactly where the resistance can be found."

A sharp prick jabbed into the side of my neck. I reached up and fingered a small dart. My vision blurred and my limbs grew heavy. I staggered where I stood.

Someone grabbed me from behind, but I no longer possessed the strength to fight against them. Instead, I was hoisted over their shoulder. My hood flopped forward, and someone reached up to tuck in my loose strands of hair.

"I'm asking you to trust me, Mike. Whatever happens from now on, I'll keep you safe."

Twenty-Four

Strong lights filtered through my fluttering lashes. Their brightness compounded the headache that consumed my thoughts. I lifted my hand to my eyes, trying to shield them. The air carried a damp, musky scent. But at least I could breathe without coughing. I shivered as the cold seeped up through a thin layer of woven fabric wrapped around a steel frame. No blanket or padded insulation.

My eyes focused on the distant gray wall and the concrete floor. Overhead, lights dangled from chains bolted to the dark gray ceiling.

Was I surrounded by rock? Where the hell was I?

I sat up and looked around at the glass-fronted cabinets that lined the walls. From my vantage point, they looked to be filled with medical supplies.

Pain radiated from my right wrist. It was wrapped in a gauze bandage. Confused, I undid the bandages, only to see a small centimeter slit that had been neatly stitched together.

What the hell?

A blurry person floated around on the other side of the room, humming to themselves as they worked. They sang the familiar chorus refrain of my favorite song. I had to have been dreaming.

As I shifted my weight, the stretcher creaked. The person on the other side of the room looked in my direction, then headed toward me.

"Ah. You're awake. That's good." A woman with long, curly auburn hair came into focus. Though most of her hair was pulled back in a ponytail, there were enough loose strands that framed her face, giving her a familiar quality. I couldn't work out where I knew this woman from, but I *did* know her.

"I never know exactly when someone is going to wake up when they're brought in here," the woman said. "There are so many factors involved, including a person's size, their metabolic rate, where they were when they were given the sedative, and the last time they ate."

She pulled over a tray from the end of the stretcher. "If it's okay with you, I just need to check a few things—make sure that you're not having an adverse reaction to the sedative." She grabbed a long rectangular device with a bulb and a gauge hanging from it. "Please take off your jacket and roll up your sleeve. I need access to your upper arm."

"Where am I? And what the hell did you do to me?" I held up my wrist, making sure that this unknown woman could see my undressed wound.

The woman took my wrist and examined it. "That should heal quite nicely."

"What did you do?"

"If you really must know, they tried to remove your pharmachip while in the field—unsuccessfully, I might add. I told them it was a stupid idea—that they should have waited until I had the chance to fully examine you—but sometimes Cedrick gets his own ideas. As for your current location . . . We call this place the Sanctuary. Cedrick brought you here to keep you safe from the Pregutor."

I looked into the woman's eyes, trying to see any sign of deception, but there was none. "What is that for?" I indicated with my head to the rectangular unit in the woman's hands.

The woman smiled. "It's a blood pressure cuff. We don't exactly have access to the latest and greatest technology down here, but we make do. Now please, I really do need to monitor your vitals."

I pulled tighter on my sleeve and shook my head.

"It's okay. Any signal that your pharmachip might be giving off will be shielded by all this rock around us. They won't find you. I promise. As long as you're down here, you're completely safe."

I glanced up at the rock ceiling, then looked back at the woman. She appeared to be sincere in her motives. There was no pressure to do anything that I didn't want to do.

Reluctantly, I removed my jacket and rolled up my sleeve. The woman then wrapped the rectangular padded fabric she called a blood pressure cuff around my upper arm.

"This could get a little uncomfortable, but it's okay. It's all perfectly normal." The woman grabbed some sort of listening device from the tray and put the earbuds in her ears, and pressed the microphone end to the inside of my elbow. She then pumped the bulb attached to the blood pressure cuff.

The pressure around my arm was so tight that it felt like the circulation to my fingers had been cut off. As the woman twiddled a silver nob located at the top of the bulb, the pressure released. A throbbing developed in the crook of my elbow—slow at first, but strong—but it eventually vanished.

When the woman removed the blood pressure cuff, I rubbed the inside of my elbow, then pulled down my sleeve and put back on my jacket.

"Well, you will be pleased to know that your blood pressure is perfectly normal." The woman then clipped a light device to my finger, which read a number of 98. "And so is your blood oxygen." She then held up her finger. "Keep your head still and follow my finger with your eyes only."

The woman conducted a series of simple tests, tests that I had been subjected to multiple times in the past, all designed to check my stability and inner balance. Being surrounded by all the medical supplies . . .

"Are you a nurse?"

The woman smiled. "No."

"So, you're a doctor."

"I am."

"Maybe that's where I recognize you from. Were you ever a doctor at the hospital in Sector 14?"

The smile on the woman's lips faltered. "I was actually— up until about a year ago." She packed up the things that she had used, laying them out on the tray again in a carefully ordered fashion.

"Why would you give up a job in a state-of-the-art facility to work in a place like this?" I scanned the surrounding area. It looked to be more equipped to handle triage, not full medical care.

"If you must know, I was fired. And no, I didn't do anything dangerous or reckless—not unless you want to consider questioning the orders issued by the Pregutor as dangerous or reckless."

I blinked and shook my head. "Why would you question the orders of the Pregutor? The system is flawless."

"Is it really? So, you would trust your entire existence to some artificial intelligence that has no working comprehension of human compassion? Numbers and statistics are good for some things, but sometimes you have to follow your gut. You can kill people if you just blindly follow orders—especially when it comes to medicine. A machine can give you the numbers, but how you interpret those numbers . . . There are so many factors in play, including the human psyche. Some doctors seem to have forgotten that."

Although I had no medical training—other than basic field first-aid—I knew exactly what the woman was talking about. If medicine was just a matter of pure numbers, then I wouldn't have been hearing voices.

"So, what orders of the Pregutor did you question?"

"I questioned the drug protocols being administered to patients." The woman continued with her busy work, making handwritten notes on—

—Paper? Where did she get paper?

But instead of focusing on the ancient technology surrounding us, I turned my full attention to the woman, desperately trying to work out how I knew her. I envisioned her face hovering above a coffee table. And she was covered in blood and very dead.

"Elizabeth Eason. Your name is Elizabeth Eason. But that doesn't make any sense. The Angel of Death was killed in a covert operation to stop her from turning those with White Rabbit syndrome into weapons."

The woman slowly inhaled, then exhaled, before responding. "I guess it's a good thing that to live down here, you have to be a ghost." The woman rubbed the inside of her right wrist and bowed her head, forcing herself to take multiple deep breaths—like she had regretted something I wasn't privy to. She then tried to smile, but it was weak. "Yes, my name is Elizabeth Eason, but I prefer to go by Beth, if you don't mind." She pulled out a tray from the cabinet and unwrapped what looked to be a needle and some sort of tube. "I need to take some bloods. You'll need to take off your jacket again."

I shook my head. "There is no way that I'm going to put my life in the hands of a killer."

Beth smirked. "Hands of a killer, eh? Based on what I was told about you, only one of us is a killer—and I know it's not me." She sighed, then moved the tray to the side. "Look, I know you don't want to trust me, and you have every right to be suspicious of me, but I'm all you've got. There is no one else. Take a good look around you. You're in the Underground. Everyone here has been exiled by the Pregutor. We're threats to society and everything that Rhodon is doing. Some of us even have death warrants hanging over our heads."

I held my breath. My belly did flip-flops. I was likely one of those with a death warrant over her head.

"So, what's it gonna be? Are you going to let me take those bloods?"

"And how do you do that?"

"I need to jab a needle into your arm and pull out a vial of blood myself."

"A needle? Couldn't you use some sort of scanner?"

Beth laughed. "If we had one. Sure. Slight problem though. Even if we had one, we wouldn't be able to use it. The medical scanners are hooked up to the central system back in Sector 14. This place is off the grid. If we were to hook up to the central database, the Pregutor would know where to find us. Sorry, but we have to do this the old-fashioned way. Look, if you're worried about me learning the truth—that you have audimentia—I already know that. Cedrick wouldn't have brought you here if you didn't. But I need to check every aspect of your health. I need a baseline. I could have taken the bloods while you were still unconscious, but out of respect to you, I didn't want to perform any invasive procedures without your knowledge. That includes jabbing you with a needle."

"And trying to remove my pharmachip isn't invasive?" I waved my wrist again in front of her, to make my point.

"Cedrick and I have already had words about that. What he did was stupid. If he had actually removed your chip, he would have killed you. Removing a Class 3 pharmachip like yours is a delicate operation. In his rush to take matters into his own hands, he put your life unnecessarily at risk." Beth sighed. "Look, what's done is done. I can't go back and change the past. And neither can you. All we can do is move forward. And right now, I need a baseline to help me monitor your health. Will you let me take the bloods?"

We stared at one another for what felt like eternity, a fight of the wills. But there was no aggression in Beth's presence. No irritation or annoyance. Just a sense that she cared about the people around her. And even though she didn't know me, for some bizarre reason, Beth's caring nature extended to me too.

I sighed and removed my jacket. "Is it going to hurt?"

Beth shrugged with an *I-suppose* expression on her face.

"Do what you have to do," I said, "as long as you're one hundred percent certain it's safe."

Beth smiled and got to work. It didn't take her long to collect three vials of blood. When she was done, she told me to press on the puncture wound where the needle had been. "It's going to take me a while to run the test. I would like to say that you're free to wander around, but you're not. There are guards posted outside the door with orders to shoot if you try to leave the med bay."

"So, there are guards outside, but not in here?"

Beth smiled. "My hospital, my rules. You're not a prisoner, Mike, but we do need to protect ourselves. Until I've completed a full medical workup, ensuring that you're not a carrier of some disease that could endanger the population, we can't allow you to leave this room."

"I can accept that." Whole sectors of the population had been wiped out because of some tiny microscopic bug. I could never forgive myself if the group of people trying to help me suffered because I was a carrier of some infectious disease.

Beth patted my arm. "It'll be okay." Then she headed to the corner of the room to begin her little experiments.

I sighed. Little experiments. That's what I was—an experiment—but an experiment in what?

I put my jacket back on and brushed my fingers down the sleeves. It was great that Beth had the confidence that the surrounding rock would keep the pharmachip signal from getting back to the Pregutor, but why take any chances? Out of habit, I quickly patted down my person. The breather was still in my left pocket, but in the pocket where I normally kept my display glasses when I wasn't wearing them was the card.

The Queen of Hearts. I couldn't be one hundred percent certain if this was the same card that I had left at George's aunt's place, but the uniqueness of it was too similar to be a coincidence. I stared at the card and its red hues.

In my mind, I was standing in front of George as he looked down at me with loving eyes. We were in Sector 14, in one of the side alleys just off the main plaza. And he was demanding to know if I was hearing the voices again. "I want you to make me a promise," he had said. "If you are ever presented with the opportunity to get out—to escape this life—take it."

I looked across the room to Beth, the woman who was supposedly dead, a woman whose death I had orchestrated by delivering the weapon to kill her. But here she was—alive and well. A ghost.

Was this my chance to fulfill my promise to George? I fought to hold back the tears, knowing even if this was my chance to get out, George would forever be just a memory.

I cupped the card in my hands and held it to my chest. "I promise," I whispered, wishing for George's ghost to hear me. After a few deep breaths, I put the card back in my pocket.

Not quite certain what to do while I waited for Beth to perform her experiments, except perhaps to contemplate my nonexistence, I wandered around the small medical facility. There were cabinets labeled with suture kits, medical gloves, and needles. Glass-fronted fridges stood side by side, filled with vials of various drugs. On the other side of the room, near where Beth worked, stood another glass-fronted fridge with tubes of red fluid, possibly blood samples from others. Bookshelves ran along the back wall with binders stuffed in every nook and cranny. It was tempting to take out one of the binders and read what might be written on the papers inside, but the pages were likely filled with medical mumbo-jumbo and symbols that made no sense to the normal person.

Beth continued her work in the corner, occasionally starting up another whirring machine and tapping on an old-style button keyboard. She scribbled more notes on that paper pad of hers, then carried on tapping at the keyboard.

I meandered around the room, deliberately staying clear of the door. I didn't want to give the guards outside any reason to believe that I might have been trying to escape—not that I had anywhere to escape to.

Ticking sounds began to blend in with the other quiet noises. An old analog clock hung on the wall, marking the passage of time with its wiggling little arm moving from position to position. I hadn't seen an analog ticking clock since . . . well . . . ever. I knew how to read the device, but even the clock tower in Sector 14 used a holographic digital display. It didn't tick. And on the smaller clock faces mounted on the walls of offices and meeting rooms, the movement of the second hand iterated forward smoothly—no jiggle.

I smirked. How old was the equipment in this living museum piece?

Just watching the jiggling hand seemed to hold a fascination of its own. The jiggling was more pronounced when the second hand was horizontal. I stared at the clock, watching the seconds . . . minutes . . . hours pass by. It all seemed to blend into one. And for the first time since I woke up, I wondered exactly how long I'd been here.

Had a day passed? Had two? The clock read just after nine o'clock, but was it morning or night?

In the city sectors, the changes in the ambient lighting under the overhanging clouds helped to distinguish between night and day. My optical display glasses and my connection to Alice kept me on time for my various appointments. And in every transport tube station, holographic displays hung in front of the tracks with a schedule for the next trains. But here—

"So, Doc, how's the patient?" Cedrick entered the med bay, rubbing his hands together like he was scheming.

"As far as I can tell, she's as healthy as they come."

"Does that mean she can get out of this place?"

Beth cocked her head to the side, like she was thinking it over. In the end, she nodded. "As long as she comes back here at night. There is still a significant level of mintonal in her system, and though she is feeling well and healthy now, that could change quickly."

"Understood." He clapped his hands together and grinned. "Let's get out of here. There's a few people waiting to meet you."

TWENTY-FIVE

I RACED AFTER CEDRICK AS he headed out the door—only to be met by a wall of men, the guards Beth had told me about. Big and mean looking; many of whom had their arms folded across their chests, emphasizing the size of their biceps. And not one smile among them. Instead, there was a wall of scowls. And I was fairly confident that it was my presence they were scowling about.

Cedrick held out his arm in a flourish, urging the wall of guards to part. "Ignore these brutes. If you don't give them any reason to be grumpy with you, they won't act. Besides, you're with me. I'm more dangerous than all of these guys put together."

I glanced sideways at Cedrick, rolling my eyes. His mind reading abilities might have given him the advantage in a fight, but with his spindly limbs, these guards would snap him like a twig.

One guard snorted and shook his head as he stood back to let Cedrick and me pass.

I followed Cedrick down the hall, followed by the guards. They kept their distance, but if I did anything they didn't like, there was no question in my mind they would have been on me faster than I could blink. They might not have worn a uniform, but their bearing gave off the impression of confidence and power. And they might have been big, but big didn't mean slow. I had no idea what these guards were capable of, and I wasn't in the mood to find out.

The stone architecture of the med bay was exaggerated in the halls. The grayness of the walls was interspersed with dark and light layers, nature's record of the geological history of the region. The low ceilings carried cabling for the lights bolted to the rock, only highlighting that the halls were really just carved-out tunnels. At some point in history, concrete had been poured to create a smooth floor—although now it was riddled with cracks.

"How deep underground are we?"

Cedrick smiled. "Far enough. This facility used to be a war bunker. We're not sure when it was abandoned, or why, but it's completely off the grid. Fully self-sufficient, complete with its own water reclamation plant and power generation. The place was fully kitted out to house hundreds of people to survive a nuclear holocaust."

"Oh." It was the only response I could think of. It was bad enough that the reliance on nuclear power grew in the early twenty-first century, when it became clear that the burning of oil and coal were only making the level of carbon dioxide in the atmosphere skyrocket. But the military boys still liked their toys . . . and they were all determined to show the world who had the more destructive weapons. Never mind that it was the microscopic bugs buried in the melting icecaps that showed the entire planet who was boss. And every attempt that governments took to fight the losing battle only made the atmosphere worse.

If I really thought about it, this network of underground tunnels wasn't all that different to the domes covering Sector 14 and the rest of Crystal Hills. It was still an attempt to keep out the atmospheric dangers. The only difference was that in Sector 14 you could forget about the truth, living a life filled with lies. Here, the truth was out in the open.

Or at least, I hoped that was the case.

As we continued our tour, Cedrick pointed out where to find the amenities and other creature comforts. But my focus was on the people.

Teenagers carried baskets of soiled clothes toward wherever it was they did laundry, glancing at me as they wandered past, but they were encouraged to move on with a quick head gesture from one of our shadowing guards. There were those with legs and knees wrapped in bandages who hobbled down the corridor, taking a wide berth around us. And the older ones stood in the junction of various passageways, staring at me, mirroring the scowls of the guards.

A group of children ran down the hall, giggling and shouting at one another, pushing their way around guards. Any warnings of staying clear were ignored, a few of them brushing their fingers against my hand as they ran past. With each touch, the world around me shifted. A green sheen to my vision. The scent of sweet flowers. Piercing laughter. Then images of a loving embrace.

One child tripped over, sprawling out in every direction. And the child's arm flung against my leg. A buzzing humming grew in my mind and the edges of my vision grew dark as I looked into the child's eyes.

Doctors in white coats floated before me. Needles and scanners. Beeping monitors. Yellow gowns. Guards in their black uniforms with purple and blue stripes.

"Oh no, you don't."

The lights from the surrounding world flooded my vision, forcing me to blink as I stumbled backward against the wall. The coldness of the rock helped to ground me in reality—in this moment. My vision returned to normal, giving me a clear view of the guards surrounding me, ready for a fight. But they kept their distance—a muted reminder of who I was.

Cedrick held the child in his arms on the other side of the hall. "You know better than that. Mike's new here. She deserves a much better welcome than you probing in her head. Now off you go. The others will be waiting for you in the fields. And next time, be more careful."

The child scowled but nodded all the same, then took off at a run, chasing after the other children who ran past. "Wait for me!"

Cedrick stood tall and urged the guards to return to their casual positions, giving me space. He stepped closer, and whatever field he was giving off with his mental powers enveloped me, muting the buzzing hum. "Sorry about that. The children are still learning that it's rude to enter into a person's mind without their permission."

I raised my eyebrows and cocked my head to the side. "A lesson that you still need to learn yourself."

Cedrick smirked. "Point taken. Come on."

After taking a few deep breaths, re-centering myself, I continued to follow Cedrick on our tour of the facilities.

"Cedrick, is everyone here a . . ." I wasn't quite sure what term to use.

"A telepath? No. Some are just empathic, able to glean the truth about our emotions, feeling them as though they were sharing those emotional states. Others are stronger, able to influence the mood of those around them. There's only a small number among us who can read the mental thoughts of others."

"What about our shadows?" I jerked my head in the direction of the guards following us at a distance.

Cedrick sighed. "Yes, our guards are among the telepaths. And until you get the approval of those in power, those guys will be following you everywhere. Even to the bathroom."

Good thing I was comfortable in my own skin and used to walking around naked in front of strangers.

Cedrick smirked, as did a few of the guards.

I scoffed and shook my head. "You all heard that, didn't you?"

One by one, they all nodded.

"Great. That's just great. I'm never going to have a private thought again."

"With some training, you will. But at the moment, your thoughts are like screams, demanding to be heard. You want to be seen for the person you are, and not just someone who has White Rabbit syndrome. You are so much more than that."

I looked at Cedrick and each of the guards in turn. "Which is why you're all scared of me." The silence that hung over the group was only accentuated by the silence that came from their minds.

"Cedrick, you promised to tell me the truth." I glanced up at the rock ceiling. "I'm surrounded by guards, not because I happen to be a telepath, because if that was the case, then you would be living a life surrounded by guards too. No, I'm surrounded by guards because I'm highly trained, and you don't know what I'm fully capable of. You've only seen a glimpse of it, but it was enough to make you scared."

"I'm not afraid of you." Cedrick stepped closer to me, close enough that I could feel the heat radiating from his body. "But the others are." He took a slow, deep breath before continuing. "You're surrounded by guards because there are a lot of things about you that are unique, and until the ones in charge of this place know they can trust you . . ." He sighed and shook his head.

"Your word is not enough, and that frustrates you."

"Now you're the one reading a person's mind without permission," he said with a smirk.

"No, just reading your body language." I took a closer look at my guards. They stood tall, heads on a swivel, looking in every direction for any potential issue. They didn't wear any uniform or tactical gear like members of STAR wore back in Sector 14, but these guards still possessed one quality in common. "Our guards are older than you."

"And they're meaner too. I've found myself flat on my back sparring against them more times than I care to count."

"But you and I are immune to any influencing abilities they may have." I paused, then added, "It doesn't go the other way, does it?"

Cedrick smiled, but it didn't quite reach his eyes. "Which is why I too will be accompanying you everywhere you go until the powers that be say otherwise. But I'm not here just to protect them from you. I'm here to protect you from the children. After what happened earlier, my presence is going to be prudent. Dare I say it, the buzzing hum you hear is going to get louder."

"Great." I pursed my lips, taking note of the accusing eyes that stood in the passageways. "Thanks for the warning. I hope your doctor has a decent supply of something to cure headaches."

"She does. But I suggest you don't wander too far from my side—at least not until you can properly shield your mind. As the mintonal in your system wears off, you're going to hear more stray thoughts. I can use my own powers to help shield you, but—"

"I get the hint. Some secrets are not meant to be shared—including exactly who I am."

The remainder of our tour seemed to be filled with nothing but endless halls that formed a complex underground maze. And all the corridors looked the same, complete with their cracked concrete floor and carved-out rock walls. There wasn't even a marker of any sort—a color, a number, or a letter—to help identify the individual corridors. If I didn't know better, I would have sworn that Cedrick was guiding me in circles, deliberately trying to confuse the hell out of me.

Snorts rippled from the guards behind us. Yet another reminder that they could hear my thoughts.

When we finished our tour of the nondescript maze, I was happy to be back in the med bay, with nothing better to do than to stare at ancient medical tech. Sure, it meant that I would be subjected to more monitoring and other medical tests, but there was an isolation about the place—a quiet—that wasn't found in the halls. The moment I crossed the threshold into the med bay, the buzzing hum disappeared, making it easier to breathe. I even took off my jacket, trusting that there was no chance the tech in my body could send a rogue signal.

For three days, I followed Cedrick on his *tour*. Each day, he appeared to get more and more excited about the things he was showing me. I had no idea how Cedrick and the guards following us were able to keep track of where we were, but somewhere in the maze was the algae farm, the water reclamation plant, the laundry, and the all-important showers.

An actual water shower.

They had rules limiting the shower usage to a maximum of four minutes, but even that was enough to melt off the filth and tension that remained from my memories of what happened to George. I didn't even mind having the guards present while I was under the water, but they kept their backs to me so I could have some sense of privacy.

Fat lot of good that did when they could read my mind like an open book. The only real comfort I had was the discovery that my grief and tears made my guards—and Cedrick—uncomfortable.

After a week of the monotonous tour, Cedrick came into the med bay super-excited. "I have some good news. I finally managed to convince the others to trust you."

"Does that mean that during our wonderful tour, we won't be followed by our faithful shadows?"

"Um . . . Yes and no."

"What's that supposed to mean?"

"It might be better if I just show you."

Cedrick led the way through the halls, eventually following thuds accompanied by the occasional grunt. The hall opened up into a large room lined with padded mats on the floor, and crates of boxing mitts and other goodies along the walls. A punching bag swung in the corner, secured by chains to the ceiling. In the center of the room, there was a group training in unarmed combat maneuvers, including the guards who had been following us for the past week.

I sighed in defeat. Of course, they would eventually want to know what I was capable of. I should have realized that the price for my escape from the Pregutor would be to become a warrior in whatever cause Cedrick wanted me to fight.

"I thought you said that you weren't going to insist that I go and fight the bad guy for you." I glared at Cedrick.

His smile slowly vanished. "I . . ." But he just stared at me, pleading.

"I'm not a warrior for hire."

"No, you're not," said a deep voice from the center of the group training in the middle of the room. The speaker had his back to me, but there was something familiar about him. "But you are the best fighter that I've ever seen. You know how to turn an opponent's strengths against them, turning those strengths into a weakness. Even when you faced off with an opponent twice your size, they always managed to find themselves flat on their backs—especially Marcus and George." The man in the center of the room turned around. His arms were folded across his chest and he wore the mischievous smile I had always admired.

I stared at the man from my youth. I struggled to breathe, gasping as I fought against the tightness in my chest. I just stood there, staring, unable to move and afraid to blink for fear that he was just a figment of my imagination.

His smile was larger than life as he slowly came toward me. He stopped just in front of me and tucked my purple hair behind my ear. "Hey, baby girl. I hope you haven't been causing too much trouble."

Twenty-Six

My heart raced ahead, and my chest grew tighter as I continued to stare at Lucas Tellis. No matter how hard I tried, I couldn't fathom how he could be here. There were so many things I wanted to say to him, but my brain was unable to make the connections necessary to get the words out. In the end, I was only able to say one word: "How?"

"With careful planning and the skills of one talented hacker."

I closed my eyes and leaned my head into the hand that caressed my cheek. Images flooded my mind about the many times I had looked up to my old trainer—including the food-covered smile from the first day we met, when I was five years old. If he was a dream, if my mind was playing tricks on me, I never wanted to wake up. "We thought you were dead."

"Then I guess it's a good thing that to live down here, you have to be a ghost."

Finally able to breathe, I stepped back from him. The images of the past vanished, replaced by the images of his dead body with a note pinned to it. *Abram Shutton's son lives.* Anger flashed through me. "You should have told us you were still alive. Jody nearly broke down when she saw your body."

Lucas frowned. "I had no choice. I had to leave her there. It was the safest place for her."

"There is always a choice, Lucas. You taught me that. Why would you lie to us?"

Silence hung in the air as the others in the room just stared at us. But my entire focus was on my former trainer, focusing on his eyes. I allowed my vision to go black around the edges. "I want the truth, Lucas. Why did you let us believe you were dead?"

He gritted his teeth. The muscles in his neck strained into cords. His fingers curled into fists, and he started to shake. He was fighting me, resisting me, but I wasn't going to let him get away with his secrets.

"That's enough!" Cedrick's voice boomed off the surrounding walls, and I fell to my knees. I covered my eyes to shield myself from the sudden brightness. When I was able to regain my focus, I stared up at Cedrick and my guards. All of whom were pointing guns at me—even Cedrick.

"Holster your weapons," Lucas ordered. "Now!"

One by one, the guards put their weapons away, but Cedrick was reluctant. Instead, Lucas stood in front of me, shielding me.

"Put your weapon away," Lucas ordered again.

The silence that filled the room was only broken by a growing hum. No doubt Cedrick was trying to dig into my mind, trying to figure out why Lucas would protect me. But Lucas had always protected me. From the very first day I met him back in O'quv Lageri, Lucas was like the big brother who never once let anyone tower over me. Whenever I was scared, he had my back.

However, there were dangers that even Lucas could not protect me from. Which was why he made sure I knew how to protect myself—using every skill I had at my disposal, including my mental abilities.

I knelt on the ground behind Lucas, trying really hard to control my breathing and to calm my nerves. I mentally sang the chorus of *Purple Rain*, just like Lucas had taught me all those years ago. Something simple to focus on when my fear threatened to consume me.

As the stare-off between Lucas and Cedrick dragged on, I didn't dare move. Lucas might have been shielding me from a bullet, but there were other dangers in that room. There were other telepaths in that room—and not just Cedrick. And if Lucas was in charge of their training, none of them would have needed a bullet to do me serious harm.

Lucas turned and smiled. "You know you mentally sing out of tune, right?"

I couldn't help it. I just snorted and laughed. And cried. No longer caring what would happen, I got to my feet and wrapped my arms around his torso, and buried my head into his shoulder. The tears drenched his shirt. And he just swayed back and forth, letting me grieve.

"I should have fought harder to pull you out sooner," he finally said, as my tears diminished to a few sniffles. "I wanted to get all of you out, but I couldn't."

I pulled back from him and looked up into his face. "You could have at least told us you were still alive."

"No, I couldn't. Look around you, Mike. Take a *good* look around you."

At his insistence, I stepped back from him and looked at all the men and women gathered around the edges in small groups, talking among themselves. Most of them were happy to ignore Lucas and myself—except for Cedrick, who stood with a massive scowl on his face and his arms folded, his frustration and irritation clearly still brewing under the surface.

"The men in this room form the entire defensive force of Sanctuary," Lucas explained. "If I had told you, any of you, that I was still alive, none of you would have been content to just let me be—especially not Jody. She might be a member of PentWave, but you and I both know that her actions are ruled by her heart. If she had known I was alive, she wouldn't have stopped looking for me until she found me, leading STAR to our doorstep. Answer me truthfully, Mike. How long do you think the men and women in this room would have lasted against STAR now that Marcus has joined their ranks? How long would they have lasted against you?"

My chest grew tight. My throat threatened to cut off of my air supply. The buzzing hum gained strength.

"Be truthful to yourself, Mike. I know you were slated to join STAR. The incident with George was your final test."

"A test I failed." I looked up at him with determination and ire in my stare. "Because I couldn't let it go. He was a good man. He didn't deserve to die like that."

"No, he didn't, but you weren't given much choice. It was either him or both of you. Either way, he was dead."

The anger returned, and every head in the room snapped in our direction. All talking silenced.

"Are you aware that it was the failed drop in Sector 5, the one that supposedly resulted in your death, that was the reason why the Pregutor issued the order to kill him?"

"That failed drop wasn't a drop at all. It was supposed to be his extraction. He was supposed to go with Cedrick, but George didn't want to leave you. You were his Queen of Hearts."

My jaw dropped as I gaped at him. My anger vanished, only to be replaced with grief as I envisioned the card in my jacket pocket back in med bay. It all came down to that stupid card, and I still had no idea what it meant. "To answer your question from before, if I had been with STAR, everyone in this room would likely be dead."

Lucas weakly smiled. "That's why I had to let you and the others believe I was dead. To protect Sanctuary."

Twenty-Seven

Everyone started shouting, and the intensity of the buzzing amplified, making it difficult to focus on anything that anyone was saying. I tried to block it out—to block out the ones who were trying to get into my head.

The edges of my vision flickered between dark and light, forcing me to continually blink to clear my vision. But no matter how hard I tried, my vision blurred, the constant shifts in light intensity blinding me. I closed my eyes and pressed my hands against the side of my head. The buzzing only continued to grow—like someone was driving a hot poker into my brain.

Every telepath in that room had to be focusing their thoughts on me, trying to break in. But I couldn't let them know my secrets. Not yet.

I fell to my knees. Waves of nausea gripped my stomach. I tried to focus on the chorus of *Purple Rain*, focusing on a single thought, but the pain poker was too much to ignore.

"Please, someone—anyone—make it stop."

Arms circled around me, holding me close. Exactly who I didn't know, nor did I care, because whoever it was hummed along with my mental refrain. The warmth of his breath helped me focus my thoughts on his tenor voice.

I leaned into his body and embraced the warmth; the nausea eased. As I continued to focus on his voice, the buzzing hum solidified into a single note, a drone that underlined the world. It possessed a musicality that was inviting. With a slow, calming breath, I embraced the note, and soon, other notes joined the first to build a chord that sounded so much like the first strum of the guitar.

Calmness washed over me, and the darkness that had been threatening to swallow me whole brightened to a soft white setting. White walls with varying shades of white in the furniture. The tiled floor was also white. But the woman in the middle of the room, singing along with the music, was dressed in a vibrant blue—the only color in the room. The woman turned to face me and smiled from ear to ear, holding in her hands a single purple rose. "Sing with me."

The vision ended as the song's chorus came to an end. The world around me fell silent. The only sound left was the soft breathing that helped me to recenter myself.

"Better?"

Slowly, I lifted my head and looked at the one holding me—and gasped.

"George?" I tried to push him away. It was bad enough that Lucas had faked his death, but I refused to accept that George had faked his death too.

When he let go, I fell to my side. Pain radiated through my hip. And George's features morphed into someone else.

"I know you're confused right now," Cedrick said, "but you need to trust me. If you don't, we'll both go insane. Right now, I'm deep inside your head, just like you're deep inside mine."

I gawked at him, trying to make sense of what he was telling me.

"Cedrick, take her back to the med bay," Lucas ordered. "Make sure she starts her training right away. I can't have you continually shielding her mind with your own."

Cedrick stood over me, offering his hand. Any irritation or frustration that had poured off him before was gone. There was only concern.

Cautiously, I took his hand, and with one swift movement, he pulled me to my feet, catching me in his arms. He then led me through the halls and into an empty med bay. I didn't bother to ask where Beth was. I got the distinct impression from Cedrick that she wasn't expected to return for several hours.

He paced a little patch in the corner where a couch and coffee table had been set up. Images of the woman in the blue dress dancing in the white room, holding the purple rose, sat on the surface of his mind. And he glanced at me each time he turned.

"You have questions," I said, trying to ease the silence.

"They can wait."

"No, I don't think they can."

Cedrick stood before me, his hands at his side. "The questions aren't mine. I don't need to ask who or what the STAR are. I already know. I was inside your mind when you ran from them. I know how afraid you were. Especially of Marcus."

"I'm not afraid of Marcus. I just don't want to fight him."

"Because you think of him as a brother. You don't want to see him hurt. I get that. But he doesn't think of you in the same way. Right now, you're a wanted criminal, and he won't stop until he brings you down."

I took a deep breath. "It's a little more complicated than that." But I really didn't want to entertain those ideas. "Since you don't have any questions of me, can I ask a question of you?"

Cedrick nodded.

"The woman in the blue dress. Who is she?"

He averted his gaze and tried to hide his smile. "My mother. Lucas is always saying that the best way to protect our minds, to shield our thoughts, is to focus on a moment of strength and joy. Whenever I'm scared, I think of her, dancing and singing in the kitchen."

"She's singing *Purple Rain*."

Again, Cedrick nodded. "It was her favorite song. And whenever she sang it . . ." He stood there breathing, silent, so I completed his thoughts for him.

"You felt safe. What happened to her?"

"She died when I was fifteen." He took several more deep breaths and continued to pace around the little lounge area. There was more to the situation than he was telling me, but just as I didn't want to go into the details about my relationship with Marcus, it was clear he didn't want to speak about his mother.

"Cedrick, what happened back there?"

"You might be a strong telepath, but you're certainly not practiced at shielding. All of them wanted answers, and they were trying to dig into your mind for what you know. You were doing a reasonable job of keeping them out, but you needed help. So I helped. And I need to apologize for that."

I blinked and shook my head.

"You made me promise to never enter your mind again without your permission. But there wasn't the time to be nice about it."

I couldn't resist the smile. "We'll let it go this time."

Cedrick smiled too, his not-so-innocent dimple showing again. "I know I said that I didn't have any questions, but can I ask one, anyway?"

"Ask away."

"I know what the song *Purple Rain* means to me, but why do you keep singing it? What does it mean to you?"

I inhaled as deeply as I could and slowly exhaled, allowing the tension held within my body to leave with the exhalation. There was no point in hiding it, because if he was really inside my head all the time, he would find out eventually. "When I was a little girl, I was sent to this camp for children with White Rabbit syndrome. Everyone there knew what it was like to be different, to be an outcast. You still had the odd person who was a jerk and a bully. But there was this one kid, older than me . . . He was always looking out for me, even though I didn't need his help to stand up against the bullies. All I had to do was to wish for the bullies to leave me alone, and they would. But there was something about George . . . He just knew when I was afraid. When I needed someone to take me for *me*."

I smiled and stared off into the distance. "One night, after a really intense day, George snuck into my dormitory and encouraged me to . . . break the rules. We ran outside and played in the rain." I threw my head back and continued to smile. "It burned. It was raining purple rain that night, complete with traces of acid, but we didn't care. We just sang and danced, and we played in the puddles." Slowly, my chest tightened again and tears hung in the corners of my eyes. "We got into so much trouble for that. They had to treat us for second-degree burns all over our bodies. But it was worth it. Just to be able to dance in the purple rain like that—without a care. In that moment, we were both free of this disease—and living life."

The grief threatened to consume me again, but I needed to get this out—so he could understand. "George and I became couriers together—always watching out for each other." I got to my feet and headed to where I had left my jacket and pulled out the double-headed Queen of Hearts. "George used to carry cards like this, and I know this card belonged to him. I had left a card like this at his aunt's, when I went to tell her of his death, but I can't remember how I originally was given the card." The memory of George's face floated before me, slowly morphing from the fun-loving soul into a vacant creature, going up in flames. I closed my eyes, wishing for the images to go away.

Cedrick stood beside me and placed a caring hand on my shoulder. "I'm so sorry, Mike. I should have insisted that George come with me. I should have dragged him kicking and screaming if I had to. But Lucas said that it would be okay. We left George there in the hope that he would get you out before the Pregutor suspected anything."

"And now he's dead." I shoved the card back into my pocket. "Because of me."

"No."

"Yes. You just said that you left him there because he was hoping to get me out. But the Pregutor knew the truth and issued the orders for his death—orders that *I* was given to carry out. Unless, by some miracle, he's a ghost walking around here like Beth and Lucas are, the truth behind George's death is something I'm going to have to live with for the rest of my life."

Cedrick backed away and sagged down onto the couch. "Use his death as fuel."

"Come again?"

"He meant a lot to you. You felt safe with him. His memory makes you free. Use it."

I stood there, carefully thinking over his words. The vision of the woman in the blue dress in the white kitchen was so vivid in his mind. "Like you use your mother."

Cedrick nodded with a soft smile. "It's time to dance in the purple rain."

The tears hung in my eyes as I sat next to Cedrick on the couch. He gently hummed the chorus of the song, and the two of us enjoyed the mashup of memories: me with George in the stinging rain and splashing around in the puddles, and Cedrick with his mother in the white kitchen.

TWENTY-EIGHT

For a week, Cedrick and I were confined to the med bay. Lucas ensured that there were suitable sleeping arrangements for both of us and delivered our meals, but continued exploration of Sanctuary was no longer an option. Something about how everyone was now desperate to know more about STAR and my connection to them. Apparently, it had gotten so bad that Lucas had to station extra guards outside the door just to keep all the nosy jokers away. And because Cedrick had been shielding my mind with his own, he was a prisoner too. Our only escape from med bay was our scheduled visits to the bathroom. For a solid week, we did nothing but work on random mental exercises, as I worked to gain more subconscious control over my mental abilities.

I sat on the couch with my feet tucked up under me, my eyes closed. I was trying really hard to *empty* my mind, but every time I tried to think about *nothing*, my thoughts drifted to *everything*: to George, to Cedrick's mother, to Jody, to Tam . . . even to Marcus. And every time my mind drifted, Cedrick made this weird grunting sound, reminding me of my task.

It was frustrating to know that he could read my mind without much effort. But that was what the training really was about: trying to develop the skills to keep Cedrick—and everyone else—out of my head. What was even more frustrating was that I struggled to read his mind. Lucas kept insisting that I was stronger than Cedrick, but every time I tried to get into Cedrick's head, I encountered the woman in the blue dress dancing in the kitchen.

I sighed and got up from my spot, and started pacing the small lounge area. "You know, the one thing that doesn't make sense in all of this is the quiet."

"What do you mean?" Cedrick readjusted himself in his own tucked-up seated position.

"Well, whenever I'm out there"—I pointed to the hall—"I'm inundated by a buzzing hum. It's getting quieter by the day, but there's a drone note that sits under everything else. The moment I cross the threshold into the med bay, the drone note disappears and everything becomes silent. Except when Beth is in here doing her little experiments in the corner. I never knew that doctors always thought in terms that no one understands."

Cedrick laughed. "It's her way of keeping the telepaths among us out of her head: confuse the hell out of us with those big terms and meaningless words."

I snorted and shrugged. "But when she's not in here, it's so . . . silent."

Cedrick smiled. "Even with me in here?"

I looked at him sideways and pursed my lips. "Don't get me wrong, *Purple Rain* is seriously my favorite song, but there is only so much dancing in the kitchen I can stand."

Again, he laughed.

"So, why is it quieter in here compared to out there?"

"Because the med bay is surrounded by a special energy field that disrupts our mental abilities. No one out there can hear what is going on in here, but the same is true the other way around. No one in here can hear what is going on out there. It's why Lucas wanted you to stay in here until you can shield your mind properly."

"So, the med bay is surrounded by some sort of psychic shield?"

Cedrick nodded. "The way it was explained to me, telepathic abilities function on a frequency, a bit like a radio signal. If you could block that frequency, you block telepathic communication."

I stopped my pacing and plopped back down on the couch. "So, it's quiet in here because telepaths are unable to hear anything inside the field?"

Cedrick shrugged with that *I-guess-so* expression on his face.

"Then why can I hear you? And let me tell you that you are horribly out of tune."

He snorted. "Probably because I'm inside the field too. I'd hazard a guess that if I went out into the hall, you wouldn't be able to hear me anymore."

"Perhaps we should give that a try."

Cedrick shrugged and gave me that knowing smile. "I'll give you five minutes . . . and I promise I won't think about my mother dancing in the kitchen." With a swagger and arrogance in his step, he headed for the door.

"So, you'll be thinking of your mother dancing in the bathroom instead?"

He looked over his shoulder and glared at me, then shook his head and disappeared into the hall.

I smirked. What would Cedrick think about all of PentWave dancing naked in the shower room as we sang *Purple Rain*? George had practically screamed out the chorus, me right alongside him. And Marcus—

I shook my head, trying to dislodge the thoughts of Marcus. I didn't want to think about him. Instead, I was supposed to be focusing on Cedrick.

Cedrick . . . There was so much I didn't know about him—about his past—but there was also so much about his person that was on the surface. The way he was able to put aside his irritation and frustration so quickly to help those around him. The way he genuinely cared about what happened to others. And the way he would blush every time Beth walked by.

The way that Beth would try to hide her smile as Cedrick did everything he could to hide the fact he was staring at her. He would radiate with an energy and pride as Beth walked by him, brushing her fingers across his shoulders, drawing his attention. And he was more than happy to grab her, kissing her with all the passion he felt.

I blinked. I had never seen Cedrick kiss Beth before. I hadn't even seen the oogly eyes toward one another. Yet, the image of Beth and Cedrick kissing in that *want-to-take-your-clothes-off* way was too strong to ignore.

With a scrunched-up nose and a grimace, I watched the scene play out in my head between Beth and Cedrick. "Oh, get a room," said one of the guards, only making Beth laugh, laughter that she still possessed as she walked into the med bay, followed closely by a red-faced Cedrick.

"Afternoon, Mike," Beth said. "How's the training going?"

"Fine." I leaned back on the couch and unfurled my legs. "So, the two of you . . ."

Cedrick turned and gawked at me, wide-eyed. "Wait. You . . ." His thoughts became a jumbled mess of his relationship with Beth.

I pursed my lips and slowly shook my head. "Joy. So, if it's not your mother, it's your sexual escapades with Beth."

Beth just stopped and stared at me. "How did you . . .?" She glared over her shoulder at Cedrick.

He took a step back from her and put up his hands in surrender. "I didn't say anything. I swear."

"You didn't have to," I said. "It's written all over your face. But seriously, dude, the others are right. You really need to get a room."

For a moment, Cedrick's eyes grew even wider and his jaw dropped. He then sighed in defeat as he slumped down on the couch next to me. "Crap."

"My thoughts exactly."

Twenty-Nine

LUCAS STOOD WITH HIS ARMS crossed and a big, fat smile on his face. He never said a word, but if I had ever seen an *I-told-you-so* expression, that was it.

"How could you be taking this so calmly?" Beth insisted. "The tech in this room was supposed to keep the others protected. It's supposed to keep me protected."

"It does."

"But it doesn't work against me." I sat in the corner of the couch with my knees pulled close to my chest. "What makes me so . . . *special*?" Of course, *special* wasn't the word I really wanted to use, but Lucas had grilled it into me years ago that thinking of myself as a freak was unacceptable and entirely pointless. It was my unique abilities that made me so useful to the Pregutor and Rhodon Corporation. It was because of my special abilities that I had managed to stay out of Ward 27.

Or was it?

I stared off into nowhere, thinking about everything I knew to be true and all the things I had learned since I had been here. I unfurled myself and stood before Lucas. "When I was little, the doctors told me that I inherited audimentia from my mother. That the condition made her go crazy— crazy enough to kill herself. But my mother didn't go crazy, did she? They wanted me to think that so I would be compliant, so they could control me. They gave me those drugs to weaken my abilities, because they knew that if I gained full control over them, there would be nothing that could stop me." How could I have been so blind?

Lucas finally dropped his arms and nodded. "The tech in this room wasn't designed for you. It was designed for the rest of us. It never did work against you."

Beth huffed, like she wanted to protest, but she stayed quiet. And her thoughts were suddenly filled with more medical technobabble that no one else understood. Cedrick wore that *see* expression. Yep, the meaningless words were definitely Beth's way of keeping the telepaths out of her head.

Cedrick sat on the couch in the space I had vacated. "But I thought the tech surrounding this room was supposed to block all telepaths. It blocks me, and I'm a fifth gen too."

"Think of it like a radio," Lucas said. "Some radios are able to pick up rogue signals even from neighboring frequencies. It's a matter of line of sight, connection, and signal strength. Now that the mintonal has been flushed from Mike's system, she's at full receiver strength, able to pick up neighboring frequencies—even ones that are weak."

"Well, the neighboring frequencies suck." I shivered on the spot, trying to dislodge the passionate kiss between Cedrick and Beth from my mind.

Lucas laughed. Meanwhile, Cedrick grew redder in the face, and Beth groaned, giving off the distinct impression that she wanted to smack Lucas.

"Here, I'll do it for you." I punched Lucas in the shoulder, making him stumble backward. He winced as he rolled his shoulder, trying to ease the pain.

"I might have hit you harder than I should have, but Beth isn't the only one irritated with you. How can you be so over the moon about this?"

"You don't remember, do you?"

I tilted my head slightly to the side. "Remember what exactly?"

Lucas backed up to the corner and sat on a metal stool. "When was the last time you and your team had training exercises in the interrogation room?"

"A few months ago."

"And what happened?"

"It was quiet at first, but we were still able to pass messages to each other."

"And who was the connection strongest between?"

I sighed in defeat and rolled my eyes. "Between Marcus and myself."

"Was there anyone on the team who couldn't get it to work?"

I took a few deep breaths as I recalled how each member of PentWave took turns being locked in the room with one-way mirrors, trying to see out—mentally and visually. We had all passed whatever test the Pregutor had ordered, but just. "George struggled to forge the connections with Jody, Trent, and the others, but he had no problem with Marcus or myself."

Lucas nodded. "That makes sense. The two of you were always the strongest."

I wanted to ask him if he knew about what the Pregutor had planned for Marcus and myself, but I was more interested in what he knew about the tech shielding the room. "You said the tech wasn't designed for me. What did you mean?"

"It was designed for fourth gens, and before you ask, I don't know why it blocks Cedrick and not Mike. But I know the Pregutor was using Mike's team to expand the technology. If you and Marcus were able to get past it, that means they still hadn't perfected it." He stood to his full height, then brushed the creases out of his pants and pulled down his vest, so it sat over his back and belly better. "Beth, feel assured that the shield is working. Cedrick . . . Mike . . . We have a lot of training to do. Let's go."

As he headed for the door, Cedrick and I exchanged looks and shrugged.

"Sorry, Beth." Cedrick gave her a kiss. A sense of relief radiated off of him, like he was grateful that he no longer needed to hide his love for her.

I just rolled my eyes. Yep, they definitely needed to *get a room*.

We chased Lucas through the halls to the main training room, followed by the guards who had been posted outside med bay. Lucas gave the orders to form the sparring ring around the mats in the center of the room.

"You know, I'm not a soldier for hire." I crossed my arms and glared at my old trainer.

"No, you're not. You're just the best fighter that I've ever trained. Now get your ass on the mat."

Cedrick stepped onto the mats, but Lucas ordered him to stand back.

"You're not up to her skill level. Trust me on that."

The look on Cedrick's face . . . a mixture of hurt and disbelief. But I knew what Lucas was getting at. I had sensed it the day I arrived. Cedrick might have been a strong telepath, but his long, spindly limbs were gangly at best.

While my guards could have snapped him like a twig, I could pummel him and rip his heart out.

"Well?" Lucas stood in the center of the mats in an open stance that challenged me to attack him. There was no way he was going to let me get out of this.

I sighed as I stripped off my extra layers, giving me the freedom to move without my clothing being a hindrance. "It's been a long time since you've sparred against me, old man. I'm not the frightened little girl anymore."

"What are you trying to do? Bore me to death? Just shut up and get on with it."

"Okay . . . You asked for it." I dashed forward. Within the span of a breath, I had crossed the short distance that existed between us, my attention focused on his eyes. The edges of my vision darkened. *Just go down, old man,* I ordered, using my powers.

With a whir of movement, my vision blurred. And I found myself staring up at the ceiling.

Lucas stood over me with pursed lips. The light behind him gave him a halo. "You're right. It has been a long time since you and I sparred, because you seem to have forgotten what happens when you focus all of your attention on your opponent's eyes. You lose sight of their feet. And thank you for the suggestion to 'just go down,' by the way, because it was exactly what I had planned—for you."

Cedrick and the others laughed. "Are you sure she's the best fighter that you've ever trained, Lucas? Because if she's the best, then any fight against the Pregutor's lackeys will be a walk in the park."

Lucas smugly smiled. "Are you gonna take that?" He reached out his hand and pulled me to my feet. "Now, do it again, and this time, do it properly."

I narrowed my eyes at him and pouted. Without warning, I launched another attack. Only to be facing the ceiling again.

Snickers rippled around the room.

"Feel the air movement around you." Lucas pulled me to my feet again. "You know all of this, but you clearly have been running packages around the city for far too long. No wonder Marcus was given that position over you."

My lips pressed together, and I glared at the older man. The heat of embarrassment flushed through my body, turning into the heat of irritation. I rolled my shoulders, trying to loosen whatever was slowing my reaction time. With a count of five, I inhaled as deeply as I could, drowning out the murmurs from around the room. I kept my focus on Lucas, but this time, I deliberately held just enough of myself back, refusing to sink into the darkened vision of his mind.

As I finished my out breath, I launched another attack. Lucas spun around with his sweeping kick, and I jumped into the air and dove over him, somersaulting as I landed and kicking out, kicking Lucas in the head. I followed through with a few more strikes and grabbed his arm as he went to punch me. I then used my size to dive under his other arm and spun him around, driving his wrist and elbow to the ceiling, controlling his descent to the ground. If he didn't go where I wanted him to go, my movements would have broken his arm or dislocated his elbow. Maybe both.

Lucas tapped the floor, a recognized signal that I had won the match, and I let him go. But instead of pushing himself up from the mats like I had expected, he rolled onto his back and continued fighting. He struck out, entangling my legs in his own. And I went down hard, hitting my head. The stars weren't quite distinct enough to count.

"You let your guard down," Lucas said, as he let me go. "You've let your feelings for me get in the way of seeing the potential danger."

He held out his hand to help me up again, but I batted it away as I rolled over and pushed myself up. The stars still hung around the edges of my vision, and I wasn't entirely stable on my feet.

"You need a break?"

"No." My response was probably a little more forceful than it needed to be, but I had a point to prove—that I hadn't gone soft. "The enemy won't let you take a break just because you see stars," I said, reciting one of his many lessons from years back. "They'll just take advantage of the disorientation."

Without hesitation, I launched another attack, this time restricting my movements to what would allow me to have at least one foot firmly planted on the ground. Lucas landed a blow that forced me to stagger backward, purchasing some distance between us. He then whistled, and four others joined us on the mats.

I dashed to the side of the mats, ensuring that none of the five fighters that I now faced could get behind me. If I had to fight them from all sides with my vision still seeing the odd star, I would have gone down and quickly. But these fighters had been trained the same way I had been. They fanned out, dividing my attention.

I forced myself to take slow, steady breaths. I hummed the chorus of *Purple Rain* over and over again. And I waited for the onslaught to begin.

A buzzing hum began to build in my head, growing to a screech. I had no way of knowing whether it was just the telepaths I faced on the mats, or whether the others had joined in, but I couldn't let any of them in. I continued to focus my thoughts on the five soldiers in front of me and the chorus of *Purple Rain*. While I might have been on the defensive, I had to stay in control. The last time I had felt this level of mental intrusion, I had Cedrick's help to shield my mind. This time, I had to do it on my own.

The physical attack turned into a series of spinning kicks and punches. The fighters I faced worked in conjunction with one another. At times, I was forced to block the strikes from two soldiers at once. And when the third strike timed itself just right, I had to bear the full brunt of it.

With each punch that got through to my head, with each kick I wore to my chest, the stars became brighter and I struggled to breathe. The screeching in my head only added to the headache that was brewing as a result of the physical strikes.

As the space between my attackers and myself shrank, now coming from all sides, I was no longer able to stay ahead of the strikes. The kick to my knee forced me to the ground, allowing the others to converge even tighter around me. In the end, all I could do was curl up into a ball and cover my head, protecting the soft areas of my body the best I could.

The onslaught seemed to drag on and on. And I sank into my memories of dancing in the purple rain with George. Soon my memories of George were overlaid with the woman in the blue dress in the white kitchen. A gentle hand squeezed my shoulder, encouraging me to unfurl. Cedrick's weak smile was barely discernible in my blurry vision. I graciously accepted his help to get to my feet.

"No more training on your own." Lucas pulled me to face him, lifting my chin and shining a penlight in my eyes. "Tomorrow, you're to join the rest of us. And I want you to give it your all. You might not be a soldier for hire, but you're being hunted . . . just like the rest of us."

THIRTY

EVERY MUSCLE IN MY BODY protested against the smallest of movements as I rolled into my cot in the corner of med bay. Beth had given me some pills to help deal with the pain, but I was going to be covered in bruises for weeks. My bruises would have bruises.

I closed my eyes, and a blaring alarm emanated from a small digital clock with red numbers. Six in the morning? But my eyes had closed for only a second.

Sighing in defeat, not really looking forward to whatever torture Lucas was going to put me through, I rolled from the cot, groaning as the pain radiated from my ribs. I took shallow breaths. This wasn't the first time I had felt this level of pain. At least I wasn't seeing stars anymore.

On the little side table was a small tray of pills and a cup of water, along with a note from Beth.

>>The next time you want to beat yourself into a pulp, talk to me first. I have a few drugs in the cabinet that can simulate the pain all over without the beating. BTW, Lucas is now in my bad books. He should know better.<<

I smirked—then immediately regretted it. My cheek screamed out in pain from the small smile. My hand shot to the sore spot on my cheek. I leaned over and looked at my reflection in the small mirror that hung next to the cot. My cheek wasn't just sore, it was purple. And not the nice shade of purple either.

Slowly, testing each movement before I moved, I took the pills Beth had left for me in one gulp, washing them down with water. I then did the best I could to pull on some fresh clothes. Clean undergarments. A clean black T-shirt. A thin purple sweatshirt with the hole around the collar lovingly stitched closed. And a pair of black leggings with thick socks to help fill out the boots I had stolen from Marcus's locker.

I stood before the small mirror as I brushed out my hair. The dark brown regrowth was now down to my ears, and the purple on the ends had faded to a grayish pink. I had never gone this long between dye jobs. But there was no helping it. So, I tied up my hair in such a way to hide what was left of the shitty dye color, showing only my regrowth.

I then sat on the couch in the lounge area and stared at the clock mounted on the wall, watching the wiggling second hand move from mark to mark. It was an odd form of meditation, but it helped to keep my mind off the pain. However, my bladder was more than happy to make itself known.

Seven o'clock. I furrowed my brow. Cedrick normally made his presence known by then. So did Beth. But med bay was empty—except for me. And my bladder didn't care.

I went to the door, knowing that the guards would escort me to the bathroom in Cedrick's absence, but no one was there. Cautiously, I stepped outside the med bay and outside the psychic field, waiting for the onslaught of the constant hum—but nothing. The silence was a little more than unnerving. It was like there was no one left in Sanctuary.

Hoping that the guards weren't hiding, waiting to beat me up the moment I headed beyond my boundaries, I darted down the hall, wincing with every quick step. As soon as I was inside the bathroom, I locked the door and pulled down my pants.

The relief that washed over me was blissful. An empty bladder . . . and a moment of privacy. I never realized how much being able to pee without someone watching over me—physically and mentally—was actually dignifying.

At the sink, I took an extra moment to splash cool water on my face, a poor substitute for an icepack.

I walked back to the med bay and went back to my funky meditation of watching the clock on the wall. Soon the clock read eight o'clock. And now my stomach made its presence known.

I took to pacing the small lounge area, constantly looking at the clock. Nine o'clock. Ten o'clock. And still no Cedrick or Beth. And still no guards outside.

What the hell was going on? Where was everyone?

The hunger pangs became incredibly uncomfortable. I kept staring at the door, willing Cedrick or Beth to walk through it, but still no one. I bit my lip as I tried to decide if it was worth the risk of getting pummeled by the absent guards and gaining more bruises. At one point during my *tour* with Cedrick, he had shown me a food hall. Surely, no one could blame me if I tried to find it on my own.

Out in the hall, I cautiously looked around the corner at the first junction, then headed left. Cedrick always took the first left on our tours. I then continued down the hall, constantly looking over my shoulder, expecting the guards to come charging at me for escaping. Another left, then a right, then another left. And at each junction, the emptiness of the halls—and the quietness of my surroundings—only added to my unease.

A soft murmur and the clatter of plates came from the end of the hall. A sweet aroma hung in the air. My stomach growled in response.

Still cautious and expecting to be assaulted by the guards, I edged my way closer to the food hall. A sense of triumph bled through me.

"Took you long enough." Lucas came up behind me and wrapped his arm around my shoulder, making me wince. But he ignored any pain I might have been feeling and steered me toward the tables in the corner where Cedrick and my guards were all scowling. "They were told they couldn't eat anything until the last member of their team arrived. And they were told that she had to make her own way here. They were expecting you a few hours ago."

Lucas pulled out a chair and forced me to sit. My muscles continued to protest. All eyes seemed to bore into me, and I wanted to hide. "Now the entire team is here, I'll go and get your food."

A chorus of growling stomachs rumbled around the table. My stomach completed the melody.

They had expected me hours ago? But why hadn't anyone come to get me?

"Because we weren't allowed to," said one of the guards, a petite woman with a snarly attitude that reminded me of Jody. "Scouts need to be able to navigate the maze without guidance."

I inhaled as deeply as I could, ignoring my rumbling stomach—and ignoring my broken ribs. "I'm to be a scout?"

"First recon, actually," said another guard, the biggest one among them. He was so big that his shoulders touched the shoulders of those sitting next to him, giving him zero room to move his arms. I was fairly certain that if I looked under the table, his knees would have been touching the underside. "With your abilities being what they are, and with your experience with Rhodon, you'd be in the best position to get in and get out, communicating whatever intelligence you can back to the team via the communications officer."

"Who is?"

"Me." Cedrick leaned back in his chair and smiled. "During missions, I tend to be sitting in Control alongside our technical expert."

"And I take it that your technical expert was the one to hack into Sector 14's security systems, not you. So, who's the technical expert?"

"Not here." Lucas placed two plates filled with food cubes in the center of the table. Like animals, Cedrick and the others dove in, leaving a single food cube. Cautiously, I reached forward to take it.

A blue food cube. Bright blue. I had never seen a food cube that color before. Normally, food cubes were gray, brown, or green, or some combination thereof. And they were never bright.

I brought the food cube to my lips and took a tiny bite. It was sweet, much sweeter than any other food cube I had ever had. And it was actually delicious. Nothing like the algae soup I had been eating for the past few weeks. And the smell . . . like grains of honeysuckle, something I had only smelled in the gardens found in Sector 14. I missed those yellow flowers. I resisted the urge to take bigger and bigger bites, savoring the smooth texture on my tongue.

Lucas put a cup of brown liquid in front of me. Again, cautious about what could be in the cup, I raised it to my nose. The nutty, bitter notes called to me. Pulled me in, inviting me to sip. "Real coffee? Where did you find real coffee?"

"We uncovered a bag of beans in a hidden food store a few months ago." Lucas grinned from ear to ear. "Savor it while you can, because this is the last of it. Cookie has been stretching it out as far as they could, but I asked for full strength for the team today. A kind of welcome to our newest member." He raised his cup in a toast.

"Welcome," the others said, as they sipped their own cups and carried on eating their food cubes.

I couldn't help it. I smiled as I raised my own cup, then took a sip.

This was my new team, though I wasn't entirely sure what our mission mandate was. Whatever it was, I was fairly confident that it wasn't to kill people—not unless there was no other choice. But it didn't matter, because they were welcoming me for *me*—for all of *me*—including my mental abilities. And more importantly, they weren't scared of me.

Cedrick leaned over and tapped my shoulder. "I should warn you: Lucas is having your things moved to the living quarters. But you'll find it more comfortable than med bay."

"You'll have to share a room with me," said the petite woman who reminded me of Jody. "You don't have a problem with that, do you?"

I shook my head and smiled. "No. It's all good."

"I'll show you our room after our training today. The name is Nancy, by the way. And our team captain, when Lucas isn't around, is this giant teddy bear sitting next to me."

"Name's Grober," said the hulking man who had told me that I was First Recon. "But I answer to Teddy Bear too."

"And I'm Scott," said the man sitting next to him, "the team's munitions officer."

"And I'm Johnny, the medic."

They went around the table, introducing themselves and their roles on the team. Twelve of them in total. It would take me a while to remember all of their names, but thankfully, when out in the field, it would only be a handful of them at any time.

As the team continued to savor their coffee—the real stuff, even if it was the last of it—I just sat there and listened to their banter, laughing as they teased each other. It felt good. The last time I was surrounded with teasing laughter like this was when PentWave became couriers. Lucas was there then too.

Lucas sat next to me and smiled with his toothy grin, complete with bits of food cube stuck between his teeth. For a moment, I could have sworn that I was looking at a younger version of him, with the same food cube smile.

"You okay?" he asked.

I nodded. "It's just—"

"You had a memory." He said it as a statement rather than a question. "About when we first met."

Again, I nodded.

"Yeah, well, that was a long time ago, and you're more beautiful today than you were back then. You're stronger too."

I wanted to shy away from the compliment, but Lucas wouldn't let me. Instead, he put his arm around my shoulder and gave me a brotherly hug.

"How did you do it, Lucas? How did you fake your death? When that body was found in Sector 5, they positively identified it as you." I glanced at his right wrist, noting a faint scar. I then ran my thumb over my own scar. "It's the pharmachip, isn't it? Your chip was removed and implanted in someone else, a lookalike."

Lucas nodded.

"But how did you get around the DNA scanners? As soon as they found the body, they would have taken a sample to run against the central database."

"It helps that I know someone who can hack into their system and alter the records."

"So, was he already dead when you implanted the chip, or did you kill him?"

"Who?"

"Your lookalike."

Lucas sighed and bowed his head. "He knew the danger. He volunteered anyway. No one compelled him to do anything and no one—" He took a deep breath. "None of us killed him."

"And I suppose the note wasn't some brilliant idea to screw with the heads of those at Rhodon."

Lucas furrowed his brow. "What note?"

"The one found pinned to the chest of your doppelgänger. 'Abram Shutton's son lives.'"

The group around me shuffled in their seats as they glanced around the room—to the children. One by one, they turned back to Lucas and nodded. Except Cedrick. He kept his focus honed on the empty plate in front of him.

"Don't try to tell me some bullshit about how Abram Shutton doesn't have a son, because Tam told me that he did. They said that Dr. Shutton's son disappeared fifteen years ago and his pharmachip went offline. Though his body was never found. And you guys sent someone in to Sector 14 to send me a message, telling me to find Abram Shutton's son—

that he could help me." I looked at each of them in turn. They shielded their minds. Nothing could be gleaned without doing a deep probe, and I really didn't want to waste my time with that nonsense. "He's here, isn't he? He was the first ghost."

I shifted my gaze from person to person, who all seemed to be looking at each other, trying to work out how to answer me. Eventually, Lucas gave a single nod.

"So, when do I meet him?"

"You already have." Cedrick finally lifted his eyes. On the surface of his thoughts was a memory of his mother welcoming his father home after a long day at work. Abram Shutton kissed the woman wearing the blue dress in the white kitchen.

I stared at him, my jaw agape. "You're . . .?"

"Dr. Shutton's biological son. Yeah. But in my case, the apple didn't only fall off the tree, it rolled down the hill as far away from the tree as humanly possible. That man is a monster, using whomever he felt like as human lab rats—including his wife and children."

"Children? You have siblings? How is that possible?" I shifted to get an unobstructed view of Cedrick. "Provisional Government Order Number 543: To ensure that the population never exceeds the capacity of the domes, each couple will be afforded only one opportunity to conceive. Any child conceived without a permit is to be terminated immediately. After a successful permitted birth, all women are to undergo a hysterectomy and men are to have their testes removed. No exception."

The men among them squirmed a bit, only making the women roll their eyes. We were living in an environmental crisis. Desperate times called for desperate measures.

"It turns out my father had a daughter in secret before I was born. No one knew about her. Certainly not my mother."

Lucas leaned forward, resting his elbows on the table. "How is it that this is the first time I'm hearing about this? If you have a sister, we need—"

"She's dead." Cedrick took several deep breaths before continuing. "My parents were fighting about it the night my mother died. My sister had died leaving behind a daughter, and my father wanted the little girl to come live with them. But for everything to be legal, before my father could publicly acknowledge the existence of his granddaughter, I had to be shipped off to O'quv Lageri for training. My father had reasoned that come my sixteenth birthday, I would have been sent to O'quv Lageri, anyway. What difference did a few months make? My mother wouldn't have a bar of it. The next morning, I found her dead in the middle of the kitchen. Apparently, she had gotten up in the middle of the night to get something to drink and had a heart attack. She hit her head as she fell. By the time I found her, it was already too late. But before my father could send me to O'quv Lageri, I ran away."

"What about the girl?" Lucas asked. "Do you know what happened to your niece?"

Cedrick shook his head. "For all I know, she could be dead. As Mike said, Provisional Government Order Number 543: Any child conceived without a permit is to be terminated immediately. But I have to admit that it would be nice to know if she was alive or not. She would have been a sixth gen—the first one born."

There was silence. And then there was silence. And hovering over that group was the quietest of all silences.

If Cedrick's and my abilities were any indication as to what a strong fifth gen could do, a sixth gen would be unstoppable. And a sixth gen in service to the Pregutor would spell death for us all.

Lucas pushed back his chair with a squeak and stood. "I want you all to get on with your training. Grober, you're in charge until I get back."

"Yes, sir," said the beefy brick house that sat opposite me. And Lucas was gone.

Grober pushed himself up from his chair. "Alright, you lot. You heard him. Time to get on with our training. And don't think I'll take it easy on any of you. Especially you." He pointed at me. "Lucas keeps saying that you're the best fighter he's ever trained. It's time to prove it."

Thirty-One

The days quickly fell into a routine. I would get up from my bed in the dorm room I shared with Nancy (and Cedrick was right that it was more comfortable than a cot in med bay), then I joined my new team in the food hall, before heading to some random part of the complex for more training. Sometimes, it was combat skills. Other times, it was mental training. And other times, it was munitions training.

I scared Grober with how proficient I was with weaponry. I had no issue with assembling and dissembling any weapon put in front of me. And my aim was incredibly accurate, with tight clustering on multiple rounds. I tried to explain that it was my job as a courier to get those weapons around the city in parts. Sometimes, a drop required that I reassemble the weapons too.

After training, the team would return to the food hall, most of us too exhausted for anything other than mindlessly putting food cubes or algae soup in our mouths. Then it was time for showers and bed.

From sun up to sun down, my time was taken up with duties shared with my new team, even though I had no clue if the sun was up or down. It was one of the downsides of living underground: one never saw the sun. Then again, I never saw the sun above ground either, but at least we got a sense of ambient lighting, even with all the cloud cover.

As the days started to morph into one, I found the routine to be meditative. But getting a *day off* was just as welcoming, because it meant I could sleep in.

I laid in bed snoozing when I felt a familiar presence out in the halls. I couldn't explain it, but I could sense whenever Cedrick was near, even through all the rock found in this place. It was like he had spent so much time in my head that his mental thoughts were now a beacon. But there was another presence with him. Someone who I hadn't met before, yet I knew their mind.

Tempted by the new-but-familiar mind, I pulled back the covers and quickly got dressed. I headed out into the hall, following the beacon that was Cedrick and the new mind. Every time I hit a junction with multiple directions to head, I closed my eyes and focused on the energies radiating from Cedrick. Left, then right. Right, then left. Was it possible that he knew I could track him like this? Was he deliberately avoiding me?

I turned the last corner and found Cedrick in the middle of the corridor, talking to the new-but-familiar man. The balding patch on the top of his dome told me that he was older than Cedrick, but I could only guess by how much. His age likely made him one of the seniors who ran the place. And the fact that his surface thoughts were filled with a nonsensical selection of numbers and symbols only reinforced the idea that this man knew how to shield his thoughts from telepaths. But still, there was something familiar about him. If only he would turn around so I could see his face. Perhaps I would recognize him from one of the many briefings that I had been given before the Pregutor sent me out into the middle of nowhere.

Cedrick glanced in my direction, then said something to the unknown man, who disappeared before I could join them.

Cedrick smiled and clapped his hands as I approached. "I was just coming to get you. I know today is meant to be your day off, but Lucas wants the full team in the training room."

I sighed and my head flopped forward in defeat. "More training? My bruises have bruises."

"Can't be helped."

"I can still complain about it."

"You could. Wouldn't change anything."

Again, I sighed. "Okay. Let's go." I deliberately walked as slowly as possible, dragging out the inevitable. "So, who was that?"

"No one in particular. Just the one who keeps the lights on."

"So, he's important then." I glanced back over my shoulder in the direction the unknown man had disappeared. "And he's avoiding me."

"Why would you say that?"

"Because the moment I came around the corner, the moment you realized I was near, he disappeared."

"Don't try to read anything into it. Eddie's just a cantankerous old bastard who likes his solitude."

"Eddie . . . so that's his name."

There was this change in Cedrick's mental patterns, like he was putting up a wall around his thoughts. I could have broken down that wall if I needed to, but Cedrick had been open and honest with me until now. I had no reason to believe that he would hide anything from me—not if I asked the right questions.

"So, what were you talking about when I arrived? It looked to be something big." A total lie, of course, because, in fact, it looked to have very little significance at all.

"I guess it depends on your point of view."

"And your point of view?"

Cedrick stared off into the distance. "People are dying. Our kind are dying." As much as he tried to hide it, there was a sense of fear and concern radiating from him—from his mental energies.

I pulled him to a stop and forced him to face me. "What's going on?"

He sighed in defeat. "I guess there's no point in hiding it. You'll find out soon enough, anyway. There have been terrorist attacks on the general population of the city. Suicide bombers and shooters. And the ones responsible all reportedly have audimentia. The news reporters are saying that the terrorists are all acting in the name of the Rhodon Central Hospital killer. Somewhere along the line, the Pregutor decided to turn you into a martyr. It's a massive manhunt now. They're saying that you just waltzed into Rhodon Central, and, for no reason at all, killed over fifty people."

"What? But I didn't kill anyone."

"Except for that not-nurse."

"Oh yeah. Him. But I didn't kill anyone else."

"I know that. I was in your head, remember? But they're showing the footage of you using that dead security guard to open doors. They're saying that you killed him to gain access to restricted areas. And they're showing footage of you fighting your way out, narrowly escaping the bullets fired at you as you headed for the service tunnels. Mike, even though there is no footage of you killing anyone, what footage does exist is enough to sow seeds of fear."

I looked around at the others walking past us through the corridors. "Has everyone here seen the footage too?"

"No. That's what Eddie was talking to me about. He's managed to put Sanctuary on information blackout, but he doesn't know how long he can maintain it for. Some of the kids are pretty tech-savvy. The last time Eddie put us on information blackout, it lasted less than twenty-four hours."

"So, in less than twenty-four hours, everyone here will know that I'm Crystal Hills' most wanted. And some of them will likely want to turn me in for the reward."

Cedrick shook his head. "No, they won't. If anything, they'll want to protect you."

"How can you be sure of that?"

"Because it's not a manhunt for just you. It's a manhunt for all of us. According to the reports, they instigated an immediate registration act. All those with audimentia are to report to Sector 14 for immediate treatment monitoring. All health scanners throughout the city have been given an update patch that checks for the unique DNA markers connected to the condition. Over one hundred people have already been taken into custody, and the cells can't hold any more. Some of them have already been publicly executed as a matter of show. The Pregutor wants everyone to know that they mean business. Rhodon has declared war, and we have to build our army in response."

I took several deep breaths. "I won't be the poster child for this revolution of yours."

"What you or I want doesn't matter. You're already the face of this. Rhodon did that by saying that the latest attacks are in your name. The question is: are you going to let them continue to defame you, or are you going to take control of the narrative?" Cedrick sighed and bowed his head slightly, ducking down to my height. "Mike, I'm not going to sugarcoat this. People will die before this is over. But if we don't stop the Pregutor, no one else will. We're the only ones who know the truth."

I wiped my forehead and combed my hair out of my eyes.

"Come on. Lucas is waiting for us in the training room." He headed down the hall, not really waiting for me.

I shook my head and chased after him. "Lucas is back?"

"He got back a few hours ago."

"Did he find anything about your niece?"

Cedrick shrugged and shook his head. "I don't know. What I do know is that he came back with an update patch for that shield that blocks our powers. He's carrying a personal unit now." He stopped in the middle of the hall and scowled. "I can't get into his head. I'm hoping that you can."

I bit my bottom lip. "We need to know, don't we? If your niece is still alive and she's sided with STAR . . ." I looked down the empty halls and imagined how so full of life they would be in a few hours. How the children would be joyfully playing. And how the children would be at the greatest risk if STAR ever found Sanctuary. "I won't let it happen. If I have to, I'll kill her myself."

"She's family, Mike."

"If she's sided with STAR, you won't have a choice. You and I are criminals in the eyes of the Pregutor. We're a danger to everything that the Pregutor and Rhodon are doing. STAR will have been tasked with hunting us, and they won't stop until we're dead. The only advantage we have right now is that they don't know you exist. You're just a myth. A ghost.

But the moment they confirm that Abram Shutton's son still lives and is leading this rebellion . . ."

Cedrick took a deep breath of his own. "And when the public finds out that Crystal Hills' most wanted is fighting alongside him . . . Yeah, we won't have a choice." He shook his head and sighed. "I hate this."

I stepped closer to him. "That's because your heart is still pure. You care about those around you without reason. You would do anything to keep them safe. But here's a little secret. We would do anything to keep *you* safe—even me. You won't have to be the one to kill her, whoever she is. I'll do it. And I won't think twice about it, because it means you'll be safe."

"Hey, you two," Lucas called out from the end of the hall. "Are you joining us or not? I could really use the help of my two best students to show the others how to kick some telepathic ass."

Cedrick and I snorted.

"After you," Cedrick said with a flourish of his arm. And we followed Lucas into the training room.

Thirty-Two

I squatted in a low crouch, one leg stretched out to the side and my arms extended to provide balance. It had been a long time since I had worked this hard in training, using these particular moves. My muscles protested, and I would likely be nursing new bruises in the morning, but the adrenaline pumping through my veins helped to keep the pain at bay. I had to force myself to breathe through my nose, doing the best I could to keep my heart rate steady.

The last time I had to work this hard, my sparring partner had nowhere near the level of competence in their mental abilities that Cedrick had. I needed to be constantly on guard, or Cedrick would be in—and I would be on my back—again. Even now, I could feel the buzz building inside my head.

I kept my attention finely honed on Cedrick, watching every twitch of every muscle, taking note of the beaded sweat on his brow. I waited for an opening to push past the boundaries he kept around his mind.

It turned out that shielding one's mind was like breathing air. Drowning out the mental voices of other people—that took practice. And everyone standing around the edges of the room was mentally shouting at me.

Whoever was sending me mental images of what he wanted to do with me in the shower block . . . He'd better hope that I never figured out his identity.

I slowly pushed myself into a standing position, keeping the bulk of my weight on one leg. It was a precarious stance, because all it would take would be a rush in my direction, and I would be flat on my ass. But with one leg free of weight, I could kick out quickly. As I raised to my full height, I never once took my eyes off Cedrick. We stared directly into each other's eyes, but the mental connections were blocked on both ends. I couldn't get inside his head, just as he couldn't get inside mine.

Fully erect, I brought my arms in front of me, forming a circle to protect my center. With a small twitch of my supporting leg, I sprung into a full attack. Kicks. Punches. Mental jabs. I pushed forward, forcing Cedrick into the corner of the sparring mat. But Cedrick had a few tricks of his own.

The mental guard on his mind was suddenly lowered, and my vision became near black with only the tiny window of his eyes still clear. The sparring room was overlaid with the white apartment and the woman dressed in blue, but she wasn't singing—at least not out loud. Instead, she gave her young child a plate to carry to the dining room where their guest waited along with his father. The guest, dressed in white, with white hair and incredibly pale skin, turned to face the child with a broad smile.

Tam? Cedrick knew Tam?

My world spun around in circles, coming to a sudden stop as the air was forced from my lungs and pain radiated throughout my back. My vision returned in a flash, and Cedrick knelt over me, his forearm pressed to my neck. It wouldn't take much for him to shift his weight, driving a significant amount of downward force through his forearm, crushing my windpipe.

Cedrick smiled widely, disarming me with that not-so-innocent dimple. "You shouldn't have been pushing so hard. Next time, hold just a little back." He let me go, standing up and extending a helping hand to help me back to my feet.

I pressed my hand to my head and blinked a few times, trying to wash away the mental residue of our connection. "Did you just . . ."

"Lower my guard? Yeah, I did. But I let you see only what I wanted you to see. And I knew that the moment you were inside, you would be blind."

"I really need to get a better handle on that."

"Yeah, you do." Cedrick continued to smirk.

But I wanted to push back into his head—to see more of that memory.

Cedrick shook his head. "I didn't know her name," he said, answering my unspoken question. "I just knew that she was someone my father respected, and whenever she was around, my father was actually civil. He even laughed sometimes. And my mother loved her."

"Her name is Tam," I said, "and she isn't a she. They're a they. Tam was my handler and the psychiatrist in charge of monitoring my condition. And now that I know what I know, Tam was likely testing my abilities, determining when it was time to transfer me to STAR. I wasn't aware you had ever met Tam. And I wasn't aware that Tam knew how to smile."

Cedrick cocked his head to the side as he scrunched up his brow.

"Tam rarely showed emotion—any emotion. The fact that you saw Tam smile is a rare thing."

"Everyone, take a break," Lucas ordered. "Get some food. Mike, come with me. There's someone you need to meet."

Thirty-Three

I followed Lucas through the maze, winding this way and that. I still struggled to understand how anyone could properly navigate this maze without any markings on the walls, but I noticed how the air temperature dropped, and we walked down a slight slant in the floor. The quality of the rock walls became more roughly hewn. It was like we were heading deeper into the Earth.

At the end of the corridor was a giant metal door covered in rivets, but no handle—and no obvious way to open the door from the outside.

Lucas banged on the door. "Eddie! You in there?" He waited for a few seconds, then banged on the metal surface again. "Come on, old man. Wake up!"

There was a whirring from the corner of the ceiling, and a speaker crackled into life. "Go away. I'm working."

Lucas looked up at the black dome camera housing. "Stop being an old fart and just open the door."

"I said, 'Go away.'"

Lucas took several deep breaths. "Come on, man. You can't hide in there forever."

There was silence, but Lucas insisted I stay where I was. And to keep quiet.

"What do you want, Lucas?"

"You can't keep avoiding her. Eventually, you'll need to talk to her and tell her what you know. And Eddie, she knows things about Rhodon and the Pregutor that I don't—including why Steve was killed."

So many questions flew through my head—like who the hell was Steve?

Lucas glanced at me, and an image of a naked man running through the plaza in Sector 14 rested on the surface of his thoughts. But the little shake of his head told me that now wasn't the time for questions. His mental image would be the only answer I would get.

We stood in silence, looking between the door and the camera in the corner of the ceiling. I have no idea how long we stood there, waiting in silence for something to happen. However long it was, it was long enough to make me wonder if what we were waiting for was ever going to happen.

"Whoever this Eddie person is, they clearly don't want to meet me. So . . ." I turned to head back the way we had come, but Lucas grabbed my arm, then banged on the door again.

"God dammit, you stubborn old fool. She's Natalie's daughter!"

Again, questions went through my mind, but before I could vocalize them, there was a clunk and a whir, followed by a hiss. The door in front of us rolled back to reveal a darkened hole.

"Just the girl," said the voice over the intercom. "You stay out, Lucas."

"Fair enough, old man." Lucas stepped to the side and gestured to the opened door. "Don't let him scare you. He growls a lot, but he's a big softie when you get to know him."

Again, I furrowed my brow as I stepped through the door.

It was dark with extremely dim lighting, but it was enough to see the work benches lined up, each laden with tools of various descriptions. Hammers and nails on one. A soldering iron on another. Microscope on another. And lined up along the far wall was an array of monitors showing different security feeds from within the underground facility and throughout the city.

"Well, don't just stand there. You're blocking the door."

I stepped forward, and a motor to the side of the metal door whirred into action, slamming the door shut. The turning locks on the back of the door spun around, putting metal bars through the floor and the ceiling.

My stomach started doing flip-flops. If I had wanted out, my only escape was now locked.

A light came on from the ceiling, shining a bright light in my face. I blinked and held up my hand.

"Oh, bloody hell . . . You look just like her." An older man stepped out of the shadows with his arms folded across his chest. There were dark rings under his eyes, as though he hadn't slept in a long time. The frown on his face only accentuated his wrinkles. "Well, it would appear that your mother's talents weren't the only things you inherited from her. Now I understand why Abram is so fascinated with you. And before you ask, yeah, I knew your mother. I was the one who helped her escape before you were born. I tried to help her hide. But it wasn't good enough. They still found her. They found you."

He turned and headed back into the darkness. "Well, move your butt, Davison. I haven't got all day."

I was suddenly plunged into darkness as the bright light above me was turned off. Before I dared to move deeper into the room, I waited for my vision to right itself.

Everywhere in Sanctuary was dark, with no light from the outside. But this room was different. The walls were painted black, as though they were painted that way to absorb stray light. With the monitors and the colorful displays, I felt like I had stepped into some warped version of the briefing room back at Rhodon. The only thing missing was Tam in their white suit.

Eddie pulled out a metal contraption from the wall and unfolded it into a chair. It was no surprise to see more ancient technology in this place, but the chair was at odds with the holographic display hovering above the desk in the middle of the room.

The old man lowered himself into a padded chair and gestured for me to sit on the metal chair in front of him. "I suppose I better explain why I've been avoiding you. To be blunt, I can't shield my mind against someone like you—not without tech or another mind reader to help. And I didn't know if I could trust you or not."

I smirked and shook my head. "I haven't done anything to warrant your trust. Not yet, anyway."

"True, you haven't. But your mother has. And I made her a promise that if her daughter ever came to my door, I would help her in any way I could."

I stared at the man before me, not really sure what to do or say. If he really knew my mother, then he might have known exactly how she died. I was fairly certain that it wasn't suicide like I had been told all those years ago. I was tempted to use my abilities to dig inside his head, but digging around in his memories wasn't the way to gain his trust.

"You really knew my mother?"

Eddie smiled. "Your mother and I were both assigned to the Stilte Project with Blomme Industries. It's a sister company to Rhodon Corporation located in Lagniappe Fields. And with your mother's help, my job was to find a way to shield non-telepaths against telepaths."

"My mother was a telepath?" I asked it like it was a question, but I knew the answer already.

Eddie looked at me silently, like he was waiting for me to ask a question of consequence, not state the obvious.

"So, you were part of the team that developed the technology in the med bay?"

Again, Eddie smiled. "I was. But as you've already discovered, it has its limitations. For one, it wasn't originally designed to withstand someone with your strength."

"No, of course not. It was designed for my mother." I shifted in my seat, trying to bring the feeling back into my numb butt cheeks, and I forced myself to take several deep breaths. "Why would my mother help anyone to develop the technology that could block her abilities if she was trying to hide? Wouldn't having the ability to read minds help to keep her hidden?"

Eddie nodded and grunted, like he was approving of my line of thinking. "When NeuWave started, your mother wasn't hiding. She had no need to. She was proud of who and what she was. A descendant of the first generation of Rhodon's genetic experiments. She knew that the geneticists at Rhodon were working toward a future where humans could properly reclaim the surface—where we could live outside the domes again. But she also knew the truth behind where her abilities came from—where *your* abilities come from. Cedrick may have told you that your abilities were an unforeseen mutation of the genetic experiments, but they weren't. They were deliberate. But not everyone born with the abilities had the same sense of duty and moral justice that your mother did. The number of fourth gens with empathic and telepathic abilities was on the rise, and while Rhodon was working on a drug to suppress the abilities, Blomme was working to develop other tech to exploit them. Your mother happily volunteered because she knew the danger that a rogue telepath could present to society."

He leaned back and reached over to the monitors behind him. He then flung his hand toward the desk and the holographic display. A photo of a younger version of the man sitting in front of me hung in the air. Standing next to him was a smiling version of myself. But that wasn't possible.

"Is that—?"

"Your mother." He smiled. "She had a kind heart, but she was incredibly fierce—highly protective of those around her. And when she found out how far Abram Shutton was prepared to go in his efforts to force the next evolution of man, everything changed."

He took a deep breath as he sank back into his chair. "Your mother started to get sick—constantly throwing up, unable to hold anything down. She went for test after test to find out what was wrong. The results kept coming back as inconclusive. She was sent back to Crystal Hills, where she could be under the watchful eye of Abram Shutton himself. And he apparently found some miracle cure to stabilize her system. Only he didn't tell her the truth. She wasn't ill. She was pregnant. And the drugs he gave her to make her feel better were the first round of *in utero* vaccinations for the unborn child she carried. But there was something special in the cocktail that he gave her. It was designed to alter her child's DNA so Rhodon could get one step closer to creating a human who could breathe the atmosphere without a breather."

Eddie's fingers curled into a fist, and a snarl crept across his face. "Your mother had been turned into a breeding specimen. She didn't get a say. She wasn't raped, nothing like that. But during one of her so-called routine exams, she was artificially inseminated. By the time she found out the truth, she was already five months pregnant. She used her abilities to break into the facilities to retrieve her records, to find out who was truly lying to her. The head of NewWave signed the orders. Abram Shutton."

I gaped at him, unable to fully understand what he was telling me. "But Dr. Shutton—"

"Has been experimenting on you your entire life. Just like he experimented on his daughter and son. And his wife."

There was a tension that hung over the room, growing thicker as the seconds ticked by. I wanted to believe that it was fiction, but fiction or not, the man in front of me believed it was entirely true. That information rested on the surface of his mind.

"You asked how your mother could help to develop a technology that would suppress her abilities when those very same abilities could help her hide. She helped to develop that tech *before* she became pregnant with you and *before* she discovered what Abram Shutton had planned for her baby. Natalie couldn't let him experiment on you any more than he already had. Not only had he given you drugs that would alter your DNA, she knew that eventually he would turn you into breeding stock too. So, I helped her escape. You were born three months later—a little early, but healthy."

The anger and tension drained from his face. He smiled as he brought up images of my mother—a woman I vaguely remembered—holding a baby in her arms. He wasn't wrong in saying that I looked so much like her.

"You were so tiny. A sweet little bundle of joy. And you had me wrapped around your little finger. I would have done anything you asked me to do. And with that incredible mind of yours, you made me do some pretty disgusting shit." He chuckled. "Your mother reprimanded you more times than I care to count for abusing your abilities like that. The only one who was able to properly resist your suggestions was your mother—but even she struggled at times."

Eddie finally turned off the holographic display, then got up from his chair and started pacing the small patch of open space next to him. "We moved from place to place, never staying in one spot for too long. If anyone ever found out the truth about you or your mother, it would have spelled certain disaster. So, I continued my work on the tech to disrupt your abilities with your mother's help. Eventually, I got it working on a rudimentary level, but the power generation requirements were enormous. Before I was able to turn the technology into something much smaller, something more portable, a STAR unit hunted us down. That was the first time I had ever seen Natalie in action—unleashing her full fury. She influenced the entire team to kill themselves—and they did. We split up after that. She took you, and I took the tech designed to stop you."

"But my powers grew." I stared into the blank space in front of me, blinking occasionally as the lights of the room changed—becoming darker.

A vague memory came to my mind, one in which I was sitting on the floor, working on a puzzle, and my mother walked the length of the lounge area with a comm-unit in her ear.

✳

"HER STRENGTH IS beyond imagining," my mother had said. "We've had a few close calls. I don't know how much longer I can shield the neighborhood from her. We need your machine."

There was a moment of silence as my mother just nodded.

"Yes, I understand that, but she's only a child. Besides, she misses you. And so do I."

There was a knock on the door. The energy coming from my mother changed—fearful and urgent. "Michaella, you need to hide like only you can hide. No one can find you. Not until Eddie comes to get you, okay? I love you."

I SUDDENLY BLINKED as my vision returned to normal. I looked up at the caring face staring down at me, filled with concern.

"She was on the phone with you the night she was killed." It was more of a statement than a question.

Eddie nodded.

"Then you heard everything that she said to me."

"I did."

"Did you hear what happened after?"

"From the moment she opened the door."

"She didn't commit suicide like I was told, did she?"

"No."

"Do you know who killed her?"

Eddie shook his head. "I don't know who pulled the trigger, but I do know that Abram Shutton was there."

Thirty-Four

I walked through the halls in a daze, my feet on automatic with no destination in mind. All I knew was that somehow the lead geneticist at Rhodon Corporation was responsible for my mother's death. A man I respected.

I knew I was a living experiment. It was the one thing that all of us with White Rabbit syndrome had in common. But everything I thought I knew about my life—about why the Pregutor chose me for training—it was one big fat lie. Not only did Abram Shutton know the truth, he orchestrated it.

But now that I knew the truth, I had no idea what I was going to do about it.

A group of children ran down the hall, laughing and singing, pulling me out of my dazed state and back into the moment. As they ran past, I held out my hand, encouraging them to give me an awkward high-five as they ran by. With each touch, the world around me shifted. A green sheen to my vision. The scent of sweet flowers. A piercing laugh. Images of a loving embrace. And I sent them images in return—of dancing in the purple rain with George, laughing and singing out of tune. As the children continued to run down the halls, they collectively started singing the chorus of the old rock ballad.

I laughed and joined my voice to theirs. But as I continued to watch the children run down the hall in the distance, a painful knowledge squeezed my heart.

None of the children would know what it meant to live free . . . not as long as the Pregutor was hunting them.

I stood tall for the first time in a long time, knowing with certainty what the future held in store for me. I didn't know how or when, but I was going to destroy the Pregutor. And I was going to kill Abram Shutton.

Knowing my path forward, I looked around at my surroundings, stunned. All this time, I had been wondering how the others knew how to navigate this crazy maze of corridors that all looked the same. But at each junction, at knee height, was a little drawing. A child's drawing of cats and dogs. And funny-shaped horses. The odd drawing included sunshine and rainbows.

I brushed my fingers over the stick figures dancing in the purple rain.

Following the childlike drawings, I headed for the training room.

Lucas stood by the door with his arms crossed, smiling like an approving big brother as I walked in. "There she is: the best fighter I've ever trained."

"I'm still not a warrior for hire," I said, "but this is my fight. No one else here has any hope of going up against the likes of Marcus. And before you even think it, no, there is no hope of swaying him to our side. He's fully indoctrinated, believing whatever lies the Pregutor and Rhodon tell him. Even if the truth was put right in front of him, he wouldn't see it."

"So, what do you want to do?"

"Put me in. I need to train. Because when the time comes, I'm the only one who has any hope of going up against him."

Lucas nodded and called out the orders, resetting the sparring ring, putting me in the middle against the others.

I rolled my head, loosening my stiff neck and shoulders. I took several deep breaths to center myself. Standing in the middle of the mat, I prepared to face those who were older, stronger, and more experienced in hand-to-hand combat than I was. But I was the strongest telepath among them. That had to count for something.

I waited for the first attack wave. The buzzing hum grew, the telltale sign that multiple people were trying to push past my mental defenses and into my thoughts. But protecting my mind was instinct now. I pushed outward with a sharp thought, and several people staggered where they stood, shaking their heads and wincing. I smiled, knowing I had blocked the first attack. Now for the next one.

Another wave of buzzing started. At the same time, several warriors crept forward, approaching from all sides. I couldn't stay in the center for long, but I had to stay there long enough so I could work out where the weakest link was—launching a counterattack.

Nancy, my roommate, smiled and nodded once, like she was responding to a command given to her by one of the others. She then charged at me with a yell.

Instead of defending myself against Nancy's attack, I kicked at Scott, who was coming in behind me on silent footing. I then grabbed Johnny's arm and pull him past me and into Grobber's path, using Johnny's weight and forward momentum against both men. From there, I was in pure automatic mode, no longer thinking, just dodging and reacting to the punches and kicks coming my way. Blocking and counter-striking. And with each touch of skin to skin, I dove in and out of their minds, seeing where the next attack was expected to come from.

It became a dance without the music. The imaginary chorus and guitar riffs carried me through into the next steps.

As my mental song moved to the bridge, I spun around to counter the strike that was coming from behind . . . except Cedrick wasn't where I expected him to be. Instead, he came in from my blind spot with a spinning kick to the head—at full force.

The stars spun in every direction, and I fell to my knees. But unlike the previous time when I found the ground, the group backed off and gave me the space I needed to recover.

"Are you okay?" Lucas pulled me to my feet and forced me to face him. He brushed my hair out of my eyes and held my head between his hands. "Why are you holding back?"

I blinked multiple times in the vain attempt to remove the stars from my vision. "I'm not, I swear."

"Yes, you are."

When my vision cleared, I saw the one thing in his eyes I hoped I would never see. Fear.

The world around us grew silent—muted in both noise and color. The only color in my vision was Lucas. "Mike, I get it. You've spent your entire life trying to hide who you are, afraid of how people would react if they ever learned the truth. And if you are forced to fight against STAR, any chance that you had of staying hidden would be gone forever. But war isn't just coming. It's already here." He took a deep breath as he continued to stare into my eyes. "I know about what happened in the plaza in Sector 14, how you just willed a man to stop . . . and he did. And it's not the first time that I've seen you use that power."

An image rested on the surface of his mind of Marcus kneeling on the ground before me. Marcus had taken a knife to his wrists. His face wore a vacant expression.

I shook my head. "No, that never happened."

"Yes, it did. You just don't remember it. But I was there, Mike. I know exactly what you are capable of. And the Pregutor knows it too. It's why Abram Shutton is hunting you. He can't let his greatest experiment escape. Mike, if you want to survive this war, you have to stop holding back. You need to fight with everything that you've got—including your ability to compel a person to bend to your will."

I glanced at the others. They stared at me in return. I took a deep breath, wincing with the pain in my ribs. I swallowed a few times. "Lucas, you don't know what that does to a person. You didn't see what it did to George."

"So she can compel someone," Cedrick said. "Big whoop. So can I."

I slowly shook my head. "Not like this. You might have been present in my head when I escaped from that hospital, but you have never been inside my head during a drop. You haven't seen it all. Not even by half." I looked Cedrick deep in the eyes, but I concentrated on the thoughts of the others. "Don't you get it? They're not hunting us because of our telepathic abilities. They're not even hunting us because of our ability to compel others. We might all be able to read a person's mind, get inside their heads and know what their weaknesses are, but I'm not like you, Cedrick. They're hunting me because I can turn an entire army in on itself."

The energy of the room changed. I pushed Lucas to the side, maintaining physical contact. Together, we dove as Grober rushed forward and struck out at Cedrick.

"What the hell?" Cedrick jumped back, narrowly missing a knife being swung at his middle. He then blocked the next strike, only to be hit over the head from behind.

"Because of who I am, Cedrick, because of what I can do, I don't need to lift a finger to attack a person. I've never had to. And the more trained a person is, the more I can bend them to my will."

Cedrick blocked and counterattacked in a flurry of motion. He was pulled to the side, flung at the spaces that were off the mats, thrown to his stomach. He was then picked up and punched by another. Cedrick blocked a downward strike, another knife, but he missed the knife that came in from the side. As the blade pierced his abdomen, he screamed out in pain—pain that I felt too, making it difficult to breathe.

Lucas pulled me into his arms, his lips to my cheek. "Let them go, little one. I think he gets it now." His familiar thoughts push in on my mind, and I melted into his memories of the first time we met—and his toothy food cube grin.

Able to breathe again, I nodded and turned my mental attention to the group surrounding Cedrick. "Let him go," I commanded. Tears streamed down my cheeks. "Your minds are your own again."

The noise of the world crashed in on me. The buzzing hum turned to a scream.

"Cedrick!" someone shouted. "Oh shit, someone get Beth!"

Thirty-Five

I careened through the halls, running into the med bay ahead of the group carrying Cedrick. It hurt to breathe, but that didn't matter. Saving Cedrick's life had to take priority.

I pulled a surgical gurney into the center of the room and positioned freestanding lights exactly how Beth would have wanted them. I then pulled a surgical kit from the cabinets in the corner and prepped the tray with the tools that Beth would need. I even had a surgical gown waiting for Beth by the basin, ready to don as soon as she scrubbed in.

When Beth came in with Cedrick, everything was prepped and ready.

"How did you . . .?" Beth gawked at me.

"You told me. I was reading your mind as you were racing through the halls to get him back here."

Beth pursed her lips as she glared at Lucas. She was clearly still peeved that Lucas hadn't told her how the shield had never worked against me.

Lucas shook his head. "Not now. Cedrick first."

Beth nodded and went to work, looking over everything I had pulled out for her. "He may be unconscious, but we're going to need the anesthetic as well."

"I'll get it," I said. "Blue cabinet, right?"

Beth nodded. "And we'll need—"

"The needles too. In the drawers next to the blue cabinet, second drawer down."

"I guess I know who my nurse is. Everyone else out."

As Beth scrubbed in, I continued to set up the ventilation machine, seeing each step necessary in Beth's head. When Beth returned in a surgical gown, I went about my tasks of hanging IVs and getting fluid bags ready.

"I'll finish," Beth said, taking the IV lines. "Go scrub in."

I just nodded and absorbed the mental instructions from Beth. With clean surgical scrubs on and my dirt-covered clothes in the laundry pile in the corner, I darted to the sink to clean my hands. I resisted the urge to rush it, ensuring that every single particle of dirt was scrubbed out from under my nails, following Beth's mental instructions precisely. With dry hands, I donned a pair of gloves and a mask and rushed back to Beth's side, waiting for further instructions.

Beth looked at me . . . really looked at me. *"Can you really hear my thoughts?"* she said mentally.

I just nodded.

"And if I think in pictures?" Beth then envisioned how to monitor the oxygen and the carbon dioxide output on the ventilation machine.

"I'm on it," I said aloud, knowing that Beth wouldn't be able to hear my thoughts.

Behind me, Beth took in a slow, deep breath. And she gave off the distinct impression that she had a lot of questions that would eventually need answers. But not right now. Cedrick was more important.

We worked in relative silence. Occasionally, I called out the numbers that Beth asked for mentally. And there was the beeping of the machines and the whoosh of the ventilator.

But Beth never said a word. All instructions were mentally given as pictures, turning Beth and me into a cohesive unit.

With the last stitch, Beth took one last breath and placed the tools back on the tray. She then stepped back from the surgical gurney and closed her eyes.

She pulled off her bloody gloves and threw them into the biological waste. Peeling off her surgical gown and putting it into the laundry to be sterilized, she finally spoke aloud. "I don't think I've ever had surgery go so smoothly before. You did a fantastic job setting everything up before I got here . . . even if it did mean that you could hear past the shield. I'm still irritated by that, by the way."

I sighed as I disposed of my bloodied surgical gear the same way she had. "I know you don't like it, but it saved his life, didn't it?"

Beth smirked as she nodded. It was like she was struggling to process how the world was changing. "He'll live." She collapsed onto the stool that rested against the wall. "Though he's going to be weak for a while. I may have to give him a transfusion at some point, but we have plenty of people around who share his blood type. What the hell happened?"

"Training exercise."

"I might have to have a word with Lucas about his training exercises. I think it's safe to say that this one went horribly wrong."

"Actually, it went exactly as planned." I sat on a stool next to Beth, turning my attention to the man on the gurney in the center of the room. How could I have let this get so out of hand? Because of me, someone I had come to think of as a brother was now badly injured. "Lucas kept telling me that I couldn't hold back, that I had to fight with everything that I've got."

"Are you telling me that you stabbed him? How the hell did you manage to stab him that many times and come away from it without any injuries of your own?"

"I wouldn't say that I've got no injuries of my own. I probably broke a rib. But how I stabbed him . . . I compelled someone else to stab him for me." I turned and stared at Beth directly in her eyes. "I compelled all of them to stab him. He didn't stand a chance."

"Are you telling me that you're capable of controlling the thoughts of an entire army?"

"I don't know about an entire army, but thirty fourth gens? Yeah, not a problem."

"But how? Not even Cedrick is able to do that, not all at once, anyway."

"I don't understand all of it, but what I do know is that Cedrick's abilities and my mother's abilities were similar. And with each generation, the abilities get stronger. According to Eddie, my mother was able to compel a group of highly trained telepaths, turning them against each other. But a single STAR unit for me . . ." I licked my lips and sighed. "Now that the drugs are out of my system, it's just a jaunt in the purple rain."

Beth's eyes widened, like they were about to pop out of her head. Her hand subtly moved to cover her belly. She got up from her perch and started pacing the small lounge area in the corner of the med bay.

"Oh, my god." I stared at Beth, whose mind was racing over terminology that didn't make any sense. But I didn't need to understand the terminology to know what it was I saw. It was just a glimpse, but I saw it. "You're pregnant." I glanced at Cedrick, unconscious on the gurney. "And Cedrick is the father."

Slowly, Beth nodded, and tears threatened to spring forth.

"Beth, you said it yourself: he'll be fine. And the day your baby is born . . ." I grinned and bit my bottom lip. I envisioned Cedrick wearing the exact same expression that Eddie wore when he was telling me of my own birth. "Cedrick is going to make an amazing father."

"If only that was true." She looked at me with a *stay-out-of-it* look, but there was a hint of *please-keep-pushing* screaming out from her eyes.

"What are you talking about? He adores you. You don't have to be a telepath to see that. Surely, if you talk it over with Cedrick—"

"He doesn't know, and he can never know."

"Why not?"

"Because it would crush him."

"I don't understand."

Beth slumped onto the couch and leaned forward, resting her elbows against her knees. "When I came to Crystal Hills—when I started working for Rhodon—I was given a series of injections that were mandatory for all new citizens of Crystal Hills who were biologically female. The city can only support so many people. As such, steps need to be taken to ensure that any population growth is sustainable. The drugs I was given . . ." She swallowed and looked up at the ceiling, blinking constantly, like she was trying to keep the tears from falling.

I sat on the ground before her and placed my hands on her knees, encouraging her to look at me. "I know the drugs you're talking about. I was given them too. They were part of my annual packet."

"Not these." Beth inhaled deeply. "The drugs you were given would have been designed to prevent conception. The drugs I was given were designed to permanently alter my physiology such that I'm unable to carry a baby to full term without medical treatments from Rhodon. The government wanted a way to ensure that all children born within the walls of Crystal Hills were given the *in utero* vaccinations—no exception. If a mother chooses to not get the treatments, if they choose to avoid the *in utero* vaccinations, their body would work against them and they would have a miscarriage. Because of the drugs I was given when I first arrived in Crystal Hills, I can never have a baby . . . not unless I go back. And they would kill me the moment I set foot inside the door."

"You could be wrong. Drugs don't always work the way they're meant to. I mean, look at me. Miransine was supposed to suppress my abilities, but here we are."

Tears streamed down Beth's cheeks. "I'm not wrong about this. This is my third pregnancy in two years. The first two didn't make it past the fourth month."

I sighed in defeat. "Now, I understand. You're afraid that if Cedrick finds out you're pregnant, he'll do something stupid—like try to break into a medical clinic to get you the treatments you need."

"It's worse than that. There's only one medical center in the city that stocks the drugs I need."

"Let me guess . . . Rhodon Central in Sector 14."

The silence that hung between us was all the answer that I needed.

I continually shifted my attention between the woman before me and the man sleeping on the gurney in the middle of the room. "How desperately do you want this baby?"

"It doesn't matter what I want. My body will make the decision for me. Without those treatments, I will suffer another miscarriage in roughly three months."

"Then we have three months." I got to my feet and headed for the door.

"Where are you going?"

"To do something stupid."

THIRTY-SIX

I EXITED THE TUNNEL NETWORK exactly where Eddie told me I would. Sector 7, one of the sectors on the outer rim that still had the luxury of a protective dome. The filtration system was glitchy, so it wasn't as clean as the air in the inner sectors, but at least I didn't need a breather. I maneuvered out of the shadows and took one last calming breath before I immersed myself into the noise of the world.

"Mike, what the hell do you think you're doing?" Cedrick's mental voice carried a hint of anger mixed with fear.

I smirked. *"Sleeping Beauty finally decided to wake up. Took you long enough to join me on this merry ride."*

"Mike, please, I don't care what it is you think you're doing, but you need to come back now. You'll be captured."

"That's kind of the idea."

Silence.

I had no way of knowing with certainty what was going on back at Sanctuary, but I hoped that Eddie and Lucas were filling him in on the plan—parts of it, anyway. There were some aspects he couldn't be allowed to know. Not yet. For his own protection. In case I failed. But I was the only one who could do this.

"Mike . . ." The quality of his mental voice changed. There was a hint of sadness, mixed with desperation and a

resignation of how he had no control over what would happen next. *"Lucas says to make it good. He says to go all in and don't hold back."*

"Anything else?"

"Nothing, except that the holes have been sealed. You can't come back even if you wanted to."

I tried to smile, though I knew he couldn't see it. *"I know you don't understand, Cedrick, but trust me . . . And trust Eddie and Lucas. This is the only way forward."*

I pulled my hood tight around my face and stepped out from my hiding spot and into the crowded streets. I had expected to be overwhelmed by the thoughts of others, but the world was filled with a silence that I had never experienced before. It was peaceful. Calm. And it came with a knowledge that I was the one in control.

A passerby bumped into me, and an image flashed into my mind of a man shedding the uniform of oppression and dancing naked in the streets. I looked over my shoulder at the man who had bumped into me and grinned. Lucas wanted me to make it good, so . . .

"You!"

The man looked over his shoulder. He didn't turn far, but it was enough to capture his line of sight—a direct channel into his mind and soul.

"Yeah, you. You want to dance naked through the streets? Do it."

A dazed expression came over his face, and he took off his clothes, layer by layer. The others in the street scurried around the guy as he disrobed—and with his last article of clothing gone, he started to sing and dance.

One person wolf whistled while others laughed. But most people tried to avoid the crazy dancer in the streets.

I caught the eyes of another man, who frowned and took a wide berth around the naked, dancing man. *"Join him."* Without any hesitation, the previously grumpy man removed his clothing and joined the naked man dancing among the gathering crowd.

"All of you join them."

Some were eager to strip off as fast as they could, while others fought against the urges they were feeling. But soon, the group of naked dancers swelled to fill the entire street. Someone started playing music, exciting the crowd further.

I just stood there, laughing and clapping my hands. The feeling of freedom could be tasted in the air. The mixture of sweet perfume combined with sweat as the energy associated with the dancing became more vigorous. Energetic music drove the crowd into a gleeful frenzy. I inhaled as deeply as I could, allowing the happy thoughts to fill my mind, taking the darkness away from my soul.

The world possessed a lilac sheen, wavering with strings of pink.

"Security has been dispatched to your area," Cedrick said in my mind. *"The drones should be there any second."*

I slowly turned on the spot. In the distance, a small cluster of dark drones moved closer. But these drones were much bigger than I was used to seeing. Something hung below them, swiveling in every direction.

Shit. I rushed to pull out my breather—the one I stole from Marcus. I pulled on the straps to ensure a tight seal around my mouth and nose. I took one last look at the dancers.

"Dance until you can't dance anymore. After your sleep, you'll remember only joy, but you will be in complete control over your own lives again. And my gift to you all for allowing

me this moment of bliss: I leave you with an imprint of my mind and the knowledge on how to protect yourselves from others like me."

I wasn't sure if that last suggestion would work, if the crowd really would be protected. But if just the suggestion of dancing in the streets could cause such chaos, then perhaps I could do something to protect the citizens of Crystal Hills from Rhodon Corporation in my own way.

The cluster of drones settled over the top of the crowd and released a series of gas bombs filled with a blue-tinted gas. Whatever the gas was, it stung my eyes, but I resisted the urge to wipe them. That would only make the stinging worse.

One by one, the naked dancers fell to the ground. Feet and arms graced the pavement in every direction.

Marching footsteps echoed in the distance. It looked like an entire battalion had been sent after me, all wearing full tactical gear. And if the intel that Lucas and Eddie were able to get their hands on was anything to go by, many of them would likely be carrying portable energy shields, shields supposedly designed to block my abilities.

I meandered down the street away from the unconscious dancers. The blue air thinned.

Armored security guards surrounded me on all sides, leaving me with nowhere to run. Not that I had any intention of running.

"I hope you know what you're doing, Mike."

"We're about to find out. Just in case this goes horribly wrong, look after them, Cedrick. If I fail…"

"Just focus on what you need to do. You've committed to this, so do it."

I tapped on the device that hung around my neck, an amplifier unit that Lucas had given me before I left. "I wouldn't come out from behind your shields if I were you. Or you might enjoy a little dancing in the streets like these people did." Never mind that the shields wouldn't have protected them either. Not from me. But I didn't want to tip my hand too early. Besides, all I wanted was to get their attention, and I certainly had that.

There was a small thump against my shoulder. A tranquilizer dart rested on the ground by my boot. I picked it up, still fully loaded.

"Holy cow, that's some jacket you have."

I smiled. *"Standard issue."* When you didn't want your operatives to wear something as obvious as tactical vests, you gave them jackets with Kevlar lining—a little detail that not all of PentWave or STAR knew about. But I knew. Tam made sure I knew. I might have hated everything that Rhodon stood for, but they did provide their undercover operatives with the best gear possible.

I looked up at the central drone and gave it a little wave. And I held the dart in my fist, preparing to use it as a weapon.

A transport unit flew overhead, and a group of soldiers dropped to the ground in the middle of the cordoned off area. They fanned out to surround me. Their deep navy blue jackets bellowed in the slight breeze. Thin purple stripes ran down their sleeves.

The STAR.

I was used to fighting against other telepaths now, but this fight wasn't going to be like the sparring matches back in Sanctuary. For one, these telepaths all held rifles. The muzzles pointed in my direction. My jacket might have had a Kevlar lining, but any bullet strike was still going to hurt like hell. And if enough bullets hit me, it could still take me down. All the STAR needed was an excuse to open fire.

Two of the STAR broke formation, stepping closer, their weapons still raised. Even though I couldn't see their faces, I knew exactly who the Pregutor had chosen to send after me.

"So glad you could join my little party, Marcus." I tried to keep my voice cheery and light, although my heart was breaking. "I was hoping you would come. But I'm surprised to see Jody here. I wasn't aware you had joined STAR."

Jody didn't respond. If anything, she just stood there, like a robot ready to attack. But a sense of pride, layered with a hint of sadness, radiated off her person. It colored the air around her with a greenish-blue haze.

"What the hell are you doing, Mike?" Marcus lowered his hood. He had on a new breather, more state-of-the-art than the one I stole from him. The air around him carried a reddish-orange haze. And specs of black shot out in every direction.

I tried to remember if I had ever seen color surrounding either of them before. But maybe this new vision was just an extension of my abilities. How many other aspects of my power had I been cut off from because of those stupid drugs?

"I thought it was obvious," I said. "I was hosting a party."

"Mike, this is not like you," Jody said, also removing her hood.

"How do you know?"

"Because I know you. You would never do anything that could expose the rest of us."

"We were already exposed. Terrorist attacks throughout the city are being blamed on those with audimentia—people being killed, publicly executed, for crimes they didn't commit. And according to the news reports, some of those attacks have been done in my name. Can you blame me for wanting to have a bit of harmless fun instead of violence?"

The others looked at one another, slowly shaking their heads. They were clearly having full on conversations with one another. I wondered how much of it was conversation aided by technology and how much of it was telepathy.

"Stand down, Mike." The mental energies coming from Marcus were all wrong. He wasn't the smart-ass I knew so well and had come to . . . *respect* was too strong a word; *tolerate* was more like it.

"Or what? You'll take me down yourself?" I shrugged. "Good luck with that. I'm a better fighter than you are."

Marcus laughed. "You really think so?" He readjusted his grip on his rifle, raising it to take aim.

I laughed as I put my hands out to the side in a pathetic display of surrender. "You have to fight with a gun? You don't even have the guts to face me with nothing but your hands and fists. Like I said, I'm a better fighter than you are."

If looks could kill, Marcus's eyes would have been shooting laser beams.

He lowered his aim and unclipped his rifle from his jacket and passed it to Jody. He then pulled out a baton from under his jacket and twirled it around, loosening his wrist.

Like on command, the other STAR took three steps back. Half of them passed their rifles to the team member on their left, pulling out batons too, stepping forward again to form a tight circle around Marcus and me.

I lowered my hood, giving me full use of my peripheral vision to hunt down the weakness in the group surrounding me. I held no delusions; this little stunt was going to earn me more bruises, but if I wanted to survive, I needed to slip into the mind of the enemy—starting with the weakest link.

Marcus sauntered toward me. The cockiness poured off him in a salty perfume and a haze of yellow. I so wanted to put him back in his place, to smack him from side to side and land him flat on his back. He lunged at me, swinging his baton and spinning around with a series of kicks.

It was a rookie move. Something easily dodged.

Was it possible that his fighting abilities had always been this rudimentary? Even in our youth, I had no problems staying ahead of him, but now I wasn't even breaking a sweat. Without any effort, I ducked, bent backward, or jumped to the side, kicking him in the abdomen and occasionally his head. A few times, I came close to using the tranquilizer dart against him, bringing my fist around to press the needle into his neck. But Marcus had always been physically stronger than me. He was able to use his brute strength to stop me from pushing the dart into its target. He even tried to grab my arm and twist it up behind me, but I flipped over him and then under him in ways he clearly didn't know I could do.

I somersaulted past his onslaught of kicks and found myself face to face with a STAR soldier. I was close enough to him that if he had chosen to strike out, I would have been hit. But I was the one in control.

I smiled and stared directly into his eyes. *"Time to help me, jerk."*

Without warning, the soldier struck the man standing next to him. I ducked as my reluctant comrade swung his leg over my head, kicking Marcus behind me. He then charged at Marcus, taking him off my hands.

I spun and dodged out of the way, catching the eye of a soldier standing among the outer circle. Time to call my army.

Soldiers behind the wall of shields dropped whatever units they held and charged the STAR that stood around the fighting pair in the middle. Chaos reigned. No one knew who was on whose side. With the mental defenses of the STAR distracted, I seized the opportunity to enlarge the fighting group. Some of the soldiers fought against my suggestions, unwilling to fight for me. But this was the true nature of my power.

A roar sounded behind me, and I kicked out, not really knowing, or caring, who was attacking me. To my pleasant surprise, my foot came in contact with Marcus's solar plexus, sending him flying to his ass. But my clear dominance in hand-to-hand combat didn't stop him. I spun around and kicked the pistol from his hand before he could properly take aim and fire.

Marcus performed a kick-up jump, launching himself back onto his feet. He then wove his hands in front of him into a guarded posture, like he was inviting me to strike.

The buzzing hum started to build in my mind, the familiar tentacles of someone trying to reach into my thoughts, pushing hard.

In the distance, the refrain chords of *Purple Rain* echoed off the surrounding buildings.

"And there's my cue. Cedrick, tell Eddie to start running the Bandersnatch protocol."

"He's on it. And he says to wish you luck. And Mike . . ." The hesitation in his voice was almost too much to bear. He didn't understand why I was risking everything like this, but he would . . . eventually.

"I'll see you on the other side." Then I turned my full attention to the danger in front of me.

My army of unwilling soldiers kept anyone not under my control off my back, giving me the freedom to focus on Marcus. The buzzing in my head grew louder, and the edges of my vision started to go black. I had to make it look good.

Marcus struck at me again with a series of punches and kicks. One of his punches connected with the side of my head, and my concentration wavered. The mental connection between us threatened to take me under. But I knew how to properly defend myself against the mental attacks. I was the one in control.

"Enjoy the dance, Marcus."

I let him into my memories of when we were children. Our mutual dislike of one another was no secret to authorities at O'quv Lageri. Yet, they still assigned us to the same training unit. It was difficult to get past our differences, but when we did, we were an unstoppable force. And somewhere along the way, Marcus had become like a brother . . . a brother that I hated, but a brother nonetheless. And I knew he thought of me as a sister, something I had gleaned from him when we last walked side by side . . . as he escorted me to the chair room.

The world shifted from the red of anger to the green of guilt.

And I bore another strike to the side of my head, making my vision blur.

I staggered on the spot. As I turned to face Marcus again, I stared directly down the muzzle of a pistol pointed at my head. I might have been a better fighter, but at this distance, he would have had no issue creating a new hole in my head.

"I don't want to hurt you, Mike."

"And I don't want to hurt you." I could have dug into his mind and had him turn the gun on himself. Perhaps one day I would, but not now. Right now, it was more important to let this play out however it wanted to.

"Please, Mike, I'm begging you. Stand down."

I nodded once. "Since you asked me so nicely. Oh, and Marcus . . . You can tell them to stop the music now. It doesn't work anymore. I know the truth."

A familiar presence radiated behind me, but before I could process it, something blunt hit me over the head and I fell to the ground. I rolled over onto my back. Even through the blurry sight, I could still make out the person dressed in the white suit standing over me.

"You don't know all of it."

Thirty-Seven

THE WORLD WAS DARK. There was no sound. And the back of my head throbbed. No matter how much I wished for it to be different, the pain and the darkness wouldn't go away.

I tried to move my head, but something held me firmly in place, pressing up against my ears. I tried to lift my arms, but my wrists were restrained, pressed tightly to my sides. My legs were held out flat. There was a slight rocking motion, back and forth, like I was in a transport of some kind—likely restrained on a transport gurney. Likely blindfolded with noise-canceling headphones on, unable to hear what was going on around me.

But I had other methods of hearing.

If I was right about this, they likely gave me with a high dose of Miransine in an attempt to suppress my abilities. But even highly doped up, I could still hear the strongest of minds around me. Though they didn't know that.

I counted to five as I inhaled, then counted to five again on the exhale. All the while, I focused on the world beyond the darkness.

I was fairly confident that the Pregutor believed that Marcus was strong enough to break through my mental defenses. So, he had to be nearby. And even though something had changed in him, I still knew him. The odds were Jody was with him, lending her mental strength to his. I searched for the two mental voices I had known since childhood, inviting them in.

"How could Mike betray us like that? It's not like her."

"Jody, focus. If she wakes up, she'll hear your wandering thoughts."

"How can you be sure of that?"

"Because she was always the strongest among us. That's why they sent both of us after her—because only together, we're stronger than she is."

"Are you sure about that? Are you absolutely sure? I don't think all those people were dancing naked in the streets of their own accord. And what about those guards who attacked us from behind?"

There was a mental silence, followed by a mental growl. *"Just stay focused. This will all be over soon."*

The motion of the world changed. There was a sudden jolt to the side, then a tilting motion that moved back and forth.

The pressure from around my ears released, and the darkness lifted from my eyes.

"I know you're awake," Marcus said. "You can stop pretending. You were listening in on my conversation with Jody."

I slowly inhaled and opened my eyes. The sudden brightness was painful to start with, and I squinted, turning away from the bright light. Slowly, figures and random shapes came into focus. The circular muzzle of a pistol came into focus first.

"One move—just one—and I'll take great pleasure in blowing a giant hole through your brain. Good luck in trying to compel me to do something that I don't want to do then."

I looked down the length of the barrel to the person holding it. Marcus possessed a level of calm that I had never seen in him before, but there was something else there too. Loathing. Hatred. Anger. The red cloud surrounding him deepened in color . . . to almost a black.

I used my peripheral vision to take in the rest of the scene. Guns pointed at me from every direction, all wielded by those wearing black uniforms with blue and purple stripes running down the sleeves. Some faces I knew; I had grown up with them. But other faces I had never seen before. Most appeared to be in their late teens, but a few were in their thirties, possibly even their forties. I couldn't know for sure, but the older ones in the group had to have been part of the experiments when my mother was conscripted. It meant that I was more powerful than they were, but they had the experience to back up their skills. I wasn't ready to test my abilities against the older ones yet.

How many of them knew the truth like I did? How many of them were in full control of their mental abilities? Without the drugs to hinder them?

Tam stepped through a parting in the black uniformed soldiers. Their white suit blended into the white walls. "Michaella, you have been sick. You should have told me about the voices. I could have done something about it."

"Like strip away my memories again?" I stared at Tam, ignoring everyone around us.

"If such a thing was even possible, why would I do that?"

"Because you didn't want me to remember what happened to George. You didn't want me to remember what happened to my mother."

Silence hung between us. I could have pushed past whatever barriers Tam used to shield their thoughts, but what would be the point? Not only would I tip my hand too soon, but I wouldn't remember anything that I had learned. They were going to strip my memories away again. That was why Eddie and I had taken the precautions we had.

Never mind that they would know about those precautions too, but it was worth the risk.

"I know you believe I am the bad guy here, but you need to trust me. I have always had your best interests at heart."

"If that was true, then why did you lie to me?"

"I have never once lied to you, Michaella."

"Really? Because the way I see it, you've been lying to me for years. You knew my mother. And I'm not talking about what was just in the medical files. You knew her personally. She trusted you." I continued to focus solely on Tam. The way they looked at me . . . I had never noticed it before, but there was a hint of pain in Tam's eyes—guilt. I focused on the memory fragments from the night my mother died, recalling the details like I was five years old again. "You were there the night she was killed, weren't you? It was you who knocked on the door. You showed up that night, trying to convince her to stop running. You said you had a way to protect me from Abram Shutton's experiments. But you lied to her. They found us because you led them straight to us. You knew all along what they would do to me, who they would turn me into, and you wanted it to happen. When those men broke down the door, she turned to you and asked you what you had done."

The quality of the memories shifted, becoming dark around the edges. And the viewpoint changed. I was no longer the little girl cowering in the closet. Instead, I looked directly into my mother's face, hearing her words. As her lips moved, I vocalized what she had said all those years ago.

"How could you betray your own daughter?"

Tam's expressionless face was plastered into place, but I could hear the mental response as clearly as if Tam had said it aloud. *"Because it was the only way to protect you."*

"I am sorry, Michaella, but we now need to transfer you to the chair. You have two choices: you either volunteer to go into the chair yourself, or we put you there forcibly. But if you resist . . ."

I smiled. "I could find myself in Ward 27. Don't worry, Tam, I'll go voluntarily. You'll learn all my secrets whether I like it or not. This way, I can at least maintain some sense of dignity. But in return for playing the good girl, I'd like to ask one favor."

"I cannot make any promises."

With a slight nod, I continued to smile. "When I come to—after you've stolen my memories—please tell me that George is dead, so I don't try to go hunting for him, believing you've shipped him off somewhere. As long as I know he's dead, and that you're not lying about it, I'll probably be more compliant."

"I can do that. He was your friend, after all. You have the right to mourn your friend." Tam looked at the others. "Release her restraints. Help her into the chair."

Marcus holstered his weapon and came forward, releasing the restraints that held me to the gurney. He then wrapped his fingers tightly around my upper arm and pulled me into a seated position. The tension that radiated off him, radiating through his fingers, pushed in on my mind. And he was having doubts.

"It's okay, Marcus. What will be will be. Sometimes, we have to be willing to follow the White Rabbit down the hole, even if that hole doesn't lead to Wonderland. I know what

I'm doing. I won't resist. What would be the point? Besides, I still need to prove to you that I'm the better fighter."

He smirked. "You can think that all you want, but we both know the truth."

"Do we?"

I wanted our locked gaze to last an eternity, but not because of any warped sense of false hope that he would suddenly flip to my side. No, I wanted to know what lies they had told him to keep him faithful.

"I don't want to fight you, Marcus," I said. "Not yet, anyway. There are more important things to focus on right now—like getting into the damned chair." I smirked, but he didn't return the smile.

His grip on my arm loosened, and he gave a slight nod. "What will be will be." His voice was soft and his lips hardly moved, but the underlining message was clear. If I did anything that would negate his trust, I would suffer the consequences. He moved back to give me the room needed to swing my legs around and stand.

The others in the room shifted their stances, adjusting their grips on their pistols. Tam stood by the chair with a syringe—no doubt a sedative.

I sat in the chair and waited patiently as Marcus applied the restraints to my arms and legs. I pressed my head against the headrest while Tam injected the contents of the syringe into the crook of my elbow. Tam then reclined the chair slightly and applied the restraints to my forehead.

I looked up at Tam. "You can tell me. I won't remember it, anyway. Was my mother really your daughter?"

Tam gave a short nod, but never said a word.

I closed my eyes, trying to hold back the tears. My entire world had just changed. Only time would tell if it was for the better.

Thirty-Eight

The bongo drums inside my skull echoed louder and louder, the pulse beating at my temples. I tried to press my hand to my forehead, but my wrists were handcuffed to the railing at the sides of the bed.

I groaned as I opened my eyes, assaulted by the brightness of the room. My head pounded even more.

"Michaella? Michaella Davison? Can you hear me?"

"I prefer Mike." I inhaled, and the sterile notes of disinfectant curled the hairs on the inside of my nose. "Where am I?"

"You're in the hospital. Don't you remember?"

"How can anyone remember anything with their head pounding like this?"

Something cold washed into my veins.

"This should help. The relief should be almost instantaneous."

As the owner of the voice promised, the headache lessened. The light no longer stung, though my vision was still blurred. All I could make out were blobs of color—a hint of orange-peach lined up next to something white and gray. A window perhaps?

I looked down at myself. Even through the blurry vision, I could see the pale yellow of the scratchy garment I wore. Not my color at all.

"How did I get here?"

"They brought you in two days ago, unconscious. How you came to be unconscious is unknown."

A warm hand rested gently on my forearm, drawing my attention to the nurse. Slowly, the woman's smile came into focus.

"Why am I handcuffed to the bed?"

"Because, my dear, in your unconscious state, you were thrashing around. At one point, you removed your IV. Your fists pack one hell of a wallop, even in your unconscious state." The nurse pointed to the red hues around her cheek that were slowly turning purple. "But don't you worry about that. It's not the first time I've worn a black eye because of a patient, and it likely won't be the last time either. It's one of the downsides of working in this ward."

"And which ward is that?" Though I wasn't sure if I wanted to know the answer.

"I'm sorry, Michaella, but you've been admitted to Ward 27."

"Ward 27?" Goosebumps ran up and down my arms, although the room was a comfortable, moderate temperature. Ward 27 was the last place on Earth I wanted to be. "Why?"

The nurse took a deep breath as she checked the IV. "Your audimentia has progressed to the final stages. You're hearing voices, aren't you? And those voices are trying to convince you to harm yourself and others, aren't they? It's okay. We'll make you better. There are new treatments available now. I'm sure we can help you get back up on your feet, living out the remainder of your days quietly."

I looked at the nurse intently. *"Let me go. Remove these handcuffs."*

The nurse smiled and gently patted my forearm. "I should inform the doctor that you're awake."

The door to the room closed slowly behind the nurse, followed by a click and a soft buzz. Even if I hadn't been handcuffed to the bed, there was no doubt in my mind that I was a prisoner, locked up behind a door that required an electronic keycode to open. If only I could remember what I had done to deserve being locked up in this place.

I took several slow, steady breaths, mentally singing the chorus of my favorite song. If I was going to figure out how to get out of this mess, I had to stay calm and level-headed.

Damn it. Why was I in Ward 27?

I pushed my head deeper into the pillow as I tried to remember what happened. Everything was a blur. The only thing that was clear in my memory was Tam's face in their white suit. Everything else was hazy—like my peripheral vision was blocked by something. But Tam had been a big part of my life for as long as I could remember. If I could just focus on Tam, then maybe . . .

Keeping my eyes closed, holding Tam's pale features in my thoughts, I conjured a scene where Tam was surrounded by guards with Marcus at the back. There was something about Marcus's face . . . A contorted snarl. Murderous eyes. Pure hatred and loathing. In my mind's eye, Marcus lunged forward with his hands around my throat—and I struggled to breathe against the imaginary grip.

My eyes shot open. I had to recenter myself again . . . humming *Purple Rain.*

I took mental stock of my body. Every inch of me was sore, like I had been in the fight of my life. And given my current situation, I probably had. Faint bruises graced my upper left arm, barely visible under the sleeve of the hospital gown. As I contorted around to get a better look, I envisioned a tight hand squeezing my arm, cutting off the circulation to my fingers.

Marcus's hand. When had he done that?

I then turned my attention to the nurse who had left the room. According to the nurse, I had given her a black eye while in an unconscious state. Was that even possible?

An image of a nurse lying on the ground at my feet flashed through my mind. If this was a memory, could that have been the incident that landed me in Ward 27?

I closed my eyes again, trying to discern the details of the unconscious nurse at my feet. But the nurse wasn't a woman. She was a man. And he wasn't a nurse. He had a mustache. All medical personnel were meant to follow clean shaven protocols.

The door creaked open, and an older doctor walked in. Dr. Abram Shutton. He was the specialist who had been treating my White Rabbit syndrome since I was a little girl. I only ever saw him when my symptoms were out of control, and the fact that he was here now was not a good sign.

"Michaella," he said with a smile. "How is my favorite patient today?" He moved to the side of the bed where the monitors were, scanning through the readouts on the various screens. He waved his hand in front of him, like he was flicking through paperwork on his virtual display. "You promised me that you would come to me if your treatments were no longer working as they should. I told you that you were approaching the limits of Miransine. We can't give you anymore, or it will cause other problems."

"Like shutting my heart down, right?" I tried to say it with a chirpy voice, but it felt hollow considering the handcuffs.

"Right." Dr. Shutton wore a regretful smile—the look that all doctors got when their patient tried to see the positive in a bad situation. He sighed and rested his hand on my forearm. "Why didn't you come to me? I have been your doctor since you were five years old. No one knows more about your case than I do."

"No offense, Doc, but that makes you old."

He chuckled. "I guess that does."

I looked up into his eyes. They were the kind eyes that got me out of the foster system and into the NeuWave program, getting me the medical treatment I needed. It was because of him that I was accepted into O'quv Lageri. It was because of Dr. Shutton that I had a well-paid job with Rhodon Corporation. I owed him everything. I owed him my life.

"I didn't want to disappoint you."

"Oh, Michaella, you could never disappoint me. You're like a daughter to me. I will always be proud of that little girl who came into my life all those years ago." He caressed my cheek, and I sank into his touch. There was a brief image of a young boy staring out the window, but before I could process what I was seeing, the physical contact between us was severed. The image of the boy was gone.

"Now, let's get you out of these handcuffs and have some tests done. And let's find out what is really going on inside that head of yours. There are a few different treatment regimens I would like to try to help stave off the final stages of audimentia a bit longer. I'm not ready to mourn over your body just yet."

"Do I need to remind you that you're old and that the odds are I'll outlive you?" I smiled, trying to ignore the fears that had hung over me my entire life.

"Here's hoping, child. Here's hoping."

"Doc, can I ask a question?"

"Just the one?" His light spirit had always managed to keep me calm—especially considering he was treating me for a disease that would eventually kill me.

"Okay, more than one, but I would really like to know why I've been admitted to Ward 27."

The old man took a deep breath. "I didn't want you in here, but until we know the true extent of how far your disease has progressed, we can't take any chances. No doubt the nurse has told you that you were becoming a danger to yourself and to others. But it was more than that. In your delusional state, you killed a man."

"What?" It was like the air had been sucked out of the room. I thought I had problems inhaling before, but now I couldn't breathe in or out. My chest grew tight, holding in the last of my oxygen.

Again, images of the hairy-faced not-nurse on the ground came to mind. Blood pooled around his head.

"Michaella, it'll be okay."

I looked up at the doctor, focusing on his kind eyes.

"I pulled a few strings and managed to placate law enforcement. As long as you remain under my care, you won't be prosecuted. You weren't in control of your own actions. The voices were."

"So, that's it then. I'm a resident of Ward 27 for the rest of my life—however long that may be."

"No." Dr. Shutton encouraged me to sit up, then pulled me into a hug. "Like I said before, you're like a daughter to me, and I will not have my daughter locked up in this place forever. Now, let's get you tested, so we can work out what we need to do next."

The nurse returned with a wheelchair, and a guard armed to the teeth. There was a pistol strapped to the guard's right thigh, a sheathed dagger strapped to the left. An expanding baton sat in a pocket on the guard's belt, along with a taser ready to draw at a moment's notice. But that didn't account for any of the skills the guard might have had in hand-to-hand combat.

With a helmet and goggles in place directly over the breathing mask, the guard's identifying features were concealed. I had no idea who they had brought in to keep me under close watch, but judging by the blue and purple stripes running down their sleeves, I didn't want to piss them off.

"Is that ride for me?" I tried to keep my tone light.

The nurse smiled, and Dr. Shutton helped me jump down from the hospital bed and into the chair.

"Do I need to be handcuffed to the chair?"

The doctor shook his head. "I think we can forgo the prisoner treatment this time."

I glanced at the guard. Despite anything that Dr. Shutton said, I held no delusions. I was still a prisoner.

Thirty-Nine

Dr. Shutton and the nurse helped me up onto the scanner bed. The technician ran through their briefing about what to expect. I had lost count of the number of times I had heard this particular briefing long ago. But it was protocol, so I dutifully listened as the technician went through their canned speech. They then passed me a set of headphones. "Is there anything in particular you would like to listen to during the scan?"

"Can I listen to *Purple Rain* by Prince and the Revolution?"

The technician looked at me, shaking his head slightly. "I don't think I've ever heard that song before."

"It's an old song from the late 1900s," Dr. Shutton said, smiling. "You'll find a copy of it in the Apollo archives. Be sure to use the file labeled V8M. That's the extended version, and I know she's particularly fond of that one."

The technician nodded, then ensured that I had put on the headphones correctly and encouraged me to lie down on the scanner bed.

It wasn't long before there was a slight shudder as the scanner bed slid into the circular orifice and the music started playing in my ears. So glad I wasn't claustrophobic.

The clunks and other loud noises of the machine could be heard over the top of the music, even through the headphones. With how health-conscious society had become over the years, surely the doctors would have preferred to use technology that was quieter to run, but nope. As Dr. Shutton often said, "Sometimes the old ways were the best ways." At least the scans wouldn't take too long. It was unlikely that I would get to hear the full eight-minutes-and-forty-five-seconds song.

But maybe they would just let me stay here to hear the ending, anyway.

I focused on the strumming of the electric guitar and the beating of the bass drum. The subtle rattles of the snare strum were muted just as the symbols chimed. In the intermittent silences between stanzas, I relaxed, enjoying the choir as they sang the chorus. I resisted the urge to sway along with the music. As much as I wanted to listen to the full song, I also didn't want to stuff up the scans. I needed to stay as still as possible.

The bridge of the music hit roughly four minutes into the scan. As I listened to the music with my eyes closed, a woman I had never seen before danced around in circles in a white room with no carpet. The woman's blue dress billowed in every direction as she spun around. She held a single purple rose in her hands. The music grew in volume, as the woman started singing as loud as she could—terribly out of tune, but that didn't matter, because she was filled with joy. The woman in the vision turned to face me, grinning from ear to ear. The purple flecks in her blue eyes were captivating. "Sing with me."

In my mind's eye, I went to step forward, but dark blood leaked from the center of the unknown woman's forehead.

The pristine white world melted away. Blood pooled at the woman's feet, and the walls became the dark grays of undressed concrete.

The woman's long blond hair darkened; her eyes transitioned from blue to hazel. And the blue dress vanished, becoming a pair of jeans and a T-shirt.

I jerked my eyes open. My heart raced ahead. The closed-in walls of the scanner tube pressed in on me. "Get me out of here. Get me out!"

I banged on the scanner tubbing as the scanner bed made its slow transition out of the scanner. As soon as I could see the ceiling, I climbed the rest of the way out and bolted to my feet—ripping off the headphones and truncating the song that was still playing.

"What happened?" Dr. Shutton dashed into the room, followed by the technician. "Michaella, your brain activity spiked just before you panicked."

I hugged myself as I paced on the spot. My breaths came out in a rushed panic. "I . . . Um . . ."

"It's okay. Just take your time. Breathe. Now, what happened?"

"There was a woman . . . singing to *Purple Rain* . . . and she . . . She was covered in blood and dead at my feet. That's who I killed, wasn't it? You said that the reason I was in Ward 27 was because I killed someone. I killed some random woman that I didn't know."

He shook his head. "No. You killed a man pretending to be a nurse. It was why I was able to convince the courts to release you into my custody. We don't know who the man was or how he got into the sector without proper authority. All we know was that he was here for you. He was sent to do you harm—by whom, we don't know. But you were trained by the best." Dr. Shutton smiled. "Why don't we finish up with the tests so we can get you medically cleared as soon as possible? Perhaps you can help the investigation team work out who the man was."

I nodded. "Do I have to go back into the scanner?"

"No, I think we've got enough."

FORTY

I STOOD ON ONE LEG with my hands out to the side, staring into the space beyond Dr. Shutton.

"And onto the other leg," the doctor said.

I did a funky hop and went straight into the next pose. It was a classic balance test, and one that I could ace on the worst of days. It helped that I had never been sick in my life . . . except for whatever symptoms came with White Rabbit syndrome. And that would one day kill me.

"Okay. Up on the table."

I jumped onto the examination table with my feet dangling over the side. Dr. Shutton stood before me, using firm fingers to check around my jaw and neck. He then stood back from me and pulled out a penlight.

"Keep your eyes forward." And he shined the light in my eyes.

As the light waved from one side of my vision to the other, his face morphed into the face of a young woman. I blinked, and the delusion vanished.

"Well, you will be pleased to know that everything appears to be normal."

"Except the fact that I'm having blackouts and killing people during those blackouts." Symptoms that I could only assume were connected to my audimentia.

Dr. Shutton pursed his lips and patted my knee. "We'll figure it out."

Reluctantly, I nodded.

He pulled out a scan wand and encouraged me to turn over my right wrist. He paused for a moment, running his thumb over my pink scar. It was like he wanted to ask me about it. Even if he had asked, I wouldn't have been able to tell him anything. I couldn't remember getting it. Instead, he scanned my chip and brought up my medical notes on a virtual display.

He continually waved his fingers through the air, like he was flicking through my notes. His frown deepened. He grunted a few times. I wanted to ask what was going on, but after years of being under his care, I knew that this was part of his process.

"I need to check a few things," he finally said. "Consult with pharmacology on possible drug protocols. Will you be okay in here on your own? I won't be long."

I smiled and nodded.

Dr. Shutton smiled in return. He patted my knee again, then went to the door. "Your blue hair is looking lovely, by the way. Brings out the color in your eyes." He didn't wait for a response, but rather disappeared out the door. I caught of glimpse of the armed guard outside.

Blue hair? I jumped down from the examination table and darted across the room to the small mirror hanging above the sink. My dark roots blended into a dark blue, which shifted into purple around my ears. It was such an odd dye job. Definitely not something that I would have done myself. My entire head should have been purple—except for my new hair growth. How long had I been in Ward 27?

I took a deep breath and wiped my hands over my face, stimulating the blood flow.

I glanced at the medical equipment resting on the bench beside me. I had never seen some of the devices before. The long rectangular fabric device with a bulb and a gauge hanging from it was of particular interest.

As I brushed my fingers over the device, I envisioned the fabric rectangle wrapped around my upper arm, cutting off my circulation. And I was looking into the face of the young woman again.

"It's a blood pressure cuff," said the woman. "As you can imagine, we don't exactly have access to the latest and greatest technology down here, but we make do."

I curled my arm, rubbing out the sense of throbbing left by my imagination.

A ticking sound filled the quiet space. As I turned around, I stared at an old analog clock hanging on the wall, marking the passage of time with its wiggling little arm moving from position to position. The white medical room morphed to a dark gray cavernous space packed with glass-fronted cabinets lining the walls.

There was a buzz, and a door opened. The white room reasserted itself. Abram Shutton walked in. "Well, it will take us some time to find the right dosage, but I'd like to try a new drug. And if it works, we can get you out of here."

"Sounds great." My response wasn't overly enthusiastic.

"Are you okay?"

"Yeah, I'm fine." But the fact that the blood pressure cuff had vanished along with the gray cavernous room was concerning.

"Are you sure you're okay?"

"Just looking forward to getting my audimentia under control." That was, of course, assuming that the delusions were a symptom of audimentia. And if they weren't . . .

I really didn't want to think about the alternative. "So, tell me about this new drug."

Forty-One

THE DIRT ROAD WOVE THROUGH the trees. The sunlight filtered through the cedar canopy, flooding the world with a yellow warmth and washing away the leafy greens. With each inhale, the woody earth scents instilled a calm like nothing ever could—not even my favorite song. Shame it was just a simulation—a virtual environment designed to provide mental relaxation as I ran on the treadmill. But I didn't care. In that simulation, I was free, able to forget the realities of the world.

A dark figure stood in the middle of the road, hazy in the virtual world. "Mind if I join you on your run?"

I reached up to my temple and took off the virtual reality glasses. Marcus stood there in a pair of black shorts and a black T-shirt. The logo insignia of Rhodon Corporation rested proudly on his chest—a white rose in full bloom.

I stepped down from the treadmill and wiped the sweat from my brow and the back of my neck with a small towel as I guzzled down some water. I glanced over my shoulder at the security guards by the door—my ever-present shadows.

"I never thought I would see you in this place." I picked up some dumbbells and started doing bicep curls.

"Tam thought you could do with a training partner. You know . . . something normal."

"If I wanted a training partner, I would have asked for George." I was probably a little curt with my response. Definitely confrontational.

Marcus nodded but said nothing. It was no secret that I tolerated him at best.

I sighed, exhaling in a rush and closing my eyes. "I'm sorry. I didn't mean to be a bitch."

"Yeah, you did. Just like I mean to be an asshole at times."

I snorted. But my chest grew tight. I backed up to sit on the bench press, leaning forward, trying to open my chest so I can breathe more easily.

"So, how's it going?" Marcus asked.

I shrugged. "As good as to be expected, considering I'm seeing and hearing things that aren't real. The only reason I've been allowed to use the training room is because Dr. Shutton is confident that the new drugs he has me on will manage my symptoms better than any drug I've been on before—although I'm not sure I like the side effects."

"What sort of side effects?"

"My vision. Colors are muted, not as clear as they once were. Just now, I was using the cedar forest simulation. I don't remember it being so yellow. Then again, it has been a long time since I've used it." I took another sip of water, then laid down on the bench and put my hands on the bar above me. "Since Tam's asked you to be my training partner, you might as well spot me."

Marcus nodded, then moved to a position by my head and helped me to lift the weights off their support. I brought the weights down in a controlled motion, then straightened my arms. Marcus counted out the reps.

"If you're talking about Cefretin, I'm on it too. When I first started taking it, colors would flicker. Red one moment.

Yellow the next. Then back again. I thought I was losing my mind. But it does eventually stabilize, and my vision has never been so sharp. I'm not exactly sure what the drug is supposed to do, but I feel good. They put me on it when I transferred to STAR."

"You're part of STAR?"

"Um . . . Yeah . . . Don't you remember? You would have been in STAR too if—" He took a deep breath and shook his head.

"If I hadn't had gone insane and killed a man." I sighed and lifted the weights back into their support home—with Marcus's help—then sat up. "It's okay, Marcus. You don't have to say it." I looked up at him and for the first time in . . . well, ever . . . Marcus didn't exude that asshole vibe. Instead, he bit his bottom lip, and he stared at me with eyes that seemed to be waiting for something to happen. If I didn't know better, I would have said he was concerned about me. "Didn't they tell you why I've been admitted to Ward 27?"

He shook his head as he pulled at the bench opposite me, turning it into a seat of his own.

"I've been suffering from blackouts. I can remember what I had for breakfast, but I don't remember what I did last week."

"So, you honestly don't remember my promotion?"

I shook my head. "Congratulations, by the way."

"Mike, what is the last thing that you remember clearly?"

I took a few deep breaths, walking through my memory—or what I had of it. "I remember the drop to a coffee shop in Sector 4. Apparently, the package was a gun."

"But you don't remember anything after that, do you?"

Again, I shook my head.

"You don't remember going to Sector 2?"

"Why would I go to Sector 2? There's nothing there except hovels and slums. The place doesn't even have a working dome and air filtration system. The Pregutor would never send any of us there. What danger would the residents of that shithole ever be to Crystal Hills?"

Marcus looked at me with a level of intensity that was a little unnerving. It was like he wanted me to admit to something—if only I knew what that something was. "George used to visit Sector 2 all the time. He has an aunt who lives there. I would have thought that you would have gone with him on a couple of those trips."

I took a controlled deep breath. "If I've been to Sector 2, it would have been during one of my blackouts, because I don't remember it." I kept my eyes on him, focusing intently. His eyes drew me in. And what was surprising—I wanted in.

The edges of my vision darkened, and the world around me shifted. He showed me a burned-out store with a charred apothecary sign swaying in the breeze. Shards of glass spread across the ground among the remnants of weeds and dried flowers. A tiny bell repeatedly dinged.

I blinked, and my vision returned to normal. Marcus continued to look at me with that concerned expression of his. And I really didn't like it. Ever since we were kids, we had been rivals, forced to work together by circumstances—and White Rabbit syndrome. Why would our rivalry change now?

"Mike," a soft voice called out, almost a whisper. *"You're almost out of time. You need to remember exactly who you are."*

I glanced over my shoulder, searching for the owner of the voice—though I knew in my heart that the voice was inside my head.

I took one last swig of water. "I'm done with training for the day. I should get cleaned up before my psych evaluation."

"Training tomorrow?" Marcus asked.

"Sure. Why not? I would be stupid to turn down the opportunity to kick your ass." I didn't wait for a response. Instead, I followed my guards out the door.

I would have been lying to myself if I said that the entire exchange with Marcus wasn't weird and unnerving. There were too many things about it that made me question reality.

Why did he invite me inside his mind like that? And why did he want to show me that, of all things?

Why was he fixated on Sector 2?

The guards led me to an open locker room isolated from the rest of the facility. In the center of the room was a pile of folded white garments waiting for me to change into, along with a pair of slip-on shoes. To the side of the room, running along the entire wall, was a tiled area with small bays with no doors. In the center bay, a collection of cleansing solutions and washcloths waited for me.

Not thinking twice about it, I removed my soiled clothing and walked to the small shower bay. I didn't even care that the guards stood at the entrance, watching me in my naked form. Lack of privacy came with being an employee of Rhodon.

As I worked the dry bath solution all over my body, I focused on the image of the burned-out apothecary. Could that place have been in Sector 2? Was that what Marcus wanted me to remember?

I closed my eyes and allowed the clean feeling to wash over me. My mental image of the apothecary cleaned itself up too. And George exited from the shop, carrying a brown bag in his arms. He stopped in front of me, grinning. He then sighed and put the bag of herbs on the ground at his feet and pulled off his breather and goggles. Coughing, he tried to take a deep breath.

"Not everything is as it seems, Mike," he said. *"Do it, and never regret it."*

As I continued to stare into the gaze of the phantom in my mind, life drained from his eyes. His vibrant soul morphed into an empty shell.

"You know what to do." The dream version of myself pulled out a package from the inside of my jacket and passed it to zombie-George. There was another ding of the tiny bell, followed by an explosion.

I screamed and wrapped my arms around my head, curling up slightly as I tried to take shelter from the unknown explosion.

"Are you okay?" the guard asked, pulling me back to the present.

I forced myself to take several deep breaths before answering. "I'm fine, but I need to see Tam. Now."

Forty-Two

I PACED AROUND THE SMALL space in front of the white couch. A white couch in a white room with white carpets. Even the person sitting on the other side of the room was white—sitting tall in their white suit and slick white hair. The only color that existed in the room was my pale pink skin and my horrible blue and purple hair.

I continually rubbed my hands along my arms and down my thighs. "Why do you insist on lying to me? I want to know where George is, and I want to know now."

Tam pursed their lips and looked down at their notes. "Michaella, please sit down. I can see that you are agitated. Our minds have a way of inventing stories to protect us from the pain of the truth. In addition, our minds do not always remember things as they really happened. I believe that is what is happening in this case."

"So, you're telling me that George isn't dead?" I glared at Tam, just barely able to contain the rage. The only thing staying my actions was the armed STAR in the corner, who was prepared to use lethal force if they had to.

There was a knock on the door and one of Tam's apprentices popped their head in. "You wanted us to inform you when we found him."

"Is he ready now?" Tam asked.

"Yes."

"Good, send him in."

The temperature in the room changed as the door fully opened. "So, you're not as invincible as you had us all believing."

I held my breath, and my heart raced ahead. I was afraid to move. Tam wore a soft smile and nodded.

"Here I was thinking that it would be me who found themselves locked up in this place, not you."

I continued to hold my breath as I closed my eyes. Every muscle in my shoulders and neck tensed, and I rocked on the spot, praying for the voices in my head to go away. Had I really spiraled so far into the depths of crazy that I was hearing the voices of the dead too?

Gentle pressure encapsulated my shoulders, pulling me close. "I'm real, Mike, not in your head."

Barely able to hold it together, I cautiously opened my eyes and turned to look at the man standing in front of me. His smile was larger than life.

"I'm real," George said. "You're not losing your mind."

"But you're dead." My voice came out as a little squeak.

George chuckled. "How can I be dead if I'm right here next to you?" He caressed my cheek, and I melted into his touch, cupping his hand with my own.

I closed my eyes again and inhaled as deeply as I could. His musky aroma smelled like the rain, but without the acid that burned the skin. I then opened my eyes again and took in everything about him. His coffee-colored eyes sparkled in the overhead lighting. His crooked smile foretold of the mischief he was planning. And his hair . . . It wasn't the red curly locks I was used to, but rather a dark yellow, almost mustard. But that didn't matter, because he was there. He was really there.

"But I watched you die."

George's smile carried a hint of concern. "Whatever you think you saw clearly didn't happen. Because here I am."

"It is what I have been trying to explain to you," Tam said. "Your mind was doing whatever it needed to do to protect itself. Filling in the narrative so your mind could make sense of what you were experiencing. But it was not the truth."

George caressed my cheek, pulling my attention back to him. "Tam tells me that we have a fun job ahead of us, trying to work out what you thought you saw versus what's real. And it starts with the fact that I'm not dead. I'm right here."

I didn't know what to believe. Standing before me was the evidence that George was very much alive. Yet, I remember him walking into that shop just as it exploded. But if my memories of George were faulty, what else was not real?

"I will leave the two of you to talk." Tam headed for the door, encouraging the security guard to follow. "Someone will be right outside if you need me."

"Thanks, Tam," George said, "but I have it from here."

Tam nodded and left.

I continued to stare at George. With tentative movements, I reached up and brushed my fingers through his yellow locks. "When did you decide to change your hair color?"

He furrowed his brow and slightly shook his head.

"Don't get me wrong, this yellow suits you, but I thought you preferred red."

He licked his lips. "The red would have stood out too much."

"Um . . . That was kind of the point, wasn't it? To add a bit of color to this place. Too much blue and yellow. Your words. Not mine."

He shook his head. "No, not stand out around here. Stand out during my mission."

"What mission?"

Again, he shook his head. "Doesn't matter." He turned me to face him full on. "What does matter is that you're finally awake and lucid. You had me worried. For weeks, you've been muttering gibberish, talking about random underground tunnels. Mike, you're the only one who keeps me sane in this place. How could you go off on that suicide mission and let it screw with your head?"

I shook my head, not really understanding what he was referring to. Mind you, I still had big holes in my memory.

"I still can't believe that the Pregutor sent you to Sector 2."

Now it was my turn to furrow my brow. "Why would the Pregutor send me to Sector 2?"

"Why does the Pregutor send any of us on a mission?" George sighed as he encouraged me to sit down on the couch next to him. "The target was an apothecary. And when the shop blew up, you were still in the vicinity. The seals on your breather gave way. Mike, you were exposed to some nasty hallucinogens, and in your delirium, you started seeing things that weren't there. The Pregutor sent Marcus and the others to retrieve you. From what I've been told, you put up one hell of a fight. Jody got a lump the size of a fist on her head because of you. And Marcus . . ." He grinned. "You gave him a black eye."

"Marcus had a black eye?" I didn't recall seeing any evidence of a black eye that morning. How long had I been locked away in Ward 27?

George laughed. "I really don't know why he thinks he can take you on in unarmed combat. You're lethal when you want to be."

I couldn't help it. I smiled.

"Ah . . . That's better." He caressed my cheek again. "Don't ever scare me like that again. Do you hear me?" He pulled me close, and I nuzzled into his chest, inhaling deeply. "If anything ever happened to you, I don't think I could go on living. You're the Queen of Hearts."

I pulled back from him slightly and stared up at him. "What does that mean?"

"Just that I love you. I always have." He brushed back the strands of my hair and kissed me on the forehead.

I was so confused, uncertain about what was real and what wasn't. It was like I was two headed, with one head flipped upside down. "So, I was admitted to Ward 27 because I've been suffering from a drug overdose? What about the man I killed?"

George shook his head. "I don't know anything about that. But if you killed someone, no doubt they deserved to die."

I licked my lips and closed my eyes again, inhaling his musky scent. "If Marcus and the others were sent in to bring me out of Sector 2, why weren't you there?" I looked up at him, not quite certain what I was expecting.

He smiled weakly. "I was on assignment myself. In Skáki Valley."

"Skáki Valley? But that's a war zone. The Pregutor has never sent any of us there before. Why now? And why you?"

George grinned. "They wanted someone with my *unique* skill set, if you catch my drift."

"You mean someone who's a smart-ass and doesn't know when to keep their mouth shut?"

George snorted. "Well, there is that."

"No, seriously, George, what were you doing in Skáki Valley?"

"Mission critical, Mike. I can't tell you any of the details. But I have to head back soon. The job isn't done."

"How soon?"

"Tonight."

There was a silence that hung in the air as we stared at one another. If he had been in Skáki Valley all this time, and if I had known that was where he had been sent, it was more than possible my brain created a narrative in which he was dead. Very few went to Skáki Valley and returned to tell the tale.

And I, too, would have changed my hair to yellow. George's red hair would have painted a target on his head.

I wrapped my arms tighter around him. "I can't believe the Pregutor would send you to Skáki Valley."

"It's not any more dangerous than being in Sector 2." He pushed me back so he could see my face. "Speaking of which, I have a favor to ask you."

"Anything. Just name it."

"If anything should happen to me, I want you to tell my aunt the truth—or at least as much of the truth as you can. She doesn't have the clearance, so she can't know everything, but she should know that it would be you looking after her from now on."

"You're talking like you're not coming back."

George's smile turned into a frown. "I'm not going to pretend that I'm not scared, Mike. I mean, this is Skáki Valley we're talking about. Tell you what, I'll contact you as soon as I can, just to reassure you that I'm still alive and kicking."

I smiled. "You better." I pulled him close again, no longer able to hold back the tears. "You're not dead."

"Nope. Heart's still beating, and I'm right here."

"Yes, you are. You're real."

Forty-Three

Seeing George worked wonders, remembering the good times we shared as children. We reenacted our mischief, but without the trips to medical to get treated for burns. Laughing at my own stupidity. I wished he could have stayed, continuing to be my source of grounding, but when the Pregutor gave orders . . .

The following day, I awoke early and headed for the gym, my guards in tow. Marcus was waiting for me in his black training gear. We never once said a word to each other. We didn't have to. We had trained side by side for years. Soon, we fell into our old routine.

In the afternoon, I was subjected to another battery of tests. Dr. Shutton put me in the upright scanner multiple times, running different scans for different things. When the tests were done, I was back in Tam's office, answering whatever crazy questions my handler asked.

The next day, I did it all again.

For a solid week, I followed the same routine. And on the seventh day, when I went to the open locker room, instead of white clothing waiting for me, it was a black uniform. I stepped closer and stared at the sleeve, folded in such a way to ensure that the colored stripe was proudly displayed. Initially, I thought it was blue. But as I blinked a few times, the purple color became so strong. I brushed my fingers along the colored stripe, afraid that I might be seeing things again. But the uniform was real. My uniform.

Excited, I stripped off my soiled clothing and darted to the open cell to use the dry bath solution. While the cleanser felt wonderful on my skin, I had always wondered what it would have been like to stand under a shower head with running water. It would have been nice to feel the pounding drops of liquid seep soothing warmth back into my muscles.

As I cleaned my hair with the dry shampoo, I envisioned an open shower room with gray rock walls . . . and my guards standing with their backs to me. I looked over my shoulder to where my guards were standing. The room might not have been gray, but they were indeed standing with their backs to me. My smile grew.

Feeling clean, I darted across the locker room to where my uniform waited for me. I almost didn't want to touch it, but my eagerness could not be contained. I rushed to don the uniform and my boots. When I was fully dressed, I stood before the mirror, admiring the purple stripes.

"How do I look?" I asked my guards.

They turned around and smiled. "Like you're our sister," one of them said, making me blush. I grinned from ear to ear.

I followed the guards out of the locker room and down the hall with a skip to my step. But the guards didn't lead me to the treatment facility like I expected. Instead, they led me directly to Tam's office.

Tam dismissed the guards and encouraged me to sit on the couch. "It is good to see you in that uniform again."

"It's good to be wearing it again."

"Well, you will be pleased to know that Dr. Shutton has recommended that you be allowed to return to duty. The tests from the last few days indicate that the new treatment protocol is working. Before I give you the all clear, I still have a few questions to ask."

"Fire away."

"Have you heard any strange voices or had any strange visions in the last few days?"

I shook my head, still smiling. "Nope." It was a relief to know that I wasn't going crazy.

"No visions of explosions or people dying?"

"No." My smile diminished.

"And what about your training sessions with Marcus? How have they been going?"

I bit my bottom lip. "They've been okay."

"What do the two of you talk about while training?"

"We compare notes about our experiences of the side effects of Cefretin. But other than that . . ." I shrugged. "We tend to train in silence."

"So, no other conversation?"

I shook my head.

Tam scrutinized me with those white eyes, the expanse of white only broken up by the black dots of the pupil. "Do you like being a courier?"

"I'm not quite sure what you're asking me."

"Before this all began, your application to join STAR had been approved. Is that still something you wish to pursue?"

I licked my lips and did the best I could to stay in control of my emotions. "Yes, if they'll have me."

"Then I have good news for you. Your selection training begins tomorrow."

"Are you serious?"

"I am always serious, Michaella. You know that."

"Yes, but I thought . . ." I took another controlling breath.

"You thought what?"

"I thought that after my latest relapse, I would be excluded from selection."

"You have Marcus to thank for that. He said that the two of you were so in sync that there was no need for either of you to communicate your needs. Your silent training sessions have shown him what he has been missing all this time . . . in a partner. He requested that you be assigned to STAR immediately. You are to be assigned to his unit."

My jaw dropped.

"A word of warning," Tam continued. "Training with STAR is not like anything you have ever faced before. And you will not be granted the stripes of STAR until the unit commander deems you ready—if at all. Do I make myself clear?"

I nodded and tried to swallow back the nervous lump forming at the back of my throat.

"I need to hear you say it, Michaella."

"Yes. Crystal clear."

"Then it is time to get you settled into your new quarters." Tam stood and brushed out the creases in their pant suit. They gestured toward the door, encouraging me to lead the way.

We walked down the hall side by side, Tam setting the pace. Alone. No guards to make me feel like a prisoner. And with each step, I felt more free.

"Tam, if you don't mind me asking, any idea when I'll be allowed to return to my apartment?"

Tam sighed. "I should have told you sooner. Because you were away from your apartment for so long, your landlord leased it to someone else. Unfortunately, we were unable to procure you a new one."

I sighed too. "So, I'm in the dormitories for the foreseeable future."

"I have arranged a single room for you. One with a private bathroom."

"Not all bad then."

"And Dr. Shutton has ensured that your medication has been delivered to your new quarters, complete with instructions. He will want to continue monitoring your blood levels, hoping to decrease your dosage to the minimal amount possible. It would be unfortunate if you were to build up a tolerance to this new drug."

I nodded. "Yes, it would." I really didn't want the voices or the visions to come back.

We headed into the depths of the building, to several stories underground. They were familiar corridors leading to my old team room. Being still early in the morning, the corridors were near empty, except for the odd technician in their black uniforms with yellow stripes vanishing through holographic walls.

The white walls were eventually replaced with gray rock. My eyes darted in every direction, taking in the view—or more appropriately, lack of view. The corridors were well lit, but that only highlighted the dark rock that the corridors were carved out of. And even though I had never been in these passageways before, there was something familiar about them.

"How deep underground are we?" I asked.

"Far enough. The STAR facilities are fully self-contained, complete with water reclamation and power generation."

"Designed to withstand a nuclear holocaust."

Tam stopped in the middle of the corridor and turned to face me. "Why would you say that? You know that anything nuclear was banned in the 2090s."

"Not everything. We still use nuclear medicine. Otherwise, we wouldn't be able to see inside the body. X-rays use nuclear material—just not at a fissionable quantity."

Tam raised their eyebrows in that questioning way, but didn't say anything. Instead, they nodded, then carried on walking. I followed, wondering if I had said something inappropriate.

I turned my attention back to my surroundings. A blue rose bud logo sat in the middle of the walls—the STAR logo—but there were no other markings to indicate where we were, not even at the junctions. No letters, numbers, or symbols. Yet, I couldn't shake the feeling that I knew exactly where we were going, not needing to be told which way to turn.

I couldn't explain it. I had never been inside the STAR facilities before. And as far as I could remember, I had never been this far underground.

Tam stopped before a blue door. They entered in a keycode into the external pad, then encouraged me to put my pharmachip over the scanner.

"Welcome, Michaella Davison," said a computerized male voice. I would have preferred it to be Alice, my personal unit, but that was something that I could change later—especially if this was going to be my long-term home.

The door opened to reveal a small suite, with a large bed, a desk, a set of drawers against the far wall—and more space than I could have imagined. "Wow. Is this all for me?"

"It is."

"I have to admit, I was expecting a portable cot inside a coat closet. But this is amazing."

Tam smirked. "Well, enjoy it while you can. Clean uniforms are already stocked in your drawers. And I have ensured there is a small library for you to read in your free time. Some of the books are from my personal collection."

"Thank you." But there was something about the way Tam held themselves, more rigid than normal. "But there's something else," I said, "something that has you sad." I said a silent prayer, hoping it wasn't bad news about George. No one survived in Skáki Valley. But perhaps George would.

Tam tilted their head to the side. "We can deal with that later. Right now, I want you to enjoy your new surroundings. Someone will be by later this evening to give you the full tour of the facilities."

"Thank you, Tam."

Tam nodded once and closed the door.

I stood in the center of the room and relished the space. My apartment back in Sector 11 was so small that I could touch the walls on either side if I put my arms out wide. But in here, I could properly pace if I wanted to, six steps from wall to wall. Six long strides. Perhaps being kicked out of my apartment and being forced to live here wasn't such a bad thing after all.

I went to the desk and grabbed a small bottle of water from the stack sitting there. I ran my fingers over the books. Paper books. I hadn't read from one of those in a long time. And knowing that some of these paper books were from Tam's personal collection made them extra special.

I pulled out the title from the right-hand end: *Alice's Adventures in Wonderland* by Lewis Carroll. And this particular version was published in 2035. "Oh, my god." It was a book that was nearly two hundred years old. It had to be Tam's most treasured possession. Not wanting to damage such an important book, I carefully put it back where I found it.

I then turned my attention to the dark terminal that sat in the corner of the desk. And I sighed with pleasure. I had been out of the loop with the outside world for a long time. "Computer, bring up the newsfeeds from the past twenty-four hours."

"Access denied," the male computerized voice said.

I blinked. "Excuse me? Those are public feeds with no restrictions. So . . . Bring up the feeds."

"Access denied."

"Okay. Be that way. Computer, bring up the bio-authorization system."

"Retinal scanning login has been deactivated for this terminal."

I pursed my lips. "Okay. Maybe voice activation will work. Computer, bring up an external port. Authorization: Davison Kilo-Alpha-One."

"Access denied."

"What?" I half-chuckled as I wiped my hands down my face. "You little piece of shit. All I want to do is read some news. You know, see what's going on in the world. But no, today, you decide to be a temperamental little beast."

I took several deep breaths, determined to not throw a tantrum. Clearly, the terminal was faulty. But there had to be somewhere in the facility where I could find a working terminal.

I got to my feet and went to the door, but when I pressed the open button, the door wouldn't open. "What the hell?" I pressed the button again, but nothing happened. I half-laughed as my shoulders sagged. "This can't be happening." I then banged on the door.

"Hello! Is anyone out there? I'm stuck. I can't get the door open. Hello! Can anyone hear me?" But no one seemed to hear me or have any desire to answer me.

I turned around and scanned the room, hunting for the security cameras. All dormitory rooms had them. The concept of privacy went out the window in the mid-twenty-first century. And if you were an employee of Rhodon Corporation like I was, you waived any right to privacy when you signed your contracts. They had to be watching me. If only I could get their attention.

Mounted in the far corner of the room, facing the bed and pointing away from the bathroom, was a small dome roughly a centimeter in size. "There you are."

I grabbed one of the chairs from the table settee and dragged it to the corner. Climbing up, I waved my hand in front of the camera. "Hey, you in there." I tapped on the dome. "You paying attention? I'm stuck. Come and let me out."

There was a beep behind me, and the door slid back. "Oh, thank god."

"Mike, what are you doing?" Marcus asked, as I climbed down from the chair and put it back by the table. But before I could answer, the door slid shut again.

"No . . ." I raced across the room and pushed the door button, but it wouldn't work.

"Mike, what's going on?"

My shoulders sagged, and I rested my forehead against the sealed door. "The door won't work. And now you're stuck in here with me."

"What are you talking about?" Marcus pressed the door button himself, and the door opened without any issues. "The door works fine."

"It works for you, but it doesn't work for me?" I shook my head and started to walk out into the hall, but Marcus grabbed my arm before I could cross the threshold. "What the—?"

He shook his head ever so slightly, then tilted his head toward the world outside the door. It was so small a movement that could have easily been missed, but the message was clear.

Across the hall, two guards faced the door, armed to the teeth, and looking like they had something sour for lunch. Itching for a fight.

With Marcus's encouragement, I stepped back from the door and allowed it to close again. Turning to face him, I glared at him with all the fury bottled inside.

"Why am I being held prisoner again?"

Marcus scoffed. "You're not a prisoner, Mike."

"Oh really? Then why are there guards outside my door?" I stepped away from him, moving out of his arm's reach. "And when did you start to conceal carry inside Sector 14? And don't try to lie to me about it. I can see the print at your ankle. Shitty place to carry a primary weapon, if you ask me. You wouldn't be able to draw it in a hurry if you needed to."

Marcus smiled in a disbelieving way. "I don't know why I believed them when they said you wouldn't notice it. You always were the observant one." He pulled up his pant leg, showing off the pistol, then he let his pant leg drop and flicked his ankle around in a sad attempt to have the folds of the fabric look natural. But no matter what he did, you could still see the outline of the holster.

"Why am I being held a prisoner? I thought I was going to be training to be part of STAR—based on your recommendation."

"You are," he said with a smile. "But until they can trust you . . . um . . . you're being held a prisoner."

I scoffed. "That's just great. So, is this how you were treated?"

"No. I was in the main barracks from word go."

"Then why am I being treated differently?"

He just stared at me, like he was expecting me to come to the conclusion myself.

"Let me guess, they're scared of me." It was my worst nightmare coming to life. "But you're not." I said it more as a statement than a question.

He sighed and shook his head. "I don't want to fight anymore. You and I have been at odds with one another since we were kids. I'm tired of it. Can't we pretend like the last fifteen years never happened?" The look on his face was one I had never seen before, not on him, anyway. He was actually pleading with me.

I bit my bottom lip. "On one condition: you tell me why you're here and not someone else. I want the truth."

"Because, believe it or not, I care what happens to you. You're like my sister, Mike. And I was scared that we would lose you."

I stared at him, trying to decide if he was being sincere or not. "You knew about my mission to Sector 2, didn't you? The one I can't remember. That's why you were asking me about Sector 2."

Reluctantly, Marcus nodded. "I know about some of it."

"You were the one who pulled me out and brought me here—so I could get medical treatment."

Again, he nodded.

"Why?"

"Like I said, you're my sister. I might hate your guts, but . . ." He averted his gaze and took several deep breaths. Then he looked at me again. "I love you. As hard as it is to believe, I love you. And I don't want to lose you."

I stared at him—gawked, really—unable to process what I was hearing.

"Well, say something."

"Like what?"

"Anything. I just told you that I love you and you're just staring at me. Like I've caught some sort of contagious bug."

"Don't be silly." I tried to hide my discomfort. "You've never been sick a day in your life . . . except for the symptoms of White Rabbit syndrome."

"Forget it. I knew you wouldn't understand." He went to open the door and leave, but I grabbed his arm before he could activate the sensor.

"Why don't we just agree to say that it never happened? That the past fifteen years never happened? A clean slate. I know that you put your neck on the line by recommending that I be transferred here—Tam told me. And I'm guessing that if I don't prove that your trust in me was warranted, we'll both be removed from the program." I left it unsaid what that removal would entail.

He took a deep breath and wore a slight smile. "Why don't I show you our new home?"

Forty-Four

The days and nights that followed were filled with nothing but scrutiny and the boring humdrum of training. And everywhere I went, I was accompanied by shadowing guards, who made it perfectly clear on more than one occasion that they would have loved to put a bullet through my head. But at least my main guard, Marcus, was actually being human for a change.

It was a pleasant surprise to discover that Jody was part of STAR too, occasionally joining us for training. She was in the same unit as Marcus. It was like PentWave again, but without the animosity between Marcus and me . . . and missing a few team members. Perhaps one day the old team would be whole again.

But every day during our training, Marcus and I would show the unit commander how much in sync we were—scaring those around us. It was a small bit of justice, but there was no way anyone could say that I didn't belong there. I even knew how to navigate the facility without being told which way to go, often turning the corner before Marcus did. I knew these halls. In my mind, I had walked them numerous times, walking alongside someone I trusted completely. Although, in my head, it wasn't Marcus walking next to me . . . or Jody. It was someone else. And I half-expected to be bowled over by a child as they ran through the halls. But there were no children in STAR. And every time I was escorted to a new sector of the facility, I had to blink multiple times, believing I was seeing faces that weren't there.

The new drugs were supposed to keep the visions away, but these visions . . . No, I had to believe that the new meds were working the way they were meant to. Just in case, I couldn't tell anyone about my visions.

At the end of each day, I was escorted back to my cushy prison cell, where I had nothing better to do than read or sleep. The next day, the routine would start again.

I sat in the middle of the bed with my legs tucked under me, waiting for my escort to arrive. While I waited, I read through *Alice's Adventures in Wonderland* for what felt like the one hundredth time, turning the pages with delicate care.

"Who are you?" said the Caterpillar.

This was not an encouraging opening for a conversation. Alice replied, rather shyly, "I—I hardly know, sir, just at present—at least I know who I was when I got up this morning, but I think I must have been changed several times since then."

I stared at the words, imagining myself in Alice's shoes. Alice's world was filled with nonsense: talking white rabbits in waistcoats, and cats who could vanish, leaving behind nothing but their grins. At least my visions made sense, sort of. But I still couldn't tell anyone about them—not even Marcus or Jody. If anyone ever found out, Alice's confrontational conversation with the Caterpillar would be nothing compared to what I would face.

There was a beep at the door and a whoosh as it slid open. I put the book to the side and stood in my fitness gear, ready for more training. But Marcus wasn't dressed in fitness gear like I was. He was in full tactical gear. And he carried with him a small duffel.

"I take it that we're not doing the normal fitness training this morning."

"Nope." He threw the duffel on the bed. "You've got two minutes to get into full gear." He didn't wait for a response. Instead, he headed out the door again.

I groaned and looked up at the ceiling. I had no idea what sort of training Marcus and the others had in store for me, but if it involved full tactical gear, it couldn't be anything good.

I opened the duffel and pulled out a vest, a helmet, and a weapon's belt. The belt was loaded with a stunning rod and a taser gun. Basic gear to disable an assailant but not harm them.

Yeah, whatever Marcus had planned was definitely not anything good.

I rushed to my drawers and pulled out a black uniform, getting changed as fast as I could. When Marcus opened the door again, I was cinching up the last straps of the vest, ensuring a snug fit that wouldn't hinder any movements.

"So, do I get to know what torture you have planned for me today?"

"We have a mission. The briefing started five minutes ago."

My jaw dropped. "A mission? Doing what?"

"I don't know. Like I said, the briefing started five minutes ago. As soon as I walked into the room, I was ordered to get you. The captain said that it was critical that you be included. But don't think that this means he trusts you. Give me your wrist."

"Which wrist?"

"The one with your pharmachip."

Hesitant, I held out my right hand, exposing the inside of my wrist. He briefly thumbed my pink scar, then waved a wand over my pharmachip.

The world suddenly spun out of control. I didn't know which way was up. And Marcus grabbed hold of me so I wouldn't fall on my ass. It took a few seconds to stabilize, and when it did, the beating of my heart felt weird. Like it wasn't quite my normal rhythm.

"You okay?" Marcus asked.

I nodded as I cautiously straightened up. I placed my hand over my heart. "What the hell was that?"

"Our chips are now linked. If my heart stops, your heart stops."

"So, that's what I'm feeling. My heart struggling to find the common rhythm of our hearts. And I take it that this is precautionary?"

Marcus nodded. "Mike, I don't know what the mission is, but I know we're going outside. The captain wanted assurances that you wouldn't go rogue on us. So, umm . . ." He took a deep breath. "Just don't do anything stupid, okay? I'm not in the mood to spend the night in the infirmary."

"I can't make any promises. The last time they chose to link us like this . . ."

He hung his head. "Yeah, I remember."

"So, the pact is in place? We can't kill each other—not today, anyway."

Marcus snorted. "Not today."

"How long will our hearts be connected?"

Marcus was silent, like he was trying to decide how to answer.

"You better not say for the rest of our lives."

Again, he snorted. "No, but until they can trust you, I'm your babysitter. Look, I'm not happy about it either, because it means that where you go, I go. But there is an upside to all of this."

"And what's that?"

He stepped closer to me and gently brushed the hair out of my eyes. "In moments like this, I can feel it when your heart starts racing. Be honest, Mike, you like being this close to me."

I scoffed and rolled my eyes. "You always were so full of yourself. But I will admit that in the last few days, I've seen a side of you that I don't find so repugnant. You're actually human."

"And you like humans."

I smirked. "Yeah, I do."

It was like he was thinking of leaning down to kiss me, and if I was honest with myself, I wouldn't have stopped him. But there was still too much history between us to just let the animosity die.

"We better get to the briefing," Marcus said. "The captain's getting impatient."

"Just one question: in the field, how do you know that I won't kill you anyway, ending both our lives?"

"I don't. But somehow, I don't think you want to do that." He stepped back from me and started down the hall. "Let's go."

We walked through the corridors, side by side. No hesitation in our joint steps. Our movements were perfectly in sync. The feeling of walking next to the stranger that I trusted completely returned. At every junction, I could have sworn that I saw a child's stick drawing, only for the drawings to vanish the moment I tried to focus on them.

The corridors shifted from gray rock to the white corridors of Rhodon Corporation. And my weird visions decided to reveal a room filled with row upon row of floor-to-ceiling computer banks and flashing lights. But when I tried to focus on the room, I saw nothing but a blank wall.

If my visions decided to plague me while on the mission . . . No, it wasn't worth thinking about.

We stood outside a metal door with an identification panel mounted on the wall. Marcus held out his hand to the reader, pressing his palm flat, ensuring that his pharmachip was also exposed. He stepped forward to the retinal scanner and stared at the blue light that came out from the wall. "Agent Gahan and Agent Davison reporting as ordered." A light shot out from the ceiling, a line scanner.

"Five modes of ID checks," I said. "Whatever is behind that door is clearly very important."

"It's the command center."

"Briefings are held in the command center?"

"Briefings as important as this one are."

I didn't get the chance to ask him any more questions. The door retracted from the wall and slid to the side. Marcus gestured for me to go first.

It was like walking into a larger version of the PentWave briefing room. Black walls absorbed the light from the world. Maps hung on the walls, with the sector borders highlighted in yellow and blue. And monitors lined the back wall, showing security feeds from around the city.

The table in the center of the room possessed a three-dimensional virtual display of the city and the surrounding regions. Blue and yellow dots were scattered everywhere. There was a large cluster of blue located in Sector 14—deep underground. I couldn't be sure, but I guessed that the cluster was highlighting the location of STAR. There was another blue cluster located just outside the city walls. Before I could ask questions about the second cluster, the display changed and was replaced with a plain black surface.

Marcus encouraged me to stand next to him. Jody appeared on my other side. My two friends in this mess. Without them, I wasn't sure if I would have had the strength to get through this—whatever this was.

An older gentleman moved to the head of the table. Though his navy uniform still blended into the background, it stood out among those in the black tactical gear. His stern expression and graying temples added to the sense of authority the man possessed. "Now that everyone is here, we can get started. The mission is simple. You're to head into Sector 10 and hunt down a rogue agent."

The captain waved his hand over the dark table. A holographic head of my former trainer spun in a slow circle. The petite woman standing next to me gasped.

"I take it you know the target," the captain asked Jody.

"I do, sir. Lucas Tellis. He was our trainer, but I thought he was dead—killed by the resistance."

"Well, it turns out that he's working with the resistance. His supposed death was a ruse." The captain glanced in my direction, then flicked his hand like he was turning the page of some three-dimensional file. Another image of Lucas came up with his arm around the shoulders of another man, smiling.

I stared at the man with Lucas. Those black curls that flowed around his shoulders, and the dimple in his right cheek when he smiled. And his eyes . . . blue with flecks of purple. I didn't know how or from where, but I knew him.

He was the man I kept seeing in my visions—walking next to me through the halls.

"Who's the skatá kefáli?" Marcus asked.

"A ghost," the captain said. "In truth, we don't know who he is, where he came from, or how he got here. His image isn't found anywhere in city records. Not even in the records from Lagniappe Fields or the central government. All we know is that he's dangerous. And passive security scans show that he has White Rabbit syndrome."

The room plunged into silence as everyone turned and stared at the commander.

"Untreated?" I asked.

"Hence why he's dangerous. And hence why we're sending *you* after him." The captain looked directly at me. His stature made it perfectly clear that he was referring to me specifically, and not the rest of the team. The captain then shifted his attention to Marcus. "Gahan, you're to lead the team in the field. The scout is to be by your side every step of the way."

"Sir, I'm honored you would trust me with this mission, but why me? Lucas knows every single one of my moves. He trained me. Surely, he would be able to evade anything I come up with in the field."

The captain looked at me again, this time with an intensity that was unnerving.

I glared at the captain with the same focus and intensity that he was showing me. "The captain wants us specifically out in the field because he fears that this unknown has the same abilities that we do. He thinks this unknown is an influencer, but he fears that the unknown is immune to the abilities of the rest of the team." I briefly bowed my head, then looked up at Marcus. "Just like we're immune to the others. Isn't that right, captain?" I turned my attention back to the captain, who looked like he wanted to burn into my soul with his laser eyes—if he actually had laser eyes.

"Are you inside my head?" the captain snarled.

"No. Just reading your body language. That's why you're nervous around me. Because you can't control me. But you're hoping that Marcus can." I smirked. "I hate to tell you this, but he could never persuade me to do anything—except hate his guts."

The captain looked at Marcus. "Is this going to be a problem?"

"No, sir," Marcus said. "She's just a smart-ass who doesn't know when to shut up."

I smiled. "I learned from the best." My smile turned into a frown as I looked at the holographic image of Lucas and the unknown. "It's a shame the best went rogue." I took a deep breath, then turned my attention back to the captain. "We'll find Lucas. And we'll find this unknown. I assume you want them alive."

"If possible, but not necessary. If it comes down to it, you're to do whatever is necessary to protect yourselves. We don't know who else might have become a ghost. Jody was right before. All reports showed Lucas as dead. It was a DNA match to his chip. But a week ago, we got proof he was still alive." The captain waved his hand again. The display shifted to show Lucas standing in the middle of the street in Sector 10, waving at the camera. Lucas then continued down the street, handing out cards of some kind.

"What's he giving out?" Marcus asked.

"One of these." The captain threw a card onto the table in front of us.

"A playing card?" Marcus said.

"The Queen of Hearts." I fingered the double-headed card. I knew this card. George used to play with a deck of cards like this, and this card was part of that deck. But there was something specific about the Queen of Hearts. If only I could remember what it was.

"Does that card mean anything to you?" the captain asked.

"I'm not sure. Possibly. Then again, maybe not."

"Well, it clearly means something to Lucas and the rebels, because for the past week, these cards have been showing up everywhere throughout the city. The public has started to paint it on the walls. A Q and a heart. The rebels are making a move, and we need to strike them down before they gain any more momentum."

"Sir, is it okay if I hold on to the card?"

He looked at me, like he was demanding that I explain myself. In his navy suit, he was like the Caterpillar, demanding answers.

Alice's words rattled around inside my head. Softly, I quoted, "I can't explain myself, I'm afraid, sir, because I'm not myself, you see. I'm afraid I can't put it more clearly, for I can't understand it myself to begin with; and being so many different sizes in a day is very confusing."

"What are you mumbling about, girl?"

"The card. If I'm given the opportunity to reflect on it— to analyze it—I might be able to work out its significance."

"Whatever." The captain waved his hand, dismissing the team and the holograms hovering above the table. "Just get it done. Marcus, a private word before you leave."

"Yes, sir." Marcus looked at me with that *are-you-crazy* look, but didn't say anything.

Jody grabbed my elbow and steered me out the door. "If you want to make an impression with the captain, questioning his orders and showing off isn't the way to do it," she growled. "It's bad enough that we get treated like we're children. You have no idea how hard Marcus and I had to fight to be accepted."

"Because they're afraid of you. Because they can't influence you."

"Yeah, and you had to go and throw that in their faces." Jody sighed and shook her head. "Just do me a favor and stop quoting children's books."

"You know the book?"

"Of course. *Alice's Adventures in Wonderland*. It was Lucas's favorite. He read it to me every night when we were together." She looked off into the empty space beside us. "Why would he lie to us like that? Make us believe that he was dead?"

"Maybe he did it to protect you."

Jody stared at me, demanding further explanation. But unlike the captain and the confrontational Caterpillar, Jody was just as lost as Alice.

"He's working for the resistance," I said. "We have no idea how long he was working for them before he disappeared. Tell me honestly, if you knew he was still alive, would you have allowed him to just stay hidden? Or would you have tried to go after him and attempt to bring him back?"

Jody licked her lips.

"Perhaps he didn't tell you that he was still alive because he didn't want you to have to make a decision: to become a fugitive yourself."

Jody's face slowly contorted into a snarl. "No, now I'm forced with the decision to either kill the man I love or let him be tortured to death by the Pregutor."

Marcus joined us in the hall, a steely look in his eyes. "Let's go. Lucas's last known location was in Sector 10."

Forty-Five

I tried to enjoy the moment, riding in a hover drone to the outer sectors of the city for the first time—that I could recall, anyway. For all I knew, this was a once-in-a-lifetime experience. I wasn't a full member of STAR yet. In many ways, I was still a prisoner. But if I played the right cards, my temporary status would become permanent, and I would be granted communication implants.

The right cards. I pulled out the Queen of Hearts from my vest pocket, trying to figure out why this card specifically and not one of the others. The only Queen of Hearts I could think of was the Red Queen in *Alice's Adventures in Wonderland*. But the Red Queen was evil, a tyrant that needed to be brought down. Was it possible that the Queen of Hearts was what the rebels were calling the Pregutor?

There was a slight shudder in our flight movement, jolting me out of my reflective thoughts and reminding me of the current task. We were hunting my former trainer. But that in itself was a problem.

From everything that I could remember about Lucas, he was a loyalist, dedicated to the path set before him by the Pregutor. What could have happened that made Lucas turn his back on everything he taught me to believe?

I glanced across the drone to where Jody sat. She stared off into nowhere. A small tear hovered in the corner of her eye. I didn't need to dive into Jody's thoughts to know what was on her mind. She was plagued by the same thoughts about Lucas that I was.

There was another shudder, and the drone banked slightly to the right.

"We're coming up to the drop point," Marcus said, his voice muted as it came through the rudimentary comms unit I was given when I boarded the drone. It felt weird to hear his voice through only the one ear. That would change soon—I hoped.

The virtual display of my goggles sprang to life with a map of the sector. "Lucas was last spotted here." A bright yellow dot appeared on the map. "The drop point is here." A neon blue dot appeared on the other side of the sector. "It's roughly a twenty-minute trek across the sector, and we're to clear all buildings along the way. No physical contact with residents. Surface scans only."

"What if there are undetected telepaths?" I asked. "Won't they feel the scans?"

Marcus looked at me, not saying a word. He then smiled and turned his attention back to the rest of the team. "As I was saying, surface scans of every soul found. You are looking for anyone who might have seen Lucas or the unknown with him. Everyone, prepare for the drop."

I shook my head slightly, trying to comprehend the smug look on his face. Meanwhile, I joined the rest of the team as they secured their fold-down seats and lined up for the drop, clipping in to the drop system.

The full team pulled on our breathers, securing them in place. While Sector 10 had a breathable atmosphere inside the dome, it wouldn't take much for that situation to change. Failsafe protocols: the Pregutor had the ability to cut the power to the air filtration systems if need be.

"Drop in three . . . two . . . one."

There was a buzz, and the floor of the hover drone fell away. The entire team zoomed toward the ground. Our descent slowed for the last few meters. Even then, I hit the ground harder than I expected. The rest of the team managed to stay on their feet while I fell to my knees. Clearly, I was going to need more drop training if I was going to be doing this on a regular basis.

Detached from the drone, the team spread out in multiple directions, taking different routes to the point where Lucas was last seen.

Marcus grabbed my upper arm and pulled me to my feet. There was no doubt in my mind that he wore a smirk behind his breather mask.

I followed Marcus down the street, Jody right behind us. "You never answered my question about undetected telepaths."

"You didn't feel my scan, did you?"

"Excuse me?"

He turned around and stood in my path. "It's been a long time since you and I went against one another in our mental training. From what I can tell, you're out of practice at keeping me out. Either that, or you want me in." He stepped closer to me. He brushed a small tuft of blue hair out of my eyes and tucked it up under my helmet. "Is that why I was able to get past your defenses so easily?"

I didn't know how to respond. Instead, I focused on my breathing, doing the best I could to keep my heart rate steady.

There was that hint of a smug smile in his eyes again. He touched his hand to his heart, a clear reminder that what I felt, he felt too. And it would remain that way as long as our hearts were linked.

"Oh geez, get a room." Jody huffed as she headed down the street. "What I don't understand is why the captain thought you would be any good on this mission."

"It's not our place to question the captain's orders, Jody," Marcus said. "Though I do wish that she had at least the basic skills."

I had to force myself to take several deep breaths—yet again. "Did you ever stop to think that the reason you were able to do a surface scan undetected was because I'm allowing for surface scans to happen? So *I* can remain undetected? Your surface scan never once encroached on the mental shields that protect my secrets."

Jody and Marcus stopped their trek through the city streets and just stared at me.

"What are you talking about?" Marcus asked.

"When you scanned my mind, what did you see?"

He shook his head. "You and George singing in the purple rain. And you both sing horribly out of tune."

I smirked, and Jody snorted.

"I remember how much trouble you got into for that," Jody said.

"I still have the scars." I turned to face Marcus, preparing to remind him of lessons that he never fully understood. "The best way to shield your mind is to focus on one thought—one memory that gives you strength. If you do it often enough, you become so practiced at it, it becomes second nature. George is often on my mind because of how much I miss him. But in my memories of George, there is nothing that is a secret, especially not from the two of you. You were there for most of it." I hoped George was okay in Skáki Valley.

"A surface scan of my mind will only bring up the memories that I don't care if you see. If a surface scan brought up nothing, you would know I was trying to hide something. And hence, you would know that I was the one you were looking for. So, I let you in, but only as far as I want you to go. Anything that I want kept secret, even from you, will require a deep scan. The moment you try to breach that barrier, I'll know that you're in my mind. It's like a buzzing that won't go away, and the deeper the scan, that buzz starts to hurt. On the drone, everything was buzzing, so a surface scan could have easily been missed among everything else going on. But trust me when I say that even with all the distracting buzzing from the drone, if you had attempted a deep scan, I would have known. And I have defenses that you know nothing about."

I stared into his eyes, careful to not be drawn in, to remain alert of my full surroundings. We were in dangerous territory, and I couldn't let my senses be diminished in any way. The moment I started to see the memory that he used to protect his own mind—when he was given rank among STAR—I pushed outward with a sharp thought.

Marcus winced and staggered on the spot. "What the hell was that?"

"A gentle reminder of who I am." I stepped closer to him, but there was no way that my sudden closeness could be considered affectionate. "Even as kids, you were never able to get into my head if I didn't want you there. Your abilities might have grown over the years, as has your control over them, but so have mine."

I continued to stare at him, with slow breaths in and out. I shared with him a memory that Lucas had shared with me about when Marcus and I were kids—when Marcus tried to kill me, strangling me. In the here and now, he reached down to his weapons belt and pulled out a pistol, raising it with the muzzle pressed to his temple.

"What the hell?" Jody pushed me to the side, severing whatever eye contact I might have shared with Marcus.

Marcus blinked a few times and shook his head, then he noticed the gun in his hand. He didn't say anything. He just holstered the weapon and continued down the street in a huff.

"You could have killed him," Jody hissed.

"He was never in any danger, and he knows it. Ask him."

"She's right, Jody," he called out, the irritation strong in his voice. "Our hearts are linked. If I die, she dies." He spun around on the spot and glared at me. "Don't ever do that again."

I sighed and stepped closer to him, this time in a submissive way. "I'm sorry I scared you, but it was the only way I could think of to get my point across. You're working on the premise that any telepaths we encounter won't know how to shield their minds properly, so a surface scan would go undetected. If anyone tried to block us, we would know, potentially helping us to hunt down the ones we're looking for. But this is Lucas we're talking about here. He's the one who taught me how to do what I just did to you. And if this unknown with him is like us . . . If he's like me . . ." I licked my lips and bowed my head. I might have hated Marcus's guts, but I didn't want him dead—not today, anyway. His cocky attitude was growing on me.

Marcus took several deep breaths of his own. He then put his finger under my chin, encouraging me to look at him. "I get your point, but did you really need to do it in such a spectacular fashion? You scared Jody."

"I wasn't scared." Jody crossed her arms in front of her—a rather impressive feat, considering how bulky her tactical vest was compared to her body frame.

Marcus rolled his eyes. I snorted.

"Let's just get to the rendezvous point." Marcus headed down the street, continually looking in all directions, no doubt, still running surface scans on every mind he encountered. Jody followed him, doing the same.

I shook my head. He said he understood, but he didn't. I wasn't sure if he would ever understand.

We continued our trek through the sector in silence. To any onlooker, we would have appeared to be a standard security unit, scanning for any visual dangers. But the real danger we were looking for would never be found this way.

I tried to stay focused and calm, but as we got closer to the rendezvous point, the anxiety flowing through my body amplified. It didn't help that I was feeling both my anxiety and Marcus's.

We turned the final corner and emerged into a large plaza, but this plaza was nothing like the one located in Sector 14. For one, this plaza was filled with nothing but concrete and eroding steel.

Marcus and Jody kept their rifles raised, shifting their aim to match the directions they were looking. Other STAR units converged on the plaza from the other side, scanning the surrounding area just like Marcus and Jody were.

As we continued deeper into the plaza, square patches of the ground appeared lighter than others in a regular checkered pattern. Bronze and stone figures were scattered around, each figure centered in one of the square patches. A horse statue had been pushed over. In its place was a statue of a white rabbit in a purple waistcoat, looking over his shoulder at the regal bronze queen figure standing next to the king. They were surrounded by their court of knights and bishops. Around their feet was a bed of purple roses.

Stone tables lined the right-hand edge, each with a smaller checkered board etched in the stone. On each table stood a lonely figurine: a regal queen fashioned out of some sort of red material.

Slowly, I approached the lonely Red Queen on one of the tables. The queen's skirt was edged in hearts.

"I don't like this," Marcus said, his voice coming through the comms unit clearly. "It's too quiet. And none of this was here in the footage we saw of Lucas."

"And what's the deal with the rabbit in the blue waistcoat?" Jody said. "And where the hell did they get all those blue roses? It's not like they're naturally that color."

I furrowed my brow as I took in the rabbit statue again. It was definitely wearing a purple waistcoat, but why would Jody think it was blue? And those roses at the feet of the king and queen were also purple.

"I see something at the rabbit's feet." Jody edged closer to the White Rabbit with her scope on her rifle raised to her eye. "It's a playing card. The Queen of Hearts."

The energy of the plaza shifted, and a chill washed through my veins. The hairs on the back of my neck prickled.

A buzzing noise grew, and I looked in every direction, including up at the surrounding buildings. The buzzing wasn't painful—yet—but someone was definitely trying to get inside my head.

"What do you want?" I said mentally, projecting my thoughts outward.

"I don't want anything," Marcus said through the comms.

I pressed my hand to my radio transmitter on the rudimentary comms unit. "Shut up. We're not alone."

"How do you know?"

"Remember when I told you how I would know if you were trying to break past the barriers that I use to protect my secrets? How it's like a buzzing?"

On the other side of the plaza, Marcus spun around and glared at me. I nodded once in response to his unspoken question. Though I couldn't hear it, I knew he was swearing repeatedly to himself.

And I knew he didn't understand what I was saying earlier. Perhaps now he would.

"Who are you?" I called out with my thoughts.

The response came in the form of a looped vision of George and me dancing in the purple rain. It was like the owner of the unknown mind was trying to tell me that I could trust them.

"Lucas." I continued to scan the plaza.

"Not Lucas." The deep, mental voice was somehow familiar, calming, but no matter how hard I tried, I couldn't remember how I knew this voice.

The image in my head morphed into a woman in a blue dress dancing in a white kitchen and singing *Purple Rain*. It was the same woman I saw while in the MRI. The image shifted again to a darkened training room. Lucas stood at the edge of the training mat, watching the match in the middle like a proud father. And I was surrounded by people I didn't know—yet I felt at ease around them.

The image shifted again, and I was sitting at a table surrounded by my unknown team, playing a game of cards. In the vision, my hands gathered the cards and started constructing a tower with them. "It's like a House of Cards," I said in the vision. "If constructed in the right way, it can be strong." I placed a cup of water on the top of the tower to demonstrate my point. "But all it takes is for one card to have a weakness, a crease or a fold, and the strength of the entire structure is compromised. Eventually, it'll come crashing down." The card tower fell, getting everything wet. The vision ended with the Queen of Hearts in the middle of the small puddle.

I suddenly inhaled as the buzzing vanished, and my sense of reality returned. I scanned the plaza. In the distance, Jody held the card from the base of the White Rabbit statue.

"Jody!" I sprinted from the edge of the giant chessboard, determined to get to Jody before the House of Cards came crashing down. Before I could close the gap, an explosion shattered the White Rabbit, and I flew backward.

I blinked multiple times and shook my head, trying to dislodge the disorientation. The world was filled with nothing but ringing. Heat pressed in on me, and I raised my arms to shield myself from the rising heat. I continually shook my head, trying to dislodge whatever was affecting my hearing. And I hunted for Jody.

A petite figure was sprawled on the ground a short distance away. "Jody!" But my voice was muffled—even to my own ears. I crawled the short distance, continually wincing against the heat. The explosion must have hit a gas line. The fire suppression systems inside the dome should have been able to put out the fire by now, but the fire seemed to only grow hotter.

"Jody!" I grabbed the vest of the woman and pulled. Who would have guessed that a petite woman would weigh a ton when unconscious?

Another pair of hands rushed to my aid, pulling Jody over their shoulder and carrying her to the edge of the plaza, well away from the heat. I chased after them, staggering. I never realized how much of my balance was tied to my hearing.

The unknown man placed his fingers on Jody's neck. *"She'll be okay."* His voice was crystal clear, even though I still heard nothing but ringing from the explosion. *"But I don't think Grober will be. Lucas is going to be furious when he finds out that his girlfriend got caught in that explosion."*

I stared at him. No one but Marcus and I knew about Lucas's relationship with Jody. No one.

"Who are you?" My own voice was still muted by the ringing. I stared directly into his eyes, and the edges of my vision started to go dark. I pushed into his mind, demanding an answer.

He shook his head, like he was dislodging a thought. *"Are we really going to do this now? Here?"*

It was unnerving how I could hear him so clearly inside my head, yet my own voice was distorted.

"You're him. The unknown we're hunting." I darted forward and grabbed the pistol from Jody's weapons belt, then stood tall and held the gun pointed at the unknown man. "Get up slowly and put your hands up. You're under arrest."

The unknown man just shook his head. *"Not today. You're forgetting something."*

"And what's that?"

"Pistol safeties are DNA encoded." He then bolted to his feet and took off down the alley leading away from the plaza.

I took a shot at him—or at least I tried to—but the stupid weapon wouldn't respond to my commands. Instead, I dropped the gun by Jody's side and chased after the unknown, down the dark alley.

Forty-Six

LEFT, THEN RIGHT. Right, then left. Deeper and deeper into the maze I went, just barely able to keep up with him.

As I ran, I activated my comms. "This is Agent Davison requesting backup. I'm in pursuit of the unknown."

"Where are you?" Marcus asked. His voice was muffled, but the fact that I could clearly make out his words had to be a good sign.

"How the hell should I know?" My muscles burned as I continued to run.

"It's okay. I have your position on locator. We'll be there soon. Just don't lose him."

I had no intention of doing so.

The unknown turned the corner just ahead.

As the blood pumped through my body, I became more clear-headed and focused. My hearing returned, and the pounding of my boots on the concrete was a comfort. I controlled my breathing, in and out through the nose.

I rounded the last corner, only to come face to face with him standing in the middle of the alleyway. Behind him was a dead end.

But he wasn't afraid, or at least he didn't show signs of fear on the surface. Instead, he stood with his shoulders pulled back and his hands held in a guarded position, one hand stretched out in front of the other. He stood with his weight resting primarily on his hind leg, like he was ready to kick out with his front leg the moment I attempted to get close.

"Stand down." I reached down to my weapons belt, pulling out the only weapon I had that was worth a damn—a taser gun.

"What do you plan to do with that? You know the trigger system is just like the pistol safeties, right?"

"Yeah, but this one was given to me." Two prongs shot out, aimed at his chest. But before they could make contact, he shifted his weight to the side, dodging the electrified prongs.

I didn't wait for him to regain his defensive posture. Instead, I launched myself forward and came at him with everything I had. Adrenaline pumped through my body, taking away any fatigue, helping me to ignore the pain of his blocks and counter-strikes. I just kept punching and kicking, occasionally running up the alley walls to help gain some height as I aimed for his head.

I reached out to his mind, pushing my will onto him. But whoever he was, he was good. He was well trained. I was inside his head, but all I could see was the woman in the blue dress dancing to the tune of *Purple Rain*.

Kicks flew in both directions, high and low. I was forced to jump over his sweeping kick, but I misjudged the landing and was pushed up against the wall. My arm was pinned behind my back.

The unknown pushed into me. With his breather removed, his breath was hot on my ear. "I don't want to fight you, Mike. I never have."

"Who are you? How do you know my name?"

"You really don't remember, do you? Lucas said you would forget, but I had hoped that he was lying."

The pressure holding me against the wall vanished. Slowly, I turned around, taking off my helmet, goggles, and breather too. They were getting in the way, anyway, disrupting my peripheral vision.

He looked at me with wide eyes. "Woah, talk about a shitty dye job. What would possess you to do that two-tone number on yourself? At least the purple was fun. But that blue . . . It's so washed out and muted. It's definitely not you. I beg you to get rid of it."

I couldn't help myself. I smirked. I hadn't thought much about my hair, not since I had been released from Ward 27. But now that he mentioned it, it really was a bad dye job, and not something I would have chosen myself. Purple was my color. Purple all the way.

And somehow this guy knew that.

I continued to look into his mind, determined to find answers.

The woman in the blue dress, the woman I remembered from my vision in the MRI, was joined by another face I recognized: Dr. Abram Shutton. He held the woman in his arms as he spun her around in circles. And in the background, there was Tam, laughing and enjoying a glass of wine. And my mother was standing right next to Tam.

I blinked and pulled back from his mind. I stared at him, taking in his physical features. That's when I saw it. He was a younger version of Dr. Shutton.

"Who are you?"

"That's a bit hard to explain."

"Try."

"Okay. You asked for it." He sped forward and grabbed my arm, ensuring that his bare hand was in direct contact with my skin. He then stared at me with an intensity that I couldn't resist. And the world around us went dark.

"PUT IT ON my tab," the man said in our joint vision. He sat at the other end of the bar, taking in everything about me, especially my purple hair, bright as anything. And my purple jacket.

The vision shifted as we darted through the streets, avoiding the police drones stalking overhead. The man pushed me into an alleyway, up against the wall. "Do you trust me?" Before I could respond, he kissed me—a kiss that consumed my senses.

The vision changed again, and we were walking side by side through underground tunnels—followed by a group of men who were trying to look mean and scary, but they were really teddy bears, every single one of them. The way they interacted with the children was proof of that.

And again, we were looking into each other's eyes as our joint memories of *Purple Rain* merged into one: me with George, and him with the woman in the blue dress.

I fought to regain hold of my senses, to wrench back control of my own mind. "Get out of my head," I roared, and I pushed him away with every ounce of strength I had, both physically and mentally.

As my vision returned to normal, he stood hunched over, breathing hard. "I'd forgotten how strong you were—even drugged up like you are. But I can't let you go, Mike. You have to remember who you are."

Breathing hard myself, I stumbled to the side, tripping over my helmet, crushing the optical gear and comms unit—destroying my only way to call for help.

"I won't let you into my mind again." But the energies in the alleyway shifted, and a familiar presence came out of the shadows.

Lucas, my old mentor, stood there with a pained smile on his face. "You don't have a choice."

I was surrounded on all sides. The buzzing hum grew to debilitating levels. I blinked, trying to stay alert, focused, but the darkness encroached on the edges of my vision, pulling me under.

I sat in a dark room with Lucas and another man who I didn't recognize, but somehow, I knew him anyway. We sat around a dimly lit table.

"How can you be sure this will work?" Lucas asked, his voice like a memory.

"Because she thought of it." The unknown man threw a card into the middle of the table, but not just any card. The Queen of Hearts.

I fingered the card, caressing it, and my mind drifted to George. I took a deep breath and looked directly into Lucas's eyes. "Cedrick can't know until it's too late. But eventually he'll have to know, because only he will be strong enough to break in past the barriers. And he'll need the help of the rest of the team."

"He'll be ready when the time comes."

"I better let the White Rabbit know what's going on." The other man laboriously got to his feet and limped to the back of the room, where there was an old-style mechanical keyboard and a bank of monitors.

Lucas and I got up from our seats and headed toward the door.

"Lucas, before we leave the control room, I have a question for you. How long have you been working with the resistance?"

He bowed his head and gave me a pained smile. "Since the day I was ordered to wipe every trace of what you could do from the servers." He headed out the door without another word.

I looked back over my shoulder as the connection with the White Rabbit was established and the doors to the control room closed.

MY CHEST FELT tight. A rush of air filled my lungs. Something pressed against the side of my neck. "I have a pulse."

"Her eyes are fluttering."

"Mike! Mike, can you hear me?"

I groaned. My head was pounding, like someone decided that inside of my skull was a set of bongo drums. Slowly, I opened my eyes.

"Welcome back to reality." Marcus stared down at me, blood running down the side of his face. His helmet and breather were gone.

I sluggishly moved my head from side to side, taking in the soldiers surrounding us. I did the best I could to push myself up, against Marcus's protest.

"Did you get them?" I asked.

"They're gone. They vanished just as we got here. No idea how they managed to slip past us. We've even lost track of them on the security feeds. Mike, what the hell did they do to you? Your mind was a chaotic mess."

I licked my lips and shook my head.

The medic pushed Marcus to the side and forced me to look at him, flashing lights in my eyes and scanning my pharmachip for additional stats.

"I don't know," I said. "One minute, I was . . . and then . . ." I could barely process it myself. I pushed the medic away and pulled Marcus close. "The unknown—he's the strongest telepath I've ever met. He's even stronger than you."

"Did he try to compel you to do anything?"

I shook my head. "No, he just . . . He was trying to embed false memories. But I don't think he could compel me even if he tried. Help me up."

"Mike, you really should stay seated. You hit your head hard. You need to get checked out."

"So should you." I pointed to his head and the gash on his forehead.

Marcus winced as I touched it. "It's nothing that I haven't had before. But no doubt the doctors will make a big fuss when we get back to the barn."

"Yeah, well, they can fuss over me all they want . . . but we can't go straight back. We have something we need to do first. If we're going to have any chance of plugging the leak, we have to go after them now."

"What are you talking about?"

"The resistance." I closed my eyes, trying to ignore the pain in my head. "I don't know how much of what he showed me was true, but I can tell you with certainty that the resistance has an inside man working from within Rhodon Corporation. And I know who it is."

Forty-Seven

Marcus and I marched down the hall, shoulder to shoulder. Neither of us wanted to do what we were about to do, but there was no other option worth considering. Rhodon Corporation had a leak that needed to be plugged. I wanted to believe that I was wrong about what I saw in Lucas's head, but I knew in my heart that I wasn't.

The moment we arrived back in Sector 14, we progressed through the bare minimum of decon. As soon as we were given the all clear, we dressed in clean full tactical gear, and headed straight for the underground entrance of the Rhodon Corporation buildings.

A dozen STAR marched with us, each of them fully armed for what we were all hoping would be nothing. Everyone we passed in the halls pressed themselves against the white walls. Streaks of purple bled into the air, and I had to work hard to shield my mind from the fear and apprehension of others.

Members of our group peeled off to guard the stairs and the service elevators on the ground floor and the basement. Marcus and I led the remainder of our small team up the only remaining elevator to the clinic levels.

A calming melody played as we rose to the upper levels. Marcus and I smirked and continually shook our heads.

When the elevator doors opened, we continued our march into the psychology offices.

The receptionist looked up at us as we entered. Whatever smile she had vanished. "Can I help you?"

Marcus and I just ignored the woman and headed for the inner door, but the receptionist was quickly out of her chair to stand in our way.

"You can't go in there. Tam is in a private session."

"Exactly what we wanted to hear." Marcus pushed the woman out of the way, partially restraining her as he passed the woman to one of the other guards with us.

Unhindered, I opened the door and barged in.

"What is the meaning of this?" Tam was on their feet in a flash.

"Tam Haworth, I regret to inform you that you are under arrest by order of the Pregutor."

"Arrest? Under what charge?"

"Intent to commit espionage."

"Excuse me? What are you talking about?"

"We know the truth, Tam. Lucas told us everything."

"Lucas?"

"Lucas Tellis. You remember him, don't you? You were the one to falsify the records, faking his death. And you have been feeding the rebels inside information for months, possibly years. Don't try to deny it." I stared intently at Tam, staring directly into my former handler's white eyes. "He told me everything . . . White Rabbit."

The room was suddenly bathed in an orange and purple haze. The patient that had been sitting on the couch tried to push their way out the door, right into the arms of the waiting guards. Tam glanced around the room, like they were trying to size up the true severity of the situation, but there was nowhere to run. We had Tam cornered with no escape.

Tam slowly backed up against the blank wall, their hand out behind them. When they came in contact with the wall, they tapped out a distinctive pattern, and a bright light flooded the room. Sirens blared, causing me to cover my ears from the piercing noise. When the light cleared, Tam was gone.

"Where the hell did they go?" Marcus yelled, just barely audible above the siren.

"Out an escape route." I rushed to the wall, running my fingers over it.

The siren cut out. A faint ringing was left in my ear.

I was getting tired of hearing nothing but ringing.

"What do you mean, you can't track them?" Marcus's voice was muffled by the ringing. "I don't care what you need to do. You find Tam Haworth now!" He then turned to the other STAR with us. "Take these two down to the interrogation rooms and alert the captain that our mole has fled."

I continued my tactile search of the wall. There were several indentations, barely detectable, arranged in a square pattern. "There's a keypad here."

"Someone get one of the technicians up here," Marcus ordered.

"Wait, I have an idea." I stood tall and pressed my back against the wall, just like Tam had done. I then took off my glove and pressed my hand to the wall, right above the indentations. Closing my eyes, I focused on my last image of Tam, concentrating on the rhythm they had tapped out on the wall. Trusting my memory—not that it had been much help lately—I tapped out the same pattern.

The bright flash returned, and the siren started again. And the wall gave way. I grabbed Marcus's arm, pulling him with me as I fell backward through the small open doorway. It closed behind us, plunging us into darkness and muting all sounds from the office. I activated the night vision of my goggles, bathing everything in a sheen of green.

"How the hell . . .?" Marcus shook his head. "Never mind. I don't want to know." He then reached down to his ankle and passed me his secondary weapon. "You remember how to use one of these, don't you?"

I rolled my eyes. "Just tell me that the damned thing doesn't have a DNA-encoded safety."

"Why do you think I'm giving you that one and not my favorite toy?" Marcus looked both ways down the hall that ran behind the wall. "We should split up."

"No."

He looked at me with a quizzical smile. "Don't tell me you're afraid of the dark."

"Don't be a smart-ass." I pressed my lips tightly together and looked down the hall in both directions. "They went that way."

"How can you be so sure?"

"Did you notice the shift in the color in the room just before Tam disappeared?"

"Yeah, I did. What the hell was it?"

"I don't know, but I think it was something that Tam did. And that direction has the same shift in the spectrum."

"You can see that? Even in the night vision?"

I looked down the hall again. Nothing I could say would ever properly explain what I was seeing, but the hall possessed a slight haze. The energy coming from the space left an anxious feeling in its wake. "Trust me, they went that way.

Do you want me to take the lead? I mean, in my inadequacy, I could shoot you in the back. It's been a while since I've used one of these things." I held up the pistol and checked it to ensure that the safety was off and that the weapon was hot.

He snorted. "Let's go. We need to find Tam before they get out of the sector." He didn't wait for a response. He just held his pistol before him and led the way down the hall.

I tried to envision what navigating this hall would have been like without night vision goggles. It was pitch black, with no stray light at all. Tam would have needed to run their fingers along the walls, so they knew they were running in a straight line. And no doubt, Tam had run this particular path multiple times, practicing their flight, in case their duplicitous activities were ever discovered.

The path led to a set of stairs spiraling downward. By my calculation, we had to be in the center of the Rhodon buildings. And this set of stairs likely led to the employee tunnels that ran under the sector.

Marcus and I continued down the stairs. Even though I was confident that *down* was the right direction, I occasionally directed my attention back the way we had come.

In the vision that Lucas implanted in my mind, the unknown man had called Tam the White Rabbit, and here I was following the White Rabbit down a dark rabbit hole. But Wonderland was not waiting for us at the bottom. Instead, it was likely to be some Pregutor hell. Yet, just like Alice, curiosity drove me on.

The stairs bottomed out, and there was only one path to follow. Footfalls clacked against the concrete floor in the distance. And Tam, in their white suit, seemed to be a shrinking figure in the dark tunnels.

Marcus took off at a run. I chased behind him.

At the end of the hall was a door that was sealed using an old rusted mechanical wheel. Tam reached the door and tried to open it, twisting the wheel, but it wouldn't budge. The two-inch rods that held the door securely in place were still jutted into the ceiling and the ground.

Marcus stood solidly in the middle of the hall with his pistol raised. "Put your hands up and slowly turn around. Don't make me shoot you."

"Do what he says, Tam." I held up my own weapon trained on my former handler. "I beg you to make this easy on yourself."

Tam looked over their shoulder, their hands still on the rusted wheel. "It is not surprising that you would be the one to work it out. But you have to know that I will not allow myself to be captured. Too many lives are at stake."

I reached up to my goggles and deactivated the night vision, turning on flood lights instead. Tam's white suit only added to the brightness in the space.

"Just tell me why." I pushed in front of Marcus. "Why would you turn your back on everything that Rhodon Corporation stands for?"

Tam held their hands up, shielding their eyes from the bright light. "You tell me."

I continued to look into Tam's colorless eyes, searching for anything that would explain Tam's actions. Resting on the surface of their thoughts was a memory of the night my mother was killed. And I could see it as though I was there—inside Tam's body. Living it. Feeling it.

✳

Tam stared into my mother's eyes. As my mother's lips moved, I vocalized what my mother had said all those years ago.

"How could you betray your own daughter?"

It was Tam's memory that answered. "I never once betrayed you. It was because of me that you met Eddie in the first place, and he has done well in keeping you hidden. But the Pregutor knows where to find you. If you want to live—if you want your daughter to remain free—you have to trust me."

"How can I trust you? You were the one who fed me to the wolves."

Tam took a deep breath and nodded slightly. "I know there is a lot of bad blood between us, but I beg you, Natalie, for the sake of my granddaughter . . . Please. Time is running out. We need to leave. Now."

Natalie's eyes shifted to something behind Tam, but before Tam could turn to see what Natalie was looking at, a gunshot went off.

I blinked as the vision vanished. I was looking into the pained, pale eyes of my former handler. And in the middle of Tam's chest, a red spot grew among the white.

"Tam!" I rushed forward and caught Tam and eased them to the ground. I then pressed my hands to the center of Tam's chest. I looked up at Marcus, who stood there with his gun aimed before him.

"Marcus, don't just stand there! Help me!"

He blinked a few times, then holstered his weapon. "What do you want me to do? That was a clean shot."

"Use that communications implant of yours and get someone down here. Now. Tam needs urgent medical care."

"What's the point? Tam betrayed us."

I glared at Marcus. "Betrayal or not, it's not up to us whether they live or die. Besides, we need information. We need to know who their contact was with the rebels."

"We already know that: Lucas Tellis."

I continued to glare at him, but Tam reached out their hand and grabbed my arm, drawing my attention. There was no pain in Tam's eyes. Instead, there was a calmness to their being, like everything was how it was meant to be.

Tam reached up with a bloodied hand and caressed my cheek. "You look so much like your mother. I am sorry that I was unable to fulfill my promise."

"What promise?"

"To keep you safe."

The scent of roses overpowered my senses. "Remember," Tam whispered.

My vision went dark as I was plunged into Tam's memories again. Everything that I saw and felt was how Tam remembered them. Their thoughts. Their internal sensations. Their emotions.

TAM SCREAMED AS they ran for their daughter. They cradled Natalie in their arms as blood pooled beneath them.

"How could you?" Tam screamed at the man standing in the doorway, the smoking pistol still in his hand.

"She was going to run again," Abram Shutton said, "with the girl."

"She was your daughter! And you killed her!"

"She was an experiment. Just like you and I."

Tam took a deep breath and pushed their dead daughter off their lap. With shaky legs, they got to their feet. "Is that all you and I ever were? An experiment? Because I remember it quite differently."

"If that were so, then why did you lie about who her father was? Why did you allow me to have another family?"

Tam wanted to say that it was for some noble reason of protecting the man they loved, but they couldn't say that. In truth, Tam had always known where his heart lay. He was loyal to the Pregutor, determined to seek the ultimate human being, one who could reclaim the surface of the planet. That would always be his number one driving force. And if Tam hadn't protected their daughter in the only way they knew how, their granddaughter would have become an experiment too from the moment she was born.

"Where is the girl?" Abram demanded as he holstered his weapon. He pushed Tam out of the way, so he could head deeper into the apartment. Tam slipped on the blood beneath them—their daughter's blood.

"She's not here!" Abram spun Tam around and stared into their eyes. His grip on their upper arm cut off the circulation to their fingers.

Pain grew behind Tam's eyes as they fought to keep him out, but he would always be stronger than they were. Abram was a fourth gen. Tam was only a third gen.

"Where . . . is the girl?" he hissed.

"I don't know," Tam said, unable to resist his command to tell him the truth. "If she's not here, then I don't know where she is."

Abram pushed Tam back and glared. "Interesting."

"What is interesting?"

"For a moment there, you lost your sense of control. You were speaking in contractions. And your fear was palpable." His nose wrinkled and his lip curled. His sneer made it perfectly clear what he thought of them.

Tam fought to hold back the tears as they looked upon their dead daughter behind him.

"Take off your clothes."

"Excuse me?"

"I said, 'Take off your clothes.' What is there to not understand? The cleaner is going to need to destroy all evidence that Natalie was ever here, including your blood-soaked clothes. Now take them off, woman, or I'll instruct the cleaner to destroy all evidence while you're still wearing them."

Tam took a deep breath and slowly peeled off their purple jacket and began unbuttoning their blouse. As they took off every item of clothing and dumped them into a pile on the floor in front of them, Abram's sneer only grew. When Tam stood before him naked, Abram's disdain manifested as a burning smell that wafted toward Tam like smoke on their tongue.

"Do I have your permission to seek out something alternative that I might wear as we travel back to Crystal Hills? Or must I travel naked as the day I was born?"

Abram rolled his eyes. "Do whatever you feel you need to. Just be quick about it." He stormed out of the small apartment and barked orders to the soldiers outside—orders to find the girl.

The cleaners came in and started wrapping Natalie's body, preparing it for disposal. Tam's purple suit had been thrown in with the body.

Tam continued to inhale deeply, doing the best they could to keep their emotions from raging out of control. Feeling numb, they headed to the only bedroom in the small apartment. In the drawers, they found a pair of white-washed jeans and a white T-shirt, clothing that had belonged to their now dead daughter. They weren't quite Tam's style, but they would at least fit. Natalie had been the same size as her mother.

In the middle of the bed was a small stuffed animal, a purple cat with the widest, most un-catlike smile. As Tam picked up the toy, a sense of fear washed over them. But this fear wasn't their own.

Tam turned around, trying to find the source of the fear, feeling it stronger as they headed to the small closet located in the corner. Tam opened the closet door and allowed their feelings to be their eyes. An invisible figure bathed in a purple haze was huddled in the corner.

Tam took another deep breath, then knelt before the closet. "Michaella, I know you are scared. I am too. I have no way of knowing for sure what will happen, but I do know one thing: I refuse to let anything bad happen to you. I will do everything within my power to keep you safe. I promise. You and I both share the same blood, and because of it, we both know that your kitty cat is purple." Tam put the stuffed animal down on the floor in the space just before the closet. "I am only guessing here, but I bet your mommy told you that the bad men cannot see purple."

The purple cat vanished from view, taken into the haze in the corner of the closet.

"It will be okay, Michaella. Please, show yourself to me. I am unable to keep you safe if you stay hidden from me."

Slowly, the hazy form took shape. There, in the corner of the closet, was a little girl, only five years old, clinging to the purple cat.

Tam tried to smile at the little girl, but they had to fight to keep the tears at bay. "You look so much like your mother. Come here, and let me put my arms around you. I will be your shield, so the others never need to know exactly what you can do."

It took a bit of coaxing, but eventually the girl went into Tam's arms. Tam stroked the girl's hair and hummed the chorus of *Purple Rain*.

THE VISION DIED away, as did the feeling of safety and warmth. As I continued to look at Tam, all that was left was the colorless stare of death.

Forty-Eight

I sat in the middle of the locker room, trying to piece it all together. I remembered the purple cat and its stupid grin. It was one of the few things I had managed to keep from my childhood. I still had it—assuming my things from my apartment hadn't been thrown out like common trash. But while I couldn't remember the exact details about how I got the treasured stuffed animal, I always felt safe—and loved—when I held it in my arms.

And if what Tam had shown me was real, my mother hadn't committed suicide like I had been told. Instead, she had been killed in cold blood . . . by Abram Shutton. My grandfather.

I never knew about any blood connection between myself and the doctor, but if it was true, it explained so much.

So many visions. And there was no way to know if any of it was real.

"Are you okay?" Marcus sat next to me, wrapped in nothing but a towel.

"I'm fine." My voice sounded mechanical, even to my own ears. But I was struggling to maintain some sense of control over my raging emotions.

"You might want to get out of those clothes. They'll be covered in Tam's blood."

I sat up straight and looked down at my black uniform. "Yeah, they will be." Not that anyone could tell. But eventually the dried blood would make the fabric stiff—well, stiffer than normal.

"Before I forget, I just got word. Jody came through surgery just fine. She should make a full recovery."

I nodded. "That's good."

"Are you sure you're okay?"

Again, I nodded. "Just a lot to process. First, our trainer. Then our handler. What other secrets will we uncover?" I didn't wait for an answer, because I really didn't want to think about the consequences. Instead, I stripped off the bloodied uniform and dumped it into the sanitation bin, then headed for the shower.

After making sure I was clean, scrubbing under my nails too, I went back out into the locker area with a towel wrapped around me. I felt so lost. I didn't have a locker in this room, so I didn't have any clean clothing to change into. I just bowed my head and did the best I could to stay calm and centered.

"These might help." Marcus held out a stack of folded black clothing and a pair of shiny new boots. The uniform was similar to what he wore, but smaller. Complete with the blue and purple stripes that ran down the sleeves.

"Who did you steal those from?"

"Don't ask. You'll be happier not knowing."

I smirked as I took the gear and put it on.

"Gahan. Davison," someone called out from the other side of the room. "The captain needs you up in the surgical ward right away."

Marcus and I glanced at one another. We then sprinted from the locker rooms and through the halls, heading for the elevators that would take us to the hospital facility above ground. The elevator couldn't move fast enough. Both of us paced the little space, preparing to run as soon as the doors opened.

At the doors to the hospital wing, Marcus waved his wrist over the scanners and punched in his access code to override the doors. As a member of STAR, there was nowhere within the Rhodon facilities that he didn't have access to. And he didn't wait for the scanners to clear me either. He just pulled me through with him.

We ran into the ward and headed for the nurses' station. "We're looking for Jody Kristensen," I said. "She should be here." But before the nurse could answer, Marcus nudged my shoulder and pointed to a glass-walled room on the other side of the ward.

"Oh my god, Jody."

We raced into the room, taking up positions on either side of the petite woman in the bed. Tubes and wires came out of her tiny frame in every direction. Multiple IV lines fed into her neck. But it was the big tube breathing for her that hit me the hardest.

"I thought you said that she had pulled through the surgery."

"That's what I was told. I don't understand." Marcus took Jody's hand in his own. "Her hands are warm. That has to be a good thing, right?"

I shrugged, but my instincts told me something was off. For as long as I could remember, Jody had always complained about how her hands and feet were cold. I had to force myself to breathe as I stepped closer to Jody. I stared at the woman, willing to hear her thoughts, but there was nothing—not even her giddy hum.

"Gahan. Davison. What are you doing here?" The captain stood in the doorway with a doctor standing next to him.

"We were told that we were needed in the surgical ward," Marcus said. "How bad is she, sir?"

The doctor who stood next to the captain answered. "Jody Kristensen will be fine."

"How can you say that?" I asked. "She's on a ventilator."

"Just a precautionary measure," the doctor said. "I can assure you that she is breathing for herself." But there was something about the way he spoke—about the way he stood—that gave off the impression that there was more to Jody's condition than he was telling us.

The readouts that hovered above Jody's head appeared to be normal, with a regular heart rate and a stable blood pressure. But the respiratory output changed color every few waveforms, shifting between brown and blue, then back again. I didn't know what the shifts in the color meant, but I suspected that Jody wasn't breathing entirely for herself, like the doctor wanted us to believe.

"Agent Kristensen is in the best hands possible," the captain said, "but Kristensen is not why you were called to the surgical ward."

Marcus and I glanced at one another, shrugging and shaking our heads.

"The two of you did a good job today," the captain continued. "It's obvious to me that you two make a great team. We would be stupid to pull the two of you apart. So, good news, Agent Davison, you've been promoted to the rank of Lieutenant JG. You're to be assigned to STAR

Unit 99—Gahan's unit. You'll be his second, but you will have the full autonomy that being a Lieutenant JG provides. The two of you were called to the surgical unit so we could sever this funky heart connection between you, and enable Davison to get her communications and tactical implants."

"Now?" I asked.

"Now. I'll let you have a few minutes to savor the last of your heart connection, but you are to report to surgery immediately." The captain left, and the doctor pushed past Marcus to examine Jody's vitals.

Marcus sauntered around the foot of the bed, encouraging me to follow him out the door. The grin on his face spread from ear to ear. It reminded me of that stupid grin on that stuffed purple cat.

"Don't get me wrong, I'll miss our unique connection"—he tapped his hand to his heart—"but while on missions, I would prefer not to be hampered by your physical ailments. And it's good to know that we'll be on the same side, fighting alongside one another from now on."

"Yeah, it is good news." Though my voice didn't possess any of the enthusiasm that his had.

"Hey, I thought you wanted this." He forced me to face him, with his hands on my shoulders. "You've worked hard to prove to the Pregutor that you're loyal. Hell, you helped to find the leak. But if you've changed your mind, we still have time to reverse the orders."

"No, this is the right path. It's just . . ." I took several deep breaths and looked back over my shoulder at Jody. My eyes focused on the ventilator tube.

"Jody would be excited about this too. She's been waiting for you to help her kick my ass in training."

Despite my hesitations, I smirked. "I guess I wasn't expecting it to be so soon after my first operation with the unit."

"You've proved your loyalty—multiple times. Why wait?"

I slowly nodded. "You're right. Why wait? Just as long as you can bear the absence of our heart connection." I deliberately stepped closer to him and placed my hand on his belly, just above the waistband of his pants. I ran my fingers around in a figure eight.

For a moment, my heart jumped ahead. And it wasn't my heart that directed the increased pulse rate. I laughed as Marcus blushed and glanced around the ward to see who might have been watching us.

"You're mean, you know that?"

"Yep," I said, still laughing. "Let's go sever this heart connection and get me some implants."

Forty-Nine

THE PROCEDURE TO GET THE implants didn't take anywhere as long as I thought it would. A small cut behind the right ear, and the small disk was inserted into place. But it was the ocular implant that was a little more involved.

They took my eyes out of their sockets and connected the units to my optic nerves. And I had to be awake during the entire procedure. It was incredibly disconcerting as the medical unit came toward me to take my eyes out. It was disorienting to see my body at angles that weren't normally possible without moving my head.

But it was the disconnection of the hearts that was the worst. The connection process had required only the wave of a wand over my pharmachip. But the disconnection required a reprogramming of my pharmachip. It meant taking the pharmachip offline for a few seconds. Under normal circumstances, that wouldn't have been an issue, but with the hearts linked, when Marcus's pharmachip went offline, my pharmachip thought that his heart had stopped and my own chip stopped my heart in the process. I was grateful we were in the surgical unit for that.

As the last of the new implants were installed and my pharmachip program was updated, Marcus was by my side the entire time.

"Okay, we're all set," said the technician. "Implants are in place and we're ready to bring them online to calibrate them. Are you ready?"

I took a deep breath and nodded.

"First, we'll bring online the communications chip." The technician turned to his virtual keyboard and tapped a few commands into the air. I winced at the sudden squeal in my right ear.

"Sorry about that. Your hearing is better than average. We'll just dial that down a bit." And the squeal vanished. "How's that?"

"Better."

"No residual hum?"

I shook my head.

"That's good. Agent Gahan, if you could give it a try?"

Marcus nodded and tapped behind his left ear. "Comms check."

I smiled at the beep. "Coming through loud and clear. And in both ears. How is that possible?"

The technician furrowed his brow. "Um . . . You have two comms units."

"No, I don't. You only installed the one."

"Yes, we do, Mike," Marcus said. "The first unit was installed when we were given agent status as couriers. Don't you remember?"

"Oh yeah. I guess that it was so long ago it must have slipped my mind." In truth, I didn't remember it at all.

The technician continued typing commands on the virtual keyboard. "Well, the two units are now linked. Whatever one unit hears, the other unit will hear too."

"And stereo sound?"

The technician nodded.

"That's good, because it means my music won't be lopsided."

Marcus laughed. "She's just a little obsessed with certain songs," he said, answering the questioning look from the technician.

The technician shuffled in his chair and smiled. "Why don't we try the ocular implants?"

I nodded my agreement.

"You might want to sit back in the chair as we bring the implants online. The shifts can be a little disorienting. Just do the best you can to keep your eyes open."

I settled in the chair with my head against the headrest. My vision suddenly blurred into a blob-filled colored mass, filled with nothing but blue and yellow. Slowly, blobs turned into discernible shapes, but everything was still out of focus. As I continued to look forward, trying to ignore my rising concern related to my compromised vision, a crosshair pattern came into focus. For a split second, the crosshairs were clear, but it went past that and became unfocused again. The next minute was taken up with fine tuning the focus and the crosshair pattern.

"Okay . . . The unit has been calibrated for your natural vision. Over time, you'll need to get the unit recalibrated, but we can do that as part of your annual check."

I sat more upright and swung my legs over the side of the surgical chair. "So, that's it?"

"That's it. All there is left to do now is to ensure that you know how to activate the system and bring up your tactical display. Make sure that there isn't a glitch in the interface."

"So, what do I do?"

The technician smiled and deferred to Marcus.

"The implants behave exactly like your glasses and earbuds did," Marcus said. "Except now, no one can take them away from you, not without blinding you and cutting you up."

"I'll forgo the blinding and cutting up part, but I like the idea that no one can take them away. So, the interface commands are just like the glasses?"

"Yes."

I stared into the empty space in front of me and pressed my fingers to my left temple. My vision was overlaid with a virtual display with icons around the edges. As I moved my eyes around the edges of the screen, the display changed. I wasn't quite sure what I did, but suddenly my vision was washed in a sheen of green that kept phasing into yellow. The brightness of the lights forced me to cover my eyes. "Oh, wow . . . That's not good."

"You activated the night vision, didn't you?"

"I think so, yeah. How do I turn that off?"

"The icon should be on the bottom-left of the interface," the technician said. "Just move your focus to it, mentally willing the icon to change color."

With the sheen of green gone, I took several deep breaths before opening my eyes again. "Let's not do that again."

Marcus's laughter filled the room. "You'll get used to it." It was oddly a comfort to know that I could be a source of amusement.

"The interfaces are customizable, so you can move the icons around and change the activation sequence, if you want," the technician said. "Some agents prefer to use hand signals or tapping sequences to shift vision modes."

"That sounds like a good idea." I then looked up at Marcus. "So, is this what it's like for you?"

Marcus slumped a little in defeat. "All the time."

"Well, everything seems to check out okay," the technician said. "You're free to go, but if you suffer from any headaches or blurriness of vision over the next few days, come back immediately."

I nodded, then hopped down from the surgery chair. "Thank you."

The technician smiled. "You're welcome."

Marcus and I headed out into the halls. The entire time, I kept looking around, but I wasn't looking at the surrounding environment. I was taking in my new virtual display.

"This is so weird. I'm used to not having any access to my peripheral vision when I see a virtual display like this."

"When in the field, you still won't have access to your peripheral vision, because you'll still need to use goggles. But now you don't need those stupid single screen displays when inside Sector 14. Trust me, it's better this way."

"I believe you." I then stopped and turned to Marcus. "You said these things are just like the glasses and earbuds. Does that mean I'm now able to gain access to the external feeds?"

Marcus grinned. "Except you'll want to upload your personal AI to your implants right away. The personality that comes stock standard with these implants is so boring. And the voice . . ." He gave a bit of a shiver. "It's so irritating."

I cocked my head to the side and tried not to laugh. I had never seen him so . . . free and natural like this. He was being human for a change.

"So, how do I access the feeds?"

"Just like you would have done on the glasses. Tap your temples to activate the system."

Biting my bottom lip, I tapped the side of my left temple. "Computer, initialize system."

"Initializing," said a robotic voice that had zero tone inflections.

I hunched my shoulders and winced. "Oh, that *is* annoying."

Marcus just shrugged with that *I-told-you-so* look.

"Please tell me that the AI transfer is the same as on the glasses."

Marcus nodded.

Trusting that Marcus was right, I tapped my temple again, this time with three quick taps. The virtual display shifted and brought up what looked more like a faded computer screen. I could still see the actions of those around us through the virtual display.

I grabbed at virtual items hovering in front of me, moving them around so I could get to the system for the AI transfer. "Computer, bring up an external port and connect to node 1659B. Authorization: Davison Kilo-Alpha-One. Alice, are you there?"

"Awaiting instructions."

The smile on my face grew to consume my being. "It's so good to hear your voice."

"It is good to be heard."

I laughed, then looked at Marcus. "Okay, these things are not exactly like the glasses. So, what can they do that the glasses can't?"

FIFTY

We walked side by side down the halls. The whole way, comparing notes about the new implants and how they differed to the virtual display glasses. The one mode present on the new implants that wasn't available through the glasses was access to security maps for the sector. As we walked through the halls, I got instant updates from the servers about everyone's security access: who was who, and if they were in the right place. I could happily get used to that.

We stopped outside the door to the room that had been my prison cell. While I liked having the space—and the private bathroom—I hated being trapped. But now I had implants, I was moving to the squad barracks.

"Are you sure you can handle sharing a room with me?" Marcus wiggled his eyebrows.

"I don't know. Maybe." I stepped closer to him and placed my hand on his chest. Slowly, I trailed my finger down the hidden line of his abs toward the waistband of his pants. I couldn't feel it, but I knew his heart was racing ahead.

"Cruelty is your strength, isn't it?"

I shrugged as I waved my pharmachip over the sensor for the door. "Hey Marcus, do you think the captain would be willing to help me with a slight problem that I now have?"

"Depends on the problem."

"I need to move the main server for Alice. The unit's installed in my apartment in Sector 11, but the apartment was rented out to someone else when I wound up in Ward 27."

"What are you talking about? Your apartment wasn't rented out, at least not according to the sector directory." He waved his hands in the empty space in front of him, clearly going through files on his own virtual display. "It says here that you're still the leaseholder, and that your rent has been paid through to the end of the year."

"That can't be right."

"See for yourself." He scrunched his hand into a fist and flicked the file in my direction.

I tapped on the icon in front of me to open the file. "I don't understand. Tam said—"

"Tam betrayed us. Everything they were doing was a lie. Why would this be any different?"

I took several deep breaths. "It wouldn't. So, I still have an apartment."

"Yeah, but you may not want to use it when you're on duty. STAR squads are often called into service at a moment's notice. The time it would take to get here from Sector 11 . . ." He shrugged. "The squad would have left without you."

A warmth filled my being. I still had a place that was all mine, where I could hide from the world if I needed to.

I headed for the drawers where my uniforms had been stored. "Alice, bring up the public newsfeeds from the past twenty-four hours."

"Processing."

Marcus laughed from the other side of the room. "You really like reading the news, don't you?" He started stacking the books that were on the desk.

"We need to stay up to date with what's going on out there." I grabbed the rest of my things stashed around the room—a hairbrush, an electronic notebook, and a pack of playing cards—giving a small portion of my attention to the newsfeeds. Footage of the incident in Sector 10 played over and over, including the dark figure pulling Jody from the fire and me stumbling after them. But the news report was identifying the *hero* as Marcus Gahan.

"Um . . . Marcus, why would the news be calling you a hero? They're saying that you were the one to pull Jody from that fire, but you and I both know that's not true."

"We can't exactly have the public knowing that it was the unknown, can we?"

The news changed. "Marcus, there's a report here saying that you're to be awarded the Grand Cross of the Redeemer for your actions."

He kept his back to me. "That's correct."

"Marcus, look at me."

"I would prefer not to."

"Because I can read your mind and see the truth." I sighed. "But I don't need to read your mind to know what it is you're trying to hide from me. You lied to the captain about what happened, didn't you? You told the captain that it was you, because you didn't want some stranger to get the recognition. I can't believe you would lie like that." I shook my head and looked up at the ceiling. "Just tell me honestly why you lied."

"I thought it would have been obvious."

"Yeah, you wanted the fame and glory."

"No, you idiot. I lied to protect you." He spun around and stared at me with an intensity I wasn't used to. Pain and desperation radiated off him. "The unknown was right there in front of you, and you didn't act until he ran. I saw the footage playback in detail, Mike. Two whole minutes, and you did nothing but just stand there and look at him." He bowed his head and took several deep breaths. He then looked up at me, and I saw something else that I never thought I would see in his eyes. Desire. "I lied because I would never forgive myself if anything happened to you."

He rushed forward and pulled me into a kiss, and I didn't resist. But I didn't feel anything. I thought I would. I wanted to. But now that my lips were in contact with his, I felt nothing, except perhaps annoyance and confusion.

When the kiss was over, he pressed his forehead to mine. "I should have asked them to keep our hearts linked. At least that way I would know what you're feeling." He stood back from me, looking into my eyes. "But you don't feel anything, do you?"

"Marcus, I . . . So much has changed. Lucas. Tam. Jody."

"It's okay. I always knew it would be hard." He backed away and went back to stacking the books on the desk. "Perhaps one day you'll be ready to forget him."

"Forget who?"

"George." There was pain and disappointment in his eyes. "I know you loved him, but . . . I thought that maybe you could find a little room in your heart for me. I should have known that I could never compete against a memory. No matter how much time passes, it will always be your memories of George that give you the most strength."

I tried to swallow back the lump forming at the back of the throat. "You're talking like George is never coming back."

"Of course, he's never coming back. He's dead."

"Just because he was sent to Skáki Valley doesn't mean he's dead. I know that his chances aren't great, but . . ." I stopped when his expression became slack-jawed and his eyes grew wide.

"Is that what Tam told you? Is that what they took from you?"

"What are you talking about?"

"The chair. Before you were admitted to Ward 27, you were in the chair. A full memory download. But they clearly chose to take away some of your memories too. That has to be it. That's what they took from you. Your memories of George. Of how he died." He stepped closer to me, like he was ready to catch me should I fall. "He wasn't on a mission in Skáki Valley. He died in Sector 2—in an explosion that destroyed an apothecary."

"No, that can't be right."

"Mike, you were there when it happened. You saw it all."

I closed my eyes, desperately trying to hold back the tears. "It's not possible. Why would he . . .?" My chest grew tight, and my breathing became labored. I pressed my hands to my chest, just above my heart. "Alice, play *Purple Rain.*"

As the electric guitar strummed the opening chords, I stumbled backward and fell onto the bed. The snare drum sounded, and I started rocking back and forth. The bass drum and the lyrics came in, and I focused on George as we sang in the purple rain. Slowly, I was able to take a deep breath.

Pressure on my knee drew my attention. "I'm sorry. I thought you knew."

"Why was I there?"

Marcus shook his head. "I don't know. The records have been sealed, even from me. The only thing I know with any certainty is that you were there when it happened. You were making a delivery."

I gasped. And like a tidal wave, I was pulled under by the vision—and my memories of George's death.

Fifty-One

For hours, I sat on my new bed in the barracks in the dark. Marcus's light snoring echoed around the small space. I was grateful that he was sound asleep, because I couldn't take much more of him trying to cheer me up. No, I wanted to dwell on George and everything that he meant to me. I wanted to cling to what memories I could before time eroded them away.

That was assuming that they didn't force me into the chair again, taking away the memories of what I had relearned about George's death.

I thought of his boyish smile. His barking laugh. The glimmer of mischief in his eyes. George was my home—my center. Now he was gone.

I brushed my fingers along the scar behind my right ear where my cochlear implant had been put in—the radio receiver that no one could take off me without surgery. "Alice, play *Purple Rain*," I whispered, trying not to wake anyone. Soon, the music streamed into the implant where only I could hear it.

With the first strum of the guitar, I laid on my bed and pulled the covers over my head. I closed my eyes and focused on the musical chords, conjuring memories from our playful jaunt in the purple rain as it burned our skin. I fingered the pock scars that ran down my arms as I remembered how badly we would sing the chorus of our favorite song together. His arm draped over my shoulders. And as our horrid rendition of the song ended, he would always say the same thing. "I'm here. Not letting you go. Never forget that."

I tried to hold on to him, holding his loving smile before me. In the dark, I reached out to caress his cheek. Before I could make contact, the joyful and fun-loving man morphed into a walking zombie, devoid of emotion. He turned away from me and headed into the apothecary just as the store had exploded. Before I could scream and do anything to save him, he was standing in front of me again, his fun-loving nature radiating from his soul—only for him to become the walking zombie again, exploding before my eyes.

My mind dwelled on the idea of watching George die. The tears escaped. I couldn't shake the vision.

Unwilling to accept any longer the torture my mind had concocted, I threw off the covers and got dressed.

"What are you doing?" Marcus mumbled from the other side of the room.

"I couldn't sleep. I'm going for a walk."

"Do you want me to come with you?" His words carried an undertone of 'Please don't make me come with you.'

I smirked. "No, I'm all good. You go back to sleep."

Marcus mumbled something else, but soon soft snores came from the direction of his bed.

I headed out into the main plaza and sat on the bench in the middle of the rose garden. The white roses were bathed in the moonlight that was nothing but a projection on the dome overhead. While I still preferred the idea of having my own apartment, living in the barracks in Sector 14 had its advantages. Where else in the world could you get a clear view of what the sky had looked like more than two hundred years ago?

"How many times do I have to tell you that it's not real?" George's voice was so clear in my head. I closed my eyes, trying to hold back the tears. *"I want you to make me a promise. If you are ever presented with the opportunity to get out—to escape this life—take it."*

"I promise," I whispered. My hand rushed to cover my mouth in a poor attempt to hold back the sob.

A ding sounded in my ear. A message counter hovered in the air before me. I blinked a few times, slightly disoriented by the new vision display.

"Alice, what's the time?"

"The time is 0200."

"So early?"

With my mind racing ahead, searching for answers, I reached out to the new message counter and gestured to open the message. Words typed across my vision.

>>Do me a favor. Make sure my aunt gets this. Signed, George.<<

Then an image of a playing card grew in my vision, but not just any playing card. The Queen of Hearts. Double headed and regal.

I sat up straighter. Every time I turned around, something else was leading me back to the Queen of Hearts. But why? What did it mean?

"Alice, confirm who sent this message."

"George Tuthill."

"What?" That wasn't possible. George was dead. "Alice, when was this message sent?"

"On May 14th, 2220, at 0819."

I held my breath. That was four months ago. Long before George died.

"Alice, why am I only just now getting this message?"

"The message was suspended. Subject to the Bandersnatch protocol."

"The what?"

"Please restate the question."

"What is the Bandersnatch protocol?"

"Unknown."

"If it's unknown, then how do you know about it?"

"Unknown."

"Is there anything at all that you can tell me about the Bandersnatch protocol?"

"Please restate the question."

I forced myself to take calm, slow breaths. It was times like this that Alice was annoying as hell.

"When was the Bandersnatch protocol enacted?" I might not have known what the protocol was for, but I could at least work out its origins.

"The Bandersnatch protocol was enacted on July 3rd, 2220."

"That was two months ago."

"Correct."

I shook my head, trying to piece it together. If the Bandersnatch protocol had been enacted two months ago, that still didn't explain why I was only just now getting this message. I racked my brain, trying to think back to what might have been significant about two months ago. Then my shoulders sank. Two months ago, I woke up in Ward 27 a prisoner—without communications and with no memory of how I got there.

"Alice . . ." I licked my lips, not sure I wanted the answer to my next question. "Who designed the Bandersnatch protocol?"

"You did."

I closed my eyes, desperately trying to maintain some sense of composure. I couldn't remember designing the protocol, but maybe that was the point.

The Queen of Hearts. The playing cards. The White Rabbit. And now Bandersnatch—a creature that was under the command of the Red Queen. It was all connected.

Clues. To my memory. And if I wanted to remember the truth, I had only one choice: to deliver the card to George's aunt.

Besides, the woman had the right to know that her nephew had been killed while in the line of duty.

Fifty-Two

I HEADED FOR THE EMPLOYEE tunnels and the locker rooms. I didn't know where the STAR locker rooms were, or if STAR used these corridors, but that didn't matter. As far as I knew, I still had a locker among the couriers. Everything I would need for an excursion across the city would be there.

Without any real plans or thought about the morning hour, I stripped my Sector 14 clothing, dumping them in the sanitation bins, then headed for my old locker.

There was a small amount of dust on the security panel, but that was to be expected. I just wiped away the dust and waved my pharmachip over the panel. With the locker door open, I brushed my hand down the fabric of my purple jacket. It would likely be the last time I would ever wear it. As a member of STAR, my jacket would be navy. Perhaps they would let me keep my purple jacket for personal reasons.

I quickly donned my street clothes, rolling my ankles to ensure a good fit in my boots. I then threw on the jacket and grabbed my glasses with peripheral seals and breather. But that was when the rashness to make a move across the city at this hour backfired. I stood on the platform for the transport tubes staring at the display for when the next trains were due. The next transport wasn't due for another two hours.

I flopped my head forward. What did I expect for so early in the morning? Sighing in defeat, I looked over my shoulder at the employees' tunnels. I could always go back to bed, making the trek across the city in a few hours' time, but I was already dressed and alert. Instead, I put on my breather and glasses, activating the peripheral seals, then headed for the foot passageways that ran alongside the transport tube tracks.

I put one foot in front of the other. My footfalls on the concrete created a rhythm that lulled my mind into a sense of peace. I turned the corner and went through the first checkpoint of many that existed between Sector 14 and Sector 2.

Just inside Sector 12 was George's favorite shop. I shook my head and smiled as I remembered how George used to get so excited when there had been a new shipment of Frenz— the most disgusting candy I had ever tasted. But George was happiest when Frenz turned his teeth blue.

A few streets over, I stood at the edge of a quiet park. In my mind's eye, I watched George play soccer with the neighborhood kids. He tried so many times to get me to join in, but I was having too much fun watching him. "Besides, it wouldn't be fair to the kids to have to compete against both of us," I had told him, and he accepted my excuse.

I entered the next sector checkpoint and remembered how George would skip down the streets, shouting out nursery rhymes and children's poems. *The Walrus and the Carpenter* was a favorite.

Any irritation I had initially felt being forced to walk across the city at the early hour eroded away. Each stage of my journey allowed me to relive another memory of George. I had never realized how much of my exploration of the city had been with George as he did his George things.

As I passed through the final checkpoint into Sector 2, I looked up at the archway entrance. The faint outlines of the mural artwork showed a young family walking into a dome-covered garden. The dome depicted in the mural was missing sections, just like in reality. There was no protection from the outside atmosphere. But just like in the mural, there were still traces of the garden beds that would have once been filled with flowers. Although instead of flowers, sticks grew out of the ground. I had always thought that the sticks were dead, but now, as I looked closer, reddish-brown spikes covered the stems, and there was a small collection of browny-green leaves unfurling at the ends.

"They're a type of fern," said an old man who was tending to the pseudo-garden.

"Excuse me?"

"The plants. I noticed you studying them. They're a type of fern. They're hardy, resilient plants, willing to grow almost anywhere, even in ground that is filled with acid and few nutrients." The man encouraged me to come closer, to focus on the small curled plant that was just poking out of the ground. "This little guy is only a few days old. But if we let him grow, in a year's time, he'll be as big and strong as that guy over there." He pointed to another flowerbed on the other side of the path. A small shrub with large unfurled branches stood in the center, providing shade for a bench where people could rest their feet.

I looked between all the *ferns* and the gardener. And it wasn't until then that I noticed the gardener wasn't wearing a breather unit. He didn't even have tubes to feed oxygen into his nose. And he seemed to be breathing perfectly fine.

"How long have you been in Crystal Hills?" I asked.

The old man cocked his head to the side and rubbed his chin. "Oh, I'm not sure. I was still a child when my parents first came here."

"And you've been here ever since?"

The old man nodded.

"Did you not want to move into the inner sectors?"

"And leave my garden unattended?" The old man winked and smiled. "I've led a good life. And I've done what I was meant to do."

"Which is?"

He smirked. "To tend to my garden every day, waiting for one to finally see the beauty that these little sticks can have. It might not seem like much, but all it takes is for one person to see the truth." He pulled something out of his pocket and placed it down in the garden next to the newest spring of life. He then groaned as he got to his feet. With one last smile, he headed down the path, away from the sector checkpoint.

I took in the beauty of the little plant one last time, but my eyes gravitated to the card resting next to it. I half expected to see a Queen of Hearts, but this card was a Joker. It was the one card that didn't really have a place, yet in certain games, it was the most powerful card in the deck. I considered pocketing the card, but there was something about its placement that was important. It was like the card was telling everyone who passed by the baby fern that this fern would ultimately become the most powerful plant around.

I allowed my systems to do one final scan of the surroundings. There were no airborne contagions—other than those found naturally in the atmosphere. Taking a deep breath, I removed my breather. I held my breath for a few seconds, questioning my sanity. But I took off my breather for a reason. If the old man could get away without wearing a breather, then I could too.

I counted to five, then exhaled and tested the contaminated air for myself. As my lungs filled with the toxins, I half expected to start coughing. Instead, I had zero problems with breathing. It wasn't the clean air found back in Sector 14. No, this air had a burned taste to it. But I was still breathing it.

I knelt next to the flowerbed and smiled at the baby fern and the Joker card. I was breathing the same air that the little plant was forced to process. And if the old man was right, the plant would thrive despite the hostile environment.

Residents came out of their environmentally sealed homes and headed down the streets toward various places of work. Some people wore breather tubes, while others wore a breather unit. And others wore no breather at all. As I continued to watch the pedestrians on the street, I noticed something that I would have never noticed if I didn't take the time to admire the fern. The people who wore no breather at all were wearing some shade of purple. Those with the breather tubes wore blue. Those with the full breather units wore monochromatic colors that blended into gray.

I looked up at the sections of the dome that still remained. And my jaw dropped. The cracks within the dome structure weren't random. It was the distinct pattern of the four suits of cards. A diamond. The spade. A club. And a heart. And in the center of the pattern was the Joker.

It was a symbol for anyone who cared to look.

Just like the little fern, the residents of Sector 2 would continue to thrive in this hostile environment.

"Alice, what is the time?"

"0800 hours."

I nodded to my invisible companion, hoping that it wasn't too early to visit an old woman.

Fifty-Three

I knocked on the door with my gloved hand, hoping that the old woman was already awake. The minutes dragged on, and there was no response. I knocked again.

A washed-out holographic head of an elderly woman appeared in the middle of the door. "What do you want?"

"Renee Tuthill? My name is Michaella Davison. It's important that I speak with you."

"Do you have any idea what time in the morning this is?"

"Yes, and I'm sorry for that, but it's really important. It's about the Red Queen." I licked my lips and hoped that I was right about the connection. "It's about Bandersnatch."

The face disappeared, and nothing happened. I didn't want to walk away, so I just stood there, staring at the door.

There was a click and the door to Renee Tuthill's apartment creaked open. "Are you alone?"

"Yes."

"And the playing cards? Do they know you're here?"

I glanced down at my right wrist. "Yes, and no. I didn't tell anyone I was coming here, but my pharmachip was scanned as I entered the sector."

There was an audible sigh as the door opened farther. "Then you better get inside. We won't have much time. And you don't want to be here when they come."

The apartment was narrow, just barely wide enough for the bed that ran along the back wall. There was a small lounge area centered around a table, and a tiny kitchen contained a small cook top and a food storage unit. But it was the decorations around the tiny apartment that caught my attention.

Everywhere I looked, there was a poster or figurine that linked back to *Alice's Adventures in Wonderland*. A Cheshire cat with his wide grin. Pictures of playing cards with heads and limbs, painting the roses red. Figurines playing croquet with flamingos. And the Queen of Hearts upon her throne.

"Have you always liked *Alice's Adventures in Wonderland*?" I asked.

The old woman pulled tight on the white shawl that draped around her shoulders. "You ask me that every time you come to see me. And the answer is still yes."

I blinked. "Every time I come to see you?"

"You don't remember, do you? Hmm . . . That doesn't surprise me. Well, in any case, make yourself comfortable. And I suggest you put *that* in your pocket." The old woman pointed to the breather still in my hand. "You're going to need it when you leave. Best to keep up appearances. We wouldn't want the authorities to know that you don't need a breather now, do we?" The old woman stared at me, waiting. It was like she expected me to protest in some way, to deny what was so obviously true.

I pocketed the breather, then forced myself to take a deep breath. A sweet cinnamon smell danced around my nostrils and made me feel . . . at home. "I know that smell. It's cinnamon and . . . some kind of fruit."

"It's apple peel, along with a hint of chamomile. I'm in the process of making some tea from ingredients grown in the hydroponic bays on the other side of the sector. But I don't think you'll have the time to stay long enough to have some, not unlike last time you were here."

"And when was that?"

The way Renee looked at me was like she was trying to determine if there was any trickery on my part. "You really don't remember, do you?" She busied herself in the tiny kitchen area. "You've been here many times over the years. At first, it was only with George. He was so nervous about bringing you to meet me," she added with a chuckle. "He loved you, but he wasn't sure what sort of future the two of you could have. Over time, you gained the confidence to come and see me on your own. I think you saw this as one of the few places you could truly be yourself without the playing cards watching your every move. And when George died . . ." Renee bowed her head and closed her eyes. "You have been here so many times over the past two years, and each time you come, it's to inform me of my nephew's death. That's why you've come, right?"

I gawked at her, unable to blink. "George died two years ago? But . . ." I had seen him only a few weeks ago. And he was real. I struggled to breathe as I thought through the last time I saw him—with his yellow hair instead of his favorite red. Could he have been just a figment of my imagination? Could he have been a simulation? "Two years?"

Renee shuffled to sit next to me, taking my gloved hand in her own. "The day he died, you came to see me, carrying a bag of fresh and dried herbs from my favorite apothecary. You said that George would have delivered them himself but was caught in the explosion that destroyed the store. You wanted to personally deliver the news, not relying on some stranger to do it. You couldn't tell me how you knew that

George was innocent of any wrongdoing, but you knew that the news was wrong. You returned a few weeks later to inform me again of George's death—like you had forgotten that I already knew—but there were playing cards with you, and we were unable to talk freely. You returned again a few days later. And, again, the month after that. Each time, it was with the same message. And it was important to you that you be the one to deliver it."

The old woman sighed. "Even though you always came with the same message, I was never angry about it. I have always known about the memory wipes. Whenever George visited, he would frequently forget that he had already delivered my medicine. He was good at hiding it, but then he started to reiterate things that happened long ago. And he was always commenting on how fast my condition was deteriorating, when in reality, my deterioration is the slowest that medical science can make it. I just assumed that whatever had happened to George's memory was happening to you too. The last time you were here, you confirmed it.

"About two months ago, you returned again to tell me of George's death, but that time was different. While you couldn't remember the previous times you had been to see me, you remembered other details—details that you thought were important that I knew about—so I could remind you when the time was right. You told me about Project NeuWave, how it was a genetic experiment designed to force the next evolution of man. The geneticists wanted to create a human able to reclaim the surface of our planet—to live outside the domes. But the moment you start to play with DNA . . ."

The expression on Renee's face was the same combination of caring and regret that I had seen on Tam's face when Tam died. "I know the truth about your mental abilities—a secret that the Pregutor has been hiding from the world. Those with White Rabbit syndrome all possess some form of extrasensory perception. A few are empathic, able to influence the emotions of others. Others, like George and yourself, are influencers, able to implant a thought that people are compelled to follow. But in your case, there is no one alive who is able to withstand your suggestions—not even George." Tears hung in the corner of Renee's eyes. "You implanted the idea into his head that he blow himself up."

The old woman struggled to her feet, then shuffled to the back of the apartment, only to return with a small black box. "I wanted to be angry with you, but you were just as much the victim in this as he was. The Pregutor and Rhodon have been killing those with White Rabbit syndrome for years, determined to wipe out any threat before they became a threat. And they have been using you and others like you to hunt them down. George was part of an underground movement to smuggle those with White Rabbit syndrome out of the city. Unfortunately, the Pregutor found out before he could get to safety himself. When you started to piece it together, you fell down the rabbit hole, but it wasn't Wonderland that you fell into. It was a nightmare orchestrated by the Pregutor."

She passed me the box. "The last time you were here, you gave me that. You said that it was important that I kept it hidden until you came back again—without the playing cards. You were afraid for your life, and you had no one else you could trust. I asked you, 'Why me?' Then you reminded me of your established pattern. Something would happen and they would wipe your memories. You would then learn of George's death, and shortly after that, you would come to see me to inform me of my nephew's death—yet again. You decided to take advantage of that established behavior so you could hide the information that you would need. But Michaella, every time you came to visit me, I would be visited by those wearing blue and purple stripes shortly thereafter. They would question me for hours, insisting that I go over every detail of your visit. I told you this the last time you were here, but you said that they wouldn't come—that you had used different means to enter the sector. You told me that you were working with the resistance."

Renee smiled weakly as she placed her hand on top of the box. "You were right. They didn't come. They don't know about the box. But they will come this time. They know that after you learn of George's death, you eventually come to see me. As much as I would love it if you would stay to have some tea, you don't have the time."

She reached forward and caressed my cheek. "This time, our parting will be our last." An image of the old woman drinking a cup of tea and falling into a deep sleep sat on the surface of her thoughts. "They're mind readers, Michaella. I don't have the ability to keep them out. But whatever happens from here on, I'm glad that you kept visiting me after George's death. I know you'll do what's right, and I'm pleased to help you do it. I don't know what is in this box— I've never opened it—but I do know that it contains the key to Wonderland. And Alice will help you get there."

Cautiously, I looked at the box, uncertain what to do. I was curious about its contents, not once doubting that I had planted the box with Renee myself. But I couldn't shake the image of the old woman falling into an endless sleep. But if she was right about being visited by STAR after each of my visits, the sleeping death was the only way the old woman could shield her mind.

"What if they come before you fall asleep?" My voice cracked with the truth of the situation.

"Don't you worry about that. I have my ways of making it fast."

"But why?"

"You know why. Oh, Michaella . . . I see a world on the edge of a blade. Without balance, it will fall. And you, Michaella, are the source of that balance. The world needs you. And if the Pregutor learns the truth before you have a chance to enforce that balance, we all suffer." She leaned back and pushed the box into my hands. "I have done what I was meant to do. Now, it's your turn."

The lights flashed, and Renee got to her feet, pulling me up with her. "Time is up," the old woman said. "You need to leave, and you need to leave now. I wish you could stay, but the playing cards are here. If you want to get that box out of here before they learn you have it, there's no time to waste. Don't worry about me. I know how to look after myself." She pushed me toward the door, but before I could get too far, Renee pulled me into a big hug. "Thank you for telling me the truth about my nephew."

Fifty-Four

I KEPT LOOKING AT THE door to the old woman's apartment, then down the hallway toward the exit, torn. On the one hand, I wanted to save the old woman before she killed herself. But on the other hand, if I didn't move, and move now, then the old woman's sacrifice would have been meaningless. Everything Renee had done was about protecting the box and its contents.

There was a click on my comms, then nothing. I had forgotten about the new implants, but now, it was like there was traffic on the secure channels. Cautiously, I reached up and pressed the slight bump controlling the comms disk under my skin.

"Unit 86 in position. Front door to the building clear."

"Unit 47 in position. Rear exit, all clear."

"Unit 58 in position. We have eyes in the sky."

"Unit 99 in position. Stairwell clear. Waiting for the command to go." That last one sounded like Marcus, but his voice didn't come from just the comms. There was a muffled echo with every word.

I snapped my head in the direction of the main stairwell to the building. Unless I wanted to get caught, I couldn't go that way. Instead, I darted down the hall toward the fire exit.

I pulled out my glasses and breather unit. Even though I didn't need them anymore, they still had their uses. With the peripheral vision seals and breather unit in place, I pulled up the hood of my jacket, tightening it over my forehead. With a snap, the hood attached itself to the glasses. I then pulled on the sides of the hood to attach it to the sides of my breather unit. Finally, I pulled down on my sleeves to ensure that there was no chance a stray signal from my pharmachip could be detected. With one last deep breath, I darted down the stairs.

"Davison just disappeared off the grid," someone said across the comms. It sounded like the one who had the eyes in the sky.

"All teams go," the commander ordered. "We can't lose her."

I continued toward my only exit strategy, praying that I wouldn't encounter another team coming up those stairs.

At the bottom of the stairwell, there was a door that led to the outside world. I rested my hands against the push bar for the door and wished that I had taken the time to connect Alice to the city security feeds. But it was too late for that now. Any new connection to the city's security network would give my position away.

With a slow exhale, I pushed on the door release and edged it open. I couldn't see anyone through the crack in the narrow alley, but that didn't mean that they weren't waiting for me. I opened the door farther and poked my head out. Empty.

The comms chatter suggested that they had all exits from the building covered, but why would they miss this one? And if they were after me, then why would they give me the implants I needed to monitor their comms channels? The furrow in my brow deepened. It had to be a test. And I had a horrible feeling that I had already failed.

Unless . . . I thought back over everything that had happened in the past few days, starting with the failed mission. What if this wasn't a test at all, but a trap? The question was: for whom?

A bang echoed over the comms, followed by shouting and the sound of things smashing to the ground. Then Marcus cursed. "Sir, the contact is dead. There's an unlabeled vial next to the body and a needle sticking out of her arm. I don't know what she injected herself with, but I'm guessing that she knew we were coming."

"Of course she knew we were coming, you moron. We always come."

"Yes, sir. What about Davison?"

"Let her go, Gahan. We'll pick up her signal again when she tries to leave the sector."

I closed my eyes and bowed my head, saying a silent prayer for the old woman. It was the only moment of grief I could allow myself. I still had to get out of the sector.

I continued out into the streets, hoping that I could blend in with the gathered crowd watching from behind police barriers. And for the first time ever, I wished my jacket wasn't purple. But that couldn't be helped now. At least my jacket was keeping my signal dark.

An explosion blew out the windows from the twelfth floor of Renee's building, the floor where Renee's apartment was. The gathered crowd screamed as they ran from the falling debris. The comms chatter was chaos, as everyone was trying to work out what had happened and ascertain who was injured and who was dead. As chaotic as it was on the comms, the chaos on the street was the perfect place to hide—especially considering the falling debris provided a cloud that shrouded the crowd from the overhead drones.

"You're welcome, Mike," said a stray voice that I couldn't identify. *"Now, get out of there."*

With no time to process whether the voice came from the comms or somewhere else, I took off after the frightened crowd, deliberately turning back occasionally, just like the crowd was doing.

As the running crowd thinned, I decreased my pace to a brisk walk. My eyes darted in every direction. And my virtual displays went into overdrive, showing medical dangers coming from every direction, including the toxicity in the air. The comms chatter died down, though I still couldn't make out the details regarding who had survived the explosion and who hadn't. All I knew was that the active search for me had died away in the disaster. The captain kept repeating that they would pick up my signal when I tried to leave the sector.

So, that was my next hurdle. Leaving the sector without detection. Not really certain what I was going to do when I reached the sector checkpoint, I continued my trek in that direction, anyway.

I continued down the streets, scanning in every direction, hyper-aware of any danger. Wall art covered the concrete monoliths that lined the streets. At first, I didn't take much notice of it, with its rudimentary, random figures having no real connection to the lines around it. But as I got closer to the sector checkpoint, the connection between the different pieces started to form.

Some of them were spray-painted words. Quotes.

>>We're all mad here.<<
>>Sometimes I've believed as many as six impossible things before breakfast.<<

»Curiouser and curiouser!«

And some of the pieces were images. A young girl in a blue dress, reading a book under a tree. A man in a top hat having tea with a hare and a mouse. And a little girl chasing after a white rabbit down a rabbit hole.

I stopped in the middle of the street and stared at the giant mural of the little girl pushing her way through the roots of the tree. And there, where the rabbit hole should have been, was a dark alley.

I pulled out the box Renee had given me. "I don't know what is in this box," Renee had told me. "I've never opened it—but I do know that it contains the key to Wonderland. And Alice will help you get there."

I shook my head and put the box back in my jacket pocket. Coincidences didn't exist. So, I followed Alice down the rabbit hole and away from the sector checkpoint.

Fifty-Five

THE ALLEYWAYS THROUGH THE SECTOR were a maze, turning this way and that. But I never questioned which way to go. Every time I came to a junction, I followed the Alice wall art.

Left, then right. Right, then left. And across the way.

With each turn, I fell deeper into the rabbit hole, falling into . . . Well, I had no way of knowing where this rabbit hole would lead, but I was fairly confident that it wasn't Wonderland. Just as long as I didn't find the Pregutor's lackeys waiting for me.

I turned the last corner and stared at a black wall. A dead end. I scoured the walls, hunting for my next clue, but Alice headed toward the black wall. I flicked through my vision filters, trying to find any hidden detail. But there was none. It was just a concrete wall painted black.

I wanted to curse and swear, but the constant comms chatter in my ear was a reminder that I needed to get out of the sector. I bowed my head and sighed in defeat. I then leaned against the wall—and it shifted.

Standing upright, facing the wall, I brushed my gloved hands over the surface. Not finding anything of note, I controlled my breathing, and did the only thing I could think of. I pushed on the wall, and the wall moved again.

It couldn't be that simple.

Not afraid to look a gift horse in the mouth, I pushed harder. A door-sized section of the wall recessed, as though going down the pictorial rabbit hole. As soon as a gap appeared large enough to slip through, I darted inside. The wall slab moved back into place, plunging me into darkness. Even my comms went dead. There was nothing but static.

I didn't know if that was a good sign or not, but coincidences didn't exist. Whatever tunnel I was standing in had to be shielded.

Cautiously, I reached up to my hood and detached it from my goggle-like glasses and breather. I pressed on my comms disk and turned the unit off. There was no point in continuing to listen to nothing but static. And I pulled off my glasses and breather, putting them in my pocket.

My ocular implants automatically shifted to night vision. The counter-weight pulley system ensuring the door to the tunnel remained closed was now obvious. And there was a giant wheel on the back of the door connected to metal rods. It was like the system was designed to seal the door from the inside, so nothing outside could get in, but those inside could get out. It was tempting to seal the door, but what if others needed to follow Alice down the rabbit hole?

I scanned the surrounding area using my new ocular implants. The tunnel appeared to be large enough for a truck to move through, roughly five meters high by ten meters wide. Down the center of the floor, rails were cast into the concrete. Pipes lined the corners of the ceiling. What the pipes were for was a mystery. The space was cold, but my heat sensors showed pockets of life in the distance. Rats.

"Alice, are you there?"

"Awaiting instructions."

I sighed in relief. At least my portable AI system was still active. "Alice, you wouldn't happen to have a map of these tunnels in your archives, would you?"

My command, which wasn't really a command, was met with silence. That in itself didn't instill much confidence.

"Alice, do you have a map or not?"

"Negative. Unable to access archives."

I sighed in defeat. "That's okay, Alice. We'll just have to do this the old-fashioned way. Keep a record of our path through this maze and extrapolate the possible structure."

"Working."

After inhaling several breaths of the stale, damp air, I headed deeper into the tunnel.

At first, there was nothing much to see. Concrete walls with more pipes and more tracks in the ground. And there didn't appear to be much direction to the tunnel structure, either. Except it sloped downward. There wasn't any evidence of the decline, but it was enough to note changes of pressure in my ears. And the air became staler. I was tempted to pull out my breather, but I needed to conserve the cartridge for as long as possible. Just in case I got stuck down here.

As I continued deeper into the tunnel, wall art graced the concrete walls, but this art was different to that found outside. There was no connection to the beloved children's story. Instead, these images told the history of Crystal Hills, starting with the construction of the underground facilities where people took shelter from the toxic atmosphere, and eventually leading to the construction of the domes. There was even a portion of the wall dedicated to the rise of the Pregutor and Rhodon Corporation.

I pulled out my glasses and activated the flood lights, blinking as my ocular implants readjusted to the sudden increase in brightness. Purple clouds covered the domed city, and there were lines of people trying to enter to safety. There were images that depicted the vaccinations of those coming in, and images of soldiers taking the children away.

But it was the image of a figure with purple hair strapped to a chair that caught my attention. Next to the chair was a figure in white, complete with white hair, but in the center of the chest was a red dot. And there was the Red Queen holding out her hand, like she was asking for me to trust her.

"Alice, are you able to determine when these drawing were done?"

"Pigment and dust accumulation suggest that these drawings were drawn approximately twenty years ago."

"Are you sure?"

"With eighty percent certainty." Alice's eighty percent was more like my one hundred and twenty percent.

I followed the Red Queen, uncertain of the dangers that awaited, but if it meant that I could figure out what was going on, then it was worth the risk.

The purple-haired figure underwent various medical procedures, including the implantation of a comms unit behind her left ear—the unit I didn't remember getting. There were fitness tests and fight training. There was even the image of a little girl standing before a boy who took a knife to his own wrists.

The final image in the sequence was of two children splashing around in the puddles, dancing in the purple rain. One was dark-skinned with short red curly locks and the other fair with purple hair tied up in a ponytail.

My chest grew tight, and I struggled to draw in air. I pressed my hand to the wall, to the red-headed figure, and allowed myself to grieve for all I had lost.

I had no idea how long I sat at the base of that wall, curled up into a ball. And I had no idea where I was, either. But regardless of how the drawings of my life came to be on that wall, I couldn't continue to sit there, wasting away to nothing.

I was the one in control of my life. Not the Pregutor. Not Rhodon Corporation. Not Marcus. Not Tam. Not Dr. Shutton. Me. Just me. And if I wanted George's and Renee's death to mean something, I needed to find out what the hell was in that box.

I pulled out the box and cradled it in my lap. It didn't seem like anything special. Just a black box with a sensor pad on one side, small enough for a thumbprint. I pulled off my glove and pressed my right thumb to the sensor pad. A small screen came to life with a single-word instruction: »Passcode?«

Coincidences didn't exist.

"Bandersnatch."

The screen flashed yellow, then there was a small hiss as the unit opened. Inside was a card—the Queen of Hearts—and a small thumb drive. I pocketed the thumb drive. I wouldn't have been able to do anything about the little device without access to a terminal with an external port. I had one in my old apartment in Sector 11, assuming I could get there. But at the bottom of the box was an old photo: an image of PentWave taken the day we were all given our courier uniforms.

We all looked so young—and so full of hope. Jody looked like a midget as she stood between Trent and Marcus. And there was Frank, as he tried to look all macho, but totally failing. And George and I stood with our arms wrapped around each other's shoulders. But the photo wasn't right. For one: George's hair was yellow. Two: my hair was blue.

I had always dyed my hair purple. Always. Because the bad guys can't see purple.

A timer went off in the corner of my vision along with a note—a preprogrammed reminder that I was overdue for my next dose of Cefretin. And that's when it hit me.

Ever since I had started taking the new drug, the colors within my vision hadn't been right. Flickering. Fading. Greens looked more yellow and . . .

Purples looked blue.

My heart raced ahead. As far as I knew, every member of STAR was on Cefretin. That was why Jody couldn't see the White Rabbit's purple waistcoat. And George's hair . . .

I stared at George's yellow hair that was meant to be red.

How could I have been so ignorant? The bad guys couldn't see purple not because they were *bad*. They couldn't see purple because of the medication they were on. And they were *bad* because they bought into the lies they were being told by the Pregutor and Rhodon Corporation.

And the best way to explain all of that to a child was to tell them that the bad guys can't see purple.

I leaned against the cold rock, feeling a sense of clarity that I had never felt before. When I had last seen George, I had asked him about his yellow hair. For a fleeting moment, he was stunned. But he had an answer ready. A lie. Because he wasn't George. He had to have been an artificial construct—a simulation designed to lure me away from the truth. But there was no construct around me now. And I knew the truth in my heart.

I picked up the card and stared at the Queen of Hearts. And I finally understood what it meant and why it was connected to George. The Queen of Hearts was a representation of the boundary that existed between reality and imagination. And the city was being littered with these cards, because the truth was coming out.

As I continued to stare at the card, I smiled. I had seen so many cards over the last few days, but this one was different. The card's backing was purple, not blue like the others.

"The bad guys can't see purple." I reached up to my left temple and gave my fingers a twist. The display on the glasses zoomed in on the purple pattern on the back of the card. It was a series of lines in a distinct pattern, one that I recognized. I twisted my zoom back to normal, ensuring that I could see the full card on my glasses virtual display. "Alice, scan in the pattern on the back of this card and overlay the map of the tunnel network that you've created so far. Is there any part of this pattern that matches?"

"Affirmative."

"Show me."

The virtual display kicked in. At the edges of the small structure, the lines were a perfect match.

"Alice, overlay a map of Crystal Hills."

Coincidences didn't exist.

The edges lined up perfectly. "Alice, assume that the line structure from the card is a map of these tunnels. Plot us a course to Sector 11."

"Course plotted."

"Alice, show me the way home."

Fifty-Six

I COULDN'T RESIST THE CARIBBEAN rhythms, doing a little salsa move, shimmying my hips to the beats. For a moment, I was free.

"Connection reestablished to the servers," Alice said. "You should be advised that security has been alerted to your emergence. However, no security units have been dispatched as yet."

"What about STAR?"

"Unknown. I do not have access to those systems."

"Then we better get moving." I would have loved to continue enjoying the music, but I had to stay ahead of STAR. Even with my hood up and the signals from the tech in my body partially blocked, the odds were they knew exactly where I was heading—though they wouldn't know why. I couldn't shake the feeling that this was all a trap—and that I was the bait. But this little piece of bait had ideas of her own.

I took off at a brisk walk, determined to avoid drawing any more attention, and headed straight for my apartment building.

In the lobby, the building superintendent sat comfortably behind his glass wall, his attention fixed on the newsfeeds displayed on the back wall. My image showed on the screen, complete with that shitty two-tone dye job. I had forgotten about my hair. Hopefully, I still had some dye in my apartment.

"We're full."

"I'm not here to rent a room. I already have one."

The superintendent turned to look at me, then blinked as he looked back at the woman on the monitor. He bolted to his feet and reached for the phone unit on the desk, but he made the mistake of looking at me one last time.

The edges of my vision darkened. His look of panic vanished as he became a zombie. "You never saw me," I said aloud. "I was never here. And you're going to go back to looking bored as you change the channel to something else. Do I make myself clear?"

The man nodded slowly. He went back to his chair and put his feet back up, then changed to the channel to some show filled with canned laughter.

I closed my eyes and took a deep breath. When I opened my eyes again, my vision was back to normal. I climbed the stairs to the upper floors, not wanting to risk getting caught in the elevator. I exited onto the sixth floor. There were only four doors. My apartment was the last door on the left.

Dust accumulated on the security pad, but there was no dust on the floor for about an inch just outside the door. I tapped my right temple three times, shifting my vision to ultraviolet. A lattice of lasers covered the space before the door. In the middle of the lattice was the logo for Rhodon Corporation: a white rose in full bloom.

"Alice, is there still no sign of security dispatched from Sector 14?"

"Affirmative. No one from security has been dispatched to your location."

"And still no sign of STAR?"

"Radio channels from STAR remain silent." Though that didn't mean anything. If I was right—that the Pregutor was using me as bait in a trap for the resistance—then STAR would likely let me continue to roam the city unchecked while they got the rest of the pieces for the trap in place.

"Alice, are you able to get access to the systems controlling this laser lattice?"

"Affirmative."

"Deactivate it. And start a timer. Countdown twenty minutes." Although I knew in my heart that this was a trap, I prayed that it wasn't a trap for me.

The laser lattice vanished. "Twenty minutes, starting from now."

I pulled out a small light screwdriver from my inside pocket and went to work, pulling the sensor pad from the wall. It didn't take long, and soon wires were the only thing keeping the dusty panel from falling to the floor. I then hot-wired the door, and it opened with a whoosh.

Once inside, I scanned the interior, looking for any other presents left by Rhodon. But everything in the tiny room looked exactly how I had left it. A collection of bottled water sat on the shelf at the end of the room, just above the sink. A small fridge was tucked into the space just under the sink. And my spare boots were lined up under the cot. The sheets had been tightly tucked in, with a stuffed purple cat resting on the pillow.

I picked up the purple cat and smiled. "I'm glad they didn't throw you away, Violet."

Putting the stuffed toy aside, I pulled out the thumb drive and went to the personal console unit—the main interface for Alice. When I plugged in the drive, the screen came to life, and I stared at a version of myself. The woman on the screen still had a shitty dye job, but it was more like her natural hair had been allowed to grow past her ears.

"Hi Mike. If you're watching this, then your plan worked. Unfortunately, your time is almost up."

Fifty-Seven

I RUBBED THE COLOR WAND over my fringe as the video continued to play in the background. There were so many details missing from my memory. With each new learned fact, I knew in my heart that it was all true. According to the video, it was my choice to have my memories taken away from me—again. And I had good reasons to do it too.

With the last strands of hair redyed, I looked in the mirror and smiled. It wasn't my favorite color, but the shitty dye job was finally gone. My hair was all one color again. And for the first time in weeks, I was in control over my own life. I grabbed the scissors from the side of the sink and finished tidying up the frayed ends.

The video played on a continuous loop, going over the details of my self-appointed mission. Maps of the Rhodon facilities were loaded into Alice's remote systems in my implants, including details on how to bypass certain security systems if my security clearance had been revoked. And there were notes about how I was supposed to get the drugs out of the sector. The only thing missing from the plan was what would happen if everything went belly-up.

Because in big operations like this, things never went to plan.

"I know it's a lot to remember," said the video version of myself, "but you're not alone. If you get stuck, reach out to Cedrick. He'll be able to help. Just use your mind, Mike. Cedrick will be listening—waiting for you to reach out to him. But be warned. He might be a little hurt that you didn't tell him you were leaving. The two of you have become really close. Not romantically close, but still close."

I reached over to the video display and ended the playback. I then took several deep breaths and closed my eyes, not sure if I was ready for this.

"Cedrick," I called out, "assuming that's your name. Are you there?"

"I'm here." His voice came from somewhere inside my head. And there was a hint of relief mixed with hurt to it. *"Took you long enough. We're running out of time here if we're going to make this work."*

"Are Beth and the baby okay?"

"For the moment, yes, but Beth is coming to the end of her fourth month. If you don't get that drug soon . . ."

"I know. She'll lose the baby."

"You could have told me. You didn't have to do this alone."

"I'm not alone. You're here with me now . . . inside my head."

There was a sense of a smirk, though I couldn't see it. *"Well, speaking of which, you don't need to talk aloud. I can hear you perfectly clearly without it."*

I smirked too. "Of course you can. But by vocalizing my thoughts, I don't feel so crazy. It doesn't feel like I'm talking to a voice coming from inside my head. It feels like I'm talking to someone on comms."

"I can appreciate that."

I took a few deep breaths, trying not to freak out about the enormity and the idiocy of what I was about to do. "Please tell me that you know all the details of this plan. If my implants fail or get overridden by the Pregutor, I'll lose all the information stored in Alice's program."

"It's okay. I'll be with you most of the way. But there are sections within Rhodon where our connection will be cut off, which is why you went through all of this. You wanted to ensure that you knew the full layout and the full plan in case we couldn't establish a connection. And it was why you had Eddie make that card. Talk about a brilliant way of getting those maps to you."

The Queen of Hearts card sat next to the black box on the bed. The recordings told me how to shift my optical filters so Alice could scan the multiple layers of information imprinted on the card—on both sides. "Well, Alice has the maps ready to go, but some layers came with a time delay instruction for Alice's processor. You wouldn't happen to know what that was all about?"

There was a slight hesitation coming from Cedrick's mind, like he was asking another person. *"Eddie says that it was your idea. You knew you wouldn't have access to Alice's main processor. So, you asked Eddie to build in instructions to purge certain portions of her local stored memory at certain points during the operation, giving you access to only the information you needed in that moment."*

I blew out a steady stream of air. "Like the time-delayed message from George." I still struggled to fathom that he had died two years ago—and I had no clue.

"Yeah . . . Sorry you had to go through that."

"Don't be, because it was that message that made me go see Renee." I took the thumb drive out of the port next to my monitor. "I need to destroy the box and the thumb drive. Any ideas?"

"In the bottom of the box. Hidden compartment."

Examining the box, flipping it over this way and that, there was nothing obvious on the outside to suggest a hidden compartment. However, the internal space seemed to be a lot smaller than it should have been. I pulled out the felt lining to reveal two vials of what looked like innocent, clear fluids. "Is this what I think it is?"

"Glynferix and theridoxite."

"An acid bomb." I inhaled as deeply as I could and controlled my exhale. "There's enough here to destroy the entire building—and some."

"Well, it's what you said needed to be done. It was your plan, not mine." And there was that sense of hurt again.

"Of course it was. Alice, how much time is left on the clock?"

"Two minutes and thirty-six seconds."

I grabbed my jacket and secured the hood to my breather and glasses. I tossed the thumb drive onto the floor and smashed it with the heel of my boot, twisting my ankle to ensure that the casing was fully destroyed and the circuit board was exposed. I then poured the contents of one of the vials over the remains, dissolving the componentry instantly. I placed the Queen of Hearts card on top and watched the acid slowly eat away at the card from the center. The box was then added to the pile, and I poured the contents of the other vial into the box. Small wafts of smoke rose from the acid eating the box.

Without any further thought, I headed for the door. "Time to get the last thing I need to get out of fucking

Wonderland." In the hallway, I pulled the emergency alarm and headed for the stairs.

FIFTY-EIGHT

I STEPPED OFF THE TRANSPORT tube and stood on the platform, waiting. Not exactly sure what I was waiting for, I had to trust in the plan. It was my plan, after all. If the plan was flawed, I only had myself to blame.

Cautiously, I reached up and lowered my hood and put my breather and glasses in my pocket. It was a risk, but if I wanted to *blend in*, I couldn't be wearing those things.

The ground under my feet rumbled, a sensation I had only felt when on missions for the Pregutor, the result of a building collapsing somewhere nearby. Although Sector 11 wasn't really nearby. I said a silent prayer for any lives extinguished because of my actions.

Guards in full tactical gear came out from the main guardhouse and formed a line in front of the sector entrance. "I'm sorry, folks, but we have orders that no one is to be permitted in or out of the sector. Essential personnel only."

The gathered crowd shouted about how they would be late for their shifts. Some even pointed out that surely medical personnel were classified as essential. But I knew what the guards meant. Only those with the clearance and training to bring down a rogue like me would be allowed to pass.

There was a little hum inside my head, followed by Cedrick's voice. *"Now we get to find out if everything you went through was worth it."*

I couldn't agree with him more. I pushed my way to the front of the group. "Let me through."

"I'm sorry, ma'am, but you'll have to wait like everyone else."

"No. You're going to let me through." I reached over my shoulder and pulled my hair away from my right ear, turning my head so the guard could see my blue rose tattoo. When I turned back to face him, his eyes were wide, and the color had drained from his face.

"You're . . ."

"Yes. Now let me through."

"Yes, ma'am." The guard stood to the side to let me pass . . . and I didn't even need to use the scanners. The crowd behind me shouted and pushed forward in protest. A single gunshot was fired into the air. I just kept my attention on my own tasks, knowing that more violence would be needed before the day was done.

"Hurdle one down." There was a hint of amusement in Cedrick's mental voice, like he couldn't believe how just the tattoo was enough to get into the sector and past the security scanners.

"Fear," I responded. *"It's a great motivator."*

I marched through sanitation bays of pink fluid and toward the main locker rooms, where I removed all of my clothing and threw everything that I owned into the bins earmarked for incineration, including my breather and glasses. With my implants, I wouldn't need my virtual display glasses to access Alice's systems. And with the genetic modifications that Rhodon had done over generations, I didn't need the breather anymore either.

Though the Pregutor didn't know that.

There was no one at the health scanner, and the unit doors were open on both sides. I stood at the precipice of what could have easily been the end of the road if I had gotten the protocols wrong. I took another deep breath, then stepped through the scanner—and right out the doors on the other side. No scan.

"Hurdle two down," Cedrick said.

I headed straight for the uniform station, where a pile of black clothing was waiting on the counter, complete with a weapons belt and tactical gear. There was no radio or a display unit, but I didn't need them. None of STAR did.

"The guards at the entrance must have alerted the staff that you were coming through."

That was my assessment as well. But something was off about the whole situation. For one, where were the staff who manned the desk so I could sign that I'd taken possession of the weapons?

The halls were empty. I had never seen them this empty. And while it was a good thing, it still made me nervous.

I donned the black uniform right there, ensuring that the issued boots were a good fit, so I could run if I needed to. And I checked the issued weapons. A laser pistol without a DNA safety, among other goodies.

There was a slight whistle in my head. Cedrick didn't need to say anything else.

I just smirked. *"I'll see if I can bring it home with me."*

Home. I had never called Sanctuary "home" before, but that's what it was. A warm glow filled my being . . . and I was fairly confident that the source wasn't entirely my own mind.

Fully armed, thanks to the security protocols for the sector and the privileges awarded to those with the blue rose tattoo, I continued down the path and into the main sector area, entering the main plaza.

I tapped my temple. "Alice," I said softly, "continually scan comms, including the restricted channels. Search for any reference to the progress in Sector 11 . . . and keep an ear out for any reference to me."

"Processing."

I gave my temple a complicated tap pattern, one that had been preprogrammed for this moment. My vision was overlaid with a tactical display, telling me where everyone was within the sector. No one was in my vicinity. My path toward my destination was clear. And my nervousness continued to grow.

With my head swiveling back and forth, constantly looking in every direction, I headed across the plaza to the main medical building. My target wasn't the hospital but the med labs, where new drugs were manufactured. According to Beth, a certain amount of the base drugs was kept there in case the main supply was cut off. Rhodon couldn't have their key personnel getting sick in a crisis.

Every step of the way, the halls were empty.

"I don't like this," I said. *"Cedrick, are you there?"*

"I'm here."

"Do you have eyes?"

"Yeah. Eddie's patched in to the security cameras. And yeah, I don't like this either. It feels like a trap."

"Trap or not, we don't have a choice. Beth needs that drug. Just . . ." I exhaled, hoping I was wrong about this. *"Just keep scanning."*

"We'll do one better. We'll pray."

I smiled but stayed focused on my tactical display. With my path to the med labs clear, I stood outside Med Lab 6 and stared at the security panel. And I prayed that my training from before becoming part of STAR would pay off.

I pulled out the knife I had been issued and wedged it into the seal between the security panel and the wall. With a twist of my wrist, the panel popped right off. For an organization that prided themselves in being the most technologically advanced organization in the world, you would think that they would put at least some of their money into the security systems. Yet, these components were as cheap as anything.

With the wires exposed, I went to work in overriding the security on the door. The door latch hissed, letting me know it was in manual mode. I pushed the security panel back into place to make it look like I hadn't done anything to the door at all. But if anyone in security had been watching, they would have noticed the changes to the door status. I had seconds to get what I needed and get out. A minute, tops.

I rushed to the cabinets on the right-hand side, the refrigerated units with glass fronts. As I scanned through the vials in the unit, I held my gloved fingers to my temple, using the program that had been loaded into Alice's systems to help identify the exact drug needed. I scanned through each cabinet in turn, knowing that my time was running out, but nothing was coming up a match.

"Damn it! Cedrick, can you hear me?"

"I'm here."

"I can't find the fucking drug. I've looked everywhere. It's not here. We must have chosen the wrong lab to raid."

"No, Beth says you have the right lab." There was a brief silence. *"We have an idea, but you'll need to look at each label slowly—without Alice's tactical display in the way."*

"If I disable the tactical display, I lose the proximity sensors."

There was another moment of silence. *"I don't think we have a choice. Beth needs that drug. And all that data is confusing me. I don't know where to look. And before you ask, no, I've never worn one of those devices before. Never needed to."*

I took a controlled breath. *"Remind me when I get back that Lucas is to put virtual tactical displays into your training."* I then tapped out the pattern at my temple that turned off my ocular implants. My vision was entirely my own. *"Do I need to read the labels out?"*

"No, just look at them. I can see what you're seeing, and Beth is right next to me."

I nodded, then remembered to mentally vocalized my thoughts. Cedrick wouldn't have been able to see me nod. *"Going to the first cabinet again."* I pulled out a vial from each group, one at a time, ensuring that I looked at the label long enough for Cedrick to check with Beth before moving to the next group.

Time was ticking by, though there wasn't a ticking clock in this lab. And I resisted the urge to check the time with every vial that I looked at.

"That's it," Cedrick said, as I looked at a vial from the fifth group in the third refrigerated unit. His voice contained a little too much excitement.

I pocketed a handful of the vials, placing them into my tactical vest. Beth only needed the one vial, but there was no way I was going through this again if another woman in Sanctuary became pregnant.

"Put your hands up and slowly turn around."

"*Shit.*" The sentiment came from both Cedrick and me.

"*Mike? Just d—*" And Cedrick was cut off. The silence was unnerving.

"I suggest you do as ordered, Davison, or we will shoot you."

Slowly, I raised my hands and turned around. Five guards were scattered around the room, all of them in tactical gear . . . and none of them wore any visible comms or tactical display units. I didn't know any of the STAR in front of me, except for the man in the middle of the formation.

"Don't even think about using your funky mumbo-jumbo on us." The captain made a show of the little portable unit in his hand. "Do you know what this is?"

"Of course. That little device is a shield of sorts—a psychic shield. And I'm guessing by the cocky smile on your face that the design has been recently upgraded, so it can block the likes of me. But I'm also guessing that you have no idea how that thing actually works." I slowly stepped forward, closing the distance between the captain and myself, my hands still up in surrender. I ensured that I had his full attention, that he was looking directly into my eyes. "You see, while the device is designed to block psychic intrusion, it wasn't designed to keep people out who were already inside the field."

I tilted my head to the side and burrowed into his mind. I went just far enough that my own vision remained unaffected, but the captain dropped the device and fell to his knees, silently screaming. Blood streamed from his nose. I then turned to face the others, who also screamed as they fell to their knees. I didn't let up my assault until every one of the STAR around me was on the ground unconscious.

With the STAR incapacitated, I stared at the doors to the med lab.

"Fuck! Cedrick, are you there?"

I scanned the room, looking for the little device the captain had dropped. If I wanted Cedrick's help, I had only two options: find the little device and shut the damned thing off, or find a way to get outside the field generated by the device. As the seconds continued to tick by, with no ticking clock, I had a bad feeling that I was going to have to make a run for it.

I reached up to my temple and tapped out the sequence to reactivate Alice's tactical display. When it came online, something was off. The tactical display didn't see the bodies around me. I shifted through the various visual modes. Infrared. Ultraviolet. Night vision. Nothing but an empty room. With each shift in mode, I waved my hand in front of me. I had no issues in seeing my own hand, but the STAR . . . I could only see them with my true vision.

Shit! With my tactical implants proven to be useless, I deactivated the display again.

"Alice, are you still monitoring comms?"

"Affirmative."

"Has there been anything on the comms regarding myself or Sector 11?"

"Negative."

Bullshit. I closed my eyes, trying to work out when Alice's systems would have been compromised. It had to have been when I resurfaced in Sector 11 and Alice reconnected to the servers.

My shoulders sagged. Even if that wasn't how it happened, it didn't matter. I was now truly on my own. No

Cedrick . . . and no Alice. "Alice, execute Protocol White Rabbit. Authorization Davison-Kilo-Gamma-Delta."

There was a high-pitched squeal in my ear, followed by a low-voltage jolt. I winced.

"Goodbye, Alice," I whispered, then turned my attention to my current problem. How to get out of Sector 14 while being technologically blind and without help.

Fifty-Nine

I KNELT BESIDE THE UNCONSCIOUS STAR and rummaged through their pockets, taking a pocketknife from the captain and a hunting dagger from one of the others. There was no point in going for the DNA-encoded pistols and tasers. But it was the smoke bombs found on the fourth guard that gave me an idea.

I lined up my new arsenal, pocketing what I wouldn't need right away. I then pulled out my laser pistol and prepared it to fire. Assuming the laser pistol was on full charge, I would get possibly twenty shots out of it, but each shot would be delayed by a fifth of a second—an eternity when in the heat of a fight.

I drew in calming breath after calming breath, focusing my mind on the reasons why I was doing this. Beth and the baby. Cedrick and his trust in me. Lucas and his faith. Tam, the one person who had always looked out for me. For Renee. And George: my reason for existing. My grounding. My best friend in all the world.

And the Pregutor took him away from me.

My fear melted away into a snarl. I knelt just inside the door and pulled the pin on the first smoke bomb, rolling it out of the small opening and into the corridor. I waited three seconds, then rolled out the second smoke bomb. Three seconds later, I rolled out the third. And with one last calming breath, I ran out the door and took aim at the shadows in the smoke.

Pandemonium erupted, as the guards in the corridor seemed to struggle to work out which way to move. With so much smoke, it would have been difficult to distinguish friend from foe. To me, they were all foe. I didn't wait for them to gather their strategies; I just ran for the exit, firing at the guards in my way, a laser bullet through their heads.

I sped across the short distance and attacked the guard who stood between me and the door. My strikes were targeted at the soft tissue exposed by the gap in the side of the tactical vest and at the man's neck. I spun him around and used him as a human shield as I fired the last shots from my laser pistol at the heads of the remaining guards. There was a brief moment of silence, and my human shield finally fell to the ground.

I quickly checked the charge left on my laser pistol. Ten percent. If I was lucky, I had two shots left. While the weapon was great at piercing through any armor that a person might be wearing, the thing lacked longevity. I holstered the laser pistol, then made a run for it.

"Cedrick? Can you hear me?" But no response came. Knowing my luck, the dead guards around me had all been issued with one of those little devices that blocked my telepathic abilities. Or maybe there was a larger device that covered the entire sector. I shuddered at the thought. Something like that would mean a full out war between STAR and the telepaths outside the core.

Rushed footsteps echoed in the empty corridors, and I darted down the side passage and ducked into an empty office, keeping the door slightly ajar.

"I need a full stock take of that lab," Abram Shutton ordered. "She went to that lab for a reason, and I want to know what it is." I had always respected the man, but had that respect been misplaced? If the vision Tam had shown me was to be believed, the man killed my mother. His own daughter. He had turned her into an experiment. I didn't want to know what experiments he had in store for me.

The junior technician with him nodded, then headed off in a direction I couldn't see. But Abram Shutton headed for the office I was hiding in.

I pushed myself into the darkest corner of the room. When the lights came on, I darted across the room and held the laser pistol to the back of his head.

"Give me one good reason why I shouldn't pull this trigger."

"It's nice to see you too, Michaella." He started to turn, but I pressed the pistol tighter against his head.

"Don't move."

"Surely, you want to be able to look into my eyes."

"And why would I want to do that?"

"So you can compel me to do whatever you want me to do. That is how your abilities work, is it not? By looking into a person's eyes, you see into their soul."

"I don't need to look into your eyes to know the darkness that consumes your soul. The only thing I don't understand is how you could do it. How could you turn your own daughter into breeding stock?"

"So, Tam finally told you. What else did they tell you?"

"Does it matter?"

"No, I guess it doesn't." He took a deep breath. "Now what? You should know that even if you compelled me to help you get out of here, you would never make a clean escape. The moment you chose to destroy that building, you became Public Enemy Number One."

"I was already Public Enemy Number One. You have been hunting for the Red Queen for months."

"You?" Despite my instructions to not turn around, he turned to face me. "There is no way you could be the Red Queen."

I backed up from him, ensuring there was enough distance between us so he couldn't easily seize any of the weapons on my belt. At least, not without charging at me first. At which point, I would pull the trigger.

"Let me guess," I said. "You didn't get that little piece of information from the chair download. But I know you got other information. So, what do you know?"

He stared at me silently—almost defiantly. It was like he was daring me to dig into his head for the answers I sought. But before I could even attempt to dig into his head, something bit my neck. I reached up and pulled out a tranquilizer dart.

My eyes drooped, and I wavered on the spot. I blinked several times and tried to stay focused, but my grip on my pistol slackened. A guard came up from behind me and easily disarmed me, pushing me to my knees.

"You're getting sloppy, Mike. Shame on you for not keeping an eye on all entrances into this office—including the hidden ones." The voice sounded muffled and drawn out. The world started to spin. "Are you okay, sir?"

"Well done, Gahan. You shall be rewarded."

SIXTY

THE RESTRAINTS HELD ME IN place. Not that I had the strength to get up from the chair, anyway. A white blob moved against the white background. A silver-topped receptacle was waved in my face.

"Why do you need this?" Dr. Shutton's voice was unnervingly calm. Almost fatherly. But there was evil sitting under that calm. An evil that killed my mother. "I know it's not for you. So, who did you steal this for?"

I looked at his blurry face and smiled. Didn't say a word.

"No matter. I'll know soon enough." He put the vial down on the table on the side of the room—at least I thought it was a table—then he waved his hands in front of him, activating his virtual console. A slight hum filled the room.

I sank into the chair. Soon my memories would be taken from me—yet again. The system arms extended around my head . . . and the lights went dark. Emergency lighting bathed the room in a faint blue.

"Go find out what's going on."

"Sir, we're under orders—"

"Go. I'll be fine. Don't worry about her. Just get me the power back. Now!"

Several black-clad blobs disappeared out the door and into the hall. And all I could do was wait for the inevitable to happen. Even if the power outage continued for the rest of eternity, it wouldn't be long enough.

The lights flickered back on, and there was a loud clunk as the chair system restarted its startup sequence.

One guard returned, closing the door behind them.

"I take it the issue has been resolved."

"Not quite," the guard said, a familiar voice, though in my daze, I couldn't identify who.

The black-clad soldier rushed across the short space. Through my blurry vision, I couldn't really see what happened, but the doctor in white was lowered to the ground, and the soldier was coming for me.

I pulled on my restraints with all of my strength. Unfortunately, there wasn't much to be had.

"Mike, calm down. It's me." The black-clad soldier came closer and loomed over me. Something warm flushed into my arm, and my vision cleared. Marcus stood over me with a wrinkled brow and strained muscles in the side of his neck.

I pushed myself deeper into the chair and started to twist my wrists, trying to gain the room to set myself free. "Get away from me."

"Mike . . ." The pain that came from his eyes pulled at my heart, but I didn't have time to be sensitive to his feelings. "I'm getting you out of here."

He reached down to my wrist and removed the restraint holding me there. As soon as my hand was free, my hand darted to his neck and squeezed. His eyes bulged as he stared at me. I didn't have the physical strength to hold him . . . but maybe I had the mental strength.

The edges of my vision darkened as I stared into his eyes. He resisted me—the ceremony when he was given rank among STAR sat on the surface of his thoughts—but I knew my power. I pushed harder, like a narrow pick driving in to shatter his ideal world. The vision melted in the middle, leaving Marcus vulnerable to my will.

"You get one chance to tell me the truth," I hissed, my words slightly slurred from the sedative. "What are you doing here?"

"What does it look like I'm doing? I'm helping you escape." His voice was hoarse. But he didn't turn into a zombie like I had expected. Instead, he looked at me with the same determination he had before. And he hadn't reached up to his neck to free himself, either. Instead, he used his peripheral vision to free me from the restraints. "You're going to have to let go of me if you want me to get the restraints around your ankles."

But instead of letting go, I squeezed harder, using my other hand to help. "You shot me."

"I didn't have a choice."

"There is always a choice."

"Not if I wanted to remain undercover." He finally reached up to his neck and carefully peeled back my fingers. "How do you think the captain got the Queen of Hearts card that you needed to remember who you are? Now, do you want to get out of here? Or do you want to beat the shit out of me?"

I studied him, hunting for any sign of deception. "You're really here to free me?" Though I was tempted by the idea of beating him into a living pulp.

Marcus nodded, then got to work at releasing the restraints around my ankles. "Can you stand on your own?"

I blinked several times, trying to process what was going on but failing. I pushed myself into a standing position and took a few unsteady steps. At least I was standing.

Marcus pulled my arm over his shoulder. "We don't have the time to wait for you to regain full control. We need to get out of here now."

"No, wait." I looked over to the side table where Abram Shutton had put the vial, but it wasn't there. "Where did it go?"

"Where did what go?"

"The vial. I need the vial Dr. Shutton took from me."

"You mean this?" He pulled a vial out of his vest and showed it to me. "I saw Dr. Shutton demand to know why you'd stolen it. I'm guessing that whatever it's for, it's important. Else you wouldn't have risked your life to get it. The moment you had been discovered, you could have disappeared, but you didn't. You broke in for this." He put the vial back into his vest pocket. "If you don't mind, I'll hold on to it for the moment. You don't exactly have somewhere safe to stash it."

I reluctantly nodded. My uniform didn't have any pockets, and my tactical vest was nowhere to be seen. I could have stashed the vial in my boot, but that was asking for it to be smashed.

I leaned on him for added stability as we headed out of the chair room—still not certain if he was friend or foe.

The hall outside the chair room was littered with black-clad soldiers, all unconscious or dead. Streaks of blood covered the walls.

"You did this? Alone?"

"No need to thank me. Let's just get out of here."

"Why?"

"Because if we don't get out of here now, they'll kill you."

I pulled him to a stop. "No, Marcus, that's not what I meant. You've always been loyal to the Pregutor. The happy thought that protects your mind is the day you became part of STAR. So, I ask again. Why are you helping me?"

"We really don't have the time for this."

"Make the time. Because I'm not taking one more step until you answer me."

"If you really must know, I'm helping you because of George."

It was like my mind had frozen in thought, unable to process what he was getting at.

"You don't know how many times I watched you grieve over him. And I knew damned well that if I just left you there, I would be forced to watch you grieve his death again. I'm sorry, Mike, but I can't do it anymore. I won't let them take those memories from you—not again."

I had never liked Marcus. I tolerated him, really. But now there was a desperate truth that washed over him. No deceit.

"Mike, I don't know what else you want me to say, but we're running out of time here. The comms channels are in a fury. They don't know you're gone—yet—but as soon as they work it out . . ."

I nodded. "Lead the way."

We left the dead bodies behind and headed for the old service tunnels abandoned long ago. Our joint footsteps made muffled thumps in the silence of the space. We turned right, then took a left, and faced a dead end. Before I could say anything, Marcus waved his wrist over a hidden sensor pad, and there was a slight hiss as the wall moved.

I stared at the thin, dark opening and was overwhelmed by the feeling that I had been there before. But in my vague memory, Marcus was chasing me, not helping me.

He reached into his pocket and passed me a small flashlight and a small tablet. "Everything you need to navigate the maze is here." He tapped the tablet's surface three times, activating the physical display. "The tablet is not connected to the servers, so it'll be safe to use while down there. The door at the other end is already unlocked. I . . . ah . . . broke the access panel earlier, ensuring that security couldn't remotely lock it. It's stiff though—the hinges are rusted. I'll do what I can to make sure that you have as much time as possible to get away from here. I estimate that you have roughly thirty minutes before they work out which way you went."

"Come with me."

Marcus shook his head.

"The moment they work out how I escaped, they'll know it was you who helped me."

"You let me worry about that. Just get out of here and stay safe." He pulled out the vial from his vest and gave it to me. "Go. I'll cover your tracks."

"Marcus, I . . ." Everything I thought I knew about the man was wrong. In the end, I grabbed him and pulled him close, kissing him.

The boundaries around his mind vanished. Without even willing myself into his thoughts, I was suddenly there.

I felt his uncertainty as we trained together after my memory loss. There was a hint of excitement as I was temporarily transferred to the STAR facilities. His amusement radiated as I called him out for his bullshit, pointing out the weapon he was trying to hide. And there was a sense of longing when Marcus admitted that he had loved me. He had called me his sister, but in truth, he had wished that I could be much more than that. And when I was granted rank among STAR . . .

As the kiss ended, our minds separated. Marcus leaned into me, touching his forehead to mine.

"So, you—"

"You're human, Marcus. And I like humans."

He smirked. "Maybe when this is all over, I'll get to watch you as you dance in a white kitchen."

"Excuse me?" I pulled back from him slightly and looked at him with furrowed brows.

"Just trying to imagine what life would have been like if none of this had ever happened." He caressed my face and allowed his fingers to intertwine with my freshly dyed hair. "I'm not sure when you managed to redye your hair, but I like this color. So blue. And you would look awesome in a blue dress matching it."

I did the best I could to hide my growing fear, trying to keep my heart rate from speeding ahead. There was no way he could have known about the woman in the blue dress dancing in the white kitchen. I only ever told one person about that vision: Dr. Shutton. The only way Marcus could have known about it was if he was . . .

I had to force myself to breathe. I tried to smile, though my heart was breaking. "I better go. Thirty minutes, right?"

"At least that, but I'll try to buy you more time."

"Thank you."

There was a look in his eye that suggested that he was hoping for another kiss, but I couldn't bring myself to do it. Instead, I turned from him and headed into the tunnel network. When the door closed behind me, I stood in the middle of the passageway, trying to keep myself from falling apart.

How could I have let him get past my defenses like that? He hadn't burrowed his way into my mind, but he had found a way into my heart. I closed my eyes and allowed myself a moment to grieve, knowing that he had betrayed me for the last time.

With a deep breath, I turned on the flashlight and followed the path marked out on the tablet. Even if I was walking into a trap, I didn't have much choice. I rushed through the tunnels as fast as I could, eventually finding my way to the end of the maze. The door ahead of me had a mechanical locking system, coupled with an electronic system. And just as Marcus had promised, the electronic system was busted. The only thing holding the door closed was the horizontal locking bolts.

Just inside the door was a pile of gear, including a purple jacket, a breather, and a pair of virtual display glasses. But it wasn't just any jacket, breather, and glasses. They were mine—the ones I had thrown away as I entered Sector 14. The feeling that this was all a trap intensified.

With the jacket on, and the breather and glasses stashed in my pockets, I grabbed a metal rod from the ground and wove it through the spokes of the wheel on the back of the door. As the metal door groaned, it opened, and I escaped Sector 14 through a curtain of dead vines. With the door to the underground tunnels closed again, and the vines readjusted to mask the door's existence, I joined the bustling crowds moving down the street.

"Cedrick? Can you hear me?"

"Mike? Is that you? Oh, thank the spirits. I thought we'd lost you."

"You should know by now that I'm full of surprises. Meanwhile, I need your help to get out of here."

"Exactly where are you?"

"Sector 12."

My mind was filled with silence.

"Cedrick? You there?"

"Yeah, sorry. Did I hear you correctly? You're in Sector 12? How the hell did you manage to get out of Sector 14?"

"I'll explain everything later. Right now, I need to get to safety. Just tell me where to go."

"To the Zukon foot passage. It's the fastest way to Sector 9."

"To the White Rabbit Bar," I said.

"You remember."

I tried to smile, though my heart wasn't in it. *"I do."*

Sixty-One

I stood outside the White Rabbit Bar in Sector 9, staring at the darkened windows and the built-up layers of dust outside the main door. It was a dark hovel—the perfect place for a trap—but I trusted Cedrick. He wouldn't knowingly put me in danger. However, I feared the Pregutor was using me as bait to trap Cedrick.

I reached into my pocket and wrapped my fingers around the vial. That vial meant everything and made it worth the risk. With a calming breath, I went inside. The door sealed with a hiss.

The bartender looked up. "You're cutting it a bit close."

"Excuse me?"

"Cedrick said to expect you around midday. It's nearly dark light."

"Dark light?"

"When they take the sector off the grid for the night. To conserve power. When dark light hits, there's no getting through the checkpoints. They seal them up tight. No one in or out of the sector till morning."

"So, what you're telling me is that if I stay here, I'm a sitting duck."

"That depends on your definition of a sitting duck." The bartender poured a glass of some red liquid and placed it on the bar, gesturing to the stool in front of him. "Quack, quack."

I stared at the bartender and the drink on the bar.

"You can stand there if you want, but the moment Cedrick gets here, he's likely to want to make a move and get out of here before they seal up the sector. I suggest you finish your drink before he gets here. You might not get another chance." Again, he pointed to the stool directly in front of the red drink.

Cautiously, I sat down. My fingers inched toward the glass. "You didn't put anything suspicious in this, did you?"

The bartender feigned a shocked expression, then laughed. "I learned the hard way to not try to mess with you. I want to thank you, by the way. If it wasn't for you, my baby girl would be dead. I don't know how you did it, but . . . Well . . . Thank you."

"You're welcome." Though I had no idea what he was talking about. It had to have been one of the memories the Pregutor took from me.

He knocked on the bar. "You just let me know if I can get you anything else."

I nodded and took a sip of the sugary drink. It wasn't bad. It wasn't great, but it wasn't bad. Not really wanting to sit on the tall stool with my back to the door, I picked up the drink and headed for the booth in the corner.

I didn't have to wait long before Cedrick slid into the booth opposite me. And he had a purple coat of his own. And his grin spread from ear to ear.

"You look like a Cheshire cat."

"I can even disappear, given the right circumstances. It's a magic coat, after all." We both laughed. He then turned serious. "Did you get it?"

I pulled out the vial, putting it on the table between us.

"All that trouble for this." He held up the vial to the light, like he was trying to see if it was made of gold or something. He then passed it back to me. "You keep it safe until we can give it to Beth. I'm not really used to wearing one of these jackets. So many pockets."

"Speaking of which, where did you get it?"

"You don't want to know." A hint of sorrow washed across his face, only to be replaced by that Cheshire grin again.

"The White Rabbit is dead, by the way."

"We know. But they succeeded in doing the one thing that no one else could."

"And what's that?"

"They encouraged Alice to embark on a journey into Wonderland."

"So, I'm not the Red Queen?"

"No, you never were."

I sighed in defeat. "Because I'm Alice. The white pawn who somehow managed to make it to the other side of the board and becomes a queen herself."

"Not just any queen. You're the queen who will take out the Red Queen before calling checkmate."

I smiled at that. But I couldn't hold the tears in any longer.

"Hey . . ." He moved to sit next to me, pulling me into a loving embrace. But it wasn't romantic. It was brotherly. "It's okay. Everything will be okay."

"No, it won't." I looked up at Cedrick, doing the best I could to hold it together. "They let me go. I didn't escape. I can't explain how I know." My last exchange with Marcus played over and over in my head.

"I can. The bad guys can't see purple." He picked up a lock of my hair and tucked it behind my ear. "At least your hair's not that two-tone whack job you had before."

I snorted, but the tears threatened to restart.

"I'm so sorry. I know you wanted to believe that he had changed—that he could be one of us—"

"But he was never one of us. He was just a playing card." I took another deep breath. "Can we go home, please?"

"Did you bring me the laser pistol?"

I scoffed and rolled my eyes. His grin returned, then vanished again.

"Before we go, there's one more thing we need to do."

I sagged my shoulders. "Render me unconscious?"

"No, Lucas said that won't be necessary this time."

The bartender put a portable med unit on the bar and held out the leads.

I nodded. While my comms unit had likely been fried when Alice short-circuited herself, there was other tech in my body, including the pharmachip. And any one of the tiny devices could put out a signal that the Pregutor could use to track me. Without hesitation, I pulled off my jacket and pulled off my top, leaving only a singlet. I grabbed the leads from the bartender and placed them on my skin. Then I sat on the ground.

"You did that like you've done this before," the bartender said.

This time, I was the one to grin from ear to ear. "I learned from the best." I then laid on my back. "Hit me."

There was no warning or countdown. A surge of electricity flowed through me, making my body tense.

Cedrick knelt beside me and waved some sort of wand over me. It beeped several times. "I'm sorry, Mike."

"I know. Just do it."

Again, no warning. And I was fairly confident that the jolt was higher.

Again, Cedrick waved the wand over my body. Again, it beeped.

"Third time's a charm, right?" I said. "Crank it up to full power."

"That could kill you."

"Better dead than tracked. Just do it."

I was hit with another electric jolt and blacked out.

Sixty-Two

Strong lights filtered through my fluttering lashes. The gray of the ceiling slowly came into focus, with its veins of granite running parallel to the ground. The iridescent light cast criss-crossing shadows.

Pain radiated from my right wrist, and an IV line ran into my left arm. Electronic instruments hummed around me. But it was the ticking clock that was the most welcoming sound of all.

I inhaled the musky, damp air. I was home.

I rolled to my side and pushed myself into a seated position, careful of the IV. The steel frame of the stretcher creaked and groaned under the shift in weight.

"You're awake." Beth rushed to my side, her long hair tied up into a ponytail. But it was the tight fit of Beth's clothes around the middle that brought everything back into full focus.

"Did we succeed?"

Beth beamed. "Yes." She placed her hand on her belly. "Unless nature decides otherwise, this baby will make it to full term. Thank you."

I beamed too. The fact that the baby would be okay was all that mattered.

"How long have I been out?"

"Nearly a day." Beth held her fingers to the inside of my left wrist as she looked at the ticking clock. "Your heart briefly stopped with that electrocution trick, but thankfully, a medic team was standing by. Cedrick and Lucas learned the hard way after the last time you came in."

I looked down at my right wrist wrapped in gauze. "Does that mean . . ."

"Yep." Beth smiled again. "We got it out. We also took out your communication implants. I know we didn't ask for your permission for the invasive procedures first, but I don't think you wanted them anymore."

"No, I would have asked you to take them out as soon as possible anyway. So, did you take all my implants out?"

"No. Cedrick said something about ocular implants?"

I nodded. "I don't know much about them, but they're embedded in the optic nerve bundle."

"Hmm . . ." Beth looked around the med bay and frowned. "I don't think I have the gear needed to take those out without endangering your eyesight."

"It's okay. As long as no signal is coming from them, we should be safe."

Beth smirked. "You forget that we're surrounded by all this rock." She pulled out the blood pressure cuff and went about her general exam. "Well, I don't think you need this anymore." She closed the valve on the IV line and pulled out the needle.

"So . . . How long am I to be holed up in the med bay this time?"

"As long as you promise to come right back here if you start feeling dizzy or anything, you're free to go. Nancy already has your bunk set up with the rest of the Rabbits."

"Rabbits?"

"It's what your old team started calling themselves after you left. They're probably in the training hall now. Do you remember the way?"

I bit my bottom lip and glanced at the door. "I think so."

Beth just smiled and headed back to her workstation in the corner, allowing her growing belly to point the way.

I took several deep breaths and smiled again. The fruits of my labor had paid off.

I headed out the door and into the stone hallway, not one hundred percent certain I remembered the way, but I trusted that my body did. At each junction, my feet chose the direction. The instinctive motions gave me the opportunity to take in my surroundings. Dark gray ceilings lined with incandescent lights. Smooth walls that merged into concrete floors. Little childlike drawings found at every junction. Cats, dogs, and funny-shaped horses. There were even circular suns and rainbows. And white rabbits hopped along the walls, joining in on the croquet match with flamingos.

The Queen of Hearts pointed down the hall, and the playing cards chased after the girl in the blue dress.

Whether it was the right direction or not, I followed Alice, chasing after her. To protect her.

The air in the tunnels became warmer. Drier. Whenever Alice on the wall looked back over her shoulder, I mimicked her actions, looking around at the empty halls. I traveled deeper into the underground maze. I was nowhere near the training room, but my feet insisted that I follow Alice.

Voices echoed in soft murmurs down the hall, a sense of urgency to them. I sped up my steps. As I turned the last corner, soldiers clad in black came into view. And Marcus was with them.

Shit. I reached up to tap behind my right ear, only feeling the bandage where my communications implant had been removed. Then I remembered that those in Sanctuary didn't use comms units. Even if they did, I didn't know the frequency. Double shit.

I darted into the room and hid behind a large cylinder with pipes coming out of it in every direction.

"We need to hurry up," Marcus said. "If anyone finds out . . ."

"Just shut up and let me do my job," hissed the other soldier with him. "No one will find out."

I couldn't see what they were doing, and I didn't recognize the room. But Alice had led me here for a reason. I was the only one able to stop them.

I rushed across the short distance and launched my attack. Marcus tried to put his hands up in surrender, but I didn't want his surrender. I wanted him dead. Without any thought for my own safety, I struck at him with everything I had.

My vision darkened around the edges as I prepared to dive into his mind, ripping at his mental shields and forcing him to do my will. And I continued to throw fists and kicks in his direction. The air shifted behind me, and I spun around to block a kick aimed at my head. I grabbed the unknown soldier's leg and carried the momentum to throw the soldier up against the metal piping behind them. With a grunt and a groan, I elbowed them in the face, shattering their nose. With a few more punches and kicks, they went down.

I turned my attention back to Marcus, but he was gone. Vanished from view. I started to head off to hunt him down, but an alarm blared from the console that Marcus and the unknown soldier had been standing at. And it didn't take a genius to work out that the containment field around the power generation core was collapsing.

"Crap. What do I do? Cedrick! Can you hear me?"

I waited a few seconds, but there was no answer. The pressure on the main core continued to climb.

"Think, Mike, think." I stared at the buttons on the console. Knobs and dials that seemed to have no meaning. In the corner was a small green button with a paper note taped next to it.

»Pressure release.«

I had to assume that the paper note had been put there by someone who knew the system.

The alarm continued to blare, and the pressure levels shown on the screen were well and truly in the red levels. I pressed the button and prayed.

There was a hiss from above me, and the air temperature around me dramatically increased, but the pressure levels dropped back to green levels. I sighed and sagged forward. But I couldn't celebrate for too long. Marcus was on the loose, and I had to stop him.

I turned my attention back to the soldier on the ground. They were unconscious, but still breathing. I took their sidearm pistol and gave it a quick look over. Odd. It wasn't a DNA-encoded weapon that STAR were so fond of using. But with Marcus on the loose, I thanked the idiot for not following protocol. I pocketed the spare magazines and headed off in the direction that I hoped Marcus went.

As I navigated the underground maze, I held the pistol at the ready. The temperature in the halls continued to climb. I wiped the sweat from my brow and flapped the collar of my shirt to fan my neck. I pulled back my hair to stop the wet strands from getting into my eyes.

Stick figures graced the wall at waist height, dancing in the purple rain. One of the figures wore a purple jacket, and the other wore a navy blue one. My vision temporarily blurred, but the cool rock helped me focus.

Voices around the bend grabbed my attention. "Are you sure about this?" someone asked.

"Yes." That was Marcus. "She was last seen in the power center. And she's stronger than I expected. I couldn't break through her mental defenses."

"Understood. Right, here's what we're going to do."

I didn't wait for the STAR commander to give his orders. I came around the corner firing, each bullet hitting their target. With a count of twelve, I dropped the magazine and slammed a new one into place, then kept firing. Everyone around Marcus was on the ground, either dead or dying. And I held the weapon trained on my final target.

His eyes darted in every direction, and he slightly shook his head, as he held his hands up in the air, slowly backing away from me.

"Don't even think about running. You should know by now that I don't miss."

"Mike, please . . ."

"Don't 'Mike, please' me. You're a traitor, Marcus. You would happily betray your own kind and send us all to the wolves."

Marcus shook his head, his brow knit together. "I don't understand."

"Oh, really? If you're not a traitor, then I want you to tell me the truth."

"What truth? Mike, you're having some kind of delusional break. You're seeing things that aren't real."

"So, you're not in front of me with your hands up in surrender?"

"Well, umm . . ." He looked around at all of his dead comrades. He then looked at me with tears in his eyes. And fear. "Mike . . . What did they do to you while you were in there? This isn't you. I know they took your memories, but they must have taken something else from you too. Mike, please . . ."

A painful hum grew inside my head, and my vision blurred again. I shook my head and fanned my shirt. The upper layer was soaked and stuck to my skin. I stared at him, staring into his eyes. I wanted answers, and there was no way I was going to let his mental defenses get in the way. I was stronger than he was. I had always been mentally stronger. It was why they kept me drugged up—so Marcus had a shot at controlling me.

"Tell me the truth." My voice grew deep as I pressed on his mind. "What are you doing here? What is your mission?"

"Mike, I don't know what you're talking about. I live here. Just like you. There is no mission."

"Why were you in the power plant?"

His eyes grew wide. "The power plant? Mike, what happened in the power plant? Is that why it's getting hot in here? Has something happened to the power plant?"

The overhead lights flickered, temporarily plunging us into darkness. I had forgotten how quick Marcus's reflexes were. He charged at me, and I could barely keep track of his movements in the low-level emergency lights. I fired the pistol, but my aim was thrown off by the hulking weight that pushed me against the wall. The bullet ricocheted off the stone walls and ceiling. In the corner of my vision, I saw a small figure fall to the ground, but I didn't have time to worry about who it was who happened to be in the wrong place at the wrong time. My hand was repeatedly banged and smashed against the wall until I had no choice but to drop the weapon.

Marcus had me pinned. He pressed his arm against my throat. "Mike, you need to listen to me. I'm not the enemy. I don't know what it is you think you're seeing, but I'm not your enemy."

"You have always been my enemy, Marcus. For a time, I thought perhaps you had finally grown up, had let go of the past, but you have always been my enemy."

"I'm not Marcus, Mike. It's me . . . Cedrick." He leaned in closer to me. "How else would I know that the last time we stood face to face like this, pinned up against a wall, was in that alleyway outside of the White Rabbit Bar in Sector 9? Mike, please . . ."

I continued to stare at him, staring into his eyes. It was hard to tell in the emergency lights, but I could have sworn that I saw purple flecks in his blue eyes.

"What color is my hair?"

"I want to say purple. It's your preferred color. But when you redyed your hair in your apartment after Renee dyed, you used the color that you had on hand. It does suit you, but you've always dyed your hair purple, because the bad guys can't see purple. Please, Mike, I'm begging you . . ."

My vision wavered and blurred again. Slowly, Marcus morphed into Cedrick. And he was sending the mental image of the woman in the blue dress dancing in the white kitchen singing *Purple Rain.*

"Cedrick?"

He smiled, though it was strained. "I don't know what they did to you, but I promise we'll figure it out—together." He stepped back from me and stumbled, pressing his hands to his side.

"Cedrick." I rushed forward to catch him before he fell.

"I'll be okay. But right now, you have to tell me what has happened to the power plant."

"I don't know. I . . ."

"It's okay. Lucas and Eddie are on their way there now. And Mike, the rest of the Rabbits are on their way here. Please don't fight them when they get here."

"Why would I—"

I looked down at the bodies around us. The black-clad soldiers had vanished and were replaced by those in a variety of colors, their shirts and sweaters worn at the elbows and other areas. And the small figure who got shot by the ricocheted shot . . . Nicky . . . a little girl all of seven years old. A fifth gen.

"No." I ran to the little girl's side, pressing on the red wound in the middle of her chest. But before I could call for Cedrick to help, he, too, fell to the ground. Blood pooled under him.

I screamed with both my mind and my voice. "Someone help me!"

Sixty-Three

I sat on the cot in the corner of my prison cell. Not that I could really call it a prison cell. It was more like a partitioned off area surrounded by clear plastic sheeting. Where they got the old plastic roll was a mystery. But like so many other things found in Sanctuary, it was old technology that proved to be useful in its own way.

I couldn't see much of what was happening on the other side of the plastic walls, except the lights that blinked and the shadows of the people who passed by. But I could hear everything.

"We should kill her while we have the chance," someone hissed. "Because of her, Grober and Nicky are dead. And Cedrick is in critical condition. If you don't have the guts to do it, I'll do it myself."

The shadows outside the plastic walls converged. Clattering noises were followed by the shattering of glass. "I've already told you that she's not to be touched." Lucas's voice was filled with venom, and it was clear that he meant business.

"You're a fourth gen, Lucas. Do you really expect to stop a fifth gen if they choose to act?"

Another shadow joined the group outside, limping. "Fourth gen or fifth gen, it doesn't matter," Eddie said.

"None of you can move faster than a bullet. You think I'm bluffing? Try me. No? Not in the mood? Good. Now, get out of here. All of you." There was a little more scuffling, and the crunching of broken glass under boots. "You too, Lucas."

"Eddie—"

"Out! Or do you forget about the added defenses around this room?"

There was a moment of silence. I imagined Lucas standing there, trying to be the big hero, protecting them all, but based on what I knew about Eddie, he was more than capable of taking care of himself, including around thought-implanting telepaths.

There was more crunching glass, then a slam of a big metal door followed by a beeping noise—no doubt, the verification that the door had been locked.

"You can come out now," Eddie said. "It's just the two of us. And don't dilly-dally. We haven't got all day."

Cautiously, I pulled back the plastic wall. The remains of broken test tubes and beakers littered the floor.

"Don't worry about that mess." He hobbled to the seat in front of his bank of monitors. "There was nothing dangerous in them, anyway."

"Is Cedrick really in critical condition?"

He looked at me like he was trying to assess whether to tell me the truth or not. In the end, he nodded. "Beth managed to stop the bleeding, but he's slipped into a coma. No one knows if he's going to wake up or not. And any attempt to get inside his head is met with paralyzing force. That boy has developed some nasty mental defenses."

"He kind of had to." I bowed my head, finding a loose thread on my sweater to be of sudden interest. "How many did I kill?"

There was a huff before Eddie answered. "Eleven. Most were Rabbits."

"But not all." Tears threatened to spring forth.

"No. Not all."

"I don't know what happened, Eddie. I swear. I thought . . ." I didn't really know what I thought, except that I was fighting Marcus.

"I know. When you went back in, they didn't just wipe your memories. They reprogrammed you."

"What does that mean?"

"Well, that's what we need to find out. Lucas seems to think that they couldn't break you, that you would have never taken action if you didn't believe you weren't looking at the bad guys. And I agree. You can't convince anyone to do something that isn't in their nature to do already. Your nature is to protect the ones you care about by whatever means possible. You will kill if you need to, but only as a last resort. I think they somehow implanted a thought in your head—that you would see your enemies when you saw your friends. The rest was just you trying to protect your loved ones."

"If that was true, then I should classify you as an enemy."

Eddie tried to smile, but the sorrow the man felt only grew deeper in his eyes. "In a way, I am. I'm the one who sent you in there. I'm the one who walked away from you and your mother when you were a little girl. It's because of me, you became an agent of the Pregutor in the first place."

"Then what about Beth? Should I see her as the enemy too?"

Eddie grunted, then took a deep breath as he settled deeper into his chair. "Beth is a doctor, and all doctors you have ever interacted with have been an enemy of sorts, subjecting you to procedures you didn't necessarily feel comfortable with. But in Beth's case, I think there was something else going on."

That's when it hit. "The baby. They let me go. They wanted me to deliver the medicine that Beth needed so she wouldn't lose the baby. That's what this was all about. They want the baby."

Slowly, Eddie nodded. "That's my conclusion too. And if it wasn't for the bond you share with Cedrick, they would have gotten the baby."

"I don't understand."

Eddie reached behind him and tapped on the keyboard, bringing up a recording from the security feeds. On the video, I held the pistol aimed at Cedrick, and Cedrick was doing what he could to get me to lower the weapon, but I kept calling him Marcus.

"That's when I knew what they had done," Eddie said. "Somehow, this Marcus fellow got into your head and implanted the thought needed to make it all work— including the suggestion to shut down the safety protocols on the power generation system. But this Marcus guy didn't know the systems. And he didn't know Cedrick. And he didn't know you. He thought he did, but he didn't realize that you would do anything to protect Cedrick and his child—even kill. He is your blood, after all."

"Of course. Cedrick was Abram Shutton's son. And my mother was his daughter."

Eddie nodded. "You're a sixth gen, Mike. The first one born. And Cedrick's baby . . ."

I shook my head. "No. Don't you dare say it."

Eddie winced and rubbed at his neck. "Okay, I won't. But I thought I had that thing calibrated right."

"What thing?"

He pulled out of his pocket a small field generator. "The field is only large enough to encompass one person. It works against Cedrick, not a problem. Lucas and the other Rabbits don't have a chance of getting past this little device. But clearly, I have a bit of tweaking to do . . . so I can block you. But it's getting better. I mean, I've had nearly twenty years to work on it." He smiled and winked.

I smirked. "But I've also had twenty years for my abilities to grow in strength."

He harrumphed, then nodded.

A persistent buzz came from the desk. Eddie turned around and hit the intercom switch. "I'm busy. Go away."

"Eddie, it's Cedrick," Lucas said. "You better get your ass down to the med bay. And bring Mike."

Sixty-Four

"No! Get her out of here!" Beth held a pistol aimed at me.

The woman's pregnant belly seemed to have grown in the few hours since I had last seen her. Perhaps it was more pronounced because of the tight top that didn't completely cover her bump.

Lucas stood in front of me with his hands up in surrender. "Beth, please, you said it yourself that Cedrick is in the fight of his life, fighting the demons inside his own head. One of us has to go in there and help him fight. Mike is the only one among us who is strong enough to break past his mental defenses."

"I don't care."

I pushed Lucas to the side and stood in front of him, ensuring that Beth had a clear shot of my heart. "Beth, please . . ." I licked my lips as I glanced past the woman with the gun to the man on the gurney behind her. The woman in the blue dress kept dancing on the surface of his mind. But she wasn't singing. She was shouting—screaming about the little girl hiding in the corner. A little girl holding a stuffed purple cat toy.

I took a deep breath and looked back over my shoulder at Lucas. "I didn't know it before, but I do now. Some of the defenses in his mind were not of his own making. They were put there by me—when I was a little girl—the night his mother died.”

“What are you saying?” Lucas asked.

“I was there when it happened, but I was only five.” I sighed and shook my head. In the corner of the room, a teenage boy beckoned me toward the hall. He pointed to the shouting woman in the blue dress, then continued to beckon me forward. “I wanted to protect him,” I continued, tears hanging in the corner of my eyes. “I put a block inside his mind, so he wouldn’t remember the truth behind how his mother died.”

I turned back to Beth. “We have a connection that goes beyond our abilities. The same blood runs through our veins. And because of that connection, I know that he’s seeking answers to find sense in the madness. I can help him.”

Beth just stared at me, conviction in her eyes.

“Let her help,” Eddie said, standing beside me. “She’s Cedrick’s niece.”

Slowly, Beth dropped her aim and nodded, moving to the side.

I stood beside Cedrick on the gurney and took his hand. I closed my eyes and prepared myself to walk into Cedrick’s memories. But unlike when I was in Tam’s mind, I didn’t see things through his eyes. I didn’t experience the world like he had all those years ago. My own mind had memories of its own about the events that Cedrick was trying to understand—filling in the missing gaps.

In my mind, I stood on the edge of the joint memory as an observer of past events.

✷

THE WOMAN IN the blue dress stood in the middle of the kitchen, raging.

"You have to be reasonable about this." Abram Shutton tried to cross the room, but Tam stopped him.

"She is allowed to have her emotions." Tam's calm, carefully put-together demeanor was in contradiction to the jeans and T-shirt that they wore, clothing that I recalled from the vision Tam had shown me.

The woman in the blue dress pointed at Tam and backed away from her husband and the oddly-dressed white figure. "Damned right, I'm allowed to have my emotions. And right now, I'm angry as hell. And don't you dare try using your funky calming magic on me. I should have the two of you reported to the authorities. That girl is an abomination." She pointed to the little girl curled up in the corner, clinging to a purple cat. Little Mike.

"She's my granddaughter, Selina," Abram said. "She's the future."

"You said that about our son when he was born. They can't both be the future."

"Yes, they can," Tam said. "Both of them have a chance to live outside the domes."

I ignored the rest of the conversation that Abram and Tam were having with Cedrick's mother. All that mattered was the little girl in the corner and the teenage boy hiding in the hallway.

"Psst . . . Psst . . ." The boy poked his finger out from the hall, curling it over, beckoning the little girl to join him. "Come on," he mouthed.

But the little girl kept looking between the adults fighting in the kitchen and the boy. Eventually, she cautiously got to her feet and darted across the short space into the hall.

The boy grabbed the little girl's hand and led her to a small bedroom at the end of the hall.

I followed after them.

"It'll be much safer in here," the boy said. "We might even have a chance of blocking out all the yelling. My name's Cedrick, by the way. What's yours?"

The girl shook her head.

"That's okay. You don't have to tell me. What about your cat? Do they have a name?"

Again, the girl shook her head.

"Are you shaking your head because they have a name and you don't want to tell me? Or they don't have a name?"

Again, the girl shook her head.

"Well, I can't keep calling 'em Cat. How about . . . Violet, in honor of their purple color?"

The girl cocked her head to the side, looking between the cat and the boy. I didn't need to know what was going on in the girl's head to know that she was amazed at how the teenage boy could see the stuffed animal's true color. In the end, the little girl nodded in the exaggerated way that only a little girl could.

Young Cedrick smiled, then he reached forward and pulled the little girl into a hug. "It's just you, me, and Violet now. No matter what happens, we'll look out for one another." He started to hum the familiar chorus to *Purple Rain*.

Tears hung in my eyes.

"I had forgotten about that," said a man behind me.

"So did I." I turned to see Cedrick, as I knew him now, come out of the dark shadows of his mind.

He took a deep breath as he kept watching the two children clinging to one another while the adults continued to fight in the other room. "I remember the fight between my parents, and I knew that it had been over you, but I didn't remember ever meeting you. The moment I saw you"—he gestured to me—"this version of you, I knew there was something familiar about you. And it wasn't just the fact that I was inside your head in the days leading up to our meeting. There was this . . . presence coming from you that stirred something in me. This need to protect you. And your hair . . . It . . ." He looked back at the children huddled together, the purple cat between them.

"It was the same color as Violet," I said. "I never told anyone what I had named the cat. Because the bad guys couldn't see her true color. Every time someone saw the stuffed toy, they would call it Bluey . . . or Blue. Except George. He knew it was violet."

"So that's the real reason why you keep him in your thoughts. You knew he could never be one of the bad guys."

I nodded. Then I closed my eyes, holding back the tears. "And I killed him." Then I looked up at him. "And I almost killed you."

"Yeah, you did. Beth must be really pissed."

"That's putting it mildly. As we speak, in the real world, she has a gun to my head."

His eyes bulged. "I knew that woman had a temper, but I wasn't aware of how bad it would get while she was pregnant."

I snorted. "I don't think this has anything to do with her pregnancy. At least, her anger doesn't have anything to do with it."

Cedrick shook his head and furrowed his brow. It didn't even take a second before his eyes shot wide again. "Oh.

When they took your memories, they learned of Beth's pregnancy."

I nodded. "Your father was using us all as experiments. And your mother . . ." I took a deep breath, trying to stay calm. "There's more to the circumstances behind your mother's death, which you don't remember . . . but I do."

The world around us shifted into nighttime. The two children were curled up asleep on the tiny bed pushed up against the wall. But little Mike couldn't stay asleep. She climbed out of the bed, careful not to wake young Cedrick. With her purple cat in hand, the girl headed out into the hall, pulling at her pants. She looked in various doors, like she was looking for a toilet. But the continued argument coming from the kitchen grabbed her attention, pulling her forward.

The three adults no longer used raised voices, but it was clear that the anger was still high. The room was washed with a red haze that wafted in clouds from Tam.

"Selina, I know this is not ideal—"

Cedrick's mother put up her hand, silencing Tam. "I don't want to hear it anymore."

Abram put a glass down on the table in front of his wife. "Perhaps this will help you feel better."

Selina harrumphed, but downed whatever was in the glass anyway. The woman swayed on the spot, and eventually her head lolled forward.

"Finally." Abram moved the glass out of Selina's slack grasp and pulled her from the chair.

"Abram, what did you give her?"

"A sedative."

Tam picked up the glass and smelled the contents. "How much did you give her?"

"Enough."

"Enough for what?"

"To permanently remove the obstacle from our path."

The two of them stared at one another, not knowing that the little girl was watching from the hallway.

Pushing Tam to the side, Abram lifted the unconscious woman into the air, then dropped her. A crack reverberated around the small space as the woman's head hit the sharp edge of the table.

The little girl in the hallway froze and vanished from view. A purple haze colored the space where the little girl had been standing.

"Where did she go?" the adult Cedrick said.

"She's still there," I said, my voice cracking, "terrified of the man who was supposed to be her grandfather. I'm surprised she hasn't peed her pants."

Cedrick looked at me, constantly blinking. Yeah, I had told a joke. A bad joke, and poorly timed, but a joke nonetheless.

"Abram? How could you?" Tam tried to dart to Selina's side, but Abram held Tam back.

"This is the only way. You know it, and I know it. And you can't touch her, because if you do, they will suspect you of murder. And I will be forced to tell law enforcement that you had a secret love child and Selina found out."

Tam stared at him. Though no emotion could be seen on their face, the red cloud that hung over their person slowly took on wisps of purple.

"I suggest you get the girl out of here," Abram said. "She can't be here when Cedrick wakes up."

Tam briefly continued to stare at him, then darted into the hall. But they didn't go very far. They stopped directly in front of the hazy purple blob in the middle of the hall, their eyes wide with fear. Tam looked over their shoulder back to the scene in the kitchen, then back to the girl who was hiding. Tam shook their head and pressed a finger to their lips. They then reached down and grabbed the girl and pulled her close. "Just hold onto me," Tam whispered, "and don't look."

Only a handful of times had Tam ever used a contraction. That was one of them.

The world brightened, and the teenage Cedrick came out of his room, sleepy and stumbling slightly. But whatever sleep had been hanging over him vanished when he saw his mother on the floor—dead.

The scene went dark, and silence surrounded the adult Cedrick and myself.

"He killed her," Cedrick said. "He just wanted her out of the way. How could he do that?"

"The same way he could shoot his own daughter just so he could get his hands on his granddaughter." I didn't feel anger about it. Or sadness. Or regret. It just . . . was. It was in the past, and there was nothing I could do about it. I could only affect the future.

"How is it you remember this when so much of your other memories have been taken away from you?" he asked. "Like your friend's death?"

"Because a child's mind is not the same as an adult's mind. It's still growing. Developing. The neural pathways are not properly set, and a child's mind easily adapts to forge new pathways when needed. Tracking down specific memories is not easy at the best of times, but in a child, it's near impossible. But for a child, you can make them believe what you want them to believe. You can convince a child that they didn't see what they saw. Which is why I had forgotten about it . . . until Tam showed me their own memories about that night, and the truth about my mother's death."

I moved in closer to him and picked up his hand in my own. "I have to apologize for what I did to you that night. With Tam's encouragement, I implanted the suggestion that you never saw me. And that you didn't know about Tam's involvement in your mother's death. Because of what I did, your mind became fractured, unable to properly process your mother's death. The real memories were still there, but my suggestion blinded you to some of the facts. Your mind did the best it could to compensate. Until now." I took a deep breath, inhaling the scent that I had come to associate with the man before me—a man I trusted with my life. "We both lost our mothers that night. For a brief moment, we found comfort in the only family we had left. But our family has grown, Cedrick, and only we can protect them. But we can't do that if we keep hiding in here—inside your mind and underground. Eventually, your father, my grandfather, will hunt us down. He knows about your child. There's only one way to stop him if we ever want to reclaim our freedom."

Cedrick nodded. "No matter what happens, it's just you and me."

THE WORLD AROUND us shifted in warmth. The color of the world grew in intensity. I stood in the med bay again, holding Cedrick's hand. And his eyes fluttered. Eventually, he looked up at me.

"Hey you," I said with a smile.

"Hey."

Beth ran to the other side of the gurney and started her doctor things, checking him over.

"I'm fine, Beth. Honest." He looked at me. "Thanks to you."

"No matter what happens . . ."

"It'll always be just you and me." He took a deep breath, wincing at the pain. "That stuffed toy in your apartment? Was that . . .?" He looked at me with a half laugh.

I grinned. "Yes."

Cedrick shook his head. "That thing did not look like it was violet."

I laughed. "No, it was filthy as hell."

"Are the two of you talking about that stupid purple cat that you used to have?" Lucas asked.

Cedrick and I nodded.

"I thought that thing disappeared long ago."

"George helped me hide it." I looked back at Cedrick. "Because he knew that the bad guys couldn't see the purple. They're all colorblind . . . because of the drugs they're on."

"Holy shit. I never made that connection."

"None of us did," Eddie said.

"Tam did," I said. "They showed me the truth about what happened the night my mother was killed. Tam was one of the few people I could never hide from—because Tam didn't use their eyes to see. They used their heart. And Abram Shutton tore that heart away when he killed their daughter."

"Tam's heart wasn't the only one torn when Natalie died," Eddie said. "That man tore out my heart too."

"And he tore my heart out when he killed my mother," Cedrick said. "Then tried to kill me."

"And he tore out my heart when he falsified those records and had my medical license suspended," Beth said.

"And he tore my heart out when he issued the orders that I kill George." I then looked at Lucas.

Lucas held up his hands in surrender. "Don't look at me. I thought the man was on our side, just like Tam was. Clearly, I was wrong."

I took another deep breath. "If we want to bring down the Pregutor, we have to bring down Dr. Abram Shutton."

"The only way to be free is if we kill him," Cedrick said.

"We're talking about killing your father," Eddie said. "Are you okay with that?"

"That man is not my father. You are."

"Wow. I'm honored."

"So, are we really going to do this?" Lucas asked.

We all nodded.

"Okay. But it can't be just us." Lucas turned to face Eddie. "We'll need everyone, both on the inside and out."

Eddie sighed. "I better go make the calls while you lot work out a plan on how we're going to get close enough to kill Abram Shutton."

Lucas sighed and shook his head. "I better go let the Rabbits know how deep this rabbit hole really goes."

"Lucas, wait up." I chased after him.

"What is it?"

"There's something else that you should know, and it involves Jody."

Sixty-Five

A SMALL TUBE WAS SHOVED up my nose that led from a small oxygen tank. It was the only air I would get until the seals on my box were released. If I took shallow breaths, intended to keep enough oxygen flowing around my system, the space around me wouldn't fill too quickly with carbon dioxide.

It wasn't quite like being in a coffin, because I didn't have the room to lay down with my legs out straight. There was just barely enough room to curl up into a ball while surrounded by medical supplies.

My little box was like being inside a sensory deprivation chamber. There was nothing to see except the black void before me. It was so black that I couldn't tell if my eyes were open or shut—except my brain told me they were open. There was nothing to hear except my own thoughts. And to be blunt, I didn't like my own thoughts. And I could feel the closeness of the walls. So, yeah . . . Not a sensory deprivation chamber.

I was tempted to hum the chorus of my favorite song—the song that had become my mantra—but for this plan to work, I needed to remain silent. I couldn't even reach out to Cedrick or any of the others with my mental abilities; if anyone from STAR just happened to be around, they would hear my stray thoughts.

Instead, I continued my shallow breathing and tried to keep my mind as empty as possible. To stay hidden for as long as possible.

When Lucas suggested that we smuggle ourselves into Sector 14 using the transport network they had set up to smuggle the patients of Ward 27 out of Crystal Hills—but in reverse—I wondered if Lucas had finally lost his mind. But he was right. There was zero chance that we would have been able to sneak in using the personnel tunnels. After I exploited their weakness, STAR would have fortified the system. And there was no way that we would have been able to use the underground tunnel network, either. After I had used them to escape, not once but twice, STAR would have locked those tunnels down tighter than a drum. And they would have likely pulled up the historical records, hunting for other tunnel entrances too.

No, the smuggling channels were our only shot at getting into the sector undetected.

That, of course, was assuming that Sector 14 security didn't increase the number of guards at the goods import entrance. But the entrance was exposed to the atmosphere, with all goods being imported into the sector going through multiple airlocks, including a vacuum-sealed system that sucked out all the air from the surrounding space. The assumption was that no one would be stupid enough to try to enter the sector through an entrance that meant you couldn't breathe. Even the drivers of the transport rigs were unable to move without fear of suffocation. If the systems on their rigs failed while they were in the middle of an airlock cycle, no one would be able to get to them to save their lives in time—not even the emergency medical personnel who were stationed near the entrance. Several drivers had perished in this exact fashion over the years, suffocating while delivering goods. It was the price Rhodon Corporation was willing to pay to ensure that the main medical facility of Crystal Hills remained as germ free as possible.

But if the seals on my little box failed in the middle of one of those airlock cycles . . .

I shook my head, trying to dislodge the doomsday thinking, and focused on my shallow breathing. I rolled my shoulders, wishing I had the room to stretch out a little—to relax my muscles. But when one was desperate, you used what options you had available.

It wouldn't have been so bad if I didn't have all these boxes of surgical supplies crammed in around me, doing a poor job of cushioning me as the box jolted around with its movements. Why couldn't I have been given a box that had clean scrubs and surgical aprons? I could have at least used that stuff as a pillow.

I winced as the jolting movement forced me to bang my head on the side of the box—yet again. And the sharp corner of one of the smaller boxes poked into my hip. When smuggling people out of Sector 14, there wouldn't have been all this extra stuff in the box, but it was still a tight space. I had asked Lucas how they managed to keep the patients from freaking out during the smuggling operations. His answer: They were unconscious, and not woken up again until they were out of the city.

Being unconscious now wasn't an option. As soon as the seals on my box were released, I would need to move quickly. We only had seconds to take out the security guards in the area before STAR were alerted to any intrusion.

Of course, that was assuming that STAR weren't already in the area.

I hoped that being crammed into the tight space for so long didn't cause my joints to seize up, or this would be the shortest rebellion operation in history.

Again, I had to force myself to empty my mind of the doomsday thoughts and focus on my breathing. This not knowing how much longer it was going to take before I could be let out of the box was the worst part of this plan. But a necessary evil.

Was all of this darkness what it was like to be dead? With little room to move?

"Stop it, Mike," I said to myself. Then instantly regretted the thought.

Gravity pulled me to the side of the box. Repeated jolts suggested that the box was being unloaded from the truck. Any moment now, and I would know if the ruse worked.

In my curled-up position, with little room to move, I tried to reach down to my thigh, where a pistol had been holstered. But I couldn't contort myself far enough around to even touch the handle. Why did I go for a thigh holster in the first place? If I had chosen a shoulder holster like Lucas did, I would have been able to easily grab my weapon. But no point in focusing on that now. Hindsight was an amazing thing, but it didn't help you look forward.

I wiggled around and managed to reach the knife strapped to my lower leg, just above my boots. It wouldn't be as effective as a pistol, but a weapon was a weapon.

There was a click, then a hiss. A sliver of light leaked in through the top corner of the box. I partially closed my eyes, determined to filter the flood of light bathing the darkness through my eyelashes. If I needed to fight, I couldn't afford to be blinded.

I forced myself to breathe again, focusing my thoughts. I had trained for this situation. My body knew what to do.

The box lid opened wider, and a hand inserted into view with writing on the palm.

>>Stay where you are. Still opening boxes.<<

The owner of the hand leaned over the top of the box and looked down at me with a small smile. Wrinkles framed their smiling eyes, and a purple stone hung around their neck. I didn't know what it was, but the word *amethyst* suddenly entered my mind.

"Box 436-35T," the unknown person said aloud. "All clear. It is what is says."

"Good," said a person out of sight—a voice I thought I recognized, but I couldn't identify who. But it didn't matter. The familiar voice started the adrenaline pumping through my system. I curled my fingers around my knife and prepared to do what I must.

The amethyst person backed away from the box, and a shadow moved closer. "When this is over, you and I could . . ." A wave of euphoria washed over me, and the surrounding air was tinted in a pink hue.

The back of the guard blocked out some of the light . . . and suddenly I was glad that it was my knife in my hand and not my pistol.

"*Go!*" Lucas mentally shouted.

I uncurled as fast as I could, wrapping my arm around the front of the security guard and dragging the knife across their throat. I then flipped my knife over and threw it, lodging it deep into the neck of another guard charging in my direction.

The amethyst person then grabbed the holstered pistol from the guard I still held before me and fired at the guards who were trying to raise the alarm.

Seconds down and silence filled the large bay.

"We're clear," Eddie shouted from the other side of the room. "Security cameras are looping in the system."

I finally let go of the guard's body and let it crumple at the base of the box.

"It's good to know that sometimes things go as planned," said the amethyst person. "Let's get you out of that box so we can get it ready for its next occupant."

I reached out to the amethyst person, gladly taking the helping hand, knowing that a part of the plan was to smuggle as many patients out of Ward 27 as we could before all hell let loose. I rolled my muscles and tried to stretch as the amethyst person helped me climb the rest of the way out of the box, avoiding the dead guards around us.

"Thank you," I said.

"No need to thank me, Alice."

I looked at them, confused for a moment, then saw a small Queen of Hearts tattoo peeking through the collar of their uniform.

"You know who I am?"

The amethyst person nodded. "Michaella Davison, codename Alice. The hair gives you away. And before you ask, I knew your grandmother. We trained together in our youth."

"So, that euphoria I felt before . . ."

The woman grinned. "That was me. But your grandmother was always better at influencing the emotions of others than I ever was. It's probably why they were awarded so much freedom."

"Do the emotions always come with so much color?"

The woman gaped at me. "You saw the color?"

I nodded. "For a moment, the air was pink."

She shook her head and exhaled in a rush. "When Tam told me you were special, I didn't realize how special."

"I take it that seeing color shifts in the air is not normal."

"The ability to see the color of emotions is tied to the ability to influence those emotions. If you can see them . . ." She looked around her, surveying the team that was extracting themselves from the rest of the shipping boxes. "No wonder why Dr. Shutton is so desperate to get his hands on you."

I wanted to know what else the woman knew, but before I could ask any further questions, a scream echoed from the other side of the shipping bay.

The amethyst woman ran across the room. I followed. Everyone converged around one of the boxes.

Inside, a puffy, battered mass was tightly squeezed into tactical gear. Blood streamed out of the orifices and the eyes protruded out of the skull. As I stared at the dead body, I just prayed that Scott was unconscious when all of *that* happened.

"What the hell happened?" Lucas asked.

"Seals failed," said one of the technicians wearing an amethyst of his own. "It happens sometimes. The shipping crates are not as well maintained as they should be. I'm sorry."

"Don't be." Lucas shook his head and exhaled in a rush. "We all knew it was a risk. It's just one more person for whom we're doing this—so their death has meaning."

"How can you be so callous about this?" Cedrick asked. "This is Scott that we're talking about here. In fact, it could have been any one of us."

"Yes, it could have been." I turned and faced Cedrick with a slight snarl. "I told you this would be dangerous, but you chose not to listen. If you don't have the stomach for death, then you should have stayed behind."

Cedrick and I stared at one another. A battle of wills. In the end, he shook his head and backed away. "I'm going to let that one slide, because I know you're scared. And don't try to deny it, because we're all scared."

"Okay, everyone," Lucas called out, "say whatever words you need to say so you can come to terms with what has happened, but then you need to bottle those emotions up. We're going to lose more people before this day is done. Accept it now. We're going to work to minimize those losses, but the mission takes priority. Unless we can bring Abram Shutton and the Pregutor down, we're all dead. Maybe not today, but it will happen." He looked around the entire group. One by one, we all nodded, including me. Lucas turned to Cedrick last, but when Cedrick didn't nod in return, Lucas took a deep breath. "I'm not being callous, but this is what it means to be a soldier. We'll all grieve when the job is done, but we won't grieve for just Scott. You committed yourself to this, Cedrick. You knew the risk."

In the end, Cedrick sighed in defeat and nodded.

"Good. Are the refugees ready to move out?"

"They are," called out the amethyst person who had helped me. "Just give the word."

"The word is given. Okay, everyone, let's do this. The clock is ticking."

As the teams started to separate into their different units, Lucas put his hand on my shoulder. "I need you to go with Cedrick and Eddie instead of the hospital wing as planned."

"Then how will the teams communicate?" That wasn't really the question I wanted to ask, but I couldn't bring myself to tell my mentor and former trainer that I wanted to be with him when he extracted Jody from the hospital wing.

"We won't." His eyes were glassy, like he was fighting to hold back the tears. I could see the truth in his eyes. Extracting Jody was never part of the plan.

I swallowed back the lump forming at the back of my throat. "The STAR will probably be wherever Abram Shutton and the Pregutor are, anyway. You need your best fighter to go up against Marcus. Cedrick doesn't have a chance against him."

He tried to smile, though it was weak. "Just remember that he's tried to kill you multiple times over the years. This time, don't hold back."

I did the best I could to steel my emotions. Who else would be among those we would lose this day? Scott was the first. Jody would be the second. But I refused to let Cedrick or Lucas be anywhere on that list.

I checked the straps on my vest and secured my knife back in its home at my ankle. I then headed toward the group surrounding Eddie and Cedrick. "I'm taking point. No arguments."

Sixty-Six

I FLATTENED MYSELF AGAINST THE wall as I approached the latest junction and pushed the tiny mirror out around the corner. Two guards were positioned at the end of the hall, armed and dressed in full tactical gear. But they both wore portable tactical display units, and I could just make out the black pod nestled into the left ear of the guard on the right.

Eddie, who was standing right behind me, held up a tablet displaying an enlarged map of the facility. I pointed to where the security cameras were located, then gave the signal for two guards and pointed to my blue rose tattoo and shook my head. Eddie nodded, then tapped at the screen on his tablet. The overhead lighting flickered. He nodded again, and I did my thing.

The first time I had vanished from view—implanting the thought that no one could see me—there was a soft gasp. But after the fifth corridor that I had slipped into unnoticed, the team was used to it.

The entire world was bathed with a hint of green as I walked down the hall—a color that I had come to associate with determination. The guards at the end stared past me.

I caught the eye of the guard on the right—and he was mine to do with as I pleased.

"Take out your sidearm and shoot your friend in the head. Then unlock the door behind you and kill anyone inside."

It happened so fast. Within the blink of an eye, red blood splattered up the white walls and a black-clad heap dropped to the ground. The door was opened, and the guard moved into the space beyond and stood there, not sure what to do. The space beyond was empty of life.

I took a controlled breath and willed myself to be visible to the world again. "All clear." I moved to the side as Eddie and the rest of the team passed me in the hall.

Cedrick rolled his eyes as he walked by, dragging the dead guard behind him and through the door.

"What?"

"Never mind."

"What do we do about the automaton over here?" Nancy waved her hand in front of the unresponsive guard.

I stood before the guard, encouraging him to look into my eyes. "Disable the security lockouts on your comms and tactical display. Then hand them to me."

The zombie guard did as he was told.

It had been a long time since I had one of these units, and it felt good to have the display on again. It was the familiar, even if it was a remnant of a life that I was never going back to. For a moment, I absorbed the audio feeds and the tactical information. From what I could tell, word that we had infiltrated the sector was still silent.

I turned to face the larger room. I half expected to see a woman in a blue dress standing there in the middle of the white kitchen. Instead, a vase filled with dead roses rested on the counter.

"Why did we come here?" I asked. "Shouldn't we be looking for the server room?"

"We don't know where the server room is?" Eddie pulled out his equipment and got to work using the workstation console in the corner of the room.

"It still doesn't explain why we came *here*. Did you honestly expect that Abram Shutton would be hiding in his own apartment? I can tell you now, he hasn't been here for a very long time."

"You know that with certainty, do you?" Cedrick's tone was a little more confrontational than I had ever heard him use before.

"What's your problem?" I stood before the older man, the man who, by a weird twist of fate, was my uncle. "Ever since we started planning this operation, everything I do is met with this condemnation coming from you. I'm sorry for the things I did—for how I killed Grober and Nicky—but I can't change the past. Instead, I have to look forward and do what I can to ensure that it never happens again."

It felt like eternity as we glared at one another. It wasn't like we would ever be the perfect family, with me being the doting aunt . . . er, cousin . . . whatever, to the rug rat that Beth would one day give birth to. But I didn't want to be fighting on multiple fronts either.

He turned and walked down the hall, but his actions didn't give off that leave-me-alone feeling. If anything, it was more like he was encouraging me to follow, so we could talk without being overheard by the others.

We walked into the small bedroom that once upon a time had been Cedrick's room. I remembered the details of it from our shared vision. He stood just inside the doorway, staring at the bed. The blankets were crumpled, tossed to the side.

"No, he hasn't been here for a long time," he said as I came up beside him. "The last time he was here was the morning I found my mother dead on the kitchen floor. I don't blame you for what happened to Grober, Nicky, or any of them."

"But you blame me for *her*."

Cedrick turned to face me. The light reflected off the glistening in his eyes.

"It's okay. It's because of me that she was fighting with your father in the first place. He had plans regarding me . . . and she was in the way."

He took several deep breaths. "I know I shouldn't blame you. It's not like you chose to be born. It's just . . ."

"You don't need to explain. Our worlds were flipped upside down that night because of the actions of one man. But if you don't mind me asking, there is one thing that I've never been able to understand in all of this. Why did he try to kill you? Why did you have to run?"

"Because my mother's death wasn't an accident. I've always known that. My father told the police that I was the one responsible. He said that I used my abilities to manipulate everyone in the apartment that night and that I forced him to do things he would never do. He even had video evidence to back up his story. I ran because if I didn't, I would have been put to death . . . by my own father's orders. I was just another obstacle in the way." He turned and walked out of the room, rejoining the others in the kitchen.

I stared at the crumpled sheets, tossed aside as the young Cedrick got up from the bed that fateful morning. Everything in the room was exactly how he had left it. Shoes were tucked under the bed frame, so they wouldn't get in the way when getting up. A black jacket hung over the back of the small chair in front of the desk in the corner. A stylus pen laid crossways on a small tablet in the middle of the desk, like the unit was ready for the next day's lessons. A small glass sat beside the tablet, long empty of whatever fluids it once contained.

The white walls were bare. Nothing hung on them to provide any hint that this had been a child's room. Nothing to show that a teenager had once lived here.

A small window allowed light from the rising sun to stream in—fake beams of light that came from the projected illusion that pretended to be the sky. The growing fake daylight washed the white walls and white bedding with streams of yellow.

Everything looked like it had within Cedrick's memory. Nothing had changed. Yet, something was off. The air in the room didn't feel right.

I stared at the beams of light, mesmerized by their pure quality. I reached out my gloved hand, my fingers cutting through the light like knives, creating sharp threads of shadows across the bed and the wall.

I gasped. The shadow pattern created by my hand was too sharp. Too clean. I backed up and stared at the pure light beams again. Pure light. Not even the specks of dust that would capture the bright rays as they floated through the air.

The dark screen of the tablet on the desk was pure black. Too pure. Cautiously, and doing the best I could to stop my heart from racing ahead, I reached out and brushed my gloved hand along the surface of the tablet. My fingers came away clean.

I held my breath as I took in the room again. If everything was exactly how Cedrick had left it the day he ran . . .

Resting on the nightstand was a single card. The Queen of Hearts.

Shit.

I darted from the room and raced into the kitchen. Eddie worked in the corner to hack into the systems. His movements were efficient, but not quite right—just like Cedrick's room. I closed my eyes and prayed I was wrong.

Without any further thought, I darted across the room and penned Cedrick to the wall behind him, holding my knife to his throat. The others in the room broke out in a fury, but before anyone else could do anything, I pushed the knife into Cedrick's neck, drawing blood. It ran black.

"Who are you?" I stared into his eyes, pushing into his thoughts, but all I saw was the woman in the blue dress dancing in the white kitchen . . . the same kitchen that we were standing in.

"Mike, you're hurting me." But it wasn't fear in his eyes. There was a calmness to them—a knowing—and it only made me more determined to find out the truth.

"Mike, please," Eddie called from the other side of the room. "Don't do this."

Cedrick just looked at me with his unnerving calm.

"What color is my hair?"

He stared at me, not saying a word. I pushed a little harder on the knife, drawing more black blood.

"What color is my hair?"

"Purple," he croaked out. "Your hair is purple."

The adrenaline drained from my body in an instant. I stumbled back from the man against the wall. My grip on the knife slackened. The blade fell to the ground. "No, it's not." My voice cracked, just barely above a whisper. "My hair is blue. I didn't have any purple hair dye in my apartment. So, I used the only color that I had: blue. Why are you doing this to me? What are you wanting from me?"

"Mike, something's wrong. You're not quite yourself." Cedrick moved to step forward, but he stopped when I narrowed my eyes on him.

The edges of my vision went black. All I could see were his eyes. I focused everything that I had on his eyes, targeting a pinpoint strike on his mind.

"Get out of my head!" My voice echoed off the walls. The man before me pressed his hands to his ears and fell to his knees in a silent scream. The white kitchen rippled with each rebounded wave. But I didn't let up.

Something hit me in the jaw. Pain radiated throughout my entire skull, breaking the mental connection. When I opened my eyes, I was staring at Marcus through my watery vision. I pulled on the restraints, holding me to the chair.

"How did you know?" he breathed out, wincing, obviously still feeling the pain from my attack.

"It was too perfect. You forgot the dust."

Sixty-Seven

Marcus stood to his full height, not looking in my direction. The eyes were the easiest portal into his mind, and there was no way he was going to give me that opportunity again. But maybe he had left a link within my own mind that I could exploit, riding into his thoughts using a backdoor.

I tried to focus, but my thoughts were hazy. The chair room, blurry as it was, repeatedly morphed into the white kitchen and back again. How much of the vision had Marcus implanted inside my head? And how much of it was a simulation? There had to have been some sort of drug floating around in my system, because there was no way Marcus would have been able to get inside my mind as deep as he had on his own.

Regardless, the darkness kept threatening to take me under. But I needed to stay in the real world. Assuming this was the real world.

The room wavered again, and Dr. Abram Shutton stood in the middle of the kitchen instead of his dead wife. But was he really there? Was he in the chair room?

The room morphed again, and Dr. Shutton stared at Marcus. He laughed, but it was filled with disbelief. "You said you could do this."

Marcus took a controlled breath. "With all due respect, sir, you were asking me to build an interrogation scenario using the memories of three different people, one of whom is dead. There could have been any number of things that tipped her off."

"How much of it was real?" My speech was slurred. "There is no way all of it was Marcus's imagination. He never would have blamed you for murder."

Dr. Shutton stood there in his white lab coat and his white shirt. If it wasn't for his dark hair, he would have blended into the white walls within my blurry vision. "But you do." His voice carried a threatening tone, seething for revenge. "I never knew that you were standing right there, a witness to it all. Tam did exceptionally well with your mental conditioning."

"So, it's true. You killed your wife, and you blamed your son for it. Why?"

"To use your own words: I had plans, and they were in the way."

I never quite caught the full view of his eyes. Like Marcus, Abram Shutton deliberately averted his gaze so I couldn't gain access to the easiest portal into his mind.

"Well, I'm in the way of your plans now. Does that mean you'll kill me too?"

"If only it were that simple." A thought surfaced, where he was frustrated with the experiments, unable to work out how to replicate the markers in my DNA.

I laughed. "So, that's the real reason. You can't kill me, because if you do, you destroy the only successful experiment you've ever had. There's something different about my makeup and you need live tissue to keep working on the problem. But there's more to it, isn't there?"

"Shut her up," Abram ordered, but Marcus just stood there, not moving. "Gahan, I gave you an order. Obey."

"No," Marcus said. "As much as I hate her, she's right about one thing. Our entire lives, we've been nothing but an experiment to you. You gave us one drug after another. Even after I joined STAR and was told the truth about audimentia, the drugs never stopped. At first, I didn't question it, because I felt stronger. The fact that I was finally able to get inside her head was proof of that. But whatever you've been doing has nothing to do with our abilities, does it? Like her, I want the truth. What have you really been trying to do?"

Abram Shutton started shaking. He clamped his jaw tightly shut. Blood started to stream out of his nose. For the first time, I was on the outside, watching what the compulsion abilities looked like.

"Tell me!" Marcus rushed forward and got into Abram's personal space. There were only inches between them. But from where I was sitting, Marcus had become blinded to his surroundings.

Abram Shutton reached behind his back, under his lab coat. His arm was shaking, but shakes or not, it wouldn't have mattered. The close distance would play in his favor.

Bang.

The percussive sound seemed to be compounded by the confined space of the chair room.

Marcus staggered backward. His black uniform took on a wet sheen that reflected the overhead light. He pressed his hand to his belly. His hand was instantly covered in red blood.

I hated Marcus, and I wanted to hurt him—kill him, even. But Marcus didn't deserve this end.

Abram breathed heavily as he backed away and leaned up against the table on the side of the room.

"You don't seem to have a very good track record, Dr. Shutton," I said. "You kill more of your experiments than you succeed in seeing to the end."

He pointed the gun at me. "Don't even think about trying to get into my head. I will shoot you too."

"I don't need to get into your head to know the truth. You, like the geneticists before you, were trying to help humanity survive. We can't stay where we are. The domes are failing. While they helped to stave off extinction, humans need to evolve or we will die out. So, you made us healthier, stronger. You made it so we could breathe the air outside. That's what this has always been about: reclaiming the Earth. But while you were working to save humanity, somewhere along the way, you lost your own. You should have never tried to mess with nature, forcing evolution, because nature has a bad habit of fighting back."

Abram Shutton began to shake again. He curled his wrist, slowly re-aiming the gun at himself. With his free hand, he pushed on his lower arm, trying to stop himself. "Stop it! Get out of my head!"

"It's not me doing this," I said. "You made sure that I was too drugged to get past any mental defenses that you might have. But I'm not the only one with the ability to compel a person to kill themselves."

I smiled as the dark figure in my peripheral vision staggered into view.

"Gahan, you need to let me go. You don't know what you're doing."

"Actually, I do. It may not be today, but eventually you'll try to kill us all. You have plans, and we're in your way."

Another bang filled the small space. I winced. The ringing in my ears amplified. And a white blob with dark hair fell to the floor. Red blood poured out on the pristine white surface.

Marcus staggered where he stood, like the adrenaline that gave him the strength to control Abram Shutton vanished with the man's death. He picked up the gun and checked the weapon. He then headed for the door.

"Marcus . . ."

He looked back over his shoulder in my direction, careful not to look into my eyes.

"Marcus, let me out."

"No. I don't think I will. You'll only get in my way."

I pulled on my restraints. "Marcus, please . . ."

He just shook his head and headed out the door, disappearing down the halls.

"Marcus! You bastard. Come back here! Let me out!"

I continued to pull on my restraints, trying to get free. Gunfire sounded in the distance, and the overhead lighting flickered. I pulled more frantically. I had to get free, because as long as I was strapped to that chair, I was a sitting duck.

Footsteps rushed down the hall, and I did the best I could to control my rising fear. I focused my thoughts on George and how we used to dance in the purple rain, singing at the top of our lungs.

A soldier holding a rifle came into view, and I closed my eyes, singing inside my head.

"I'm pretty sure that I've told you this before, but you mentally sing out of tune."

"Lucas?" I shook my head. Multiple soldiers stood in front of me, including Cedrick. "Grober? This can't be real. You're dead. I killed you."

The hulking bear cocked his head to the side. "Um . . . In your dreams maybe. I mean you did threaten to kill the person who had thoughts of you in the showers."

Lucas snorted as he lowered his rifle and allowed the strap around his shoulders to carry its weight, freeing his hands. "Whatever you think you saw, it was just a simulation implanted by the chair. Now, let's get you out of this thing." He and Cedrick worked to remove the restraints from my limbs and my head.

I pushed myself into an unsteady standing position and wrapped my arms around Cedrick's neck, hugging him as tightly as I could. "You're here. Please tell me that you're real and not a figment of my imagination."

"Well, I could still be a figment of your imagination, but if that were the case, then you would be a figment of mine too." He pushed me back slightly and caressed my cheek. "When I lost contact with you in the med lab, Beth and I freaked out. But apparently, someone foresaw it all happening." He narrowed his suspicious eyes. "No one told me you had already devised the contingency plan to break in and break you out. When I saw Lucas and the team gearing up, there was no way I was going to let them leave me behind. Not this time."

I hugged him more tightly. Whether it was real or not, I didn't care. In that moment, I was where I wanted to be. "You shouldn't have come, but I'm glad you did. What about Little Nicky? Is she okay?"

He furrowed his brow. "Um . . . Yeah. Why wouldn't she be?"

"Because . . ." I licked my lips. I could have sworn that I watched the little girl die, but I could have sworn that Grober was dead too. I blinked repeatedly, trying to work out what was real and what wasn't.

"It was a simulation, Mike." Lucas then pointed to the blood on the walls and to the body on the floor. "But *that* is real. What happened?"

I took a slow, steady breath. "Marcus compelled him to kill himself. And to be honest, I'm not feeling bad about it." I looked at Cedrick. "I know he was your father, but he was a murderer, willing to kill anyone who got in his way—including your mother."

"I know." Cedrick looked at me with a matter-of-fact expression. No emotion, because there was none to be had. "It was why I had to run all those years ago. He had the authorities convinced that it was my fault."

I sighed in defeat. "So that part was true."

He furrowed his brow, a silent question asking for more details.

"I hate to put a rush on the reunion, but the clock is ticking, people." Grober stood in the doorway, constantly looking out into the hall. "According to the security channels, STAR know we're here and they're making a move to box us in. If we don't leave now, we'll be trapped."

"We still need to get that drug for Beth," Cedrick said. "We need to find a way to break into the lab again and get what she needs."

I looked over at the table at the side of the room. There, in the middle of the table, were several vials. "We don't need to go anywhere near that med lab again." I quickly sorted through the vials, my vision still not quite sharp—of course, the sedative in my system—and I handed Cedrick a vial of the drug that Beth needed. "Make sure Beth gets this."

Cedrick smiled but pushed the vial back into my hands. "You can make sure she gets it yourself. Now, let's get out of here."

"I'm not going with you."

"What?"

"I have to stop Marcus. I don't know what he has planned, but it can't be good." I looked at Lucas. "And there's someone else who needs our help." I sent him an image of Jody, unconscious and in intensive care. If everything since the med lab had all been a simulation, a vision implanted by Marcus, then Lucas wouldn't know what happened to Jody.

Lucas did the best he could to hide his fear, but the color drained from his face, and his expression was carefully schooled to hide any emotions he might have been feeling. "I'll handle it. Cedrick, you and Grober—"

"No." Cedrick stared at the others, his expression stern and determined. "If this Marcus is as bad as you all seem to indicate, then she can't go up against him alone, not with STAR boxing us in too . . . and not in her *drugged* condition. I'm staying."

Grober groaned. "God, you lot are a pain in the ass. If you're all staying, then I'm staying too. Besides, Eddie will still want to find that server room. We need to destroy it, severing the Pregutor's connection to the city. Any ideas where the hell the server room might be? It's not like we can ask the dead guy."

I gaped at Grober, then stared down at the dead Abram Shutton on the floor.

Again, Grober groaned. "Don't tell me that she has the ability to dive into the head of a dead man and read their thoughts."

"No, I don't, but . . ."

"But the chair does," Lucas said. "Someone help me. Let's get him strapped in."

"No, I don't, but . . ."

"But the chair does," Lucas said. "Someone help me. Let's get him strapped in."

SIXTY-EIGHT

I STOOD IN THE MIDDLE of the white kitchen, but it wasn't white anymore. A red sheen blanketed everything—even my skin. The feeling of anger permeated the air.

A chill wafted over my arms. My breathing quivered. The lights flickered, and the world groaned as the walls bowed and rippled before stabilizing again.

This was nothing like what I experienced when I was in Tam's or Cedrick's head. It was like this mind didn't want me here. And if I was truthful with myself, I didn't want to be here. But I came here for a reason. We needed answers—answers that only Abram Shutton could give.

"Mike, can you hear me?"

"Cedrick?" I looked around but couldn't see him.

"I'm here, standing right next to you in the real world." Pressure encapsulated my hand, reminding me that what I was seeing was only in my head.

I smiled. "I feel that."

"Good," Cedrick said, *"because if I have to, I'm pulling you out. Lucas says that the connection between the chair and what remains of Dr. Shutton's mind is failing. You don't have much time."*

I nodded, then vocalized my thoughts, not sure if my physical actions were visible in the real world. "Everything is crumbling in here. But for whatever reason, his mind brought us back to the apartment."

"*What apartment? Which one?*"

"The one where your mother died. I don't know which way to go."

"*Look for anything out of the ordinary.*"

"Everything is out of the ordinary. It's bloody red in here. The air is filled with it."

There was a slight pressure on my other hand, and the world around me became surrounded by a shield of blue. Whoever was holding my hand was protecting me—like he always had. I smiled. "Thanks, Lucas."

"*He says you're welcome,*" Cedrick said.

A dark figure darted down the hall. I rushed to follow, chasing after him through the door to Cedrick's childhood bedroom. We emerged into a small research lab with a desk taking up the space on one side and an examination table on the other. A man in a red lab coat flicked through the virtual display before him. But unlike the displays in real life, I could see everything the man was seeing. I moved to stand behind him to get a clearer view.

Portraits of my former team hung in midair. Younger versions of Jody, Marcus, and myself. George was there too, along with the rest of PentWave.

A bell announced the presence of a person outside the lab door. The man tapped on an icon at the bottom of his display. "I told you I didn't want to be disturbed." Abram Shutton's voice didn't sound as aged as it had when I last saw him. This version of him was at least ten years younger.

The camera feed for the door came to life on the virtual display. Tam stood there, with black hair and a black suit. "I have those results you wanted."

"And?"

"It might be best if I show you in person."

Dr. Shutton sighed and did a funky hand gesture toward the door on the far side of the room. The door opened to reveal the black hall beyond.

Tam came forward and passed over a tablet. Dr. Shutton tapped on the screen, then entered a security code; his fingers moved too fast for me to see what the security code was. He then scanned his fingers down the screen, flicking to the next page.

"The grafting seems to be holding on Subject 99. And 97." He harrumphed. "But based on these numbers, Subject 98 should be dead. How is he still alive?"

"He has forged a connection with Michaella."

He narrowed his eyes on Tam. "You've become too attached. You should know by now that it's always a risk to get too close to the specimens."

"That specimen is our granddaughter."

A dark ire radiated off of Dr. Shutton, only deepening the red that hung in the air. "How could that be possible? My son didn't have any children, and as far as I know, he's dead. Unless you want me to report you to the authorities, I suggest you forget your connection to Subject 91 and do your job."

Tam hesitated, like they wanted to protest. In the end, Tam just stood there wearing an emotionless mask. Wafts of green hovered around them, fighting against the red, like a shield of armor.

"When can we begin the next phase of testing?"

"Next week," Tam said. "They are putting the final touches on the training facility now."

"Good. Very good." Dr. Shutton turned his attention back to the virtual display, adding notes to the files for the members of PentWave. "That'll be all."

Tam just nodded and headed out of the room into the hall of black.

Dr. Shutton then went to the empty wall space behind his desk and pressed his hand and wrist to the wall.

"Identity confirmed," said a familiar voice. "Good evening, Dr. Shutton."

My heart raced ahead. "Alice?"

"Good evening, Pregutor. Enable access to the central mainframe."

The wall behind the desk melted away. A holographic projection covering a clear door. And beyond the door was a long corridor lined with banks of computer equipment, all lighting up with an array of color.

I had seen that corridor of computers many times over the years. I had walked by it almost every day. Technicians with yellow down their sleeves would often disappear behind holographic walls, just like this one in Abram Shutton's memory—and not once did I even register what I was looking at. But now that I could see the corridor of computers in Dr. Shutton's memory . . .

The walls around me dissolved into a pixelated screen. The air shifted, losing all color. The ground crumbled under my feet. As I started to fall into the black void, a sharp tug pulled hard on my hand.

✳

I GASPED AND my eyes shot open. I laid on the floor of the chair room. Cedrick was on the floor next to me, holding me tightly in his arms.

"I've got you," he said. "You're back in the real world."

I gripped onto his forearm as I tried to slow my panicked breathing. I turned to face Lucas, who was kneeling beside us. "I know where the server room is."

"Where?"

I sat up and frowned. "In the belly of the beast."

Sixty-Nine

The air temperature dropped as we headed to the lower levels of the main Rhodon Corporation building. Twenty stories below ground, heading deeper into the devil's lair. I had walked these halls so many times over the years, and never once did I register their significance. Then again, I was absorbed in my duties as part of PentWave or STAR—not trying to blow the place up.

As we exited the service stairwell, unease grew in the pit of my stomach. The security channels were buzzing about an insurgent team, and how all security personnel were to report to stations and await further orders. Yet the halls on the lower levels of Rhodon were empty. There was no one around. Not even STAR soldiers.

But they were watching us. Recording our every move with little cameras mounted on the ceiling. Eddie had tried to hack into the system using his remote tablet, but whatever patches they had in the system demanded that he have a direct connection. So, the cameras still watched us.

If Alice was still here, perhaps I could have done something about those stupid cameras. Instead, Lucas reached out to my shoulder, reminding me to remain visible to the team.

"Sorry," I mumbled.

"It's okay. For you, it's instinct. But you're not alone."

Even as a little girl, I knew how to implant the thought that no one could see me—a suggestion that the people who saw me would forget that I was ever there. But cameras weren't people. And I had yet to figure out how to make my abilities extend through the wires.

I readjusted the straps on my vest—yet again—and checked the pistol Lucas had procured for me. One with a DNA-encoded safety. Apparently, Eddie had created an override hack so the pistol would respond to my commands, but there was every possibility that the thing would be about as effective as a rock or a small club. As much as I hated the illusions Marcus had fabricated in my head, I wished I could have had a knife strapped to my ankle too.

At the next junction, I looked left, then right. Then left and right again. I bit my bottom lip, trying to hide my uncertainty from the others. But Cedrick groaned from the back of the group.

"Seriously? I thought you knew where we were going."

"I do. It's just . . ." I forced myself to take a deep breath. I tried to remember the last time I had been in these halls, walking alongside Marcus as we headed to the briefing room for STAR. And there were all the times when I was with George, heading to a PentWave briefing. "This way." And I headed to the right.

I came to a stop in the middle of the hall and stared at the wall. "Here. The entrance is here."

"Here?" The skepticism radiated off Cedrick in an orange blanket. "I hate to be the bearer of bad news, but we're looking at nothing but a wall." He pounded his fist against the blank space to accentuate his point.

"The server room is hidden by a holographic wall," I said.

"Last time I check, holograms didn't stop matter from passing through it."

"They do if they are resting directly on the surface of a physical door."

The orange around him deepened a little, shifting more toward red and frustration. "Even if you're right, we're taking a huge risk in being here. We should just get out while we still can."

"No." Eddie leaned into the wall and brushed his fingers along the surface. "We need to take out the Pregutor. And if Mike says the entrance to the server room is here, then it's here. We just need to find the access panel."

It was clear by Cedrick's flapping jaw that he wanted to protest, but Lucas put his hand on Cedrick's chest and shook his head. "This building is filled with many secrets. Grober, keep a watch down the hall. If anyone from STAR shows up . . ."

"I'm on it." And Grober darted back the way we had come, along with Nancy.

"And you . . ." Lucas pointed at Cedrick, then headed down the hall in the opposite direction to Grober and Nancy.

I sighed, trying to ignore Cedrick's mental irritation. "He's right, you know. You and the others should get out while you still can."

"And leave you to have all the fun by yourself?" Meanwhile, Eddie continued his search.

As frustrating as it might have been, Eddie's simplistic view was really for the best.

I joined him in his tactile search of the wall. There just had to be a hidden panel somewhere, similar to the hidden keypad that Tam had used to escape. Assuming that was real and not a simulation.

"Eddie, do you know if Tam Haworth is dead?"

"Unfortunately, yes."

"And I killed them."

"Not according to the report I saw. You were there, but it wasn't your weapon that shot them."

"No, it was Marcus." I wore a small smile. But I wasn't smiling because Tam was dead or because I wasn't the one to kill them. I was smiling because at least one memory wasn't a falsehood. And if one memory wasn't false . . .

"Here." Eddie tapped the wall. "It's cooler here. Like there's a panel hidden by a simulation. I can hack into it, but it might take too long."

My smile grew wider. "In Dr. Shutton's memory, the voice of the Pregutor was Alice."

"Your personal AI?"

I nodded.

"And that helps us how?"

"Alice was a unique system. At least, I thought it was. But if I'm right, then I should be able to use a back door in Alice's system to access the Pregutor's system."

"Wait . . . What?" Eddie shook his head. "You know, I've heard crazier things. Give it a go." He stood to the side and gestured to the wall. "No harm in trying."

"Except that I might call STAR directly to us."

"They already know where we are." He pointed to the camera mounted directly above us. "They'll eventually descend on us, anyway. Might as well make some noise while we're waiting."

I smirked, then faced the cold spot on the wall. I licked my lips, imagining the ticking sound back in med bay. But my imagination wasn't as much of a comfort as I thought it would be.

Eddie put his hand on my shoulder. "Don't disappear on me now."

"Right. Sorry." I then pressed my right hand and wrist to the cold part of the wall, just like Abram Shutton had done in his memory. And I prayed. I tapped out a short rhythm with my thumb, an override code that I had programmed into Alice when I first installed the main unit in my apartment—the apartment that was now buried under rubble.

"Identity confirmed," said a familiar voice. "Good morning, Agent Davison."

I smiled. "Alice. It *is* you." I took a deep breath before giving my orders. "Alice, help me step through the looking glass."

The wall wavered, and the illusion melted away. Eddie and I stood before a clear door leading to a room filled with banks of computer equipment flashing in an array of colors.

"She got it," Eddie called out. The door opened with a hiss, and Eddie walked past me into the server room and whistled. "You have no idea how long I've been trying to get into this room, and now that I'm here . . ."

"Yeah, it's a shame to have to blow it up, right?" Lucas took out a small explosive device from one of his many pockets.

"We can't just blow it up, Lucas," Eddie said, "not while the Pregutor is still tied into the city's environmental controls."

"Which is why you're here. Find yourself an access point and get to work. Meanwhile, I'm setting the timer for twenty-five minutes. That's all I'm giving you, old man.

Everyone sync up on my mark." Each of us pulled out timer devices of our own. "And mark." There was a chorus of beeps. "Get to work, Rabbits. Who knows how long we have before STAR show up."

While Cedrick's orange skepticism had disappeared, Eddie adopted the orangey-yellow blanket of annoyance. The older man grabbed my elbow and pulled me along with him. "When STAR show up, I want you with me."

"But—"

"You can hide from view, remember? And you can hide me too. I need every second you can give me."

I nodded, then encouraged Cedrick to come with us. If everything went belly-up, I wanted him where Eddie was . . . so Eddie could get Cedrick to safety.

We headed into the depths of the server room, trying to get as far away from any door as possible. Along the way, we placed charges around the back of the computer banks, hopefully hidden from view.

Several aisles over and down the middle of a long row, Eddie settled himself in front of an access workstation and got to work. I stood with my back to the computer bank and continually looked down the row in both directions.

A series of clicks came across the radio, forming a distinct repeated pattern. Cedrick pulled out his pistol, then held it at the ready. "Time's up, old man," he whispered. "They're coming."

"Just keep them off my back as long as you can."

"We've got it," I said. *"We've trained for this,"* I added mentally to Cedrick. *"Together. Just you and me."*

The mental energies of the room shifted, and I could sense that stupid psychic shield system again. In a weird way, I wanted the sensation to be associated with a personal device that Eddie might have been carrying, but somehow, I didn't think so. Regardless, I moved closer to him. If I had to, I would shield his mind using my own. And I insisted that Cedrick move closer too. Then I wished that no one could see us gathered around the open access panel. Though if anyone had a portable stupid shield device, any suggestions I was giving off would do us no good—not while I was outside the fields, anyway.

Gunshots fired on the other side of the room, the sound echoing oddly in the computer-filled space. Cedrick twitched, but I glanced at him and shook my head. The two of us needed to stay with Eddie, regardless of what was happening elsewhere. More gunshots were fired, followed by grunts and the shattering of something made of glass.

The overhead lights flickered, but they didn't go out.

Eddie cursed, as he pulled out an additional portable tablet and some wire cutters. *Just keep them off my back.* The thought rested on the surface of his mind. Cedrick and I nodded.

Whatever commotion was happening on the other side of the room seemed to have vanished. An eerie silence filled the space.

I focused on my breathing and did the best I could to keep my thoughts on the immediate situation. I listened for the soft footfalls of those looking for us. I listened for the mental thoughts of the STAR operatives.

A buzzing hum started to build in my mind. Memories bled through the air of Marcus standing only inches from me, his heart racing ahead at my touch.

"I knew you would be here, Mike. I knew you couldn't stay away. Not from me. You like humans, don't you? You said so yourself. And I'm as human as they come."

The mental memory of his lips against mine dominated the space around us.

"Oh, come on, Mike. Admit it. You liked spending time with me. I saw the way you looked at me when we trained together. And you liked it when I kissed you. Never mind that the whole affair was only in your mind. Because I would never lower myself to be physical with the likes of you. Even if that was what the Pregutor had planned for us all along."

The images morphed into the two of us in bed together, tangled in each other's arms.

Cedrick looked over his shoulder at me, his look demanding answers. But I just shook my head.

"Yeah, I knew about that disgusting plan. But there was no way in hell I would ever want George's cast-offs."

I gritted my teeth and tensed my body. Determined to not give away our position. Determined to keep Eddie hidden. I gave Cedrick another quick shake of my head and put my forefinger to my lips. Even mental communication between us would be heard by those in STAR—by Marcus. Cedrick had to know that. I prayed that he knew that.

"So, is this how we're going to play it?" Marcus's voice continued to boom around the server room. The lack of echo was at odds with how big the place was. "You know, the one thing that I never fully understood until recently was how you always seemed to be Dr. Shutton's favorite. How you had special privileges from Tam. How you could never do any wrong. But now that I know that Tam and Dr. Shutton were your biological grandparents—"

Cedrick's head spun around so fast, and his eyes grew wide. I had forgotten how I only found out that I was the granddaughter of Dr. Abram Shutton after being in STAR, that I was Cedrick's missing niece. Everything that had happened after I confronted the man in his office was all a simulation concocted by Marcus. Cedrick didn't know that I was a sixth gen, the first one born.

"Tell me, does your uncle know that you used your abilities to force him to forget that you were there the night his mother died? That you saw everything?"

The scene from the apartment played in fast forward. The fight between Cedrick's parents. The drug-laced wine. And me, at the age of five, standing in the doorway holding my purple stuffed cat and watching Abram Shutton smash his wife's head against the table and floor. The memory continued as Tam carried me down the hall, back to Cedrick's room, where I gave the sleeping boy a quick hug, then suggested that he never saw me.

The pain in Cedrick's eyes as he found his mother the following morning mirrored the pain in his eyes as he looked at me in the server room. And I could hear the mental screams of the memory as Cedrick ran for his life, chased by his father and STAR.

"There you are," Marcus said from the other side of the room. "And you're not alone. It's not just your uncle with you. It's the traitor."

Cedrick reached down to Eddie, encouraging the old man to pack it up and leave, but Eddie just shook his head and turned his tablet around to show a progress bar. Thirty percent.

Shit.

I looked directly into Cedrick's eyes and called out to him mentally. *"Stay with Eddie. I'll draw Marcus away."*

"No, we need to stick together."

"The longer I stay here, the less time Eddie has . . . and he needs time. Please, Cedrick, stay with Eddie. Shield his mind

with your own." I then glanced over my shoulder at the camera mounted in the ceiling above us. *"I'm not leaving the room. Not while Marcus is hunting us."*

Cedrick took several deep breaths, then nodded, taking up a sentry position next to Eddie. I gave Eddie's shoulder a quick squeeze, then disappeared from his view.

"I've always hated how she can do that," Eddie whispered.

I darted to the end of the row, then headed deeper into the server maze. When I was far enough away from Eddie, I called out to the man hunting me. "You've always been so full of yourself, Marcus. All talk and no action. Just like that kiss. All in your imagination. How could you have been so foolish to believe that I would fall for that arrogance? Thank you for clarifying that a sickening moment wasn't real. In truth, I'm not sure what is real and what isn't. For example, did Dr. Shutton really shoot you? Or is that too just another false memory you implanted—so I would be denied the joy of killing you myself?"

The memories tainting the air shifted to a darker red world, one in which Marcus pulled off his vest and tried to apply bandages to a flesh wound on his lower right side. And as he lifted his shirt, a dark patch rested directly over his heart.

I laughed. "I bet that hurt like a son of a bitch. But that's nothing compared to what I'm going to do to you."

The memories in the air vanished. But I could still hear his anger. His frustration. Wisps of red bled through the air. And I followed them with my pistol held before me, turning the hunter into prey.

Marcus stood in the middle of the last aisle. And he stared at me. The words 'second choice' rested on the surface of his mind.

I grinned. "That's right, Marcus. You will always be the second choice. Just that little bit behind the leader of the pack." I aimed and fired . . . but the pistol wouldn't respond. The stupid DNA-safety override Eddie put in failed . . . just like I knew it would.

Without a thought for my own safety, I tossed the pistol to the side and raced forward to strike out at Marcus with everything I had. My vision darkened around the edges as I prepared to dive into his mind, ripping at his mental shields and forcing him to do my will.

We collided with full force—him using his brute strength, and me using my mental abilities and size to get under his wild limbs, striking where it would hurt the most. He managed to get out a pistol, but I kicked it out of his hand, just as he fired into the bank of computers next to us. Sparks flew out in every direction.

The air shifted behind me, and I spun around just in time to be kicked into a bank of computers, knocking me to the ground. The soldier who kicked me came in for another strike, but two shots were fired, and the soldier fell forward, pinning me to the ground.

Marcus stood above me, holding his pistol aimed in my direction.

"I'm in your head, Marcus. I could make you turn that pistol on yourself."

"Then do it."

Before I could implant the thought, a gunshot fired. Marcus staggered to the side, dropping the gun and holding his bleeding hand. He glanced down the hall, then ran. Before I could properly process what had happened, Cedrick was next to me, pulling the dead soldier off my legs.

"Damn it, Cedrick. You were supposed to stay with Eddie."

"You're welcome," he snapped, as he grabbed my hand and pulled me to my feet. He then passed me a fully loaded pistol. "It's Eddie's. Old-fashioned. No DNA safety. And Eddie went with Lucas, by the way. Something about Lucas's girlfriend."

I exhaled in a rush, with a slight frown, then holstered the pistol and took off at a run. "We can't let Marcus get away."

Cedrick chased after me.

Seventy

We chased Marcus through the empty halls. The lights flickered overhead. Evacuation alarms blared, making it difficult to hear anything but ringing in my ears. At the end of the hall, Marcus ran through the open elevator doors and pounded on the buttons, cursing. But the elevator didn't move. The doors didn't close. Evacuation protocols.

I grinned as I pushed myself to run faster. Cedrick was right behind me.

I continued my attempts to push into Marcus's mind but got nothing. Not even an image from when Marcus was given rank among STAR.

With one last look in my direction, Marcus darted out of the elevator and toward the emergency stairs. Cedrick and I chased after him.

For the first time since this whole infiltration began, we were surrounded by people—Rhodon employees trying to evacuate the building. They were heading down the stairs, in the opposite direction that Marcus had gone. "Make a hole," I called out with both my voice and my mind. Cedrick did the same. The path cleared so we could continue our chase.

We exited the stairwell on the level for the main lobby of Rhodon Corporation. And we chased Marcus out into the main plaza of Sector 14. The evacuation alarms stopped, and the world was filled with ringing silence. As I continued to chase after Marcus, I took advantage of the rhythm my boots made against the pathways to center my thoughts on what needed to be done.

"Marcus, stop!" I shouted mentally and physically, praying that there was nothing blocking my mental abilities.

The figure in the distance stopped in the center of the plaza. Cedrick and I converged on his location, pistols raised and aimed at Marcus.

"Put your hands in the air and slowly turn around," I called out.

Marcus did as instructed, but there was a smirk on his face. He wasn't the zombie that I expected him to be.

Marching footsteps echoed off the nearby buildings. Walls of soldiers in dark uniforms took up formations around the entire plaza, closing off every possible exit point. But these weren't standard issue soldiers. None of them wore a radio or had optical display units over their eyes. They would have had implants. And the implants were only given to the elite of the elite. They were only given to STAR.

Marcus lowered his hands and his smile grew wider. "I might not have been able to compel you, either of you, to do anything, but thank you for doing exactly what I wanted you to do. Now I suggest you drop your weapons and kick them away."

I glanced over my shoulder at the STAR who had formed a box around us. I could have sworn that I had been in this situation before—this exact situation. If only I could remember how I got out of it that time.

"You didn't," Cedrick said. "You surrendered. To him."

My eyes bounced between Cedrick and Marcus. A scowl on one face. A grin on the other. Meanwhile, I readjusted my grip on my pistol and continued to aim at Marcus. If I was going down, he was going down too.

Marcus laughed. "You still don't get it, do you? There's no one left to help you get out of this. Both Tam and Dr. Shutton are dead."

I glared at Marcus. I had a clear view of his eyes. But no matter how hard I tried, I couldn't break in. Why couldn't I break in?

"Because we've learned from the last time."

My mind was suddenly filled with hot, white searing pain, threatening to take me to my knees. No warning of a growing buzz. But I held my aim.

"Drop–your weapons–now."

Beside me, Cedrick dropped his gun and kicked it away. And his face was devoid of all emotion. His eyes were devoid of life. Cedrick was a walking zombie.

"Take her weapons from her."

"Cedrick, don't listen to him."

While Cedrick didn't move a muscle, someone else came up from behind me and grabbed me, pulling the gun from my fingers. Disarmed, I stared into Lucas's eyes. Vacant eyes.

"No. Lucas, please." But he wasn't alone. The entire team was there. Grober. Nancy. Eddie. All the Rabbits. And they were all walking zombies, no longer in control of their own minds.

Lucas stepped back from me and passed the pistol to Marcus, who only laughed again.

"Look at that. No DNA safety. An ancient weapon, but still in good condition." Marcus held out the gun aimed at Lucas's head and pulled the trigger.

I winced, but I refused to close my eyes as Lucas fell to the ground. The green grass took on a dark sheen.

Marcus stepped over Lucas's body and aimed at Grober next. "You should have listened to your friends when they tried to convince you to leave." He fired the pistol again. "Two down." Then he fired again at Nancy. "How many bullets do you think I have, Mike? Is there enough to take you all down?" He pointed the gun at Cedrick's head next. And there was nothing I could do to stop him. "When will you learn that I will always be your superior?"

A beeping alarm sounded from Cedrick's chest. Less than a second later, another beeping alarm came from Grober's chest. And another from Nancy. Then Eddie. Then Lucas. When the beeping alarm came from my own vest, I smiled and took a deep breath.

Marcus grimaced and narrowed his eyes.

"To be superior," I said, "you have to understand all the pieces at play. It's not just one move. To win at this game, you have to plan for all the steps ahead."

The beeping stopped, and the ground rumbled. Explosions cascaded around the plaza, building after building. Fire and heat filled the space with light. The ground suddenly pushed upward, throwing several guards into the air. A chasm opened up, swallowing the soldiers lined up behind Marcus.

The evacuation alarms blared again. Marcus and I just stared at one another.

Another set of explosions went off, and a boom sounded from directly overhead. A dark line snaked across the blue sky.

Ignoring Marcus and any STAR still standing, I spun around and lunged at Cedrick and Eddie, who were just coming out of their zombie-like state.

"What—"

"Move!" I ran for cover, grabbing Cedrick and Eddie as I ran past, barely dodging the falling pieces from the fractured dome. The outside atmosphere rushed in, causing everyone to double over, coughing.

Except for me. While the air had a horrible burning taste and smell to it, I was still able to breathe it.

A STAR soldier ran past us, and I attacked him, taking his portable breather unit from him. But the soldier didn't have the strength to fight back. He didn't have the air. Instead, he fell to the ground, gasping.

I held the portable breather unit to Cedrick, encouraging him to take a few deep breaths, before holding the unit to Eddie.

"How the hell are you able to breathe this shit?" Cedrick asked, just barely able to speak between coughing spurts.

"Sixth gen," I said.

"So, that bullshit that guy was spouting—"

"All true."

Another boom sounded, and a giant section of the dome fell toward the ground. I dove over Eddie and Cedrick, covering their heads.

When the dust settled, a lone figure stood tall on the other side of the debris field. Staring at me. With no breather.

"Who the hell is that?" Eddie coughed, passing the portable breather back to Cedrick.

"Marcus." I stood and faced him. As we continued to stare at one another, everything I had seen in Abram Shutton's final memory suddenly made sense. *The grafting seems to be holding.* NeuWave was about reclaiming the Earth's surface. Somewhere along the way, Abram Shutton got the idea to graft my abilities onto the members of

PentWave. All of my abilities. Including my ability to breathe the atmosphere.

I reached into my vest pocket and pulled out the vial containing the drug that Beth still needed. I knelt beside Cedrick and put the vial in his hand. I then put my hand to his face, encouraging him to look at me. My vision went dark around the edges as I focused on the purple flecks in his blue eyes. "You need to go with Eddie now. Your job is to ensure that the children left at Sanctuary are safe and that they know how to use their abilities. With Lucas gone, you're their trainer now. You need to protect the next generation." His face had become that of a zombie. I really hated to see him like that, but I had no choice.

I looked at Eddie. "Get him out of here. And make sure that Beth gets that drug."

Eddie nodded. A brief thought came to the surface of his mind: the day I was born, and when he had placed me into my mother's arms.

"I love you too, old man. Now, go!"

Without waiting for any response or waiting to see which way Eddie dragged Cedrick off in, I turned my attention back to the battlefield and started hunting for Marcus. But I didn't have to hunt very far.

Red tentacles reached out from the lone figure that stood perfectly still among the white roses.

Lightning and thunder struck. The clouds overhead possessed a deep purple hue, almost black. A twinge of pain struck my arm as a drop of rain came in contact with my skin.

The coughing of those around me turned into screams. Those able to stand stumbled toward the building overhangs and shelter.

But Marcus just stood there in the falling rain, like he knew that it all came down to the two of us.

Slowly, I walked across the plaza, navigating the fallen debris field. The ground hissed as the falling acid ate away at the grass and the other greenery. The white roses around Marcus took on a purple hue, just as the petals wilted and fell away. And I stood there, just as still as he did, not once taking my eyes off him. But there was no calmness in the way we stood there. It was pure determination.

The rain fell in thick droplets. Each drop that hit my skin burned. But I refused to give in to the pain. If I wanted to stop Marcus—to kill him—I had to do it now.

But I still couldn't get into his head.

Marcus suddenly ran forward, roaring like a raging beast. I slid one foot slightly backward and brought my hands up in front of me, guarding my center, preparing for the fight of my life.

I dodged and blocked Marcus's kicks and punches, looking for my opening—both in his physical attacks and in his mind. I flipped over and under him, but our months of training together had clearly taught him how to fight against me—how to use my acrobatics against me. Any clear dominance that I might have possessed in the past was gone. We were now equals when it came to hand-to-hand combat. But I was still his superior.

I was a sixth gen by birth. He was a sixth gen by way of DNA-modification. And it was *my* DNA that was used for the map.

I missed a blow to my head, and the stars spun as I hit the ground. My hands and forearms splashed in the puddles. I screamed as the acid started to melt away my skin.

My head was pushed down into the puddle beneath me, and I kept hearing the same thought over and over again. *"Kill her now. She deserves it. She tried to kill you, and almost succeeded."*

A memory, a joint memory, came to my mind.

MARCUS HAD HIS hands around my neck. And he was strangling me. We were children, but Marcus had no idea who he was facing. As a little girl, I dug into his mind and demanded that he let me go. As his grip around my throat lessened, I scurried out from under him and got to my feet, heaving. But I continued to glare at Marcus. He then pulled out a knife and slit his wrist. And there was nothing that anyone could do to stop it from happening.

MY HEAD WAS jerked back and bashed against the ground, severing the mental connection and ending the memory. I coughed, and I inhaled a small portion of the acidic water from the puddle.

"Not this time," Marcus growled. He jerked me over onto my back, then proceeded to strangle me, leaning the bulk of his weight into his hands around my throat.

Big mistake.

Unable to breathe, still feeling the burning acid down my throat, I reached up and grabbed one of his elbows, pulling it tight to my chest. I then thrust my pelvis into the air and rolled, but I didn't stop with him being under me. I continued to roll and tried to scramble to my feet. Marcus grabbed my foot before I could get too far, and I fell onto a shard of the fallen dome.

I kicked at his face, breaking his nose. And I continued to side-crawl across the ground. I pressed my hand to my side, my fingers splayed on either side of the shard sticking out of me. My blood was near black. Whatever had gotten hit, it was serious. But I couldn't give up. Marcus could not be allowed to win. Not like this.

I continued to kick at him, and he continued to scramble after me. A small group of soldiers, all in full breather masks, ran in our direction. And they looked directly into my eyes.

The edges of my vision went dark as their faces became devoid of life.

"Stay away," I ordered. But I suddenly had a thought. *"Go to Ward 27 and evacuate the patients from there. Help them get to safety. Set them free. Go!"*

As the guards ran off, hopefully to follow my mental orders, Marcus managed to climb up the length of my legs. Screaming, I flopped to my back and pulled the shard from my side . . . then I rammed it as far as I could into the side of his neck.

I curled my arm behind him and pulled him close to me, holding him there as his blood spurted over my hand and my face. His eyes grew wide, and I could hear his mental screams begging me to stop. To let him go.

But just like he was determined to kill me, I was determined to kill him.

My vision darkened, but his eyes didn't pull me into his mind. He didn't possess the strength to get past my mental barriers. No, my darkening vision was not a function of my mental abilities. It was my own loss of blood threatening to take me under.

He fell forward, his full weight on me. And soon, he stopped fighting me.

With the last of my strength, I pushed my pelvis into the air again, rolling him off me. His eyes were vacant. There was nothing left to hear within his thoughts.

He wasn't a lifeless zombie. He was just lifeless.

I used the last of my strength to push myself away from him, to gain a small amount of distance. Flopping onto my back, I looked up at the sky. The real sky.

The clouds were dark, almost black. But the streaks of lightning created a rainbow of color as it danced across the sky. The rain continued to fall around me, eating away at the ground and burning my flesh. Yet, I embraced every drop of rain as though it was a cooling balm washing over my skin. I just stared up at the dark clouds, continually blinking to keep the rain out of my eyes. Waiting for the end.

A silhouette obscured my vision. "You have lost your mind if you think the best way to experience the rain is by lying down in it. You should be up on your feet and dancing." He knelt next to me, and his youthful, mischievous smile came into focus. So too did the red, curly mop on his head.

"George." Tears hung in the corners of my eyes. Or was it raindrops?

He caressed my cheek. And for the first time in a long time, I felt alive.

I rolled over and pushed myself to my feet, coughing up blood. But I didn't care. Neither did he.

George sang the chorus of my favorite song—out of tune—and he held me in his strong arms, to stop me from falling as I staggered every few awkward steps.

But we danced one last time in the purple rain.

Epilogue

CEDRICK SAT IN THE MIDDLE of the coffee shop, his eyes drifting from person to person, searching for the one he was supposed to meet. The message they had received through the underground network was a little sparse on details. It just said that whoever Cedrick was meeting had information on how to track down the last few members of STAR, the ones who had escaped the chaos that happened in Sector 14. The informant had information on how to track down the last traces of the Pregutor program that had also survived.

Sure, there was every chance that this meeting was just a setup, one designed to capture Cedrick, but it was worth the risk. Mike gave her life so his son could one day live free of the experiments. If Cedrick didn't find a way to end the Pregutor's reign of terror, this would never stop. Somehow, he had to make it right. He owed it to Mike for getting her involved in this mess in the first place.

If he had just let her be . . .

So, when the message came through about someone who had information about the Pregutor and the remaining STAR, Cedrick decided it was worth the risk of exposing himself to meet with an unknown.

The digital clock in the corner of his virtual display started flashing red. Only seconds left to the appointed time.

It was still a little disorienting, having all that tactical information overlaid on top of his natural vision. But he was getting better at controlling the interface.

When the clock hit zero, a package was dropped on the table in front of him. A hooded figure darted through the line by the entryway, attempting to make an escape out the door, but more people were coming in, forcing the courier to wait.

Cedrick gathered the package and chased after the courier. That was his lead. That was his contact. Sure, the information that he desired was likely in the package, but the courier would know more. He needed to catch the courier to find out what information they had.

He activated the seals on his breather and his glasses as he ran outside in pursuit. He looked left, then right, but the hooded figure had disappeared into the crowds darting through the heavy rain that threatened to eat their skin. Dark, hooded figures were everywhere.

He looked down at the package in his hand. There was nothing special about the external envelope. Brown with no markings, no indication of who it was from—at least not on the outside. He backed up into a covered alcove, trying to stay out of the way of the passersby but stay out of the rain too. He then took a few breaths and ripped open the end of the brown envelope. Inside was a phone rod. With shaky hands, he pulled it out and allowed the scanner to scan his eye. The virtual display expanded, showing a picture of the Rhodon Corporation logo—a white rose in full bloom.

Cedrick's lips twitched into a snarl, but he did the best he could to contain his anger as he swiped his hand over the logo and activated the video that waited in the background.

The classic opening of the *Purple Rain* song began to play along with a video of Mike laying on the sodden muddy grass in the middle of Sector 14. Cedrick's chest grew tight as he took in the forms of the bodies on the ground around her. Lucas. Grober. Nancy. And right beside Mike was Marcus, the monster who had killed them all.

The video zoomed in on Mike. She stared up at the camera, smiling. And as the music continued to play, she got to her feet and started dancing, staggering every few steps, like her strength was failing her. Blood soaked the ground around her feet.

Cedrick continued to watch, doing the best he could to fight back the tears.

The video shifted to reveal a list of names. Some names were listed in red, along with the word ≫Deceased≪ next to them, including Lucas Tellis, Jody Kristensen, Marcus Gahan, and George Tuthill. Other names were listed in green, along with what looked to be GPS coordinates. However, some names, like his own, were flagged in yellow with ≫Location Unknown≪ written next to the name.

As he scanned the list, he took note of the added details. Third gen. Fourth gen. Fifth gen. Every single name on the list belonged to someone who had once been part of the NeuWave experiments. And there were notes about the treatments they had been given, links to subfiles of full medical records, including notes about their mental abilities. Sitting in his hands was all the information that he needed to track down every living NeuWave subject. And with the information in his hands, Beth would be able to devise treatment protocols to manage any complications that might have developed because of the genetic experiments.

But there was one name on the list that grabbed his attention.

Michaella Davison. It was in yellow, just like his own name. »Location Unknown.«« And the date on the record was listed as the time of the package drop.

The song ended, and an image of Mike flashed onto the screen. She looked different. Scarred. But her hair was purple again. She winked and smiled. A message scrolled across the display.

»Dance in the purple rain. You know what to do.««

Then the display went dark, leaving only a purple rose icon in the middle of the screen—an icon so he could activate the NeuWave list.

Any anger or frustration that Cedrick might have felt disappeared in an instant. Instead, he grinned from ear to ear. He knew exactly what to do.

He stepped out into the heavy rain and turned his face to the sky, embracing the burning sensation on his skin. Because it meant he was alive. "Time to dance in the purple rain." With a swagger in this step, he walked down the street, humming the chorus of the song that had become the refrain of their movement.

THE END

Acknowledgements

THERE HAVE BEEN so many who have helped me along my writing journey, with some of them holding my hand every time I got scared. Without the following people lending me their support, I would have never made it this far.

Thank you to Kathy Swailes for your regular encouragement... and the occasional kick up the backside whenever I chickened out of taking that next step. I also owe you a huge thank you for helping me get this book ready for publication.

I also need to thank Rata Turner for your comments and feedback during the various stages of this book's production, from beta reading through to comments on the cover and interior. You might not think that you had much to offer, but trust me, it was invaluable.

Thank you to E. L. Julian for the amazing cover design you did (and continue to do for my other covers). I'm so glad that I took a chance to see what you could do. You didn't disappoint.

I also need to thank Pam Sheppard for her insights on marketing and positioning. You are a wealth of knowledge, and I feel blessed to be able to tap into that knowledge.

And thank you to the various members of my writing groups. It's your spirit that keeps me going.

However, the most important people in this venture have been my husband and my two children. You have put up with the emotional roller coaster and burnt dinner meals, but you've loved me and gave me the hugs I needed to stay my course. I love you.

But I also need to acknowledge the one soul who I will never be able to thank for everything that she did for me. I hear her voice every day. And when I'm uncertain of my path, the universe finds a way of reminding me of all the lessons she taught me.

I did it, mom. They told me that it couldn't be done, but I did it.

About the Author

Kiwi Judy L Mohr is a writer, developmental editor, writing coach, amateur photographer, and a science nerd with a keen interest in internet technologies and social media security. Her knowledge ranges from highly efficient ways to hide the bodies through to how to improve your SEO rankings for your websites. When she isn't writing, editing, or doing something within the local writing community, she can be found plotting her next foray into mischief and scouting for locations to hide the bodies. (Shh . . . Don't tell anyone.) Follow her crazy adventures on her blog (judylmohr.com), and while you're there, sign up for her newsletter.

About the Type

The cover design for this novel used three typefaces. The main title used *Bedas Kai*. Hooks and the subtitle are in *Libre Baskerville*. The author's name is in *El Messiri*.

Within the interior, *Megrim* was used for the chapter numbers and titles. Within the printed version, *EB Garamond* was used for the main text, and *Jost* was used for text-based communication dialogue. In the headers, *El Messiri* was used for the header text, but the star-burst symbol is included in *Noto Sans Symbols 2*.

Bedas Kai was designed by Dharma Type and is commercially free from a variety of sources, including FontSquirrel (www.fontsquirrel.com/fonts/bebas-kai) and DaFont (www.dafont.com/bebas-kai.font).

Libre Baskerville was designed by Impallari Type. *El Messiri* was designed by Mohamed Gaber and Jovanny Lemonad. *EB Garamond* was designed by Georg Duffner and Octavio Pardo. *Jost* was designed by Owen Earl. *Megrim* was designed by Daniel Johnson. *Noto Sans Symbols 2* was developed by the Noto Project group. All six typefaces can be sourced from Google Fonts.

www.ingramcontent.com/pod-product-compliance
Lightning Source LLC
Chambersburg PA
CBHW051306190726
48290CB00001B/34